KILL SW/TCH

ALSO BY JONATHAN MABERRY

NOVELS

Ghostwalkers: A Deadlands Novel

Predator One

Fall of Night

Code Zero

Extinction Machine

Assassin's Code

King of Plagues

The Dragon Factory

Patient Zero

Dead of Night

The Wolfman

Bits & Pieces

Fire & Ash

Flesh & Bone

Dust & Decay

Rot & Ruin

Bad Moon Rising

Dead Man's Song

Ghost Road Blues

ANTHOLOGIES

V-Wars

V-Wars: Blood and Fire

V-Wars: Night Terrors

X-Files: Trust No One

X-Files: The Truth Is Out There

Scary Out There

Out of Tune

Out of Tune Vol 2

NONFICTION

Wanted Undead or Alive

They Bite

Zombie CSU

The Cryptopedia

Vampire Universe

Vampire Slayer's Field Guide to the
Undead (as Shane MacDougall)

Ultimate Jujutsu

Ultimate Sparring

The Martial Arts Student

Logbook

Judo and You

GRAPHIC NOVELS

Bad Blood

Rot & Ruin: Warrior Smart

V-Wars: The Crimson Queen

V-Wars: All of Us Monsters

Marvel Universe vs. Wolverine

Marvel Universe vs. The Punisher

Marvel Universe vs. The Avengers

Captain America: Hail Hydra

Klaws of the Panther

Punisher: Naked Kills

Wolverine: Flies to a Spider

Doomwar

Black Panther: Power

Marvel Zombies Return

JONATHAN MABERRY

———•———

KILL SW/TCH

ST. MARTIN'S GRIFFIN
NEW YORK

This is for Carol & Bill Galante, Lisa Brackmann,
and for Dana Fredsti & David Fitzgerald.
And, as always, for Sara Jo.

KILL SWITCH. Copyright © 2016 by Jonathan Maberry. All rights reserved. Printed in the United States of America. For information, address St. Martin's Press, 175 Fifth Avenue, New York, N.Y. 10010.

www.stmartins.com

The Library of Congress Cataloging-in-Publication Data is available upon request.

ISBN 978-1-250-06525-4 (trade paperback)
ISBN 978-1-250-10088-7 (e-book)

Our books may be purchased in bulk for promotional, educational, or business use. Please contact your local bookseller or the Macmillan Corporate and Premium Sales Department at 1-800-221-7945, extension 5442, or by e-mail at MacmillanSpecialMarkets@macmillan.com.

First Edition: April 2016

10 9 8 7 6 5 4 3 2 1

ACKNOWLEDGMENTS

As always I owe a debt to a number of wonderful people. Thanks to John Cmar, director, Division of Infectious Diseases, Sinai Hospital of Baltimore; Dr. Steve A. Yetiv, Professor of Political Science, Old Dominion University; Michael Sicilia, formerly of California Homeland Security; the International Thriller Writers; my literary agents, Sara Crowe and Harvey Klinger; all the good folks at St. Martin's Griffin: Michael Homler, Joe Goldschein; and my film agent, Jon Cassir of Creative Artists Agency. Thanks to Patrick Seiler of the Raymond James Group; Doug Davis and the wonderful people of Kearny Pearson Ford in San Diego; Krisztal Alexis Garcilazo; Kevin J. Bartell; Patrick Freivald; Ralph Morgan Lewis; astronomers Lisa Will, David Lee Summers, Philip Plait, and David McDonald; and Jake Witkowski (creator of the Joe Ledger Heart Attack Sandwich). Thanks to Chris Wren, Daniel Foley, Paul Bosworth, David James Keaton, Lisa Kastner, Thom Brennan, and Robert Gregg Barker, for technical information.

Thanks and congrats to the winners of the various Joe Ledger contests: Jay Faulkner, Tom Erb, Sinh Taylor, Joseph Capozzi, Tricia Owens, Otis Carlisle, Diane Sismour, James Florida, Will Divine, Christel Sparks, Linda and Sheldon Higdon, and Lou Emanuele. Thanks to Tony Eldridge of Lone Tree Entertainment and Dotonna Isham of Vintage Picture Company.

PROLOGUE

Where were you when the lights went out?

That's the question, isn't it?

What's your answer?

Were you caught by the dark, frozen into the moment, suddenly reminded that civilization and the comfort of infrastructure are just a garment we wear? A fragile convenience. Did the sudden dark remind you that all of the things we expect to be there for us, to protect us, shelter us, provide for us, are fleeting and finite?

Were you one of the cynical ones, the doomsday-prepper types who saw everything go dark and, for one moment, stood there with a smug smile, gratified by the substance of your own prophecy? And then a moment later it caught up to you that there are a great number of things about which you never want to be right.

Did you think it was all a mistake? An error? A fault in the system, or bad wiring in the grid? You were absolutely sure someone was going to come and fix it.

Any.

Second.

Now.

Were you one of the unlucky ones who slept through the first hours of it, accepting darkness as ordinary and correct, only to be called awake by something we civilized people have forgotten about? Silence.

Did you try your cell? Your landline? Your laptop? Did you go old school and turn on the TV only to find that the cable was as dead as the lights?

There was a moment, wasn't there? When you realized that the lights weren't coming back on. That maybe they wouldn't. That maybe they couldn't.

What did you feel right then, at that moment when the truth whispered to you from the darkness?

What was the content of your thoughts, the constituents of your prayers?

Tell me.

When it all went dark, did you think it would last?

And last?

Or did you think—as so many did—that this was the end? The actual "it." The stopping place, not just of the world as it was, but of your life as you needed to live it?

In that moment, what did you think? What did you believe?

Where were you when the lights went out?

Me?

I was trying to keep those lights on. Trying to hold a candle in the darkness. Losing ground with every step.

And when the lights went out I fell into the big, bottomless black.

PART ONE
THE GOD MACHINE

●———●

Stars, hide your fires;
Let not light see my black and deep desires.
—William Shakespeare
Macbeth

CHAPTER ONE

For the record, I don't believe in this stuff.

No goddamn way.

There's possible, there's improbable, there's weird, and there's no-fucking-way. This is a mile or two past that. So, no, I don't believe in it.

What pisses me off is that it seems to believe in me.

CHAPTER TWO

I was four minutes away from calling it a day and cutting out early to catch an Orioles-Padres game at Petco Park here in San Diego. Hot dogs loaded with everything that's bad for me, ice-cold beer in big red cups, and the opportunity to spend a few hours yelling at a bunch of young millionaires trying to hit a little ball with a big stick. Baseball, baby. The American pastime.

It was the first game I'd managed to catch since the craziness at Citizen's Bank Park last year. You know what I mean. The drone attacks on opening day. I'd spent a lot of the rest of the spring in hospitals. A bunch more time in rehab, then way too much sitting behind a desk doing paperwork and feeling my ass grow flat. Then I went back into the field and since then I've done nothing but run.

The Big Bad for us right now was ISIL. The press writes about them like they're a disorganized goon squad who are only a threat to the notoriously unstable governments in the Middle East. They're not. They're a whole lot scarier than that. Most of the people running them are former officers from Saddam's army. These are experienced soldiers who have been nurturing grudges. That was bad enough, but now they've upped their game and have put several special ops teams in the field. Real pros, too, and they managed to scoop up leftover Kingsmen from the ruins of the Seven Kings organization. Was it weird that ISIL was using shooters who were not Muslims? Yup. Very weird. And very scary, too, because it allowed them to come at us in unpredictable ways. A bunch of their SpecOps fighters were Americans, so even with the heightened security and paranoia here in the States following the drone stuff, we were feeling some rabbit punches from them. Attacks on power grids, an attempted sabotage of a nuclear power plant. Like that.

And our super-duper computer system, MindReader, has been picking up some hints about a really big attack planned for the US of A, and if the rumors were true then it was going to involve some kind of electromagnetic pulse weapon.

So, yeah . . . bad guys. Really *scary* bad guys, and they were causing a whole lot of very serious trouble. We had DMS teams running joint ops with the CIA and Homeland, with Barrier in the UK, with Mossad in Israel, and with a dozen other special operations crews.

Overall, I was busier than a three-headed cat in a dairy. That's not to say I spent all of my time in the field kicking terrorist ass. Mind you, I'm still a gunslinger for Uncle Sam, but now that I run the Special Projects Office I'm also management, which sucks six kinds of ass.

Baseball kept calling to me, though, and today was the first time I could reasonably justify leaving the shop early to have some actual fun.

The phone began ringing while I was tidying my desk.

If you work in a bank, an insurance company, or pretty much most jobs, you can pretend you don't hear that call. I know cops at the ragged end of a long shift who swear their radios were malfunctioning.

But when you do what I do, you have to drop everything else—your time off, your family, your friends, even baseball—and you take the call. Kind of like the Bat-Signal. You can't just blow it off.

So I answered the call.

It was my boss, Mr. Church.

"Captain Ledger," he said, "I need you on the next thing smoking. Dress warm, it's going to be cold."

I looked out the window. This was August and the Southern California summer was cooking. Temperature was eighty-eight in the shade. I was wearing shorts, flip-flops, and a Hawaiian shirt with surfing pelicans on it.

"How cold?" I asked.

"This morning it was minus fifty-eight."

I closed my eyes.

"I hate you," I said.

"I'll manage to live with your contempt."

"Okay," I said, "tell me."

INTERLUDE ONE

"Are you going to talk today?" asked the psychiatrist. "Or are you still mad at me?"

The boy sat in the exact middle of the couch even though it was not the most comfortable place. He was like that, preferring precision over comfort. It was reflected in the number of pieces of food he would allow on his dinner plate, the number of tissues he would use no matter how many times he sneezed. Numbers mattered in ways that Dr. Greene was still discovering. So far the psychiatrist had been able to determine that Prospero Bell believed that math, in all its forms, was not merely a way to calculate sums, but was in fact tied to the very structure of physical reality. He'd even made himself a hand-drawn T-shirt last year that had a quote from mathematician Carl Friedrich Gauss: "God arithmetizes," itself a variation of a quote Plutarch famously attributed to Plato: "God geometrizes continually."

Prospero was very tall for his age, but thin as a stick. As he perched on the couch, his long body seemed to be temporarily suspended, as if he was about to slide down between the two big leather cushions but chose not to fall. Always awkward and always strange, and he did not seem to ever fit into the world as it was. Dr. Greene knew that this reflected the boy's inner life. After four years of therapy, the doctor was quite convinced that this boy lived in two entirely separate worlds. The one inside, where Prospero clearly felt he belonged, and the one outside that he loathed and resented. That discomfort, and the resulting disconnect from ordinary social interactions, was the basis of their frequent sessions.

"I never said I was mad at you," said the boy. He was eleven and his voice was beginning to deepen. No cracks or squeaks, just a timbre that hinted at the baritone to come.

"You threw an apple at me last Thursday," said Greene.

"It was handy."

"That's not my point."

Prospero gave him a microsecond of a sly grin. "I know."

"Then—"

"I didn't want to talk about my father anymore and you wouldn't shut up. I didn't hit you with the apple."

"You tried. I ducked."

"No," said Prospero, "I missed. The fact that you ducked says more about you than my 'missing' says about my aim. I wanted to miss. You didn't want to duck, but you did anyway because you didn't know that I wouldn't have hit you."

Today the boy wore a green cloth jacket that he had systematically covered with symbols from cabalism, magic, and alchemy. Greene knew this because there had been three full sessions about those designs. Now there was a gray hoodie under the jacket, the top pulled up to throw shadows down over Prospero's thin, ascetic face. The boy had painstakingly drawn an elaborate and technically excellent monster on the hood. The thing had a bulbous, flabby body, stubby wings, and a beard made from writhing tentacles that trailed from the gray hood onto the green material of the jacket.

Greene met with Prospero three times a week, down from the five talks per week that marked the boy's most extreme phases, up from the twice weekly of last year when Prospero seemed to be balancing out. Greene was therapist for the whole Bell family, including the father, Oscar Bell, a major defense contractor; Oscar's current wives; and his long line of ex-wives. Greene also did occasional check-ins with Prospero's older brother from Oscar's first marriage. Greene's sessions with the rest of the family were routine, sparse, and almost pointless. They didn't need him and he privately found them intensely dull. The older boy was a clone of his father and would doubtless become fabulously wealthy building secret, terrible things for the American military. As the Bell family had since the Civil War.

Of all the Bells, Prospero was the one who logged frequent-flyer miles on Greene's therapy couch.

Greene asked, "What would you have done if I wanted to keep talking about your father after you threw that apple?"

Prospero shrugged.

"No," said Greene, "tell me."

The boy nodded to the coffee table. "There were five other apples in the bowl. I can throw pretty good." He shrugged again, point made.

There was no bowl on the table now. There was nothing there, not even magazines. Greene was moderately sure the boy wouldn't throw the table itself.

"Is it your opinion that hitting me with an apple is the best way for us to proceed?"

"We didn't have that conversation, did we?"

Even after all these years and all these sessions it still unnerved Greene that Prospero never spoke in an age-appropriate way. He never had. Even when he was five years old his intellect and self-possession were remarkable. Or maybe "freakish" was a more accurate term, though Greene would never put that in any report. Freak. It was the best word, then and now.

Prospero Bell was a freak.

None of the tests Greene or his colleagues had administered had been able to accurately gauge the boy's intelligence. Best guess was that it was above 200. Perhaps considerably above that, which lifted him above the level of any reliable process of quantification. Prospero had completed all of his high school requirements last year at age ten, and passed each test with the highest marks. The boy's aptitude was odd, though. Savantism is generally limited to a few specific areas—math, say, or art. Occasionally a cluster. But Prospero seemed to excel at everything that interested him, and his interests were varied. World religions, folklore, anthropology relative to belief systems, art, music, mathematics in all its aspects, science, with a bias toward quantum and particle physics.

He was now eleven.

But he was also deeply read in areas that were built on less stable scientific ground—cryptozoology, metaphysics, alchemy, surrealist art, pulp horror fiction. The boy was all over the place. The rate at which Prospero was able to absorb information was only surpassed by his ability to both retain and process it. He had a perfect eidetic memory, and it seemed genuine, without any of the mnemonics of someone who uses tricks or triggers to recall data. Prospero never forgot a thing he learned, and because he was so observant that meant that he possessed an astounding body of personal knowledge. Greene had given Prospero tests to determine what kind of intellect the boy had, but the results had been confounding. Prospero had marked fluid intelligence—indicating that he was able to reason, form concepts, and solve problems using unfamiliar information or novel procedures—but he scored equally high in crystallized intelligence, which meant that he possessed the ability to communicate his knowledge, and had the ability to reason using previously learned experiences or procedures. People seldom scored that high in both aspects. And he did just as well with long- and short-term memory, memory storage and retrieval, quantitative reasoning, auditory and visual processing, and others.

Greene felt that his "freak" diagnosis was the most clinically accurate assessment. There was a lot of savantism in the world, but there was no one like Prospero Bell. The question that burned hottest in Greene's mind was what the boy would do with all of that brainpower. He had hinted that he had a plan, but so far had kept that secret to himself.

Prospero's intense hatred and distrust of his father was a common topic for them, and the old man wanted Greene to determine the best way for the elder Bell to gain the trust of his son. Not the love. All that mattered to Oscar Bell was a useful trust.

But that was only a secondary goal for Greene and he didn't devote much time to it. Instead he focused on something he found far more interesting. It was also the thing that most deeply concerned Prospero.

Prospero was absolutely convinced that he was not human. Not entirely.

And he was equally convinced that he was not from this world.

CHAPTER THREE

"What's the op, Boss?" asked Bunny, the big kid from Orange County who looked like a plowboy from Iowa. His dog tags said he was Master Sergeant Harvey Rabbit, but not even his parents called him by his first name. Bunny was the muscle and in many ways the heart of Echo Team. "Those ISIL shooters find a two-for-one sale on snowshoes?"

"Funny," I said. "But no."

We were aboard an LC-130 Hercules, a big military transport plane fitted out with skis. None of us liked the fact that our plane had to have skis. I had a third of Echo Team with me. Two operators: Bunny and Top—First Sergeant Bradley Sims. My right and left hands.

"We going way down south to get out of the summer heat?" drawled Top.

"This is a look-see," I told them. "This gig is a handoff from our friends in the CIA."

"We're all going to die," said Bunny.

"There's a bright side," I told him. "The quarterback who handed it off was Harcourt Bolton."

Both Top and Bunny came instantly to point, grinning like kids.

"Seriously?" said Bunny, wide-eyed. "Wow. We made it to the pros."

"I thought he retired," said Top. "Glad to hear he's still in the game."

Guys like us don't much go in for hero worship. The exception is when the hero in question is someone like Harcourt Bolton. If America has ever had an agent on par with the movie version of James Bond, then it's Bolton. He's the spy's spy. Cool, suave, sophisticated, incredibly smart, and very capable. I may be one of Uncle Sam's top shooters, but Bolton is the Agency's sharpest scalpel. And it's not too much of a stretch to say I'm captain of his fan club. Harcourt Bolton,

Senior, was someone I knew very well. Or, should I say, I knew *of* very well. His role as a semicelebrity gazillionaire philanthropist, entrepreneur, and notorious playboy was tabloid legend. He was like Tony Stark or Bruce Wayne—a rich man who always seemed to be caught in a paparazzi photo with this year's supermodel while spending his days investing in worthy causes to better humanity. It was the kind of superstar status that never seemed quite real, because how could someone be that rich, that lucky, that smart, and that generous all in one lifetime?

That's the Bolton the general public knew. I've heard my lover, Junie Flynn, talk about getting him involved in some FreeTech ventures in developing countries. Using money and technology to save whole villages.

My guys and I knew the other side of him, however. We knew that the Bruce Wayne cover was just that. A cover. A brilliant cover, actually, because just as Bruce Wayne had that darker vigilante side with an obsession for flightless mammals of the family Chiroptera, there was a hidden side to Harcourt Bolton. He was, by anyone's estimation, the greatest spy who has ever worked for the Central Intelligence Agency. That is saying a lot. No matter what the public perception is of the CIA, they are not, on the whole, a clown college. There is a very effective little office within the CIA that makes sure the Company is regarded from a skewed perspective, because it lowers the expectations of the bad guys.

The other side to Bolton's career was the above-top-secret operations, the real 007 stuff. Like infiltrating and destroying a secret North Korean missile base that was primed to detonate the Cumbre Vieja volcano, which would have sent five hundred cubic kilometers of rock into the Atlantic Ocean, resulting in a two-thousand-foot-high tsunami. It would have wiped out the African coast, Southern England, and then the eastern seaboard of North America.

Then there was the bioweapons lab buried four stories beneath a Siberian work camp. Bolton went in alone, killed sixteen people, and blew the lab pretty much into orbit.

And the time he ripped apart a coalition of rogue Saudi princes who were financing ISIL. Bolton wore a disguise, spoke flawless Arabic, forged perfect credentials, and once he had ingratiated himself with the group, he shot all seven of them and uploaded a computer virus that stole their data and destroyed the target computers.

I could go on.

And on. I could obsess and go full-tilt fanboy on him. I would buy an action figure of Harcourt Bolton and, yes, I would take it out of the package and play made-up adventures with it. If someone told me he could turn water into wine, my only question would be whether it was red or white. And the answer would probably be the 1982 Pichon Longueville Comtesse de Lalande. Not because it's the most expensive, which it's not, but because while the 1982 is not a classic Bordeaux, it has an over-ripe, exotic quality that he's discovered would make any woman on Earth instantly disrobe. That's how Bolton would do it. Guys like him walk on water and make the rest of us look like grubby amateurs. Even my personal hero, the late, great Samson Riggs, couldn't hold a candle to him.

Bolton was the top field operator for a lot of years. Much longer than most guys manage it. He never seemed to want to retire and I could understand that. When you're at the top of your game—especially this game—there's a real fear that if you head to the showers and let a newer, younger, and less experienced player step up to bat, then he won't know better than to swing at fastballs and sliders. You stay in the game because you know it better than the other guys. Or at least you think you do. Maybe it's an ego thing—and that's got to be a chunk of it—but you know how far you've gone in the past to take the bad guys down, you know the tricks that worked for you time and again, and you don't want to take that skill set out of play. It's why so many guys like us die out there, caught in the moment when age and experience can't make up for the fact that you've lost a step getting to first base. You fall, and maybe your arrogance and fear drags someone else down, too. Maybe a lot of people. But how can you not risk it?

Bolton risked it, and he had a couple of missions go south on him. Luckily the DMS was there to back his play when things fell apart. I was the relief pitcher on the last two of Bolton's operations. I got the saves and the DMS got the credit, even if it was only an off-the-radar pat on the back by the president.

Bolton was done as a field op, though. His team was reassigned and he was given a nice desk in a nice office and people were very nice to him. Which must have been hell for a guy like him.

However, anyone who thought Bolton would just walk off the field and go sit on a porch at the Old Spies Retirement Home was sadly mistaken. Because he's a class act, and maybe an actual superhero, he shifted his gears and over the last few years he's worked his old network of contacts to get mission intel for younger CIA turks, and even for the DMS. Serious intel. If he'd been regarded as a superspy before, you can double that since then. His network was so deeply embedded in the global underworld that none of us could figure out how he did it. Someone hung a nickname on him that got some traction. Mr. Voodoo. If Harcourt Bolton says something hinky is happening—even if no one else has heard a peep about it—then you lock and load. So if he passed along intel on this job, it was on us to nut up and earn that level of professional respect.

"I'll give it to you the way I got it," I said. "The mission has two layers. Our cover story is a surprise inspection to evaluate the status of a research base designated 'Gateway.' This is a repurposed facility. The original Gateway was an old radar station from the early Cold War era. Satellites made it mostly obsolete so it was closed up. Operative word is 'was.' The base was built at the foot of Vinson Massif, the tallest mountain in Antarctica. The Russians and Chinese both have research stations in the same region."

"What's the hurry for us to get down there?" asked Top. "The neighbors getting cranky?"

"Not exactly," I said. "Our intelligence says that in the last twenty-eight hours the Russian and Chinese bases have gone dark. No radio, no communication of any kind. Nineteen hours ago our facility also went dark. We're about six hours ahead of the Russian and Chinese investigative teams. Bolton got wind of this from his network but he's in the middle of something else so he called Mr. Church."

Top grunted. "Do we think it has been taken?"

"Unknown, but on the list of possibilities," I said. "Gateway isn't a radar outpost anymore and hasn't been for over a decade. But that's where things get muddy. Bug had trouble finding out who actually opened it and what they're doing. We know it's some kind of black budget thing, but we only know that because of how well the details have been hidden. Very little of it is in any of the databases Bug and his geek squad have infiltrated. And like all of that kind of stuff there are lots of things named only by obscure acronyms, and projects identified by number-letter codes instead of names. That makes it tough to find, because something labeled A631/45H doesn't exactly ring alarm bells. Bug needs to have something to go on."

Top and Bunny nodded. This was familiar—and deeply frustrating—territory for us. Our own government is so large and so compartmentalized, and there's so much bickering, infighting, and adherence to personal and political agendas, that one hand truly does not know what the other is doing. And that gets even murkier when you factor in illegal operations, of which there are many.

"Do we know anything about what they're doing down there?" asked Bunny.

I shrugged. "Not much, and what we do know is because Bolton brought us into the loop. Not sure how he found out."

"He's Harcourt Bolton," said Bunny.

"Fair enough. Anyway, we now know the Gateway base is active and apparently serving as a research and development shop. Mr. Church had Bug do a MindReader search on Gateway and so far he's only come up with a few things, but not as much as we'd like."

"How's it possible we can't find out everything?" asked Bunny. "MindReader can go anywhere."

"In theory," I said, "but a lot of people in Washington know that we have MindReader and some of them are pretty stingy with their stuff. Can't blame them. It's not like we are actually allowed to poke our noses everywhere."

"Yeah," said Top dryly, "been a whole bunch of stuff on the news the last few years about government overreach. Maybe you read something?"

I ignored him. "The point is that more and more departments are using intranets instead of the public or military networks. Closed systems that can't be accessed from outside. MindReader can't go and hardwire a tap, you know."

Top punched Bunny on the arm. "That don't mean your browser history is safe yet, Farm Boy, so stop looking at all those naked pictures. Gonna grow hair on your palms."

"Blow me," said Bunny.

"There are other ways to hide from MindReader," I told them. "Paper files instead of computer records. That sort of thing."

"Still got to be paid for," said Top. "Operating a research base way down here? Even if it's coded, something like this has to be expensive. Got to be mentioned in the budget somewhere."

I nodded. "That's what Bug's looking at now, but it's time-consuming."

"If they ain't a radar station, then what are they doing down there?" asked Top.

"That's the problem," I told them, "we don't know for sure. The intel is thin. Bolton said his sources believe they're working on some radical technology for renewable energy. Nonnuclear but with a lot of potential. Far as he could tell it was sold to the black budget people as the thing that will take us away from any dependence on foreign oil. Don't ask me what the science is because I don't know and neither does Bolton."

"If this is energy research," said Top, "and it's non-nuclear, then why go all the way the hell down to the rectum of the world to develop it?"

"That's what I asked," I said. "Almost the same words. The short answer is we don't know. Bolton and Bug both found some oblique references to—and I quote—'side effects resulting in pervasive power outages of limited duration.'"

"EMP?" suggested Bunny.

"Maybe. Dr. Hu said that there have been a number of new energy technologies that have had side effects, and EMPs are on that list. What confuses us all is the 'limited duration' part. EMPs fry electronics. There's nothing limited about that effect. You have to replace the damaged parts." I sighed. "So you see our problem—we have bits of intel and the pieces don't fit together. We're not even sure if any of that intel is reliable or even relevant, and we can't get anyone up here to admit to knowing anything about it, and no one down at Gateway will pick up the damn phone. Bug found a code name in the same partial data file that referenced the power outage side effect. Kill Switch."

"Cute name," said Bunny, not meaning it.

"If the power outage thing is a reproducible effect, then they may have isolated it in order to develop it into a new classification of directed-energy weapon. Maybe some sort of portable EMP cannon."

Bunny whistled.

Top frowned. "EMPs," he muttered in pretty much the way you'd say genital warts. "Been hearing nothing but trash talk about portable EMPs for ten years now."

"I know," I said, "but that's the next new technology for the good guys and bad guys. We want them to use as the next generation of missile shields, and to protect against small drones launched by hostiles.

The bad guys want to use them against us because everything we put in the field or in the air has a microchip, motor, or battery."

"That sucks," said Bunny. "Couple guys sitting in a cave with a portable EMP weapon and suddenly our gunships are dropping like dead birds."

"Won't just be caves, Farm Boy," said Top. "Portable is portable. Put those same assholes in a UPS truck in Manhattan and it's lights out for the whole damn city."

"Well, for some of it," countered Bunny. "One cannon's not going to flip the switches on a whole city."

Top spread his hands in a "we'll see" gesture. To me he said, "Washington send us down here to see if the Russians or Chinese been stealing our toys?"

"Unknown," I said, "but that's an obvious concern."

Top made a show of looking up and down the otherwise empty hull of the transport. Except for our gear and a modified snowcat we were all alone. "Small team to start a war with a couple of superpowers."

"Not the plan. There's some concern that a strong military presence might send the wrong message and draw attention when it might not actually be needed. Send in a lot of soldiers and people start wondering what you have to hide. That said, though, Boardwalk and Neptune Teams are five hours behind us. They'll hold back unless we call for them, and the USS *California* is in range in case we need to open a can of industrial-strength whoop-ass. However, the president has asked us to go in first, quick and quiet. No one except the Gateway staff are supposed to know we're here. We don't want anyone or anything connected with Gateway to make the news, feel me?"

Top snorted. "The Chinese and Russians probably have every eye in the sky they own looking at this. This whole area'll probably be featured on Google Earth before we're wheels down."

"Got to love the concept of 'secrecy' in the digital age," said Bunny. "Ten bucks says that some hipster blogger will be there to meet our plane."

It was almost true, and that was somewhere between sad and scary. With the vertical spike in digital technology, anyone with a smartphone had greater capabilities of discovering and sharing sensitive information with the world than the combined professional world media of ten years ago. Social media could be used for a lot of good things, but it'd turned everyone into a potential spy or source. And, yeah, I really do know how paranoid that sounds, but it is what it is. I'm a cheerleader for the First Amendment except when I'm in the field, at which point I have the occasional Big Brother moments. My shrink is never going to go broke.

Top asked, "We have thermal scans of our base and the others?"

"They're next to useless," I said. "The mountains there are thick with metal ores, so that screws things up."

Top sat back and folded his arms. He had dark brown skin criss-crossed with pink scars. Most of them earned since he's been working for me. "Seems like they're throwing us into a situation about which we have shit for intel."

"Pretty much," I said.

"The day must end with a *Y*," muttered Bunny.

I opened my laptop and called up a few random images of Gateway that Bolton and Bug had each found. There were some preliminary floor plans that might as well have been labeled GENERIC LAB, and some photos taken by satellite showing unhelpful pictures of prefab buildings nestled against a snow-covered mountain.

Bunny made a face. "We could give an Etch-a-Sketch to a rhesus monkey and he'd come up with better intel."

"No doubt," I said. "Bug found some shipping manifests that at least tell us what's been brought out there. Lab equipment, drilling gear, six generators—two active, two emergency backups, two offline in case—and all of the other stuff necessary for establishing a moderately self-sufficient base. Staff of seventy. Ten on the science team, twenty support staff that includes cook, medical officer, site administrator, and some engineers. The rest are military but we don't know what branch, so I asked Bug to run a MindReader deep search to find out. We're waiting on additional intel now."

The whole DMS was built around the MindReader computer system. Without it we'd be just another SpecOps team. MindReader had a superintrusion software package that allowed it to do a couple of spiffy things. One thing it did was look for patterns by drawing on information from an enormous number of sources, many of which it was not officially allowed to access. Which was the second thing. MindReader could intrude into any known computer system, poke around as much as it wanted, and withdraw without a trace. Most systems leave some kind of scar on the target computer's memory, but

MindReader rewrote the target's software to completely erase all traces of its presence. Bug was the uber-geek who ran MindReader for the DMS. I sometimes think Bug believes that MindReader is God and he's the pope.

Bunny asked, "What happens if we knock on their door and some goon from the People's Liberation Army Special Operations Forces answers?"

"Then all of us become a footnote in next year's black budget report," I said.

Bunny sighed. "Like I said . . . this only happens to us on days ending in a *Y*."

I wish I could call him a liar.

INTERLUDE TWO

OFFICE OF DR. MICHAEL GREENE
EAST HAMPTON, NEW YORK
WHEN PROSPERO WAS ELEVEN

"Why do you hate your father?" asked Dr. Greene.

"You've met him," said Prospero. "You tell me."

"Let's focus on your feelings."

Prospero Bell sat cross-legged on the couch. He'd spent time setting the angles of his knees and ankles just so. He still wore his green jacket with the gray hoodie underneath. Each time he showed up for a new session there was more detail in the monster on the hood, and he'd begun adding colors to indicate light through water, as if the monster were submerged beneath a sunlit sea.

Prospero sighed. Heavily and dramatically. "Look, it's not that complicated a thing and it's wasting my time. But, since you're probably going to badger me until I talk about it, here it is. Do I hate my father? Yes. Is it because he divorced my mom? No. Mom's a complete wacko. I love her and I can't even stand to be around her. So, no, it's not that. So why can't I stand him? Gosh, let me think. How about the fact that he's always mean to me. Always. He hates me and he doesn't mind showing it."

"Your father loves you, Prospero."

"Oh, please. I'm young but I'm not stupid. It's not me he loves. It's this." Prospero tapped his head. "He loves what's up here because he knows it can make him a lot of money."

"Your father is a very intelligent man," said Greene.

"Sure, but I'm smarter by at least an order of magnitude. We all know it. And I'm getting smarter all the time. And, sure, Dad's smart, but he only uses his brains to build weapons of war. Am I against war? Not really. Wars happen. But to spend your life making it easier to kill people, and easier for very few people to kill large numbers of people, then, yeah, I don't like that."

"Because of the potential for loss of life?"

Prospero's green eyes seemed to look straight through him. "No. I don't care about people. I'm not one of them."

"Then why?"

"Because it's a waste of intellectual opportunity."

"Fair enough," said Greene, interested. "What else?"

"Well, Dad doesn't believe in anything. Not God or a larger world. Nothing. And he hates it because I do. He thinks it's a waste of my time. A distraction. He'd rather me spend all my time in the lab." Prospero snorted. "Have you seen the latest upgrades to my lab? Dad broke through the wall so that I now have the entire basement. All of it. He got rid of his billiards room to put in new sequencers and to give me table space to build whatever I want."

"That's very generous."

Prospero shook his head. "I kind of like you, Doc, so I'm going to pretend you're not that naïve. We both know that Dad will keep giving me as much scientific equipment as he can cram into the house in the hopes that I make another toy for him."

Greene nodded. Twice in the last sixteen months Prospero had built small electronic devices that, from things the father let slip, had great potential for military application. Greene did not understand the science, even when Prospero tried to explain it to him. Something about a short-range field disruptor and something else about a beam regulator. Whatever they were. Oscar Bell had been extremely excited about both, and from the things Greene had picked up, was able to obtain contracts to develop them for the Department of Defense.

Prospero had been mostly indifferent to the devices, labeling them as "junk," and ultimately disregarding them because they did not help him in his "work." He said one was a by-product and the other was an interesting side effect. Greene was trying to determine what that work was, convinced it was a key factor in understanding Prospero.

Overall, Oscar Bell was openly obsessed with his son's genius. Bell talked about almost nothing else, and that was disturbing to Greene. He did not know how this would play out over time. Bell was the least pleasant man Greene had ever met. He was acquisitive, demanding, inflexible, and probably cruel in many ways. His household staff was terrified of him and there was a high turnover rate among them. Bell was the kind of man who had no real friends and instead relied on maintaining a network of acquaintances whose shared agendas were based on financial reward rather than personal enrichment.

"I guess you know," said Prospero, "that Dad hates me because I actually believe in something. He thinks it's a distraction. He accused me of losing focus."

"Do you believe, Prospero?" asked Greene, surprised. "You've told me on numerous occasions that you reject the idea of the Judeo-Christian version of God. You said that Jesus and Mohammed and Buddha were all con men. Those are your words."

"I know. I was only ten, so that was the best I could phrase it at the time."

Greene had to suppress a smile. He said, "Would you care to restate your position?"

Prospero shot him a sly look. "Let's just say that I've opened my mind to other possibilities."

"What possibilities? Is it something your mother suggested?"

The boy seemed surprised by that. "What? No. She's a loon."

"Then what?"

Prospero shrugged. "Something else. I'm not ready to talk about it." He paused, considering, then changed the subject. "Do you remember the dream I had last Christmas? About having brothers and sisters?"

"Of course. You said that you believed there were at least fifty other children like you."

"Exactly like me. Same face," said Prospero. "Even the girls looked like me. We were all in a big room. Not a school exactly and not a hospital. A little of both. It was a horrible place, though. The people who worked there hated us. No . . . no, that's wrong. They were afraid of us."

"So you told me. Why do you bring it up now?"

The boy looked at his hands for a moment. "I dreamed about one of them again. Last night, I mean. In my dreams most of my brothers and sisters were dead. All but one. A sister."

Greene said nothing. He'd asked Oscar Bell about this and had been told, very curtly, to mind his own business. The encounter, and the boy's persistent dreams, reinforced Greene's suspicion that Prospero was adopted.

"What can you recall about her?" asked Greene, but Prospero shrugged.

"Not much. She was sad. She was older in my dream. Grown up. And she was sad. She'd been hurt. Shot, I think. She didn't die but she was sad because she couldn't have babies." The boy knotted and un-knotted his fingers. "That was all there was to the dream, but it was so real. More real than us talking right now. I don't think it was just a dream. I think I do have a sister and that she's out there somewhere. And . . . she looks exactly like me. Not like clones. Something else . . ."

His voice trailed off.

"Very well. Have you ever shared these dreams with your father?"

"No. I tried once and he smacked me across the face."

"That was two years ago," said Greene. "Your father told me that he'd hit you and that he was very sorry. Perhaps you could try to talk to him again. If not about your dreams, then perhaps about your relationship? About your feelings about his focus on your scientific achievements."

"Share? With Dad?" Prospero laughed. "Dad doesn't talk to me. Not unless it's to ask what I'm working on and how it could be used."

"Used?"

"You know what I mean," snapped Prospero. "Daddy-dear's always fishing for the next shiny toy to sell to the military. You think all of this—the mansion, the cars, the private jet, all that crap—comes from what he makes in the private sector? Please. It's all military contracts and he's always after me to come up with something because he's tapped out when it comes to his own genius."

"You're only a boy."

Prospero gave him a withering look. "We both know that's not really true."

In that moment the boy sounded like an old man. There was a world-weariness unearned by the number of years he'd already lived. It was in his eyes, too.

"So, no," concluded Prospero, "Dad doesn't say a lot to me. Not the way people do."

"Your father is a reticent man," said Greene. "Do you know that word? Reticence?"

"Of course I do. And it doesn't really fit him. Dad's simply an ass-hole."

"He's your father. You shouldn't speak like that about him."

"Really? You want me to start self-editing in therapy?"

Greene flinched. "Fair enough. My apologies."

JONATHAN MABERRY

"Dad hates me," said Prospero.

"You must know that's not true," said Greene.

Prospero gave him a pitying look. "Of course it is."

They went back and forth on that for a bit, but Greene knew it was an argument he could not win. Perhaps "contempt" was not the best word to describe how Oscar Bell treated his son, but it was close and everyone knew it. The father even intimated as much, telling Greene in private that "If it wasn't for his brains, the kid wouldn't be worth the money it takes to feed him. I sure as shit can't take him out anywhere. After what he did at the science fair? No way."

At a national science fair for grade-school kids, an eight-year-old Prospero took out his penis and urinated all over the judges' table, all the while loudly proclaiming that they weren't smart enough to judge a competition for the smelliest dog turd. It was not an isolated incident. Oscar Bell had been forced to write a lot of checks to mollify the judges, the school, and, Greene suspected, the press.

"I don't want to talk about Dad anymore," declared Prospero.

Greene accepted it, recognizing that particular tone in the boy's voice. "What would you like to talk about? We have plenty of time. I see you've added something new to your hoodie."

Prospero raised a hand and touched the tangle of tentacles that he'd drawn with such care on the gray cloth and down onto the green jacket.

"Is that from something you read?" asked Greene. "Or from a video game?"

"I don't play video games anymore."

"Oh? Why not?"

"They're designed to encourage failure," said Prospero. "The game levels get more difficult and complicated and you waste a lot of time beating them."

"Isn't that the point of those games? Overcoming obstacles and—"

"No. The point of those games is to addict people to playing them and make them desperate to win. But each time you beat a level your 'reward' is another even more difficult level. Addiction isn't growth. The game designers make them for sheep. I'm not a sheep because sheep are for slaughter."

"Prospero . . . have you been having thoughts of hurting yourself?"

"No, and don't be stupid. You know that's not what I meant. I said I was not a sheep." The boy paused. "Look, if the game designers wanted smarter kids to play there would be something better at the end of the last level than some cheap 'you won' graphic bullshit. I don't have time to waste on games. It's not what I care about."

Prospero once more touched the tentacles he'd drawn on his hood. He shrugged again.

Greene asked, "What is that thing? If it's not from a game, then where did you come up with it?"

There was a long pause during which Prospero's fingers traced the lines of ink on the gray cloth hood. When he spoke his voice was soft, distant, the way people spoke sometimes when they were quoting something that was deeply important to them. "'A monster of vaguely anthropoid outline, but with an octopus-like head whose face was a mass of feelers, a scaly, rubbery-looking body, prodigious claws on hind and fore feet, and long, narrow wings behind.'"

"What is that quote? Is it from a book?"

Prospero shrugged. "It doesn't matter. I know you're recording this. You can look it up later. All that matters is that it's something someone dreamed once and wrote down. Don't focus on the messenger, pay attention to the message."

"And what is the message?"

Prospero burned off nearly a full minute before he answered. During that time he reached up and pulled the hood forward so that the shadows now obscured his entire face.

"People are afraid of the Devil. They think the Antichrist is going to come and go mano a mano with Jesus, blah blah blah. That's bullshit. You're a Jew, so I know you don't believe it. Or, maybe you're an atheist and really don't buy into any of that apocalyptic bullshit."

Greene said, "My personal beliefs are irrelevant to this conversation, Prospero. The question is what do you believe?"

Instead of answering that question directly, the boy asked, "How would you answer if I said, *'Ph'nglui mglw'nafh Cthulhu R'lyeh wgah'nagl fhtagn'*?"

"I have no idea what that is or what it might mean."

"It's a prayer I learned in my dreams."

"I would like to talk to you about your dreams, Prospero. You know I've always found them fascinating."

Prospero leaned his face out of the shadows and the smile he wore made Dr. Greene actually recoil. It was a smile filled with strange lights and ugly promises. It was not a smile Greene had ever seen on

JONATHAN MABERRY

the boy's face before, or on any human face. It was less sane than the Joker from Batman, and less wholesome than the toothy grin of a shark. It was so sudden and so intense and so wholly unexpected that Greene flinched.

"Dr. Greene," said the boy, "I'll miss you when I leave this world."

CHAPTER FOUR

The LC-130 did a pass so we could take a good look at Gateway. The scattered buildings looked like tiny cardboard boxes, the kind Christmas ornaments come in. Small and fragile. As we swept up and around for the approach to the icy landing strip, I had a panoramic view of Antarctica. I've been in a lot of Mother Earth's terrains—deserts, rain forests, caverns, grassy plains, and congested cities—but nothing ever gave me the feeling of absolute desolation that I got from the landscape below. There was white and white and white, but mixed into that were a thousand shades of gray and blue. The total absence of the warmer colors made me feel cold even in the pressurized and heated cabin of the plane. I could already feel the toothy bite of that wind.

Suddenly Bug was in our ears. "Got some stuff and I don't think you're going to like it."

"We're in Antarctica, Bug," I said. "Our expectations are already pretty low."

"Yeah, even so," he said. "There are so many darn layers to this thing. They really went out of their way to hide it. They tried to keep the whole thing totally off the public radar, but with the ice caps melting there are too many people looking at the poles. So they have a cover story for when they need it."

"Which is?"

"Studying the Antarctic Big Bang. Before you ask, I had to look that up, too," said Bug. "Apparently a few years ago planetary scientists found evidence of a meteor impact that was earlier and a lot bigger than the one that killed the dinosaurs. They say it caused the biggest mass extinction in Earth's history, the Permian-Triassic. We're talking two hundred and fifty million years ago. There's a crater on the eastern side of the continent that's something like three hundred miles wide. The impact was so massive that it might have caused the breakup of the supercontinent of Gondwana. They've taken a lot of samples from meteor debris and it looks like the meteor was actually a chunk of rock knocked out of the surface of Mars by an asteroid that smacked it during the Permian Age. And there are some scientists who say that there was an even earlier impact about a billion years ago."

"You're saying Gateway was set up to study Martian rock?" I asked.

"Well . . . on paper, yeah," said Bug. "With a bias toward looking for microbes that might prove the existence of life on Mars. The colonists they're planning to send need to know stuff like that. But that's only the cover story, and it's the same cover story the Russians and Chinese used when they set up shop. The problem is that when I go deeper what I find are files marked VBO."

VBO means "verbal briefing only." All pertinent information is to be relayed in person. Nothing written. Or if there are papers they're typed old school and photocopied. Nothing in a searchable database. Nothing e-mailed. Ever since some skittish types in the DoD and Congress got wind of MindReader there are more and more VBO files popping up. It's making me cranky.

"This is fascinating as shit, Bug," I groused, "but it doesn't tell me what I need to know. Find out who is writing checks for this thing and tell Mr. Church that I want interrogators making life unpleasant for them until I know why I'm about to freeze my nuts off."

"Copy that," he said, and disconnected.

The pilot put us down with no trouble and informed us that the twilight temperature outside was a balmy fifty-six below. He told us that, temperature-wise, we caught a break.

Let's pause on that for a moment.

Fifty-six below.

And that is miles from what's considered cold down here. Pretty nippy by my personal standards, however.

We bundled. Mr. Church always makes sure we have the best toys, and one of the goodies we had were Therma-skinz, a pre-market kind of long johns that had micro-fine heating elements woven into the fabric of the new generation of spider-silk Kevlar. We'd stay warm and moderately bulletproof. The 'Skinz were ultralightweight and designed for combat troops who need to move and fight.

"You ready, Farm Boy?" asked Top.

Bunny looked out the window. "Nope," he said.

CHAPTER FIVE

He lay back and got comfortable. Back then comfort mattered. Back then it took a lot to get him in the mood.

No sleeping pills. He'd tried those, but that was a mistake. Sometimes the drugs blocked him; sometimes the drugs trapped him. A nightmare either way.

Comfort was the thing. A good bed with enough pillows. A recliner by the fire. The sofa in his office. Maybe later it would be easier. Cat naps. That would be good. That was a goal. A little sleep on the road, on a mission, in the field.

For now, though, he had to cater to the needs of the body in order to soothe the mind and open all those doors.

He closed his eyes and let himself drift.

Drift.

Drift.

Until he was very far away.

CHAPTER SIX

The LC-130's nose lifted on powerful hydraulics to allow us to drive the snowcat out, and the inrush of frigid air was like a punch in the face. I tugged my balaclava into place as I walked down the ramp with Bunny. Top drove the cat and the flight crew waved him down and guided him onto the access road. The crew was instructed to button up the plane and remain aboard. A team from Gateway was supposed to refuel the bird, but so far no one had come to meet us. That was troubling for all of the obvious reasons.

The closest buildings were utility sheds, all of which were dark and probably locked. The main building was a quarter mile away—a two-story central structure with single-story wings stretching off as if embracing the foot of the mountain.

"Lights are on," said Bunny.

"Doesn't mean anyone's home," murmured Top.

We had all of our normal gear and a lot of the nasty little gadgets developed for us by Dr. Hu. But Bug's information about the ancient meteor strikes made me paranoid about some kind of weirdo alien space bugs trapped in ancient ice and now melting because of the engines and general operations of Gateway. So I made sure we all wore BAMS units. These are man-portable bio-aerosol mass spectrometers that were used for real-time detection and identification of biological aerosols. They have a vacuum function that draws in ambient air and hits it with continuous wave lasers to fluoresce individual particles. Key molecules like bacillus spores, dangerous viruses, and certain vegetative cells are identified and assigned color codes. Thanks to Mr. Church we had the latest models, which were about the size of a walkie-talkie. We clipped them to our belts. As long as the little lights were green we were all happy. Orange made us sweat. If they turned red we'd be running like hell.

We climbed onto the snowcat and I'm pretty sure we were all thinking something was hinky with Gateway. When you lived at the bottom of the world, visitors were rare. You came out to greet them. And yet every door on the station remained closed. We drove in silence to the main building and Top parked us at an angle that would allow the cat to offer us protection if this turned into an ambush. He idled there for a full minute.

Nothing.

"Maybe they're putting their mittens on," suggested Bunny.

"Uh-huh," grunted Top. "And maybe they're baking us some cookies."

"Let's get to work," I said. "Combat call signs only."

I screwed a bud into my ear and tapped it. "Cowboy to Bug. Talk to me."

"Welcome to the winter wonderland, Cowboy." The fidelity of the speaker was superb and Bug sounded like he was right next to me instead of sipping hot cocoa at the tactical operations center at the Hangar, the main DMS facility in Brooklyn. "We are mission active and all telemetry is in the green."

"Okay, we're on the ground and about to leave the cat," I said. "Bunny, let's go knock. Top, watch our backs."

Top nodded and clicked the switches that made a pair of thirty-millimeter chain guns rise from concealed pods. A second set of switches folded down a pair of stubby wings on which were mounted Hellfire missiles, six per side. Like I said, Mr. Church always makes sure we have the best toys.

"Don't get trigger-happy, old man," said Bunny.

"Don't get in my way if I do, Farm Boy," said Top.

We got out. The sun was a cold and distant speck of light that seemed poised to drop off the edge of the world. Winds cut across the open plain with the ferocity of knives. The 'Skinz kept us from freezing, but the cold seemed to find every devious opening in our face masks and goggles.

I stopped and raised my head to listen to the wind. It blew across so many jagged peaks that it picked up all sorts of whistles and howls. I wasn't experienced enough with this part of the world and its sounds, but it seemed to me that there was more to that wind than the natural vagaries of aerodynamic acoustics. It actually seemed like the wind was shrieking at us.

Bunny caught it, too. "The fuck is that?"

I had no answers and didn't want to give in to any kind of discussion on the topic.

"Time to clock in," I said. "Bug, where are we with thermal scans?"

"They're online but the readings are all over the place. First I get one signature, then I have a couple of hundred, then a dozen, then none. It keeps changing. I don't think we can trust that intel. Geological survey of the area indicates heavy concentration of metal ores in those mountains." He paused. "Not sure why that's messing with thermal imaging for the buildings, though. Best I can advise is to proceed with extreme caution."

"Roger that."

Bunny swore softly and then faded to the left side of the main door; I took the right side. I reached out a hand and knocked on the door. Even when you know it's a waste of time, you go through the motions in case you're wrong. And, sometimes you do the expected thing in order to provoke a reaction.

We got no reaction at all.

I reached for the handle. It turned easily and the lock clicked open.

Bunny mouthed the words, "So much for the concept of a 'secure facility.'"

I waved my hand for Top. He turned off the snowcat, dropped down to the ice, and came up on our six, fast and steady.

We entered in silence, moving quick, covering each other . . . and then stopped. Just inside the metal doorway was a small vestibule, and the back wall of it was one mother of a steel airlock.

"Bug," I said. "Tell me why I'm looking at an airlock."

"Huh? Um . . . I don't know, it's not on the schematics for the old radar station. And there's nothing in the materials purchases or requisitions about it."

"Balls."

Top ran his hand over the smooth steel. "Ten bucks says it's a Huntsman."

I nodded. In our trade we get to see every kind of airlock they make. And, unfortunately, we get to deal with what's behind most of those airlocks. Fun times.

"There's a geometry hand scanner, too," said Bunny. "Pretty sure it's a Synergy Software Systems model. The new one that came out last December."

"Good," said Bug, "that gives me a starting point. Sergeant Rock, put on a glove and run the scanner."

Top took a polyethylene glove from a pocket and pulled it onto his right hand. It looked like the blue gloves worn by cops and airport security, but this one was veined with wires and sensors that uplinked it via satellite to MindReader. He placed his hand on the geometry scanner and let the lasers do their work. Normally they create a 3-D map of the exact terrain of the whole hand, but the sensors hijacked that process and fed the scan signature into MindReader. The computer fed its own intrusion program into the scanner and essentially told it to recognize the hand. Sure, I'm oversimplifying it, but I'm a shooter, not a geek. I'm always appropriately amazed and I make the right oooh-ing and ahhh-ing sounds when Bug shows me this stuff, but at the end of the day I just want the damn door open.

The damn door opened.

"You da man," Bunny said to Bug.

We stepped back from the airlock as the two-ton steel door swung out on nearly silent hydraulics. I expected a flood of fluorescent light and a warm rush of air. Instead we saw only darkness and felt a cold wind blow out at us like the exhalation of a sleeping giant. It was fetid air, though, and it stank of oil and smoke and chemicals. But it was more than that. Worse than that.

It was a meat smell.

Burst meat. Raw meat.

Like the inside of a butcher's freezer.

INTERLUDE THREE

OFFICE OF DR. MICHAEL GREENE
EAST HAMPTON, NEW YORK
WHEN PROSPERO WAS ELEVEN

"Prospero," said Greene, "we need to talk about your dream diary."

"I figured we would," said the boy. He sat on the floor between the potted ficus and the couch.

"When I asked you to start your dream diary it was with the understanding that you shared your own dreams."

"That's what I'm doing."

"Prospero, if these are your own dream images, then what should we think about this?" Greene had his laptop open and he turned it so they could both see the screen. Then he held up one of the boy's drawings, which showed a pair of giants kneeling in water. The giant on the left was colored in umber and other earth tones; the one on the right was in cooler blues and grays. On the screen there was a high-resolution jpeg of a painting with almost identical composition and color. "This is a very famous painting called *Metamorphosis of Narcissus*," said Greene. "It was painted in 1937 by the artist Salvador Dalí."

"Yes," said Prospero.

"You admit to having copied this painting?"

"No."

"But—"

"My drawing is different," he said. "It's not the same angle, and some of the other things are different. The decay on the stone figure is worse in mine. And in Dalí's painting there is a hand holding up a bulb from which another figure is growing. I didn't put that in because that figure's not there anymore. The sky's different, too. He painted it at twilight, but mine is clearly dawn."

Greene said, "Making changes to someone else's art is not the point. You took the theme and basic composition from Dalí and gave it to me as if it was something from your own dreams."

Prospero shook his head. "No, that's not what happened."

"It is. And I checked, most of your 'dream' images are borrowed from paintings by famous artists. The big organic machine picture is *The Elephant Celebes* by Max Ernst. The drawing of the red building is Giorgio de Chirico's *The Red Tower.* Do you want me to go on?"

"Wait," said Prospero, surprised, "are you mad at me?"

"I'm disappointed. I thought we had established a relationship of honesty, Prospero. I don't enjoy being lied to."

The boy looked alarmed. "I'm not lying. You're the only person I ever tell the truth to. The whole truth."

"Then explain these drawings. Why did you copy them and try to pass them off as your own?"

"No," said Prospero quickly. "Look at them. You think my bull-god is the same as de Chirico's? It's not. My bull is older and it has the marks of the whip and the claw. It's ready to be given to the Elder Things as payment."

"That doesn't make sense," said Greene. "Did you know about these paintings before you had your 'dreams'?"

"I knew of them before I started the dream diary for you," explained the boy, clearly upset, "but that's because I went looking for them."

"What does that mean?"

"I . . . well, I've always had dreams like this. I never dream about the stuff human kids dream about."

"You are human, Prospero."

"Don't start that again, Doc. Not now, okay?"

Greene spread his hands. In several previous sessions Prospero had expressed his hope that there were others like him here on Earth, and that if he found them maybe together they would be able to solve the problem of how to get home. Wherever and whatever home was. "Continue," he said, his patience thin.

"I had those dreams and then once I was surfing the Net, looking for people like me, you know? That's when I found this Web site about the artwork of the surrealism movement. There was a painting by Max Ernst that showed the Loplop."

Greene nodded, and located the image online, and then in Prospero's sketchbook. It showed a strange creature that was part bird, part human, and entirely unreal. The artist had done a number of drawings of the creature, claiming that it was his alter ego, which he also referred to as his "private phantom." The painting that matched—or nearly matched—one of Prospero's drawings was one of the creature in the midst of running, or perhaps dancing. The painting, known as *L'Ange du Foyer (Le Triomphe du Surréalisme)*, or *The Fireside Angel*, was subtitled "The Triumph of Surrealism."

Prospero came over and bent to touch the picture on the laptop screen. His touch was gentle and on his face was an expression of self-aware pleasure that Greene thought looked beatific. There was text beneath the image, and Prospero read it in a soft voice. "'Naked, they dress only in their majesty and their mystery.'" He turned to the doctor. "Don't you get it? This isn't me copying what they did. This is me finding other people like me. Other people who have seen the things I've seen. Not just Ernst. Others. André Breton, Louis Aragon, and Philippe Soupault." He laughed and then rattled off a long list of names. "Paul Éluard, Benjamin Péret, René Crevel, Max Morise, Man Ray, Roger Vitrac, Gala Éluard, Salvador Dalí, Howard Phillips Lovecraft, Joan Miró, Marcel Duchamp, Jacques Prévert, Yves Tanguy . . ."

Greene held a hand up to stop him. "I'm not sure I understand what you're trying to tell me."

"They saw what I see. They knew it's real. They wrote about it, painted it, told people about it. They knew, Doc. They knew that my world exists. Do you know how much I needed that? To know that I'm not crazy, that this is real?"

Greene said nothing. This was a dangerous moment for the boy and he had to decide if he had reached a new level with Prospero or if the boy had revealed just how far his psychosis ran.

Before he could organize a comment, Prospero snatched up the sketchbook and hugged it to his chest.

"I think I understand now," he declared. "Those devices I've been building? The ones my dad keeps taking from me and selling to the military? They're nothing. That was just me starting the wrong way. No . . . no, it was me getting up to speed. But this, this," he said, thumping his palm against his sketchbook so hard that it seemed he wanted to push the book into his own heart, "this is what I needed to make me stop doubting myself. God, it's like a light went on in my head the way it does in cartoons. Wow. I know, Doc. I really know what I have to do. The writers, they've been dropping clues for years. Lovecraft, Derleth, Howard? All of them, the ones everyone thinks were writing stupid horror stories? They weren't. Oh no. Oh, hell no. They were dropping clues. They were sending up smoke signals, knowing that someone like me would be out there, watching, looking, waiting for contact."

"Prospero," said Greene evenly, "I'm going to need you to calm down. Why don't you take a seat and let's do some control breathing together—"

"Shhh, Doc," said Prospero, "you need to listen now. This is so big. This is so huge my head feels like it opened up on hinges. I can feel the truth in there. I can feel the answers. They're whispering to me. They want me to find them." He cut Greene an almost conspiratorial look. "You've been a big help. You kicked me in the butt and now I know what I have to do."

"What is it you think you have to do?" asked Greene carefully.

"I have to find the books. They all hinted about them. Those writers, they weren't writing about fake monster stuff. They were making sure the clues got out there. Most people—the human herd—they think it's all nonsense and junk. But it's not. No. I need to find those books and then I need to get to work building it."

"Building . . . what?"

"My God Machine," said Prospero as if that answer should have been obvious to even the meanest intelligence. Laughter bubbled out of him. "I bet my dad would even help me. He'll have to. He'll want to."

"What is a God Machine, Prospero?"

The boy walked slowly across the room, still clutching the sketchbook to his chest. He stopped by the window and raised his face to the warm sunlight.

"It's how I'm going to go home," he said.

CHAPTER SEVEN

I heard Bunny's sharp intake of breath.

I heard Top softly murmur, "God in heaven."

Then something moved in the darkness. We crouched, weapons ready, barrels following line of sight, fingers lying nervously along the curves of our trigger guards.

Inside the chamber, a dozen yards away, we could hear something. It wasn't footsteps. Not exactly. This was a soft, almost furtive sound. A shift and scrape as if whatever moved in there did not move well. Or was unable to move well.

"NV," I said very quietly and we all flipped down the night-vision devices on our helmets. The world of snow white and midnight black instantly transformed to an infinitely stranger world of greens and grays.

The thing in the darkness was at the very outside range of total clarity. It moved and swayed with a broken rhythm, obscured by rows of stacked supplies.

"What the fuck . . . ?" breathed Bunny.

The thing moved toward us, a huge, weird shape that was in no way human. Pale and strange, it shuffled steadily toward the open door, but we only caught glimpses of it as it passed behind one stack of crates and then another. The abattoir stink of the place was awful and it seemed to intensify as this creature advanced on us.

"Got to be a polar bear," whispered Bunny.

"Wrong continent," said Top.

Their voices were hushed. They were talking because they were scared, and that was weird. These guys were pros, recruited to the DMS from the top SpecOps teams in the country. They don't run off at the mouth to relieve stress. Not them.

Except they were.

"Cut the chatter," I snapped, and from the way they stiffened I knew that it wasn't my rebuke that hit them—but the realization that they were breaking their own training. Each of them would have fried a junior team member for making that kind of error. So . . . why had they?

The thing in the darkness was behind the closest set of crates now. In a few seconds it would shuffle into view. I could feel fear dumping about a pint of adrenaline into my bloodstream.

And then the creature moved into our line of sight.

In the glow of the night vision it was green and unnatural, though I knew that it was really white. Not the vital white of an Alaskan polar bear, or the pure white of a gull's breast. No, this was a sickly hue and I knew that even with the NV goggles. This was a pallor that had never been touched by sunlight, even the cold light here at the frozen bottom of the world. This was a mushroom white, a sickly and abandoned paleness that could only have acquired that shade in a place of total darkness. It provoked in me an antagonism born of repugnance and I nearly shot it right there and then.

The creature was as tall as Bunny—six and a half feet or more—with a grotesquely fat body and eyes that were nothing more than useless slits in its hideous face.

I heard a sound. A short, humorless laugh of surprise and disgust. Could have been Top, or Bunny. Or me.

"It's a goddamn *penguin* . . ." said Bunny, his voice filled with surprise and wonder.

A penguin?

Sure it was.

In a way.

The problem is that it was too big. Way too goddamn big. Massive. Twice the size of the Emperor penguins and bigger than the prehistoric penguins I saw in a diorama at the Smithsonian. The wings were stubby and useless as if it no longer flew even through the water. The beak was pale and translucent; the body was blubbery and awkward. It waddled toward us and we gave ground, though we kept our guns on the thing. Crazy as it sounds, I was scared of it. The sight of it was triggering reactions that were way down in my lizard brain—miles from where rational thought could laugh off instinctive reactions.

The penguin shambled past us through the airlock but then it suddenly stopped at the exterior door. The sunlight was almost gone but what little there was touched its face. The creature turned toward the warmth for a single moment, and then it reeled backward from the light and uttered a terrible sound. It was the kind of strangled shriek of terror you hear only from animals whose throats are not constructed for sound—like rabbits and deer. A scream that is torn from the chest and dragged through the vocal cords in a way so violent and wet that you know it has damaged everything it touched. The penguin careened into the wall as it fled backward from the touch of the dying sunlight. Its screams were terrible.

Even after the blind animal crashed backward into the airlock it continued to scream and scream. I could see black beads of moisture flying from its beak and with sick dread I knew that they were drops of bloody spit from its ruined throat.

"Boss . . . ," said Bunny, his voice urgent with concern and horror.

"Push it back inside," yelled Top.

Bunny let his rifle hang from its strap and with a wince of distaste he placed his hands on the animal's back and gave it a short, sharp push toward the airlock, away from the sunlight. The penguin paused, though, at the mouth of the airlock, and immediately began fighting its way backward, screaming into the darkness it had come out of. Bunny shoved again, throwing his massive upper-body strength against the creature's resistance. It lurched forward, but then it turned and stabbed at Bunny with its pale beak. Bunny howled in pain as the razor-sharp beak tore through the knitted wool of his balaclava. Black blood erupted in a line from the corner of Bunny's mouth to his ear.

"Shoot the fucking thing!" bellowed Bunny as he backpedaled, shielding his eyes from another peck.

Top shoved him out of the way and raised his Glock. There was a single, sharp *crack!* A black hole appeared between the slitted, useless eyes of the penguin and the entire back of its head exploded outward to spray the line of stacked crates. The sheer bulk of the thing kept it upright for a moment, giving the weird impression that the bullet hadn't killed it. Then it leaned slowly sideways and collapsed.

We stood there in a loose circle staring at it.

Bunny said, "What . . . ?"

Just the one word and he let it trail off because clearly we had no more answers than he did.

JONATHAN MABERRY

CHAPTER EIGHT

THE FIRST PULSE
NASCAR SPRINT CUP CHASE GRID
FIVE MONTHS AGO

Sixteen cars roared around the track.

In the stands tens of thousands of fans leapt to their feet in groups as the cars swept around. The race was five minutes old. Every car was still in the game; all of the drama and potential was still ahead. Anything could still happen. And this was the start of the NASCAR Spring Cup series. With each race more of the drivers would be eliminated until that last grueling challenge between the top four. All of that was to come.

This was the first race.

Everyone was wired. The announcer and color commentator were already yelling, calling the moves, talking about the drivers and their cars, their histories, their crashes, their lucky escapes, their courage. Pit crews were in position, each of them ready, and even the most jaded among them filled with nervous energy as they watched the cars accelerate to breakneck speeds.

Even though it was early, vendors were selling beer by the hundred gallon. Hot dogs and chicken wings, chips and pretzels were being devoured by the ton.

It had all started. The race season was on.

Danny Perry, the rising star of the NASCAR world who'd come out of nowhere two years ago to win a record number of races, was there, third back on the inside, driving a Ford Fusion with the decal of a sports drink on the hood and half a dozen other advertisers crowding the doors and roof. The car had a sky blue body, and images from the interior cameras inside the car flashed the masked and helmeted face of the four-wheeled hero onto the screens. The hot money was on him to come in no lower than fourth, and maybe even second place. High enough to insure his place in the rest of the series. Some of the sports reporters were saying that he had the chops to make it all the way to the winning flag at the end of the season. He had more under the hood, they said. He had tricks he hadn't yet used, they said. He had things to prove, they said.

A lot of fans in the stands wore his colors. One group of three hundred people who had bussed in from his hometown of Greenwood had little fans with cutouts of his face on them, and each time his car roared past they waved his own image at him, and then chased him with their screams.

The cars ripped around the track, changing places, fighting each other for position, taking calculated risks, going too fast for mistakes. The interior cameras flashed one face, then another and another, onto the screens. The helmets and fireproof masks showed nothing, but the commentators made those masked faces human with anecdotes and predictions. The crowds knew the faces of their heroes anyway.

Twenty-six minutes in, just as the pack began to stretch out and lose its bee-swarm shape, Danny Perry made his move. He was known for waiting to see how the other drivers were playing it, getting the pulse of the players on the field, and then he'd make a move to take the lead. So far he'd made that play sixteen times, and each time he got the lead early he kept it. As soon as he cut through a gap that didn't look wide enough for a bicycle and shot out in front with an acceleration that lived up to the hype, the crowd went absolutely mad. Even the fans who weren't rooting for Danny leapt to their feet because this was a history-book moment. Danny wasn't racing against anyone who lived on the second or third tier of the sport. He was jousting with kings, and he'd just taken the lead in a move that made a bold damn statement.

Catch me if you can.

If you can.

The whole pace—already insane—rose up as the hunt began in earnest. It was going to be brutal. Everyone knew it.

Which is when it all went to hell.

There was no warning. No bomb. Nothing that indicated an attack. Nothing sinister.

On one side of a scalding moment of raw high-speed entertainment, sixteen stock cars raced at more than 185 miles an hour. Danny Perry had bulled his way to 190.3.

On the other side of that moment the engines of every car on the track stopped.

There were no explosions. Not at first.

The electrical conduction within the transmissions ceased. Gone. Just as the video feeds from the cameras and the big screens mounted around the track went dark. Bang. The commentators' voices were silenced. Just like that.

Only the sound of the crowd pushed its way past the moment. They were screaming, cheering, yelling. And then when the first cars spun out of control and the next wave struck them, it was only the screams that lingered.

Lingered, grew, rose, detonated into shrill blasts of horror as every car crunched together. The drivers had no chance. There was no power at all. No steering, nothing. Only the bull muscle of feet on brakes and desperate hands on dying steering wheels gave the cars any chance.

It was too small a chance, though. The speeds were too great. The shock was too much.

Engines exploded. Electricity was not flowing and there were no sparks from damaged wires. No, the sparks that touched off the fuel were from metal hitting metal. Not many sparks.

Enough.

Enough was too much.

A fireball punched upward from amid the crunched fist of the collision. The screams of the crowd changed in pitch, rising higher, sounding like a great flock of birds in pain.

CHAPTER NINE

THE VINSON MASSIF
THE SENTINEL RANGE OF THE ELLSWORTH MOUNTAINS
ANTARCTICA
AUGUST 19, 10:39 P.M.

Top pulled off his helmet and balaclava so he could see better as he applied a quick field dressing to Bunny's face. I stood guard. Nobody talked about the penguin. We probably should have, but we didn't.

Instead Bunny asked the only question that mattered. "What the hell is going on down here?"

Good question, but none of us had even a clue how to answer it.

Once Bunny's wound was dressed we began moving again. I checked the BAMS unit and got the same steady green, so I tugged down the edge of my own balaclava and sniffed the air. It smelled of machine oil, ozone, ice, and sulfur. Nothing more mysterious than that. Even the rotted meat smell seemed less evident the deeper we went into the complex.

We checked the rest of the storeroom, but it was empty.

Almost empty.

There were no more penguins and there were no people, but all along the back wall there was blood. Pools of it. Drops of it. Arterial sprays of it on the wall.

"Oh . . . shit," breathed Bunny.

Against the wall was a stack of crates that was ten boxes high and went all the way to the ceiling, the wooden boxes pressed closed. Somebody had written across the face of the stack.

THE SEQUENCE IS WRITTEN IN THE STARS

"The hell's that supposed to mean?" asked Bunny.

Instead of answering, Top leaned close to the writing, then he winced and recoiled. He didn't have to tell us what had been used to write those words. The floor was covered with bloody footprints. In shoes, in military-style combat boots, and in bare feet.

"Looks like a parade's been through here," said Top.

"Whoa, whoa," said Bunny, kneeling by one set of boot prints, "look at this. That's not American."

He was right. The tread marks of those boots were different from any of the patterns used on the boots and shoes of American military. In our line of work you learn these things. Just as you learn the tread marks of shoes worn by allies and others. This was an "other."

"Russian," said Top. "No doubt about it. Standard-issue combat boots."

We spread out and checked the rest of the prints and found two other sets of Russian boots and five different sets of Chinese boots.

"So," said Bunny, looking around, "this was an invasion? Does that mean this was an act of war or—?"

Instead of answering I called it in and told Bug, Aunt Sallie, and Church what we'd found. Bloody footprints. No bodies, no shell casings. No answers.

"That base is U.S. military property," said Aunt Sallie. "That makes it de facto U.S. soil. If you encounter enemy combatants anywhere in Gateway and if they do not surrender their weapons, you will respond appropriately to protect yourself, your team, the Gateway staff, and the physical assets on site. In that order."

"Copy that," I said.

Church added, "Get us some answers, Cowboy."

I promised that I would. Answers would be nice. Kicking some ass would be nice, too.

We followed the Russian prints out of the storeroom and down a corridor lined with closed doors. These opened into offices, bedrooms, small labs, an infirmary, and other functional rooms. No one was in any of them and there was no sign of disturbance. No blood, no damage, no shell casings. The bloody footprints had long since faded to paleness and then vanished.

Despite the coldness of the storage room, the temperature was up in all of the other rooms. Very high. The thermostat read 82.

I reached out to turn it down but found that the dial was broken. Someone had jammed a screwdriver into the gear. There were bloody fingerprints all around.

"Our bad guys don't like the cold," said Top.

We pressed on and eventually cleared the whole floor.

"Nobody's home," said Bunny. "Sort of feel happy about that."

"You know what they say about assumptions, Farm Boy," Top said quietly.

Suddenly Bug was in my ear. "Cowboy," he said, "I've been digging up more stuff on this. It's all hidden behind black budget code and—"

I held up my fist and the three of us formed a triangle facing outward.

"We're kind of in the middle of something here, Bug," I said, "so give it to us fast."

"Okay, I'm checking the profiles of everyone on the team and it's really strange. Not the individual members, but what they do. The team leader is Dr. Marcus Erskine, a particle physicist from Cal Tech. His second in command is a quantum physicist named Rinkowski, and you have four top electrical engineers, a structural engineer, an astrophysicist, a geologist, an archaeologist, a professor of comparative anatomy, a psychologist, and—get this—three people with PhDs in parapsychology."

"That's a weird damn posse for studying meteor craters or building EMP cannons," said Top.

Bunny said, "Oh, man . . ."

"Anything on the BAMS units?" asked Bug.

I checked. "Everything's in the green."

"Well, that's good, right? No Martian bacteria."

Top made a disgusted noise. "Now what makes you think our BAMS units would pick up some kind of alien space virus—?"

"Bacteria," corrected Bug.

"I'll hurt you, boy," said Top. "I can fix your mouth so it won't hold soup."

Bug gave a quick, uncertain laugh.

"Top's right," said Bunny. "I do not want to catch something that's going to make me grow a third eye or turn my dick into a cactus."

"Let's not lose our shit," I said. "You have anything else for us, Bug?"

"Just equipment manifests. Hundreds of tons of building materials. And they brought down every kind of drilling and excavating equipment in the catalog. Big stuff, too. Earth movers and a hundred-ton crane."

"For what?" demanded Bunny.

"Documents don't say," said Bug, "but there's something else. We tried to hack the Russian team's mainframe. Their system is offline, but I was able to grab some stuff that had been uploaded to their satellite. They have two separate operations going on. Cowboy . . . it looks like the Russians are building a hadron collider down there."

A hadron collider is a very large particle accelerator that's used to test all kinds of extreme theories in particle physics and high-energy physics. I didn't know a lot about them other than what I learned when I took Trident Team to keep an apocalypse cult from taking over the Large Hadron Collider in the Jura Mountains near the Franco-Swiss border. They believed that if it was ramped up to overload it would create a black hole that would destroy the entire solar system. Or something. I didn't delve too deeply into their rationale. We shot a bunch of them and freed the hostages they'd taken.

"Why in the wide blue fuck would the Russians be building a collider here?" I demanded.

Bug grunted. "You tell me, Cowboy. I just look stuff up. But, from the materials and equipment Erskine brought down with him, there's a chance he was building one, too."

"How's a hadron collider tie into renewable energy research?"

"Not sure it does," Bug said. "It's all weird, because from what we can tell, the EMP project, the crater excavation thing, and the hadron collider all seem to be parts of the same project. Don't ask me how."

I didn't, and since he had nothing else, I ended the call. We stood for a moment, facing out, weapons in our hands, heads filled with questions.

"Anyone else feel like bugging the fuck out of here?" asked Bunny hopefully. "This place is freaking me out and we don't have enough boots on the ground to do this right."

"It's not a job," said Top, "it's an adventure."

We moved off. There was a tunnel that connected the main building to an oversized equipment shed. But when we got there it was empty. No cranes, no drills. The BAMS units kept reading in the green, which was comforting. What we found was not.

What we found instead was a big goddamn hole in the ground.

It was in one corner, but it took up nearly a quarter of the floor space—maybe forty yards across. Like I said, a big hole. It dropped down into shadows.

"Look here," said Top as he squatted down on the far edge. "See this? This isn't a sinkhole, not a proper one. They started digging right here, and from the drill marks on the edge, they got down to a certain point and then something happened. Looks to me like a big-ass chunk of the floor fell in."

Top shone his light down. There was a rough ice slope angling down, steep but walkable. His light swept back and forth, then stopped on a pool of blood. Bunny touched the edge of the pool with his boot.

"Boss," he said quietly, "this hasn't even had time to freeze. Whatever's happening here is still happening."

They looked at me, and I nodded. "Rules of engagement are as follows. Pick your targets, good muzzle discipline. Let's not cap any friendlies . . . but gentlemen, I don't intend to bleed for this thing, whatever it is."

"Hooah," they said. I could see their inner hardness rising to the surface to supplant their fear. Well, some of their fear. I turned my face away, not wanting them to read whatever expression was there.

The ice slope dropped down into shadows. Everything around us was dead quiet. We were too deep underground to hear the howling winds, and all of the machinery here at Gateway was still.

The silence felt wrong, though. It was not the quiet of something empty, something over. It was the quiet of the poised fist. The tension in my chest was like a vise being tightened around my heart.

I licked my lips, which had gone very dry, and then took one single step down the slope. That's when a shrill scream shattered the silence and something came rushing at me out of the shadows.

It was a man. A soldier. Not a Russian. Not a Chinese.

The man was dressed in the camo pattern of the Marine Corps. His eyes were wide and wild, with no trace of sanity. Bloody drool flew from his lips as he shrieked nonsense words.

"Tekeli-li! Tekeli-li!"

His clothes were torn and splashed with gore and he drove straight at me, stabbing at my heart with a bloody bayonet.

CHAPTER TEN

There was no time to dodge out of the way.

He was right there. The blade was falling.

I was dead.

"Tekeli-li! Tekeli-li!"

Then suddenly the man was turning, spinning, twisting, breaking apart as bullets tore into him. I heard the gunshots almost as an after-effect. *Bang! Bang!* Shot after shot as Top and Bunny fired.

The marine slammed into the wall, rebounded, spun halfway around, and dropped face-forward onto the ground, making no attempt to break his fall. The bayonet clattered to the cold stone and the echoes of the gunshots banged and bounced all around me while I simply stood there. I had not moved at all. I hadn't reacted. Not to evade, not to defend myself.

"Cowboy," said Top. He had to repeat it again, more sharply this time, before I snapped out of it. I blinked at him, then down at the dead marine.

"What—?" I asked.

Bunny hurried over and turned me toward the light, checking to see if I'd been injured, but the blade hadn't touched me. I saw the frown of uncertainty carve itself onto Bunny's face.

"You okay, Boss?" he asked.

"I . . ."

It was all I could manage. Top came over and they both studied me for a moment, all of us ignoring the dead man.

"You in there, Cap'n," asked Top gently.

I blinked again and suddenly the strange paralysis was gone. I was myself again and I was back in the moment. It was like waking up from a dream. One of those dreams where you think you're awake but you aren't. You're trapped in that sleep paralysis that keeps you half in one world and half in the other but belonging to neither.

I pushed myself back from them and shook my head. "What just happened?"

No one answered. The facts were all there. Facts, not answers.

I squatted down next to the corpse and rolled him onto his back. He was a Latino man, maybe twenty-three or -four. Probably a good-looking kid in life, but death made him ugly; it made him strangely alien.

"Cowboy," said Bunny, still using my combat call sign, "what happened to you just now? What was that?"

I glanced up at them, then shook my head. "I really don't know."

"I never saw you freeze before," said Top. "Not ever."

All I could do was shake my head. My lack of hesitation in combat has always been one of my most important survival skills. It was one of the reasons Mr. Church picked me to join the DMS. Hesitation kills. Hesitation in a special operator can get a lot of people killed.

So why had I hesitated?

Why?

Top said, "Who is he?"

We all looked at the dead man. The name stitched onto his pocket was GOMEZ. That told us nothing. Top tapped my shoulder with the BAMS unit and I nodded and leaned back to let him run the machine over the poor kid. If Gomez's brain chemistry had been rewired by some kind of pathogen or bioweapon the BAMS unit would pick something up. The green lights didn't flicker.

"What was that he was yelling?" asked Bunny. "That wasn't Spanish."

As if in answer, we heard other voices scream out those same words.

"Tekeli-li! Tekeli-li!"

The shrieks rose out of the shadows from farther down the ice slope. Top and Bunny brought up their guns. This time I was right there with them, my Sig Sauer rising with professional speed and competence. Whatever bizarre hesitation had frozen me a moment ago was gone.

"Tekeli-li! Tekeli-li!"

A knot of figures came swarming out of the darkness. Eight of them. All of them wearing military uniforms. All of them armed with guns, with knives. All of them covered in blood. All of them with eyes that were filled with madness.

"Tekeli-li! Tekeli-li!"

Russians, Chinese, and American military, coming at us like a pack of wolves.

They opened fire at the same moment we did.

The air of that strange place was instantly torn apart as if by a swarm of frenzied hornets. I dropped low against the wall, firing, firing. Top and Bunny split apart, firing, firing.

All of us firing.

The first man was a Chinese soldier and I caught him with a double-tap. One center mass to stall him and one in the head. He was close enough for that kind of precision. His own shots went high and wild. Almost as if he wasn't aiming. He dropped down, those strange words dying on his tongue.

"Tekeli-li! Tek—!"

Bunny sawed through two others, burning halfway through a magazine. On the other side of the slope, Top was cutting a bloody swath.

It was the most savage one-sided fight I'd ever been party to. The eight of them were armed and those with guns were firing, but they weren't aiming. Their rounds hit walls and floor and vanished into the lofty ceiling, but they came nowhere near us.

We did not miss a single shot.

It was all over in ten brutal seconds. It could not have been more than that.

Three of us, eight of them.

A red slaughter.

They fell like broken dolls. Not like soldiers, not like men. They dropped like puppets. Down and down and dead.

The whole world seemed to be filled with thunder. They had been screaming those strange words, but they had not yelled in pain. Not once.

Not one sound as the bullets tore them down.

When it was over we swapped out our magazines and waited for the next wave. Waited for more.

Waited.

Amid the echoes of thunder and the billowing smoke, we waited.

The silence that fell was strange and ugly and wrong in more ways than I can possibly describe.

No one else came running up the slope at us.

CHAPTER ELEVEN

We needed to understand this. I wanted to check these men, to see if there was something about them that would explain this.

The moment wouldn't allow it. Whatever was happening . . . it was down there. Down the slope, inside those deep shadows.

I gave my men a quick, meaningful look and got very tight nods. They were clearly as terrified and confused as I was. This mission had started out wrong and it was slipping sideways, losing whatever tenuous shape it had.

I nodded toward the shadows, then removed a flash-bang from my rig, pulled the pin. I didn't need to call "frag out." We all moved back, looked away, covered our ears.

The flash-bang bounced on the dense ice, then settled into a roll, vanishing into the unknown.

Then it went off.

The bang was huge, magnified by the stone walls and the vastness of the cavern. We ran down the slope, guns ready, barrels tracking everywhere we turned our eyes, ready to fire, ready to continue this surreal fight.

The slope was littered with chunks of ancient ice that was veined with discoloration as if polluted water had been frozen here over the centuries. We saw bloody footprints, going down and coming up. We saw pools of blood and fallen equipment. We passed through the ice layer and entered the rock hardness of the mountain. As the ice gave way we realized that we were on a stone slope, and one that was far too regular to have been anything natural. And far too old to be anything our own drills and engineers had cut.

"Looks clear," said Bunny, though he stood braced to fight.

I put my high-intensity flashlight on the widest beam setting and shone it down. I heard Bunny gasp in the same instant my heart jumped inside my chest.

"Cap'n," breathed Top.

"I know," I said, my throat dry.

"I don't think Erskine's team was looking for no damn meteors," said Top.

"I know."

Bunny just said, "No."

The slope was some kind of rampart that angled downward for at least a thousand yards. It was cracked in places, and in other places byways led off from it to form slopes both angled and flat. It became clear that this was a cavern of unbelievable size. The ceiling soared above us and, except for titanic support pillars of natural rock, the cavern stretched for miles. We could see some of it, just a hint, because of weird bioluminescence—probably some species of mold—that clung to every surface. All around, on the slope, built into the walls, and tumbled ahead of us, were gigantic stone blocks. They were stacked like prefab building units and intercut with other structures—cones, tubes, pyramids, each of fantastic size, some of them taller than the Great Pyramid in Egypt. I know how that sounds, but we were all seeing it.

The flashlight had a quarter-mile reach and it barely brushed the outer perimeters of what could only be a vast city of stone.

INTERLUDE FOUR

The boy was being cooperative for a change. Even expansive. He'd recently had a new series of vivid dreams since their last session and clearly wanted to talk about them, and of course Dr. Greene wanted to hear every detail. Not because these sessions were billed at four hundred an hour, though that was a factor; no, it was because the boy genuinely fascinated Greene. In his entire professional career, including all of his clinical work, he'd never encountered anyone like Prospero Bell. No one as intelligent and no one with this unique combination of skills and psychosis.

"... and then I came through a door in the ice and I was in this immense city," the boy said, continuing a long narrative that had begun with a shipwreck and a walk of days across mud flats that gradually turned into an ice sheet. "Huge city with stone buildings made from geometric shapes. Cones and balls and blocks of all kinds. Wild, because some of those stones were bigger than the Great Pyramid. I saw the pyramids, did I tell you? We went to Egypt when I was nine."

"Yes," said Greene, "you described that trip with great precision. You have a remarkable eye for detail."

Prospero nodded, accepting that as a statement rather than a compliment. "This was bigger, and it looked like the stones were carved out of single blocks. They had to be a million tons. And just thinking about that level of technology knocks me out. Humans couldn't do that, you know. We don't even know how the pyramids were built, and each of these blocks was as big as a whole pyramid."

"Did you see any people in this city?" asked Greene.

"People?" echoed the boy. He looked momentarily confused by the question. "You know, I ... I'm not sure how to answer that. I don't know if the word 'people' applies. There were citizens, I guess you'd say. *Things* that lived there. Really strange, very weird."

"Describe them. Were they like the creatures you sketched?"

"No. They weren't my people. They were different. A separate race."

"Were they the Elder Things? You mentioned them before but you haven't explained what they are."

Prospero thought about that and began nodding. "I . . . think so. And maybe the reason I didn't go into what they are is because I wasn't sure. Not before last night, anyway. Not before this last dream. You're right; I think they are the Elder Things."

"And who exactly are these Elder Things? Are they aliens? Are they gods? What is the name of their race?"

"I don't know. They're too old for that. Names don't matter to beings like that."

"How can a name not matter? What about identity?"

"They know who they are. I guess that's all that matters. But . . . maybe I'm wrong. There are names, I suppose."

"I thought you said they didn't need names," said Greene.

"*They* don't," said Prospero, nodding, his eyes still unfocused, "but people need to call them something, don't they?"

"Can you explain that to me?"

The boy said nothing for a few moments, clearly struggling with the task of explaining the interior logic of a series of dreams. Greene knew that dreams can make perfect sense and be completely clear in the mind but often could not be clearly expressed because spoken language and freeform thought do not always share the same vocabulary.

Prospero grunted and then his eyes came into very sharp focus. "I once read that the Judeo-Christian version of God as a white man with a beard isn't based on anything in the Bible. People made that up because they need to identify with whatever they worship. Every religion does that."

Greene nodded. That had been in one of the books he'd given Prospero to read last year when they were discussing the boy's complex understanding of his own evolving view of spirituality.

"These beings," said Prospero, "don't need names for themselves, okay? But the people who worship them gave them names. Just like people made statues and carved three-D images on walls of gods and demigods and angels and all that. Greeks, Romans, Egyptians, Christians. They all carved those images on walls. What's that called?"

"Bas-relief?" suggested Greene.

"Right," he said, and Greene could almost see the word click into place in the boy's mind. He would never need to ask for the word again. "Statues, too, and icons. All of that."

"Iconography," said Greene.

Prospero nodded, filing it away. "People who see spiritual beings like these need to give them form or they can't think about them. So they paint them and draw pictures of them so they can think about them without going crazy." Prospero's hand strayed to his gray hood and touched the twisting tentacles. "Me, too, I guess."

"Are you saying that the creature you drew is one of these 'beings'?"

"Yes. No. I mean, it's not one of the Elder Things, but's part of that same world. Or . . . same universe, dimension. It's hard to explain."

"But this is something from your imagination."

"No," corrected Prospero quickly. "It's from my dreams."

"Which amounts to the same thing. It's a monster."

"Doc, why do people believe that the things we see in dreams aren't real?"

"Some of them are," conceded Greene, "but many dream images are metaphorical in nature. They represent other things. We talked about sexual imagery and—"

"No," said Prospero firmly. "That's not what I'm talking about. You're supposed to be smart, Dr. Greene. Don't go getting stupid on me now."

Greene nodded, accepting the rebuke.

"I'm asking you a serious question," persisted the boy. "But . . . let me put it another way. And you know I'm talking about the things I've been seeing in my dreams. I know they're real, even if you and my dad don't believe it. No, don't lie. Please. I can see it in your face. You think I'm crazy, and maybe I am—by your standards, by human standards—but I know that what I see aren't dreams, they're visions. Like race memory for people like me." He paused. "Let me ask you a different question, okay?"

"Okay," said Greene.

"You know that I'm really into quantum physics. You know that I understand it. It's not a hobby and we both know that up here," he paused and tapped his skull, "I'm a lot older than my age. We know that, right?"

Greene nodded.

"Okay," said Prospero. "In quantum physics, in superstring theory they talk about how there are more than four dimensions. More than height, width, depth, and time. That's part of superstring theory, that the universe is much bigger and more complex than even Einstein thought. So, go farther. What if there are an infinite number of dimensions? What if there are an infinite number of realities? Parallel worlds, each one separated by differences however minuscule or massive."

"An omniverse," said Greene, nodding again. "It's an old concept."

"That's right," said Prospero, excited. "You do understand. Cool. Now . . . what if it's not a theory? What if that's true? What if there is, in fact, an infinite number of worlds, and if those worlds are—as some people believe—right next door to us, then imagine what would happen if we could build a doorway, a kind of gate, that would allow us to move back and forth."

"To what end?"

"That's what Dad asked me and I'll tell you what I told him. It pissed him off, so let's see what it does to you."

"I'll be sure to listen with an open mind," said Greene.

They smiled at each other for a moment. Genuine smiles on both sides.

Prospero said, "If there are infinite worlds and if through quantum physics and the science of superstring theory we can access them, then why would we need to ever fight another war?"

"I don't follow. How does one relate to the other?"

"Natural resources," said Prospero. "Imagine if no one had to fight wars over limited supplies of oil, natural gas, coal. Imagine if no one ever had to fight for a place to stand, for a place to build a home. For land to raise sheep and cows and things like that. Imagine if there were infinite oceans in which to fish. If there was enough for everyone and more than anyone could ever use, why would people like my father and his cronies ever have to build bombs or fighter planes or any of that stuff?"

Greene nodded. "That is an appealing thought, of course. An end to the cause of war. By inference it would cancel out greed because there would be no limit to the things one person could possess."

Prospero brightened and nodded enthusiastically. "Then you *do* get it."

"I understand the benefits of such a scenario," said the doctor. "But it's a dream, Prospero, and dreams are only dreams."

"That's just it," said Prospero, a strange light igniting in his eyes. "What if they're not dreams? What if, when we dream, we're somehow looking from our world into another world? What if everything people dream is that? What if all dreams, no matter how weird or wild or crazy, are people seeing other versions of the world, other universes where maybe the same rules of physics don't apply?"

The boy leaned forward, his fists clenched.

"Doc, that's what is going on in my dreams," he continued, his voice dropping to a terse whisper. "The people of my world, the gods of my world, and even the slaves—the shoggoths—they all whisper to me. They want me to build the God Machine. They know I can do it. They want me to come home."

CHAPTER TWELVE

A city?

It made no sense.

None.

Bunny said, "Who built this?"

"No one," whispered Top. "You know how deep we are, Farm Boy? We're beneath a hundred million goddamn years of ice. Maybe twice that. No one had ever built no city down here. No one ever *lived* here."

The presence of the city—the sheer scope and complexity of it— made a lie of Top's words.

We stood there, dwarfed by it. It was as if the builders of ancient Egypt had constructed a megalopolis on the scale of New York or Hong Kong. Only bigger. Much, much bigger. We stopped talking about what we were seeing. It was an impossible conversation, and the echoes of our voices seemed incredibly tiny in that vastness. It made us feel like ants. It took us ten more minutes to reach the bottom of the slope.

"All that excavation equipment," murmured Top. "And the tunnel we followed to get down here. Erskine and his crew were looking for this. Maybe the Chinese and Russians, too."

"How'd they *know*?" wondered Bunny. "With all the iron in the rock, they couldn't have seen it with ground-penetrating radar. How'd they know it was here, Top? How'd they know?"

Top shook his head. "That's one more question to add to a long damn list."

He cut a sideways look at me as he said that.

Fair enough. I needed those same answers, and for the same reasons.

"Spread out and scout the area," I ordered.

Aside from a confusion of bloody footprints and a few pieces of dropped or discarded gear, we saw no further traces of people down here. That should have been a comfort, but it wasn't.

Top called, "Hey, Cap'n, you seeing this?"

"Yeah," I said, gaping at the city. "Of *course* I see—"

"No," he said, "over there." He pointed to a space between two of the titanic blocks. I hadn't noticed it at first because it was nestled closer to the ground and was dwarfed by this impossible architecture. There, half-hidden in shadows, was a machine. We approached it with caution. My heart was still beating wildly and there was cold sweat on my upper lip.

Bunny stumbled a couple of times because he kept looking at the city instead of where he was going. Guess I wasn't the only one who was out of it. And that was deeply troubling. Even with everything we were seeing, we were above becoming slack-jawed tourists. Except right now that's what we were.

"Get your fat head out of your white ass, Farm Boy," snapped Top.

Bunny twitched and gave Top a brief, blank stare that showed a lot of fear and a lot of incomprehension, then his eyes cleared and he nodded.

"This is nuts," he murmured.

"Well, no shit," said Top. He was trying to sound casual, offhand. He didn't. There was a quaver in his voice.

"Come on," I said, walking down a steep granite slope toward the object. Our shoes had gum-rubber soles but they still managed to send rhythmic echoes up into the frigid air, and distance warped the sounds as they bounced back to us. The noise sounded like the muffled heartbeat of some sleeping thing.

Because everything down there was on such a cyclopean scale, it took longer to reach the machine than I expected. And when we got there it was larger than I thought. It was built like the mouth of a tunnel, thirty feet high, with a series of inner rings that stepped back at irregular intervals. The primary structure looked to be made of steel, but there were other metals, too. Lots of exposed copper, some crude iron bands, gleaming alloy bolts, and long circular strips of what looked like gold. Heavy black rubber-coated cables were entwined with the rings of metal, and coaxial cables as thick as my thigh snaked along the ground and ran farther down the slope to where a series of heavy industrial generators were positioned on a flat stone pad. Sixteen generators. Lots of power.

The tunnel stretched back so far it disappeared into darkness. Top shone his flashlight down the gullet but the beam simply faded out after fifty yards. I leaned around the outside to see that the tunnel was built into the wall. There were blast and drill marks on the stone to show that they had bored into the heart-stone of the mountain. The throat of the machine looked like it ran deep into the bedrock.

"What the hell is this?" asked Bunny.

Top cut me a look. "Hadron collider? I mean, what else it could be?"

Bunny touched the bundles of copper wire. "Doesn't look right, does it? Different than the big one at CERN. I read about that."

"So you're an expert in damn collider design now, Farm Boy?" Top smacked Bunny's hand away from the machine. "Don't touch nothing. We don't know shit about this thing. Might be something nuclear. Don't know, can't say, so don't touch. Besides, you already been bitch-slapped by a mutant penguin. You want to get your balls blown off, too? No? Good, then stop getting grabby."

"Copy that," said Bunny, taking his hand back.

I tapped my earbud for Bug. It took a few tries and when he came on the line I couldn't understand a word he said because of the static.

"Cowboy to Bug, do you copy?" I said it again and again. Static. Maybe a fragment of a word. Nothing I could understand. Just in case it was my gear I had Top and Bunny call in. Same thing. And we couldn't hear each other on the team channel. We stood for a moment in silent frustration.

Top said, "Interference? Iron in the mountains could be eating the signal."

"What's the play?"

"Take some pictures and then we'll leave it alone," I said. "We have bigger fish to fry."

"Like finding out why everybody lost their damn minds," said Top. "And whether we're at war with Russia and China. Little stuff like that."

"Yeah," I agreed. "Little stuff like that. Kind of interested to know where the hell Erskine and the rest of the Gateway geeks are."

"Kind of thinking they're somewhere with their throats cut," said Top.

"Maybe. But there were our own people mixed in with the Chinese and Russians. I'm actually not leaning toward this being an invasion. More like a shared problem."

He nodded, looking unhappy. "Some kind of bioweapon that messes with people's heads?"

"Or something," I said, nodding.

"Sheee-eeee-eeee-it," he said, dragging it all the way out.

"Okay," said Bunny, "but what do we want to do about the city? Are we going into it?"

"Not unless we have to," I said. "Let's document this machine, then find the Gateway team."

"When we do," said Top, "I'm going to be okay with beating some answers out of someone. I'm going to go ugly on them and make it hurt."

"Hooah," said Bunny.

"I'm in," I agreed.

We each took out small but powerful ultra-high-res cameras and began documenting everything. The machine, the city, everything.

As he worked, Bunny very quietly said, "Do not let my calm, cool exterior fool you gentlemen. I am a really short step away from freaking the fuck out."

Top was leaning in to take flash pictures of the interior of the big machine. "Hell, Farm Boy, don't go thinking you hold the patent on being sphincter-clenching scared. I would give your left nut to be ten thousand miles away from right here."

"Is ten thousand miles really far enough?" mused Bunny.

The cameras went flash-flash-flash. Water dripped behind us, somewhere in the city. And several times I heard the soft, shuffling feet of heavy and awkward bodies. I couldn't see more of the penguins, but we could smell them. Bunny kept throwing uneasy glances over his shoulder. His face and shirt were still stained with his blood. It's always hard to keep your best game face bolted on when you've already been hurt by something this strange. It didn't help that our intel didn't match the situation on the ground. Or that we had no way to get fresh orders. Normally I don't mind operating without a leash, but this was beyond me.

It was beyond anything I could have imagined. The plots of nine hundred science fiction movies began rumbling through my head. Bunch of guys trapped in a remote place with inexplicable weirdness. Some unseen force picking everyone off one at a time. Those things never end well.

Top pointed into the opening of the machine. There was a tunnel that ran backward into shadows. "Looks like this thing curves down. There's something just over the edge but I can't get a shot. Think it's safe to stand up on the edge to get a better—?"

Before he could finish, the machine suddenly *pulsed*. No other word for it. There was a sound like the electrical kick of a starter. A growl that was cut off almost at once. And for a split second the first dozen rings of the tunnel flashed as LED lights hidden in the recesses throbbed once.

Then . . . again.

A third time. Each time there was that *chunk* sound, as of a giant engine trying to start and failing.

If that's what it was.

"Damn it, Farm Boy," bellowed Top, "what did you touch?"

But Bunny was standing on the far side, twenty feet back from the mouth of the tunnel, camera raised to take a wide-angle picture. "I didn't touch anything."

The lights and sound pulsed once more and then paused. That's how it felt. A pause. The activity did not feel as if it actually stopped. There was a feeling of awful anticipation as the whole cavern suddenly fell silent. Bunny hurried over and we stood there, staring down into the tunnel of darkness.

"What the hell—?" began Bunny, and then his words were also cut short as a thousand lights suddenly flared on with a brilliance so intense that it was like being stabbed through the brain. It was an almost physical blow and we all cried out and staggered back. As we stumbled, we all tried to turn and run.

But we weren't fast enough.

Out of the depths of that black throat came a massive exhalation of foul air that struck us with hurricane force, plucked us off our feet, and hurled us up the slope. That air was thick and humid and smelled of rotting meat. It exhaled at us as if the tunnel was the throat of some great carnivore. We were big men carrying heavy equipment, but in that belch of black wind we were nothing and it vomited us from the entrance. We hit hard on the stone ramp and rolled a dozen feet. I tried not to breathe in that foul wind, but the impact knocked the air out of my lungs and I gulped in a breath through sheer reflex. It was horrible. It was the worst smell, the worst taste I've ever experienced, and as soon as I stopped sliding I rolled over, tore the balaclava away from my mouth just in time, and vomited. I could hear Top and Bunny retching, too. The whole world seemed to swirl around me and my stomach heaved again. And again. Even when my stomach was empty I could not get that terrible taste of rotting meat out of my mouth.

The machine pulsed once more, and light flooded the cavern, bleaching out all colors, casting everything into sharp lines of black and white. The light was so monstrously intense it felt like I was being burned by it.

Then . . .

Nothing.

The light vanished as quickly as it had appeared. The pulsing machine noise stopped and there was some indefinable quality to the silence that let me know that whatever this was . . . had stopped.

Our flashlights and BAMS units and everything else, every piece of equipment we owned, went dead.

We damn near went dead, too. I slumped down, feeling spent and sick and weak. Feeling swatted flat. Feeling like nothing at all. Bunny groaned and flopped over on his back. Top was on hands and knees, head hung, lips slack and wet, eyes bugged and staring.

> I turned my head . . .
>> . . . and . . .
>>> . . . looked at myself.

No, it wasn't a reflection.

I was on hands and knees looking at my body, my face, my own eyes staring back at me with total shock. The other me flinched back away.

"Wh-what—what the fuck . . . ?" I said.

Or, he said with my mouth and my voice.

I—the other me—was still on hands and knees. I raised one hand and reached out toward him. Toward me.

There isn't a way to say this because there wasn't any way to be this.

My brain felt different. There were other thoughts in there that weren't my thoughts.

I saw Lydia Ruiz, one of the most senior members of Echo Team, there. Laughing. Wearing only bra and panties as she walked across the bedroom floor toward the bathroom.

Only it wasn't my bedroom. I've seen Lydia in her underwear before. I've seen her naked once when we all had to strip out of contaminated clothes. But not like this. She was in frilly underclothes, not the plainer stuff she wore when going to war. She was singing along with a Bruno Mars song, translating it into Spanish as she sang. Then she unhooked her bra and hung it over the doorknob as she entered the bathroom and leaned in to turn on the tap.

I wanted to look away. I really did. This was not mine to see. This was not anyone's to see. Not even Bunny, who was her live-in lover. Lydia was in a private moment and my being there—however and in whatever way I was there—was an intrusive and violative act.

I said, "No!"

But I did not say it in my own voice. I said it in Bunny's voice.

The *me* over there gaped at the *me* here. I blinked.

And then it was me—inside my own flesh—staring at a bug-eyed Bunny who knelt nearby, one hand extended toward me, confusion and terror in his eyes. He collapsed flat on his chest and his eyes glazed. I fell over onto my side. Now that memory of Bunny's had somehow followed me. . . .

Followed me where exactly? Home? Back?

I mean . . . what the Christ just happened?

The memory of seeing Lydia in that private moment made me feel grubby, like a peeping Tom. That was not for me to see. It did not belong to my experience. And yet the memory was there. Fading . . . but there.

I closed my eyes. This was a dream. I was probably concussed. Or something. It wasn't real. Could not be, no matter how real it felt in the moment.

I lay there, uncertain of how to even think.

CHAPTER THIRTEEN

The candidates stood behind a curved row of podiums. Seven in all, each from different states but all from the same party. All vying for the same party endorsement and the same office. Each of them holding forth on why they—and definitely not their colleagues, and in some cases friends—should become the most powerful man on Earth.

The moderator, Wilson Fryers, was the dean of the university's law college, and was both a son and nephew of multiterm congressmen. His textbooks crossed the line to become bestsellers, and his latest, *Thinking It Through: Smart Politics for the 21st Century,* had jumped back to the *New York Times* and *USA Today* lists as soon as this debate had been announced. Because of his firm hand with the candidates and his challenging questions, he was currently trending higher on social media than any of the six men and one woman who were trying to sell themselves to the voting public.

The auditorium was packed, with handpicked political science undergrads in the front rows and a lottery selection of students, press, and celebrities filling out the rest of the seats. Secret Service agents were stationed around the room and, Fryers knew, dressed in plainclothes and seeded through the audience. The debate was the last before the national convention, and the millions watching knew, as Fryers did, that this was going to come down to two key players. So far there was an even odds split on which of them was likely to get the full party endorsement. The trajectory of this debate would almost certainly settle that.

"Next question," said Fryers. "Remember, please, that each of you will have two minutes for your statement and then we will open it up to the audience for follow-up questions."

The candidates nodded, though some of them were obviously wary. The questions from the audience had been vicious. Polite, but uncompromising. Fryers loved poli-sci majors. No one asks a harder question, and most of them were better schooled in politics than the gameplayers on the stage. The disparity between what these kids wanted to know and the politicians were willing or able to say was obvious. And embarrassing. Fryers felt like Caligula at the games. There was blood on the sand and the lions were still hungry.

"This question is on immigration," said Fryers, and he saw the flinches. He could imagine seven sphincters suddenly tightening. Nobody in politics wants to field open questions on immigration. It was an enduring hot-button issue and when things were this deep into the primary process, there was no more room for verbal gaffes. Just as there was absolutely no sage answer. No matter what a candidate said it would polarize a portion of the national audience. Fryers was sure that if he asked if the sky was blue, the politicians would have a similar hesitancy, because somewhere out there was a lobby group, religious group, environmental group, or special interest group who fundamentally disagreed. It was maddening, unless you were the moderator and any kind of controversy jumped your social media and book sale numbers.

"A recent study published by *The New Yorker* indicates that small businesses, including crop farms, would be adversely affected by tightening immigration standards. Should you be elected president, would you sign or veto a bill that—"

And the lights went out.

All of them. Lights, speakers, cameras, everything.

Bang.

The library was plunged into total darkness. No emergency lights. No alarm bells. Nothing. There was a shocked collective gasp from the audience. Fryers fumbled for the battery-operated backup microphone that had been placed there for situations like this. For accidents or power failures. He found the button, tapped it, bent to speak into the mike.

"Please," he said, "remain calm."

The only one who heard his voice was him. The microphone was as dead as the lights.

Fryers froze in place, immediately trying to remember the protocols drilled into him by the Secret Service. Wait. Listen. The emergency system will kick in.

There was a scream. Of course there was. Someone always had to scream. Someone always had to panic. Always.

"Idiot," he muttered, because he knew what happened. What inevitably happened.

One scream became two. Became five.

He shot to his feet. "Everyone, please calm down!" he yelled.

The volume of panic was already rising. Fryers dug into his pocket to remove his cell phone, punched the button to get the screen. A flashlight app would be helpful. He was surprised everyone else wasn't doing the same thing.

Except the screen did not come on. His phone was dead, too.

That was . . .

His mind stalled. How could a power outage take out his cell phone? And the emergency lights were battery operated, too. The Secret Service had wire mikes and flashlights.

But there were no lights on in the hall.

None.

That's when he heard the screams turn into cries of pain and dull, angry thumps as blind people began fighting their way toward the doors. In total darkness.

Fryers tried to yell.

Tried to keep this from becoming what he knew it would become. Blind, destructive panic.

He tried.

And failed.

At the end of sixty seconds, when all the lights finally flared back on, and cell phones began automatically rebooting, and the speakers squawked with alarm bells, the crowd had already become a tidal surge of blood and broken bones.

CHAPTER FOURTEEN

Not sure how long it took us to recover.

Not sure we actually did.

Three, four minutes dragged by before I could even summon the willpower to rise, let alone the sheer muscular commitment. My head rang with the after-effects of the light. My brain felt bruised. The horrendous smell and taste still polluted my senses.

It was my flashlight that jolted me out of the daze. The light came on again. Pop, just like that. It wasn't a matter of the switch moving. The light had already been on but when that big machine did whatever the hell it did, the power in the flashlight simply died. Ditto for all of our other gear. Pop. Out. And now it was all back on. I turned my head and stared at the light as if seeing it could reveal some answers. It surely did not.

Top got to his feet first. He was the oldest of us, and probably not the strongest, but in many ways he was the hardiest. He struggled up and stood swaying over me, chest heaving from the effort, hands shaking as he checked his gear. The process of doing that kind of routine check made sense. It was a reset button to reclaim normalcy and control. Doing routine things can do that. When he was done he still looked like crap, but less so. He blinked his eyes clear, then hooked a hand under my armpit and pulled me up. My muscles were composed of overcooked rigatoni and Play-Doh. It didn't even feel like I owned a skeleton anymore. Top had to hold me up until I could stand, however badly, on my own.

It took both of us to get Bunny on his feet.

We stood in a nervous huddle, legs trembling, faces pale with sickness. Nerves absolutely shot. Burned out like bad wiring.

"Holy Mary, Mother of God," breathed Top. And he crossed himself. I had only ever seen him do that once before.

Bunny wiped pain-tears from his eyes and sniffed in a chestful of air.

The machine sat there, cold and silent and dark. Around us the impossible city loomed, mocking us and everything we believed in. Top's prayer faded into nothing.

Bunny coughed, cleared his throat. "What . . . what . . . ?"

"I know," said Top.

Bunny's head snapped around. "Top, did you . . . ? I mean . . ."

"I don't know, Farm Boy," said Top, but he was clearly in distress that ran deeper than the physical. "This is some voodoo shit right here."

"It's nuts," said Bunny, shaking his head, "but for a moment there I . . ."

Once more his words trailed away, and he shot me a very strange look. A suspicious and horrified look.

"What?" I asked cautiously. "What did you see?"

"Nothing. I didn't see nothing."

"Bunny . . . look, I saw something, too."

His eyes widened. "What?"

"I saw something, too," I repeated. "For a couple of seconds after that thing went off I saw . . ."

And I stopped, too. How exactly do you have that kind of conversation? You need to hear that someone else shared it so that it's not just you. And you're afraid that it is just you. But at the same time what if it's not just you and stuff like this is possible? You see the problem? There's no way to Sudoku your way out of it.

"Say it, Cap'n," said Top. "What'd you see?"

I wiped sweat out of my eyes and took a moment. "I saw two things and neither of them make any sense," I began. "I saw me—my body—kneeling a few feet away, looking right at me."

"Yeah," said Bunny, nodding but not looking anything but scared shitless about it.

"Then for a second I was somewhere else," I continued. "I was in your cottage, Bunny. Lydia was there and . . ."

I let it tail off. Bunny's face went from a greasy mushroom white to a livid red.

"What else did you see?" he asked in a low growl. A frightened dog growl, but definitely a growl.

"The fuck does it matter what else he saw?" barked Top. "He saw it."

Benny wheeled on him. "What makes you so sure?"

"Because I saw my ex-wife," he snarled. "Clear as motherfucking day. Sitting at the kitchen counter drinking that shit mint tea she drinks and reading stock numbers off her damn computer. Want to know where Apple stock is right now? I can still taste that son of a bitching tea."

He dragged a trembling hand across his mouth, which had become wet with spit. He looked at the moisture, shook his head, then they both looked at Bunny.

"What did you see, Farm Boy?"

"What," exclaimed Bunny, "so we're all just going to accept that this stuff just happened?"

"What did you see?"

Bunny cut a look at me and then he looked up at the ceiling far, far above us. "I had a nightmare," he said.

"What do you mean?"

"I didn't see Lydia or your ex, Top. I didn't see anyone I know." He shook his head. There was a quaver in his voice that made his teeth start to chatter. It wasn't the cold, though, and we all knew it. He was simply that scared. "It couldn't have been anything but me freaking out. It was this weird place . . . like the beach, except the ocean was black and oily, and the sky was wrong. Not our sky, you know? The stars were wrong. And . . . and there were monsters." He stopped and shook his head, unable or unwilling to continue. "There aren't words for it, you know?"

They both looked at me. As if I had any answers.

"I feel sick," said Bunny. "That air we breathed? I feel like crap."

He raised his BAMS unit. The light was no longer green. Now it flickered back and forth between green and yellow. Mine was doing the same thing. So was Top's. I peered at the tiny digital screen to see what kind of particles it had picked up, but all it said was: SYSTEM ERROR.

Top frowned. "Was it me or did the power go out when that thing flashed?"

"It went out," I said.

"And it came back on?"

"Yeah."

He held up his watch. The digital display was flashing the way those things do after a power interruption. "All my gear's in reset mode except the flashlight. It doesn't have a circuit breaker. Just a battery. It went off but came back on."

We all checked our gear and got the same results. Bunny said, "You think that machine is the EMP weapon they were building?"

Top shook his head. "Can't be the EMP cannon. It's too big."

"I know, but we got hit by something like that."

"EMP would have fried the electronics," said Top. "This just interrupted the power."

"What can do that?" asked Bunny. "I mean to everything, even our flashlights?"

"I have no idea," I said.

"Doesn't make sense," said Bunny. "If something could interrupt electrical conductivity all the way down to a watch battery, wouldn't it fry our central nervous system? I don't want to look a gift horse in the mouth, guys, but why ain't we dead?"

We had no answer for that.

Top gave the big machine a long, hateful look. "Cap'n, I'm two-thirds convinced we ought to put some blaster plasters on that thing and blow it back to Satan. We got a nice airplane waiting outside."

"Yes," said Bunny fiercely.

I shook my head. "Blowing it up isn't our job and we don't know what will happen if we damage it."

They didn't like it, but they nodded. Hell, I didn't like it, either.

"Let's gather what intel we can," I said, "find Erskine and his team, and then get the hell out of Dodge."

"Hooah," agreed Top.

"Hooah," said Bunny, but his voice was small and unemphatic.

We stood in silence, lost in the strangeness of the moment, still caught in the net of whatever had just happened to us. Three soldiers, gasping like beached trout, feeling small and scared.

That's when we heard a voice say, *Tekeli-li! Tekeli-li!*

INTERLUDE FIVE

"Did my son talk to you about his God Machine?" asked Oscar Bell. He sat on the doctor's couch, legs crossed, hands resting on his lap. Greene thought he could see a flicker in the man's eyes. Nerves, perhaps, or excitement.

"Please understand, Mr. Bell, that I encourage an air of unrestricted confidence in my sessions with your son," said Green. "However, that comes with a certain level of trust. He knows that what he says goes no farther than—"

Bell held up a finger. "Don't. You want to stick to some set of bullshit doctor-patient rules, then consider your services terminated."

That hung in the air, ugly and real.

"I . . . ," began Greene, but once more Bell cut him off.

"I don't need a blow-by-blow. I don't want to know what the kid jerks off to, and I don't want to know what he thinks of me. That's all psychobabble nonsense and we both know it. But I do want to know about the God Machine. And I mean everything."

Greene felt as if he had been nailed to his chair by the force of Bell's green-eyed stare. The man frightened him, and that went beyond the threat of a massive financial loss. Bell seemed willing to give him a few seconds to work up to it.

Finally Greene took a breath and said it. "Prospero does not believe he is a human being. Not entirely. It's his belief that he is either an alien from another world or perhaps another dimension, or that he is a hybrid of human and alien genes. It is his belief that he is not your actual son but the product of some kind of genetics experiment. He believes that you 'adopted' him only as a means of profiting from the genius he gets from his alien DNA."

Bell uncrossed and recrossed his legs. "Kid has some imagination."

"Has he said any of this to you, sir?" asked Greene.

"Don't change the subject, Doctor. Tell me what Prospero's told you about the God Machine."

"Well . . . your son has been researching the artists and philosophers of the surrealism movement and believes that their works represent visions of the world from which he comes. Notably the paintings of Salvador Dalí and Max Ernst, and the pulp fiction horror stories of H. P. Lovecraft. Your son is uncertain as to whether the surrealists are from the same world or if they somehow traveled there in dreams. I think he's leaning toward the latter opinion."

"And the machine is what?" asked Bell. "A phone so E.T. can call home?"

"No, sir," said Greene. "Your son believes that it will somehow open a doorway and allow him to return to his true home."

"Did he say anything about EMPs?"

"I'm not sure what that is."

"Electromagnetic pulses. Has Prospero mentioned that at all?"

"No, unless a 'null field' is the same thing."

Bell's eyes flared momentarily. "What did he say about that?"

"Not much. He said it was an unwanted side effect and he was trying to correct it."

"*Correct* it?" Bell shot to his feet and for a moment Greene thought the man was going to punch him. Then Bell sagged back and sat down hard, shaking his head. "Correct it, Jesus fuck."

"Is something wrong?" asked Greene.

Oscar Bell ran trembling fingers through his hair. "You wouldn't understand if I told you." He took a breath and bolted his calm back in place, one iron plate at a time. "Exactly *how* was he planning on correcting it?"

"I'm not sure. Something about a mathematical pattern that he couldn't solve unless . . ."

Bell's eyes hardened. "Unless *what*, Doctor? I need you to be very specific."

"Very well," said Greene, "but believe me, I've looked into this myself and there's nothing to it. Not even a mention on the Internet. Prospero believes that the key to making his God Machine function properly requires a sequence code that can be found in certain rare books he refers to as 'The Unlearnable Truths.' These are, according to

JONATHAN MABERRY

him, books of magic that have been hidden for many centuries. He said that they are guarded because they contain dangerous secrets."

"What kind of secrets? The God Machine isn't magic, Doctor. It's absolutely bleeding-edge science. I have forty physicists scratching their heads trying to understand what the fucking thing does, do you know that? I have guys at MIT, Cal Tech, and Stanford losing sleep over it. I've got two Nobel laureates about to go into therapy because my twelve-year-old son's designs make their heads hurt. The only thing they agree on is that the machine is real. It will do something, but wild as it sounds, Prospero understands quantum mechanics on a level that no one alive can match. No one. I sat down with Stephen Hawking and he started to cry when he read Prospero's notes. It was like he was having a religious experience, and we're talking about Stephen goddamn Hawking."

"Not to be rude, Mr. Bell," said Greene, "but what makes you believe the machine will do anything at all? From what Prospero tells me, it doesn't work."

"Doesn't work? Jesus wept. Maybe it's not doing what Prospero wants it to do, but it sure as shit does a lot of other things."

"What things?"

Bell's eyes narrowed. "That's above your pay grade, Dr. Greene."

"I feel I must caution you about placing too much stock on your son's projects," said Greene. "Since he's discovered surrealism he has become visibly detached from the real world."

"What he's doing is real to him."

"Perhaps," conceded Greene reluctantly, "but encouraging it is hardly in the best interests of Prospero's emotional and psychological health. His fascination with these 'Unlearnable Truths' has become an obsession, and I fear what will happen when he finally becomes convinced that no such books exist. He is placing a dangerous amount of faith on ultimately possessing them, or at least reading them so he can divine their mathematical secrets."

"Has Prospero told you the titles of any of these unlearnable books?"

"No. A few. Even though I could find nothing on anything called the Unlearnable Truths, there is plenty on the Net about the individual books. As I mentioned, the titles appeared in horror stories written in the early twentieth century. They don't really exist. It's only Prospero who believes they're real."

"Interesting."

"No, sir, it's not *interesting*. We're talking about Prospero's mental health."

Bell shook his head. "Mental health? I think that ship sailed a long time ago."

"Mr. Bell, we're talking about your son."

Bell stood up. "That little freak is nobody's son."

Greene stood up, too, angry but afraid of this man. He wanted to punch Bell, break his nose, throw him down the stairs. He kept his fists balled at his sides. It was clear, however, that Bell was aware of Greene's anger. He even glanced down at the white-knuckled fists.

"Let's be clear," said Bell quietly. "You're going to shift the focus of your sessions and talk only about things that relate to the God Machine, the science behind it, and Prospero's intentions for it. You will also write down the titles of every single piece of art and every single one of those unlearnable books. You'll do that right now, before I leave your office. If I like what I see, and if I am assured that you are going to continue to remember that you work for me, not for the boy, then I'll consider whether to increase your hourly rate. What is it now? Four hundred an hour? That sounds low to me."

Bell did not wait for an answer. Instead he turned and walked to the door.

"I'll be downstairs. You still have some of that scotch I gave you for Christmas? Let me go see."

CHAPTER FIFTEEN

We spun toward the sound, our combat reflexes doing what our numbed minds probably couldn't. Our guns came up, our fingers laying flat along the trigger guards. The voice was far away but it was piercing and shrill.

"It's back in the lab complex," said Bunny, and we began moving that way. Stumbling at first but finding our coordination. Walking, fast-walking, running. We left the cavern and reentered the corridor that led back into the Gateway complex, and then moved quickly but cautiously between the rows of stacked boxes. The sound continued, calling us, drawing us. But it was still far away, deep inside the structure.

"Boss," snapped Bunny, "on your ten o'clock."

We all turned. Ready to fight. Ready to kill. I could almost hear the coming thunder of fresh gunfire. The savage Killer who shares my mind with me was poised, ready to do the things that earn him the name he wears. All of my earlier hesitation was gone.

A figure came walking around the end of a long row of crates.

It walked slowly and a bit awkwardly, but it wasn't another albino penguin. It wasn't another soldier, either. This time it was a thin, fortyish man wearing a lab coat over a plaid shirt and khakis. His feet were bare. His glasses were nearly opaque from the blood that was splashed across his face. It soaked his clothes and dripped from him, and he left a long line of bare red footprints behind him.

"Stop right there," I yelled.

He kept walking.

"Sir—you need to stop right there or I will put you down. Do you understand me?" My finger was along the curve of the trigger guard, quivering, ready to slip inside and squeeze off the shot. The Killer snarled inside my mind.

The man slowed and stopped. He lifted his head as if listening to something far away, and again I thought I heard that voice cry out those same meaningless words we'd heard before. Not Russian and not Chinese. Not any language I ever heard of.

"Tekeli-li! Tekeli-li!"

We couldn't see who spoke, but it was closer now. Just beyond the range of our flashlights. A hundred yards? Less? Fifty? Twenty? The echoes were deceptive.

"Put your hands on your head, fingers laced," I told the man. "Do it now."

The man seemed to smile for a moment. "We are always what you want," he said in a voice that was muddy and thick. "The sequence is written in the stars."

"Put your hands on your head," I repeated. "I won't tell you again."

"It is there to be read."

He said those words—or at least those are the words I heard—but I swear to God that those aren't the words his mouth formed. It was so strange, like watching a foreign film with bad dubbing.

"No truth is unlearnable."

"Tell me your name," I demanded. "What is your ID number?"

The man opened his mouth to say something else, but this time instead of words a pint of dark blood flopped out and splatted onto the front of his shirt. He made a faint gagging sound and then his knees buckled and he collapsed with exaggerated slowness to the ground.

"Go," said Top as he moved up to cover me.

Bunny and I broke cover and ran cautiously toward him, checking each side corridor in the maze of crates, covering each other.

"Green Giant," I said, and Bunny grunted an assent. He took up a defensive posture while I dropped to one knee by the fallen man. I put my fingers to his throat and got a big silent nothing. "Dead."

He was a mess. Blood everywhere. A name tag hung askew from his lab coat.

M. ERSKINE

The scientist in charge of this project. From close up I could see that his skin was as gray-white and mottled as the penguin's feathers had been. Like the skin of a mushroom.

Erskine looked up at the ceiling with dead eyes and a slack mouth. And then he spoke again. "We are always what you need."

We all jumped.

"He's alive!" yelped Bunny.

"No, he ain't," growled Top.

I jabbed my fingers back against his carotid and got the same nothing as before. Top tried, too.

He jerked his hand back.

"We have waited for you since the lands split," said the dead man.

We scrambled back.

"What the fuck?" yelped Bunny.

"I know, I know," I said, my heart hammering in my chest.

"No," insisted Bunny, and he held his BAMS unit in front of my face. The comforting little green light was glowing bright red.

We scrambled back from the dead man.

"Reads as unknown biological agent," Bunny said.

"Yeah," growled Top, "but what kind? Bacteria? Nerve gas? A virus? Are we hallucinating this shit?"

Bunny shook his head. "I don't know . . . it paused on viruses for like half a second and then went to unknown particles."

Top looked at his while I covered everyone. "Mine says bacteria . . . no, I'm wrong. It's reading unknown, too."

I glanced at mine just as the reading changed from virus to unknown.

We stared at each other, then at the units, then at the dead man.

We backed away from Erskine and tried to get readings from different parts of the airflow. Every few seconds the BAMS units would shift. Virus. Fungal spores. Bacteria. Mycotoxins. And even plant pollen. But each time the meter flicked back to the display for UNKNOWN PARTICLES.

"Something must be interfering with the sensors," said Bunny.

"Can't," said Top. "They're self-contained and they have ruggedized cases."

The red lights flickered at us like rats' eyes.

On the floor the dead man spoke again, and once more his words and his mouth didn't match. His body trembled as with the onset of convulsions, but the tone was normal. No, "normal" isn't a word I can use here. Normal wasn't in that place with us. His tone sounded casual, like he was having a calm conversation with someone. The tone and words were well modulated. It sounded for all the world like a tape playback of something this man might have said at another time and under incredibly different circumstances, but somehow repeated now despite his condition.

What he said was, "There's nothing to worry about. This is a clean facility."

I could feel the shakes starting. They started deep, in my bones, in my muscles, and then shuddered outward through my skin.

"Cap'n," whispered Top, "this motherfucker is dead."

"I know."

Bunny said, "What?"

"No pulse. He's dead."

"We defeat time because it interferes with service," said Erskine. Or, at least, that's what the voice said. His mouth formed different words. Even dead. I made myself look at the shapes his lips formed. And as I read those words I could feel—actually feel—my blood turn to ice. The words his dead mouth formed were, "I'm sorry. God forgive us. We should never have opened the gate. I can see the sleeping things. God forgive us."

Over and over again. His dead, cold lips pleaded for mercy while the cooling meat of his body spoke to us in this vast and impossible place.

Bunny held his BAMS unit in one hand and had his M4A1 carbine pointed at the man's head.

"There's nothing to worry about," repeated the voice. "This is a clean facility."

Suddenly all of the red lights in the BAMS unit turned green.

I stared at my unit. The display read NO DETECTABLE PARTICLES.

I'll buy one malfunctioning unit. Maybe two at an absurd stretch. Not three. And not three malfunctioning in the same way at exactly the same moment.

Then the dead man on the floor sat up.

He didn't struggle to get up; he sat up as if he'd been doing ab crunches five times a day for twenty years. With his legs straight out in front of him, Erskine's upper body folded forward until he sat erect. He turned his head very slowly toward me. His eyes were no longer totally vacant. There was a strange new light in them, but it wasn't the kind of thing that says someone's home. It wasn't that at all.

Bunny actually shrieked. It was the only thing you could call that sound. I was so close to doing the same thing that I had to clench my jaws shut.

Erskine said, "All doors can be opened."

Top said, "What?"

"Any open door allows ingress and egress," Erskine said in that same reasonable tone. "This is a fundamental truth of all dimensions."

Blood, thick as molasses, dribbled from the corners of his mouth and ran down over his chin.

Dead things don't bleed.

But that blood didn't look like normal blood. It was so dark, almost like oil.

"The question of controlling ingress is solved at the quantum level."

The dead man looked at Bunny, then at Top, and then at me.

He smiled. With black blood oozing from his mouth, he smiled.

It was the worst thing I've ever seen. In a life spent fighting every kind of human monster, every twisted aspect of natural evil, here was a smile that shook me, stabbed me through the heart, froze my soul.

Behind us we heard a voice say, "*Tekeli-li!*"

I whirled and saw a shape, pale as one of the penguins, and I fired at it without pause, without thinking, breaking all protocols and training. The bullets tore into the flesh of a naked man. Holes opened in his flesh and black blood poured from it.

The man I shot was Dr. Erskine.

I froze, finger still on the trigger, smoke drifting from the barrel.

Behind Dr. Erskine was another man.

Another Dr. Erskine.

Other figures emerged from the shadows. More Erskines.

Then other people. Some in bloody clothes, others naked and pallid as mushrooms. The lights on the BAMS unit flared red again.

"*Tekeli-li! Tekeli-li!*" they said.

Then behind me, the first Erskine said, "Function is a by-product of need."

There was a rattle of gunfire as Bunny emptied half a magazine into him.

Then the man said, *"Tekeli-li!"*

More and more figures stepped from the shadows. Dozens of individual people. More than a hundred. Some of them were dressed in the bloody shreds of lab coats. Some were in military uniforms or engineers' coveralls. Some were American. Some wore the uniforms of Chinese or Russian military. Beyond, amid, and around them were hundreds of others. Copies of each. Hundreds of copies of each.

"Tekeli-li," they said. *"Tekeli-li!"*

Though they each spoke with their own mouths, it was all said with a single voice. One voice that spoke in perfect harmony.

One voice.

Beyond the figures I thought I saw something else. No, make that two things. Maybe I saw them. Maybe my mind was slipping gears. I really don't know.

Off to our left I thought I saw a man dressed in almost the same kind of thermal combat rig as we wore. Except he had a different kind of helmet and he seemed to be holding out a small device. I'm pretty sure it was a camera of some kind. He saw me looking, lowered the camera, turned, and vanished behind a row of metal shelves. Neither Top nor Bunny saw him, and a second later the image of him was crowded out by something else.

Something that was so wrong. So totally wrong.

It was huge and mostly hidden in the darkness, but for all its mass the thing moved with a fluid bulk. It was as if a body of viscous liquid was somehow moving without the need of containment. There was an oily iridescence about it and a stink of pollution worse than anything I'd ever experienced. And there were things coming from it. Not arms. Nothing like that. No, I swear to God that this thing had tentacles, as if it was some kind of obscene octopus. But it wasn't that. Maybe there's no word for what it is.

I saw it, though.

We all saw it. And in that moment of awful clarity I saw the machine outside of the ancient city. I saw the gateway opening and this thing came out. This tentacled abomination. It reached out of its world and into ours.

I saw it.

We all saw it.

"No," breathed Bunny. His eyes were wide and unblinking and he seemed like he was tottering on the edge of total panic.

Then all of the Erskines came charging at us. Some of them were bare-handed. Many of them held guns, knives, chunks of rock. Anything they could grab. We saw Russian and Chinese soldiers mixed in, guns in their hands, eyes empty of sanity but filled with madness. Something had taken hold of all of them and had turned this entire group of people—at least a hundred men and women—into a mindless swarm of killers.

They surged toward us, screaming their weird chant, hurling stones, firing wildly.

"God almighty," breathed Top in a terrified whisper. "If this is real . . . if this gets out . . . Jesus Christ . . ."

The swarm came howling toward us. I said nothing. I opened fire. It was a target-rich environment. We filled the chamber with thunder. We fired every bullet. We threw every grenade. We hurled every satchel charge.

Then we turned and ran.

We screamed the whole time as the collective voice screamed back at us.

"Tekeli-li! Tekeli-li!"

CHAPTER SIXTEEN

The LC-130 was still taxiing down the runway when I called in the air strike.

Top's words rang in my head.

If this is real . . . if this gets out . . .

I yelled the orders to hit the lab. To hit all of the labs. Ours, and the ones run by Russia, and the Chinese. All of it.

The USS *California* hit the Vinson Massif with six Tomahawks. I told them to empty the whole closet on them, so they sent the other six.

There is no Vinson Massif anymore. Not one you'd recognize.

We huddled in the belly of the plane, wrapped in the barbed wire of shock, hurt down deep on levels we could not name.

Behind us the missiles did their work.

And we prayed it was enough.

CHAPTER SEVENTEEN

THE DREAMER
IN THE PLAYROOM
MONTHS AGO

He walked in dreams.

It was beautiful.

So many things to see, to know. To learn.

So many secrets.

Open to him.

It was like having a key to every door.

Almost every door.

Some places were shut to him. Some minds. He didn't know why. Not even the people at Gateway understood that. No one in Project Stargate had ever understood it.

Some minds were so open they invited you in. The Mullah in that little town in Iraq was like that. His mind was uncluttered, without defenses, without guile. A simple man of simple faith living a simple life. The Dreamer could go into his head without effort. He could almost do it while awake. There were a few hundred others who were like that. The Dreamer went in and out of them with no more effort than walking through doorless rooms in a big house. The more often he went, the less effort it took to push the inhabiting consciousness to one side, to gag it and bind it and tell it to be quiet. That was fun. That was very useful.

Others were different. Some were harder to breach, and it took effort that drained him, aged him, exhausted him. A few were worth the effort. Some made even the dangers worth it, even when it left him so thoroughly spent that his mind nearly broke loose and went drifting. That was bad because there were awful places a drifting mind could go.

He knew. He'd been there. He had scars on his mind, on his soul. Some things are not unseeable.

So for those people, he had to weigh risk against reward. The way a soldier does, the way a spy does.

And then there were those other minds. The dark ones. The dangerous ones.

There were not many of them, but he had encountered a few. They were sealed against him. Or, if he managed to get inside, the things he saw there terrified him. The worst of all had been that time he had tried to crawl inside the mind of the man who called himself Church.

God.

Such darkness there.

If people only knew.

If anyone knew.

He knew, though. The Dreamer knew.

It had taken weeks to recover from that one brief encounter. Even now he had nightmares. Real nightmares, not dreamwalking. He woke up screaming sometimes.

It had been a harsh lesson.

Since then he had focused on other minds, on sailing through less dangerous seas.

Where next? he wondered.

There were so many places he could still go.

So many.

So many . . .

CHAPTER EIGHTEEN

He was the Mullah of the Black Tent.

That is what he came to be called.

He was born to a poor family near the Iraq-Kurdistan border. For the first forty-seven years of his life he was known by his given name, Maki Al-Faiz. He went to school to study Islamic traditions, known as *hadithi*, and spiritual law, *fiqh*, and over time he became a quiet, devoted, and respected man of his local mosque. Al-Faiz said his prayers and made his offerings. He was generous and humorous, but not a particularly brilliant cleric. However, since the villagers of his town were often less educated than Al-Faiz, over time they came to regard him as their mullah. When the mosque's official cleric died, Al-Faiz became the mullah in fact and from then on it was the only thing people called him. The Mullah.

When the soldiers of the Islamic State of Iraq and the Levant took over the town, some of the men of the village joined them. Some fled with their families and what few possessions they could carry. Some died.

The Mullah listened to what the fighters of ISIL had to say and although he was not deeply involved with politics, he understood that to stand with them meant that fewer of the villagers would be killed. And so he raised the black flag.

When the Americans came and drove the ISIL garrison away, the Mullah stood wide-legged before the doors of the town's tiny mosque, guarding it with his body, willing to die to keep it safe. He begged the soldiers for mercy on behalf of the villagers and this small, modest place of worship. Most soldiers might have pushed past him and searched that mosque anyway, but not the CIA man. He was in charge of this team of soldiers and he did not allow anyone to defile the mosque.

The CIA man was tall and powerful and you knew right away that this was not a green college boy who had gone off to fight. No, this tall man was a killer of men, and perhaps of many men.

He came up to where the Mullah stood and said nothing for a long time, merely staring in the cleric's face. The CIA man asked the Mullah for his name, took his fingerprints, and then abruptly turned and left, taking the other American soldiers with him.

The mosque remained undefiled.

That night, however, Al-Faiz had a dream. And in the dream he fell backward out of his body. Not all the way, but far enough that he no longer felt like he was in control of his own flesh. Not anymore. It was as if someone else had taken over control of his muscles and nerves. When his hand moved, it was not Al-Faiz who moved it. He watched as some unseen hand worked the strings and moved his body with the dexterous skill of a puppeteer.

He rose from his bed and walked out into the moonlight where several men were up late, talking by the light of a small fire. These were men who had joined with ISIL and were being trained for the war. Al-Faiz came up to them and stood at the outer edges of the fire's yellow glow. The other men greeted him, but he said nothing for a long time, and instead waited while the others gradually fell silent and turned inquiring faces toward him.

The quiet of the night settled around them and the moment gradually grew strange. Later, those gathered men would tell their friends and family—and anyone else who would listen—that weird fires seemed to burn in the Mullah's eyes. They said that when the Mullah spoke it was not in his own voice. And though he spoke in Arabic, even his accent was different. The Kurdish inflection on certain words, common to all of the people in that region, was gone.

They never forgot what he said that night, because the words of the Mullah were the match that set fire to the world.

"I am no one," he said. "I am a vessel through which God speaks. And I will tell you how we will destroy the infidels. I will tell you how to throw them into a world of darkness."

　　　　　　　　　　　　　　　　　　　　　　　　　　　　JONATHAN MABERRY

INTERLUDE SIX

BELL FAMILY ESTATE
MONTAUK ISLAND, NEW YORK
WHEN PROSPERO WAS TWELVE

"What's he building in there?"

Oscar Bell sat behind his desk and nodded to the papers. He didn't get up and hand them across. He did not do that sort of thing. Not even to a physicist whose name had appeared on the Nobel ballot four times in seventeen years. It's doubtful he would have done so had Dr. Gustafson in fact won those four prizes.

That was Oscar Bell.

For his part, Dr. Gustafson did not expect simple courtesies from this man—nor indeed any graces. He'd been warned by his colleagues and Bell's senior assistant had given him a twenty-minute talk on deportment. A younger and wealthier man might have taken offense. It's possible that a younger Gustafson might even have walked out. Youth and optimism can craft moments like that. Age and being an also-ran tended to make a person more conciliatory.

So he reached for them himself, opened the folder on his side of the big desk, and began sorting through the papers. He already knew that this would be something involving both advanced electronics and physics, but he was not at all prepared for what he saw.

What he saw confused him.

"Where did you get these plans?" he asked.

Bell sipped coffee from an expensive china cup, his face giving absolutely nothing away. "You tell me."

"Ah. Well . . . see here?" said Gustafson, rising and spreading the papers out so they puzzled together one very large schematic. "In a general sense it appears to be a hadron collider. This circular chamber is the tunnel through which the particles are run. You aim and bang and study what happened during that impact. Most of these devices are designed as large rings, of course, because you can better regulate the speed of the particles. In either case what is absolutely necessary is to get the tunnel perfectly cylindrical. Imperfections cause explosions—miner ones, of course, but damaging and time-wasting. Or your particles can strike irregularities in the wall and then the nature of the experiment is warped due to interference, and with the materials used to make the tunnel. Ultra-high-speed collisions with a loose steel rivet can spoil weeks of careful planning, and if anything is chipped off you then have particulate contaminates. It would be like doing blood work in dirty test tubes. You could never separate out the impurities from the desired particles."

"Firing tunnel and smooth bore," said Bell. "Got it. What's next?"

Gustafson shifted to a second set of papers. "Mmm, this looks like some kind of propulsion system. These are superconducting magnets with a number of accelerating structures to boost the energy of the particles along the way. Very streamlined from what you typically see, but the structural design looks good. Very good, actually. This is elegant." He named a number of other key components. "You see, inside an accelerator, two high-energy particle beams travel at close to the speed of light before they are forced to collide. The beams travel in opposite directions in separate beam pipes, like these two here and here. These tubes are kept at ultrahigh vacuum and are guided around the accelerator ring by the strong magnetic field maintained by the electromagnets. The electromagnets themselves are built from coils of special electric cable that operates in a superconducting state. So, essentially they conduct electricity without resistance or loss of energy. To accomplish this, the magnets need to be chilled to minus two hundred seventy-one point three degrees Celsius. That's actually colder than the ambient temperature of deep space. This is really a fine piece of design work." He went through more of the designs, then abruptly stopped and frowned. "Wait . . . no, that's odd. This isn't right."

Oscar Bell leaned forward. "What isn't right?"

Gustafson's frown deepened. "A couple of things. First, this here . . . I don't know what it is. It looks like the frame for an airlock, but you wouldn't need one for a hadron collider. I mean, a door to what? It doesn't even enter the main tunnel. There's nowhere to go. Strange."

"What else is wrong with it?"

"Huh? Oh . . . ," said Gustafson as he placed one sheet atop the others. It had several lines of serial number-letter codes paired with corresponding numbers given down to ten thousandths of inches.

"See this scale key? Each of these codes indicates a component of the overall machine, and the numbers on the left are the dimensions."

"And—?"

"And the scale is completely off. These plans are for a large machine approximately eighty feet in diameter. But you said that you had a model of a smaller one?"

"A working prototype," said Bell, nodding.

"I don't see how it could work. It would be impossible to generate the kind of electromagnetic power necessary to do anything or learn anything. The wires and capacitors would be too small to take any serious strain, and even if they did manage to keep from fusing, they couldn't generate the near light-speed necessary for any kind of serious particle collisions."

"You're certain?"

"Absolutely certain," said Gustafson. "And any qualified civil engineer, electrical expert, or metallurgist would agree."

Bell nodded. He stood up to take the materials back, folded them, and put the designs into his desk drawer. He removed a separate set of papers, considered them, and then tossed them onto the desk so that they slid across to the scientist. "Now tell me what that is."

With some trepidation, Gustafson opened the folder and went through each of the papers. There were more design sketches, wiring schematics, materials lists, power output predictions, and other technical data. Some of it was computer printouts, some of it was written in an awkward hand. Gustafson's frown went deeper still.

"Does any of this make sense to you?" asked Bell. "Take your time with it. Be sure."

Gustafson took ten more minutes reading through the papers, comparing one set of notes to corresponding sketches, and back again. Then he looked up, clearly troubled.

"I don't mean to offend, sir," he said, "but did you commission this work?"

"Why?"

"Well . . . if this is something you paid for, then you have been tricked."

Bell brushed lint from his sleeve. "How?"

"This is nonsense. I mean, sure, this is impressive work in many ways and whoever designed this has some appreciable understanding of physics, collider technology, and materials . . . but really."

"What is it a design for?"

"I . . . I don't know. Nothing that makes any sense," said Gustafson.

"Try to make sense of it," said Bell. "Indulge me. What would such a machine do?"

Once more Gustafson placed the papers on the desk and pointed to a sketch. "See this? This piece is a more detailed version of the airlock from those other sketches. It looks like one of the NASA designs that they are working on for the proposed Mars settlement. See here? Atmosphere filters, air scrubbers, a bio-aerosol mass spectrometer, a radiation detector. All of that by itself is reasonable for an airlock for a base on a planet with uncertain atmosphere. Though the filters here are based more on identifying air quality rather than protecting against the kind of radiation you'd have on Mars. It's not something you'd use, say, in a space station or on the moon, where there's no atmosphere."

"But—?"

"But why build something like this into the wall of a hadron collider? There is no way that makes any sense."

"If it's a hadron collider," suggested Bell.

"It is," said Gustafson. "At least that's the central design of those other plans. It's some kind of particle accelerator."

Bell nodded. "What else can you tell me?"

"Mm, well, some of these plans are for a power generator that makes no sense at all. The output predictions are way off the scale. You couldn't hit those numbers with any generator short of a nuclear reactor, but this isn't a centrifuge or a reactor. There's no mention of a reactor or nuclear fission."

"No," agreed Bell.

"And yet there are numbers for the amount of kinetic energy created by this engine that are not possible outside of fission. I mean, look here, there are references to something called refractive crystalline source generation. What is that? It's nonsense. There is no such thing."

"I see," said Bell. "So this is all nonsense?"

Gustafson hedged. "If I may be frank—?"

"Please."

"Whoever designed this is probably a genius. There are some truly elegant refinements to the standard collider components. Things I've never seen. Possibly even revolutionary. Any of those elements would be worth filing patents on right away because they, at least, are sound and, really, they're quite exciting." Gustafson shook his head. "But the rest . . . either someone is trying very hard to sell you a bill of goods, in which case if you've paid for this work you could probably sue. This is someone trying to dazzle you with bullshit. With science fiction."

"You said 'either,'" observed Bell. "What's the rest? What's the other possibility?"

"Well . . . you know the saying that there is a fine line between genius and madness? If the person who designed this actually believes that this machine will work, then he's quite mad."

"I see. But tell me one last thing, Doctor," said Bell. "You've told me what's wrong with it and why it won't work. However, you haven't speculated on what you think this machine is for. If—and indulge me on that—if the person who developed this was working toward a specific end, then what end is that?"

"You don't know? Surely he told you."

"As I said, indulge me."

Gustafson shrugged. "The power calculations, the placement of a door in an accelerator, the fact that the door is designed to scan for air quality and radiation . . . it's obvious. However deluded or misguided, it's obvious. The person who designed this is trying to generate enough power to open a door."

"Be specific, Doctor."

"This person is trying to open a door to another dimension."

Bell smiled. "Ah."

"As I said," Gustafson added quickly, "this is nonsense. It can't ever work. And if anyone was unfortunate enough to actually build this thing, it would probably blow up."

"I see."

"It gets worse, I'm afraid," said Gustafson. He picked up one of the papers. It showed a diagram of several electrical circuits connected to gemstones. Diamond, ruby, emerald, topaz, garnet, and sapphire. Beneath the diagram were several scrawled notes. "Did you take note of this?"

"I did. What do you make of it?"

"It's labeled 'crystal power sequence regulator,' and it corresponds to a key section of the firing controls for this device. From its placement in the system it clearly keeps the machine from overheating or exploding. Even if something that improbable were to work, the cost of obtaining gemstones of the type and size indicated here would be enormous. Prohibitive."

"I didn't ask you here to comment on the budget, Doctor."

"No, um, very well," fumbled the scientist, "but let me say two things. First, using gemstones to regulate this kind of power is pure fantasy. There's no valid science to support it. And frankly it's unreasonable to assume that a few carats of precious stones could in any way act as a regulator for any machine as complex and sophisticated as this. And please let me stress that as designed, those gems are key to the safety features."

"Point made. What's the other thing?"

"This," said Gustafson, placing his finger on a list of notes written in the lower left corner of the page. "These are book titles, I think. A few have bylines, so we can assume that much. And they're placed as a footnote to the power sequencer. The indication is twofold. That there is a very precise sequence needed for safe firing of this 'God Machine' and—"

"'God Machine'?" interrupted Bell.

Gustafson nodded. "There is a small notation indicating that this is the name, or perhaps code name, of the machine. Shall I continue? Yes? Very well, sir, it appears that the crucial sequence can only be found in one or more of these books. Look here, the designer says as much. I quote, 'the sequence is hidden in the prayers to the ancient ones,' and 'the Unlearnable Truths are the key,' and yet he notates that 'nothing is unlearnable.'"

Bell nodded. "I saw that. Do you have any idea what the 'Unlearnable Truths' are?"

"If I were to guess, they are the product of a delusional mind."

Bell stood up. "Thank you, Dr. Gustafson," he said without warmth, "you can show yourself out."

The scientist rose and moved awkwardly toward the door. He paused, his fingers touching the doorknob. "Sir, you asked what 'he was building in there.' Who's 'he'? Who designed this? And is he actually building it, because again, I need to caution you . . ."

His words trailed away as Oscar Bell turned his back on him and went to stand by the window, looking out on the roses in the garden. After a long, uncomfortable moment Gustafson sighed, opened the door, and left.

When he was alone, Bell crossed back to his desk, lifted the receiver, and punched in a number. The call was answered on the second ring.

"You were right," he said. "I want a team over here. I want this machine out of here before my son is home from school. All of it. The papers, Prospero's prototype. All of it. Get moving."

He made a second call to a gem merchant and a third to his banker to transfer funds. The banker cautioned against so large a transfer and warned that some holdings might have to be liquidated. Bell told him to stop whining and do it.

After those calls he replaced the phone in the cradle and then returned to the window. The early-afternoon sun turned the waters of the Atlantic into a rippling blanket of deep blue. His lips formed three words but the sound of them echoed only in his thoughts.

The Unlearnable Truths.

Oscar Bell turned and reached for the phone again.

CHAPTER NINETEEN

We sat in the empty hull of the airplane and did not look at each other. I couldn't bear to see the truth of what had just happened in the eyes of Top or Bunny. They avoided my eyes, too.

We're soldiers and we're a very specific kind of special operator. We've seen things that no one else has seen. Monsters. Genetic freaks. Doomsday weapons. That's our job, that's the kind of thing we face.

But this . . . ?

This was something else.

That gateway was ten kinds of wrong. The shapeless mass with all those tentacles? Wrong.

Swapping bodies with Bunny for a few seconds? Doing some kind of bullshit astral projection and spying on Lydia while she undressed? Really, really wrong.

The clones of Professor Erskine . . . or whatever they were?

So wrong.

When giant violent albino penguins are the least extraordinary issue of the day, then your day has slipped a gear.

We were all wasted, wired, and sick.

Really sick. And getting sicker.

Bunny suddenly staggered to his feet and ran in a stumbling lope toward the head. Almost made it. Then stomach cramps stopped him as solidly as if he'd been punched in the gut. He bent forward and vomited with terrible force all over the wall. Everything came up. Everything he'd eaten, everything he'd experienced, too. It was worse than when we'd first been hit by whatever had come blowing out of that machine. The force of it dropped Bunny to his knees and then forward onto his hands. Top and I rushed over, but we were losing it, too. Top wrenched open the door to the head and spewed inside. Into the toilet, onto the walls, the sink, the floor.

I threw up, too. Right where I stood.

The cramps really hit then. They dropped us and for a while all we could do was curl into balls and scream. The plane's crew tried to help. Tried. But there was nothing they could do.

Not for a long time.

Not until the spasms passed.

Not until we were so spent that we wanted to die. It was like seasickness times ten. I've never experienced anything as sudden, as fierce, as painful. The cramps pulled muscles and tore cries from each of us.

What the hell had we breathed down there?

What the hell had happened down there?

The plane flew on, taking us home, but if it was flying anywhere in the direction of comfort or answers, that part wasn't clear to Top, Bunny, or me.

Jesus H. Christ.

INTERLUDE SEVEN

"Dr. Greene?" said Oscar Bell. He stood at the window, holding his cell phone to his ear and cradling a glass of scotch against his chest.

"Mr. Bell," said the psychiatrist. "Good to hear from you."

"I need to cut right to it," said Bell. "In your sessions with Prospero, has he ever said anything about where these damn books are? These Unlearnable Truths? Where are they?"

"Not directly. He said that some have been destroyed."

"Christ."

"But that the essential knowledge—the knowledge he claims that he needs—is repeated in sections in the other books. As long as one possesses certain key texts from that collection, then a critical truth can be learned."

"His exact words?"

"No . . . I believe his exact words were that the books contained a message that would allow him to, and I quote, 'solve the riddle of the stars'."

"Which books would he need to do that?"

"Sir, this is—"

"Now, Doctor."

Greene sighed and then there was the sound of rustling papers. "Very well, Mr. Bell. They are as follows: *The Book of Azathoth, The Book of Eibon, The Book of Iod, The Celaeno Fragments, The Cultes des Goules, The Eltdown Shards, On the Sending Out of the Soul* . . ." The list included fourteen entries and he read them all carefully.

"Is that all of them?" asked Bell.

"Yes. Wait, no, there was one from yesterday's session. Here it is. *De Vermis Mysteriis,*" said Greene. "It translates as—"

"Mysteries of the Worm, got it. Anything else?"

"No. But, Mr. Bell, please understand, I researched these titles. They're pure nonsense—"

Bell hung up without saying good-bye.

He finished his drink, poured another, and then called a man who knew a man who knew a man. One of those kinds of calls.

CHAPTER TWENTY

Sergeant Brick Anderson sat across from Mr. Church. They were the only passengers aboard the Gulfstream G650 as the bird rocketed westward at mach point-nine-two, near the upper range of its fast cruising speed. Church was finishing a call with the president of the United States, and Brick had eavesdropped on some of it. The president was an unhappy man. He yelled. A lot. Captain Ledger's name was taken in vain, and there were threats against his life. A lot of those. The jet had flown a lot of miles while Church tried to calm the commander in chief down and convince him that Captain Ledger had not taken leave of his senses and that the missile strikes against Gateway One were not, in fact, evidence that the man had become a global terrorist or simply a madman. Church had to do a lot of maneuvering to assure the president that the actions taken were well within the scope of the powers granted to the DMS as part of this mission. Church reminded him, section and verse, of the special powers granted through the Department of Military Sciences charter, particularly in cases involving an imminent and dire biological or technological threat.

Church had the call on speaker because, Brick suspected, why should he suffer alone?

Several times Brick had to turn away to hide a grin, even though they were painful grins. No matter how this ultimately played out, Captain Ledger's ass was going to be in a sling. Church caught one of his grins and gave him a sour look, but then he smiled and mimed putting a pistol to his own head and pulling the trigger.

When the call ended Church looked ten years older. Brick poured them both glasses of wine and they sat drinking in silence for a few minutes.

"Is POTUS going to want Joe's head on a pike?"

Church considered the deep red depths of his wine. It was a Homer pinot noir from Shea Wine Cellars in Willamette. Not terribly expensive but very good. Rudy Sanchez had sent Church a case some months ago and this was the last bottle.

"It would be in the president's best interest to reread the DMS charter."

"You're saying he can't order you to fire Joe?"

Church merely shrugged and sipped the wine.

The phone rang and Brick answered it, spoke quietly, grunted in surprise, and held the phone against his chest for a moment.

"Wow," he said to Church. "It's Harcourt Bolton, Senior. Says it's important."

Church held out a hand and took the phone, once more put the call on speaker, and said, "Harcourt, it's good to hear from you."

"Right back at you, Deacon. Listen, I have a couple of things," said Bolton in his usual boisterous tone. "Heard you're having a challenging day. POTUS said something about your boy Ledger blowing the ass off the world. Words to that effect."

Church said, "No comment."

Bolton laughed. "Wasn't asking for one. Just offering sympathy. Ledger's a good kid, but he's still young. Not like us old dinosaurs."

"I have complete faith in Captain Ledger."

"Oh, hey, I'm not saying otherwise. He saved my bacon a couple of times. It's nice to know that fogies like us have hotshot kids to send out tiger hunting. Makes me wish I still had the tools for that kind of stuff. Those were good days. Damn, we pissed on walls all over the world. Geez, remember that time in Madrid when I—"

"Harcourt," said Church, "much as I would love to chat, this isn't the best time for it."

"Right, right, of course. You have some spin control to do. I know the timing sucks, too, 'cause you and your boys have had a run of bad luck lately. Big win against the Seven Kings but the last six or seven cases have turned on you. Bad luck can go in runs; believe me, I know. Sorry to see it happening for the DMS."

Brick studied the red depths of his wine, not wanting to meet Church's eyes. Bolton was right about the DMS hitting a rough patch. And it wasn't seven cases that had gone south on them, it was closer to a round dozen. High casualties in firefights, some civilian casualties, too. Failed missions, questionable intel, squandered resources, wrecked vehicles, and hostiles that slipped through the DMS's fingers. So far Joe Ledger's Special Projects Office had managed to hold a near-perfect track record, but given the bizarre verbal field report and the lack of substantiating data—at least so far—the DMS all-stars were likely to lose their shining status. It was all very stressful and so strange. Brick knew a lot of the team commanders and many of the field operators. It was not like them to be clumsy. Church didn't hire second-stringers. So far, though, there were mysteries and questions and nothing even remotely like an answer.

Bolton said, "Hey, Deke, I'm sorry as hell that it was my intel that put Ledger at Gateway. I thought it would be a walk in the park for a gunslinger like him."

"We'll survive," said Church. Brick knocked back the rest of his wine and poured more for both of them.

"Sorry, boy. Not trying to kick you when you're down. I know what it feels like when you lose a step getting to first base. That's why I stepped out of the field. Just commiserating," Bolton said, then cleared his throat. "Listen, the real reason I'm calling is to ask if you've been tracking those power outages? You know the ones I mean, the racetrack mess and the GOP debate?"

"I'm aware of them," said Church. His voice was as wooden as his face.

"You looking into it?"

"You probably know I wasn't given that case, Harcourt," said Church. "POTUS assigned a task force. Joint Homeland and NSA."

Bolton snorted. "Then you know they found exactly nothing. That team's a step down from a clown college. Their report concluded that the two incidents, though remarkable, are probably not connected. They're calling the power losses a coincidence. What do you think of that bullcrap?"

"That report has not yet been forwarded to me," said Church.

"Really? They filed it this morning. My people got it for me within half an hour. I'll send you a copy."

Brick winced, but Church merely said, "You have an excellent team, Harcourt. I take it you disagree with the team's findings?"

"Findings? Ha! That bunch couldn't find their asses with a laser-guided missile. Of course I disagree. Don't you?"

"It's not my case, Harcourt. Why are we having this conversation?"

"Geez, why are you so cranky lately? You didn't used to be like this."

"Harcourt . . ."

"Right, right. I'm calling you because it actually might *be* your case after all," said Bolton. "I called the president as soon as I was done reading that piece-of-crap report. I told him that it was wrong."

"And how did you come to that conclusion, Harcourt?"

"Easy math, Deke. I've been juggling a couple of investigations, you know, tapping my old network to see if I can shake some bedbugs out of the linen. There are a couple of case profiles I've been putting together to hand off to the young lions here at Central Intelligence. But as it turns out, two of these cases are different ends of the same case. First one is a real Dan Brown thing, you'll love it. Somebody ought to write a book. Short version is that there's a new black market that's been operating on the fringes of the Middle East. Run by a guy named Ohan, who's a non-Muslim Turk who'd cut out your mother's liver and sell it back to you for ten bucks plus installation. Sweetheart of a guy by all accounts."

"Ohan?" said Church. "I haven't heard of him." He glanced at Brick, who was already typing it into a MindReader search. Brick shook his head and mouthed the word "nothing." "How did you come up with this intel, Harcourt?"

"Oh, you know what the kids are calling me when they think I'm not listening. Mr. Voodoo. I have my sources."

Church made a noncommittal grunt.

"Anyway, Deke," said Bolton, "this Ohan character has cornered a very specialized part of the global black market. He's managed to obtain a lot of items from libraries, tombs, sacred sites, and university museums in areas overrun by ISIL. A lot of the stuff they claim to have destroyed because it doesn't fit their version of Islam wasn't so much 'destroyed' as sold. Ohan fences it for them and their cut goes into the Islamic State's war chest. Somebody has to pay for all those bullets and beheading swords. Actually, from what I've been able to put together, it looks like ISIL is using that money to step up its game."

"Step it up how?"

"That's where this story gets really interesting, because I managed to get a partial inventory list from one of Ohan's people. Call it a catalog page, or close enough. Some of the stolen tech had been in development by an international team of for-hire science nerds. Like DARPA, except they are completely mercenary with no specific national or political affiliations. Geeks R Us. Apparently some private labs in Syria had become go-to spots for off-the-books R and D. According to Ohan's list, they had stuff in development for the Russians, the North Koreans, the Iranians, the Egyptians. Fun stuff, too. Missile defense jamming systems. Laser-guided man-portable rocket systems designed to take out drones. Like that. This is quality science, Deke. This is the kind of thing that could cause real problems for us and for NATO."

"Sounds like it."

"Three items on that list popped out and that's why I called. The first is something called a 'God Machine,' which I can only assume is a code name. I showed it to a couple of big brains. You're not the only one with friends in the industry. Heh-heh. Anyway, one said that it looked like a portable version of a hadron collider, which is a contradiction in terms. Those things are huge. The other said that it was a component of a directed-energy weapon being developed under the code name of 'Kill Switch.' A kind of nondestructive EMP device, as I understand it."

"Ah," said Church.

"Now you're interested, right? Ohan claimed to have partial schematics for the God Machine and a completed prototype of the Kill Switch for sale. My sources tell me that ISIL snapped it up, which means that they're looking to take the fight to us. And get this, they didn't buy Kill Switch with cash money. What they did is give Ohan a couple of tons of priceless ancient sculptures and rare books for it."

"This is very interesting, Harcourt," said Church, "and I very much appreciate you bringing it to me. I'll talk to POTUS about having the power blackout case shifted to the DMS."

"Good luck with that. You're not POTUS's favorite guy these days."

"We still have a useful working relationship."

"Sure, but for how long?" said Bolton. "Look, it's no secret that he blames you for him not having a chance at a second term. He thinks you should have stopped the Seven Kings. He hasn't come right out and said that the drone disaster was your fault, but it's clear that's how he feels."

Church said nothing. Brick shook his head, wanting to say something but keeping his vitriolic comments locked inside.

Bolton said, "Geez, I didn't call to kick you in the shins, Deacon.

It's just that this power outage thing is scaring the crap out of me. If I was twenty years younger I'd go after this myself. Guess you feel the same way. But, bad luck streaks happen in baseball and special operations, too. They pass. Shame about Gateway, 'cause this Kill Switch thing would have been perfect for your boy Ledger."

"Captain Ledger is not the only team leader I have in play."

"Oh, I know, but he's the best now that Samson Riggs is gone." Bolton sighed. "He was good, Samson. The only guy I thought could give me a run for my money. Now there's Joe Ledger. But you know, Deke, if we're going to be honest about this, you'd never have gotten the funds to open the Special Projects Office if the president hadn't taken me out of the game. That's a fact."

Brick Anderson watched Church's face as Bolton said this. Was there a flicker of annoyance there? Or pity?

"Harcourt," said Church quietly, "this isn't a cult of personality. You did a tremendous amount of good as a field operative and now, with your intelligence network, it's possible you're even more valuable to the war we fight. No one will ever say otherwise."

There was a pause on the line, a heavy silence.

"Christ, will you listen to me?" said Bolton. "I sound like an old dog yapping at puppies. Sorry, boy. Let's put it down to stress and not enough sleep. Don't hold it against me, Deacon."

"Of course not, Harcourt."

Bolton made a sound, somewhere between an uncomfortable laugh and a self-deprecating sigh. "I hate getting old."

"We all do."

"Yeah, well, it hits some of us harder than others. You never seem to change."

"I feel my years," said Church. "It's why I stopped going into the field, too. I leave the gymnastics for younger men and women."

"You left under your own terms, though. I didn't leave the game, the game left me."

"And yet here we are, Harcourt. You've brought valuable intel to me twice in one day."

"Yeah, yeah. We're all superheroes. Got it," said Bolton. "Listen, talk to POTUS. Run down that ISIL thing. Don't back-burner it, Deke. If ISIL has gotten hold of some kind of portable EMP technology, then we are in deep, deep trouble."

"Yes, we are," said Church.

"Ohan knows who bought it. I passed this along to some guys I know in the field. Agency station chiefs who don't have their heads up their keisters. I'll send Ohan's info to you, too."

"I appreciate that, Harcourt," said Church.

"And . . . ," said Bolton, drawing it out, "there's one more thing. I don't see how it could be connected to Gateway or ISIL or the EMP tech, but those ancient books ISIL gave to Ohan? I recognized some of them and it really gave me a jolt, too. Remember that op we ran about thirty-odd years ago? Belgrade?"

"Thirty-seven years ago. What about it?"

"That was the first time you and I crossed paths. I was hunting for a couple of Kazakhstanis who were trying to sell nuclear components from the old Soviet days. And you were doing that hinky little deal with Arklight to close out those shooters from the Ordo Fratrum Claustrorum? The Brotherhood of the Lock, remember?"

"I remember."

"Remember what the Brotherhood were doing in Belgrade? Remember what they were after?"

Church said nothing.

"You never did find it. Well," said Bolton, "someone else is looking for it now, and Ohan says he has it to sell. My sources tell me there are at least two buyers bidding on it right now."

Church said nothing.

"Yeah," said Bolton, "I figured that would get your attention. Someone is trying to sell one of the Unlearnable Truths."

INTERLUDE EIGHT

BELL FAMILY ESTATE
MONTAUK ISLAND, NEW YORK
WHEN PROSPERO WAS TWELVE

The man looked like what he was.

A killer. Though Oscar Bell knew that this was a side effect of his profession, not a calling. The man was not psychotic or sociopathic, and from the reports Bell had paid for, it seemed clear the thief did not particularly enjoy killing. It was a means to an end when all other options proved inefficient.

Bell could appreciate that. The blood he had on his own hands—at however many removes—was equally cold. Emotional attachments to that sort of thing created problems.

Bell hated problems. What made him happy were solutions.

"What do I call you?" asked Bell.

"Priest," said the killer. They sat on opposite sides of Bell's big desk. They hadn't shaken hands when the thief arrived. Bell's courtesy extended to providing the man a cold beer, which sat untouched, beads of sweat running down the outside of the bottle. Bell hadn't even suggested a glass of his very old, very extraordinary scotch. The killer was dressed in a dark suit, with a white shirt and dark tie. His sunglasses lay on the edge of the desk.

"'Priest'?"

"An old joke," said the killer. "You had to be there."

"Whatever," said Bell. "You come very highly recommended, Mr. Priest."

The man said nothing; merely lifted a finger and let it drop back.

"And yet," said Bell, "your former employer was killed."

Priest smiled. "Not on my watch. My team was in Yemen when that went down." He spoke with a faint Spanish accent. Cultured and elegant, though Bell thought it was overlaid atop a more plebian one. A self-made man.

"Would things have been different had you been there?" asked Bell.

"I could not say," said Priest. "I wasn't there."

Bell shifted the subject. "Have you had time to go over my request?"

"I have."

"And—?"

"I asked a few discreet questions and received some interesting leads," said the killer.

"How interesting?"

"We do not yet have a contract, Mr. Bell. I did not mind asking those questions, but sharing the answers is different."

"Fair enough." Bell opened a drawer and removed an envelope, weighed it in his hand, and then tossed it onto the desk. Priest took it, opened it, leafed through the sheaf of bearer bonds.

"It's light."

"It's enough to pay for those answers. If I like what I hear we'll negotiate a fee for the rest."

Priest nodded. "The Unlearnable Truths aren't a myth. References to them have been heavily fictionalized, but they are real."

"And you know this for a fact?"

"I do. It's why my colleagues referred you to me. I have had some experience with rare collectibles of this kind." Priest grinned, showing a lot of white teeth. "You might say that this is kind of 'my thing,' as the saying goes. It is a very small community of people who deal in such things, and a much smaller group who know about the Unlearnable Truths. Whoever told you about these books, though, must have very specialized information sources."

"That's an understatement," muttered Bell. "Continue, please."

"Do you know the phrase 'Index Librorum Prohibitorum'?"

"I can translate the Latin. Let me see . . . 'list of prohibited books.' Something like that?"

Priest nodded. "The Index Librorum Prohibitorum was a list of books deemed heretical, lascivious, or anticlerical. Exciting, yes? Intriguing. Such a list makes you hunger to know what is in those books, does it not?"

"I will admit that I have a certain interest," conceded Bell.

"Yes," purred Priest. "The first list was authorized by Pope Paul IV in 1559."

"Ah," said Bell, "you're talking about the Pauline Index."

"Then you have heard of it."

"A passing reference," said Bell. "I'm not too familiar with it. Feel free to explain."

Priest laughed. "You would not believe what I would tell you."

Bell sipped his scotch. "I wouldn't make assumptions, friend. Now, stop dancing around it. Give me the basics. I catch on pretty quickly."

"Very well. The Index Librorum Prohibitorum has two parts. One was made public through priests whose job it was to remove restricted texts from their parishes. These priests would visit homes and inspect books to make sure that their flocks had no access to heretical, blasphemous, or obscene materials, yes? And as the years passed this became less official and more of an advisement. Banned books, book burnings. These things happen even today."

"Sure. There are a lot of very aggressive idiots in the world. I do business with some of them."

"You disapprove?"

"Whatever else I am, Mr. Priest, I am not a fan of censorship, and particularly enforced censorship. It gets in the way of the flow of information. Now, you said that there were two parts . . . ?"

"The main list is the Index Librorum Prohibitorum. That is the published list of forbidden books. But there is a second list that is shared only among the most trusted members of the inner circle at the Vatican. This list is never named except in oblique references, but in the house of the Goddess—and to a few true scholars—this most secret of lists is known as the Unlearnable Truths. Many of these books have been found and destroyed by the *Ordo Fratrum Claustrorum*."

Bell picked his way through that translation, as well. "The Order of the Brothers of the Lock . . . ? What's that?"

"They are a very ancient brotherhood of warrior priests. This brotherhood was created by a papal bull, but you will never find a record of it in any church history. They, like a few other groups, were kept secret. Only a few cardinals knew of them. Most popes, by the way, did not. I doubt Pope Francis will ever be told about it. He is too liberal and humanist. In any case, it was the mission of this brotherhood to seek out the Unlearnable Truths and to protect humanity from the secrets they contained. This they did by any means necessary. Much blood was spilled. Many heretics were burned or butchered by the Brotherhood, because, after all, sacrifices must sometimes be made to protect the flock."

"Assholes," groused Bell. "Are these jerkoffs in possession of the Unlearnable Truths?"

"They have some of them. Not all. Some of the Unlearnable Truths were burned by the Ordo Fratrum Claustrorum, others were locked away in special repositories known only to the Brotherhood. Others still remain hidden, lost perhaps. Or kept by those who seek to understand the mysteries contained therein."

"If this brotherhood is so secret, how is it that you know of them?"

Priest picked up the beer, looked at it, took a sip, and then set it down. Then he unbuttoned his left cuff and pushed up the shirt and jacket sleeve. There, on the inside of his forearm, was a very old tattoo of a burning cross set against the silhouette of a book.

"As I said, Mr. Bell, this is very much my kind of thing."

CHAPTER TWENTY-ONE

His handlers kept people away most of the time. These things had to be managed.

Abdullah was his personal aide and Akbar was his bodyguard. There were others assigned to the detail. The rules were simple. Until and unless the Mullah spoke to one of them in the other voice, then the man was to be kept in absolute isolation. This was critical because when he was not the Mullah of the Black Tent, as he came to be called, he was merely Maki Al-Faiz, a frightened man from a tiny village who did not know what was happening to him. Al-Faiz was probably mad, they decided. Touched by God, as the saying went. Al-Faiz would rave and beg and swear that he was not the same person who spoke with his mouth and stood in his body and who directed the actions of the soldiers of the caliphate. That person, the crazy man, was kept far from the public.

Only the Mullah of the Black Tent was allowed to walk free.

He, after all, had become the most important man in this war.

Akbar and Abdullah, both longtime soldiers of the caliphate, were there when Abu Suleiman al-Naser, the head of the War Council and military chief of the Islamic State, came to see the Mullah. That had been such an incredible day, a blessed day. And within a week of that meeting the soldiers of Allah had scored two massive attacks against their enemies. After another meeting with Abu Bakr al-Baghdadi, the caliph himself, special teams of soldiers were able to detonate bombs in Syria, Egypt, and Kurdistan.

The pattern was like that. A high-ranking member of the caliphate would visit with the Mullah and shortly thereafter some great victory would occur.

It was only a matter of time, Akbar confided to Abdullah, before bombs would begin going off in America.

But they were wrong.

It was not bombs that would fall.

It was planes and it was hope.

CHAPTER TWENTY-TWO

Marty Hammond didn't consider it cheating. No way. Cheating was something you did when there was some kind of emotional commitment. When there was the chance the girl—or the woman—was going to want more, to expect something beyond a dinner, some drinks, a few joints, and a hump in the hay. Cheating was what broke marriages apart, and as Marty saw it, these little encounters—his word of choice—had probably saved his marriage to Connie ten times over.

Connie was great. He loved her. Really loved her. Had since eleventh grade, and always would. They had three kids together. Bobby, who was a senior at LSU; Caitlyn, who was just starting at Emory; and little Cindy, who was still in the ninth grade. Great kids. Good-looking, too, which they got from Connie. Smart as whips, which they got from him. Or, to be fair, maybe a bit from both, because Connie was clueless but she wasn't stupid. Not by a long walk. She was smart enough in her way, but her way was St. Anthony Park in St. Paul. Connie almost never left her little town. Never willingly, anyway, and never for long. She didn't like to travel, not even to the islands. She'd gone with Marty to conventions in Jamaica, Aruba, and Hawaii, but after the third one she said that she was done. Tired of traveling. Bored with the whole thing.

That's what she called it. The "whole thing." Conventions, travel, meeting new people, parties, mixers, dinners with clients and colleagues, hotels, new places. The whole thing made her long for their home, their two acres of grass and trees with the little koi pond. Connie would rather stay behind even when the International Association of Commercial Realtors had their annual convention at the Paris Casino in Vegas. It boggled Marty's mind. It made no sense at all.

Who the hell did not want to go to Vegas? The crowds, the restaurants, the shows? Really? Ditto for Houston. There was a lot of fun to be had in Houston if you knew where to look. A whole lot of fun.

Not as far as Connie was concerned, though. She'd rather stay back in St. Paul and play bridge. Bridge, for Christ's sake? Who the hell played bridge anymore? At first Marty thought that it was a code name for Connie and her friends having hen parties where they bring in male strippers and blow them. But he had a buddy of his randomly drop by a couple of times to pick up things from Marty's home office. What he found was twelve women playing cards and eating those faggy little sandwiches. Marty believed he would actually have been okay with Connie smoking some bone-a-phone. It would be real. Bridge was not real. Bridge was a rerun of *Mad Men* or some shit like that. Old-fashioned yesterday stuff.

Marty sometimes wondered how the two of them ever managed to have kids. Connie was pretty, and when they were in the mood and in the sack, she had all the right moves. Even some mildly kinky stuff. Did anal twice. Wore a costume a couple of times. Like that. She wasn't exactly frigid, but she never made the first move. And if he didn't make a move at all, she seemed cool with it. As if sex didn't really matter. It wasn't any kind of serious thing to her.

It was a lot more than that to Marty. Hell yes. He was a man in his prime. Okay, upper end of prime. But these days fifty was the new thirty, or that's what Marty heard. He had needs. He had urges. He needed to get laid a lot more than Connie ever did, and since he was on the road sometimes twenty, twenty-five weeks a year, either he built up inch-thick calluses on his hand whacking off, or he took a more practical approach. The girls who worked the bars on the convention circuit weren't street hags. They were pretty. Some of them were gorgeous. And they were clean. You don't get to work a circuit with high rollers if you're carrying crabs. No way, Jose.

They were also commitment free. It was no different than any of the business transactions that went on a hundred times a day at these conventions. Marty got his needs met and he didn't get attached to anyone because no one at these hotels was looking for complications. A little money changed hands. They all took plastic and the billing was discreet. And when the weekend was over Marty went home to Connie. Clean and happy and without issues.

Everybody walked away a winner.

Tonight was just like all the others. He was way up on the sixteenth floor. Nice room, big king bed, and a Korean gal in the bathroom washing round one out of her snatch while he tried to get it up for round two.

"You ready for me?" she asked, her voice floating through the semi-darkness.

"Getting there," he said. Being honest about it because there are things you can fake and things you can't. And you can't fool a hooker into believing that a soft dick is a blue steel spike. It would be a professional discourtesy. Besides, he'd been with this one before. Last May and the December before that. Houston was a good conference town. The girl—Lily—knew some tricks to put some iron in the ol' putter. Yes, sir, she had a full and complete set of techniques for that. Back in December she'd helped him get it up three times. Three. He hadn't done that since the late nineties. Marty thought his heart was going to explode. So, yeah, he booked Lily again and again. And each time she proved that her skill set was mighty damn impressive. Borderline supernatural.

The drapes were open and outside the sprawl of predawn Houston was gorgeous. Lights by the million, even this early. Glittering like jewels, making him feel rich. Making him feel like he was on top of the damn world. Above the glittering skyscrapers he saw a line of jumbo jets angling down toward Bush airport. They passed directly over the hotel on their way, and somehow imagining all that power roaring above him helped Marty find that tingle that let him know tonight was going to be at least a doubleheader. If not another December hat trick.

"Here I co-o-o-o-ome," teased Lily. She opened the bathroom door and stood hipshot in the spill of light, her naked body slim and curvy and silhouetted. Marty's cock jumped. God, she was a knockout. Not one of those big bouncy broads he used to like when he was younger. No. Lily looked like she was maybe fifteen. She had to be at least twice that, but she always played it like she was a kid. A naughty, naughty kid. "Are you redeeeeee?"

His groin throbbed again. "I'm readier than ready," he said. And he was.

She giggled. He never cared whether her joy was real. Probably wasn't, but so what? She got wet and she got him hard and what more did either of them need?

"You want the light on or off?" She flicked the switch up and down, creating a strobe behind her.

"Leave it on," he said. "I want to see you."

She laughed again, and it sounded real. Happy to be admired. Or whatever. She came running toward him.

And then the lights went out.

All of them.

In the bathroom. The light on the clock. The glow of his iPad over on the desk. Out.

Bang.

The iPod went silent, too. All at once. The U2 mix he had on was gone. Just like that.

Bang.

There was a solid thump on the side of the bed and Lily's laugh turned to a sharp cry of pain as her shins hit the frame. She cursed and pitched forward into the bed. Marty could hear her but he could not see her.

Not at all.

For a single freaky moment he thought that it was him, that he'd gone blind. That the stress of sex with a woman two or three decades younger than him had pushed his ticker past the red line. He thought, Oh Christ, I'm going to die in a Houston hotel with a Korean hooker. Connie will be pissed.

But it wasn't him. He understood that a half second later.

Outside, the sky was filled with stars and the lights of Houston were still on. A splash of jewels.

"What's going on?" asked Lily, and the little-girl quality was gone, replaced by a voice that was colder, harsher, and in no way playful.

"I told you to leave the lights on," he snapped.

"I did. Maybe there's a power outage in the hotel."

As she said it the world seemed willing to prove her wrong.

Outside the lights began changing. First it was the buildings closest to the Marriott. They went dark. Bang. All at once, as if someone had found a single switch that could shut off every light.

Then the buildings across the street from them went out. And the buildings on the next block. The next. The next.

Bang.

Bang.

Bang.

JONATHAN MABERRY

All dark.

Marty and Lily froze, staring through the glass at the city.

No, staring at the blackness that had been the city. Now it was nothing. Only the upper floors were edged with thin blue lines of starlight. And Marty had an irrational thought.

At least the stars didn't go out.

It was almost the last thought he had.

He heard the sound then. Not an engine whine. No, he might have understood what was about to happen.

This was a whistling sound. Almost a shriek.

Getting closer.

Getting louder.

Something moving so fast through the dark air that the wind screamed along its sides.

Marty knew what it was. He knew.

The moment that his brain identified what it was . . . that was his last thought. He even said it aloud.

"They're falling," he said in a whisper that was filled with awe. "They're all falling."

A moment later a Boeing 737 struck the top floor of the Marriott.

Between the hotel and the airport, the rest of the planes stacked up for landing fell.

Like dead birds.

Like stricken crows. Black and falling through blackness.

Until the darkness recoiled from the fires.

But by then Marty was long gone.

PART TWO
FATHERS AND SONS

———•———

What do we know . . . of the world and the universe about us?
Our means of receiving impressions are absurdly few,
and our notions of surrounding objects infinitely narrow.
We see things only as we are constructed to see them,
and can gain no idea of their absolute nature.
With five feeble senses we pretend to comprehend the
boundlessly complex cosmos, yet other beings
with wider, stronger, or different range of senses
might not only see very differently the things we see,
but might see and study whole worlds of matter,
energy, and life which lie close at hand
yet can never be detected with the senses we have.
—H. P. Lovecraft
Excerpt from the short story "From Beyond"

CHAPTER TWENTY-THREE

THE NATIONAL SZÉCHÉNYI LIBRARY
F BUILDING OF BUDA CASTLE
BUDAPEST, HUNGARY
TWO WEEKS AGO

His name was Harry Bolt and he was not a great spy.

He was probably not a very good spy. Or even a moderately good one. He knew that. Everyone who knew him knew that. His boss did, too.

And his father definitely did.

Harry thought about this as he crouched in the dark and tried hard not to get caught, not to get seen, and not to get killed. All very important things on his to-do list. Right at the top of his priorities this evening. Harry was a disappointment to many but he was still his own favorite person. Getting arrested, interrogated, disappeared, or shot would seriously interfere with his motto of "Die Old and Rich and in Bed with a Porn Star." He wanted to get that translated into Latin and tattooed somewhere on his body.

The night was dark and the rest of his team were taking their sweet time doing their part of this job. This very, very illegal job. Being a third-tier field agent for the CIA did not come with many protections. He was alone now because the two other members of his team, Roy Olvera and Jim Florida, were nowhere to be found. Olvera was supposed to have prepped this lock so all Harry had to do was cut a wire and manually push back the metal service door to enter the underground chamber. But, no Olvera and no prep work. God only knew where Florida was. He'd gone off to upload a neutral video loop to the security cameras, but he was taking his sweet time about it. Or he was lost again. Florida got lost a lot.

That was the problem. Neither of those other two clowns took this job seriously because it was a bullshit assignment. All three of them knew it. Shit jobs like this were only ever given to field operators who had screwed up as badly or as often as the Three Stooges. That's what the other staffers at the Agency's Hungarian station called his team. Nice. He wished that it hadn't been so thoroughly earned, though. Screwups were their specialty, and Harry had to admit it.

He wondered if his father had ever screwed up any part of any mission in his entire life. No. Probably not. Demigods don't make mistakes. In truth, Harry's father was a great spy. Maybe *the* great spy. Absolutely everyone knew that. Dad was Harcourt Bolton, Senior, and Harry knew that nothing he ever did was going to let him live up to that kind of a legacy.

Harry Bolt loved his father. He really did.

Conditionally.

He also hated his father. Conditionally.

Like everything in Harry Bolt's life, his relationship with his dad was complicated. It was always complicated. Even more complicated than Harry's love life, which was so weird you couldn't sell it as a reality show. No one would believe the string of beautiful, artistic, accomplished, and absolutely bug-fuck nuts women who came and went in his life. Harry couldn't believe most of it and he'd been there, done that, and had all the scars and souvenirs.

His relationship with dear old Dad . . . well, that was even more of a mess.

Most of those complications stemmed from the challenges associated with living in the shadow of a great man. A better man, as Harry's fourth consecutive stepmother went to such great lengths to point out. A man who was, as Harry's superiors in Central Intelligence so often reminded him very quietly, a hero. A millionaire whose net worth was soon going to change its first letter from *M* to *B*. And while being the son of someone about to join the billionaire club had its perks, it also came with its burdens.

One of the problems—and there were many—was that there was no actual way to live up to his father. Ask Jakob Dylan, ask Julian Lennon. "Son of a Legend" should qualify one for handicapped parking privileges. His father's unattainable reputation was the reason Harry shortened his last name. Fewer people made the connection even though they looked exactly like father and son. Except that Dad was a little taller, a little thinner, a little better looking, and had—despite his age—six-pack abs rather than Harry's shorter stature and kegger gut.

Life, as Harry Bolt saw it, sucked moose dick.

And where the hell were Olvera and Florida? Slacker buttholes, both of them. Harry hated being the third Stooge. He squatted in the dark in a tiny electrical access corridor three hundred feet below the subbasement of the library in Budapest. He was sure that if his father was there he'd have disarmed this frigging lock with nothing more than a lift of one disapproving eyebrow, and he'd be inside already. Getting it all done.

This mission had some fuzzy edges and the best that could be said of the intel that put him down here in the dark was that it was marginally better than deciding policy by flipping a coin. Marginally, and that was Harry being generous. From a distance the job sounded pretty cool, almost glamorous. Almost "dadlike." Harry's team was assigned to track an international black marketeer named Ohan who had known ties with ISIL and who was *possibly* smuggling high-tech weapons to the extremists. The weapon, which had a cool code name— Kill Switch—was something stolen from a covert lab and was being ferried to ISIL in pieces. Harry's team was supposed to locate one such shipment and verify its contents. If the mission was successful, then the Agency would spin up its engines for an all-out assault on Ohan's smuggling network. On the other hand, if the shipment the Stooges had been tracking was a lot less important, as Harry's supervisor implied, then this was something akin to busywork. Something that looked good in any report friends of his father might see—thereby casting the Hungarian station chief in a good light—but which in reality was a big steaming pile of horseshit.

This wouldn't be the first such case. Not by a long damn way.

Harry would love to have gone up against a real ISIL field team. That would be cool. That would help him make some kind of statement about his career. Instead he was breaking into a museum for no good damn reason. He was absolutely positive that this was a waste of time.

He tapped his earbud to get to the team channel.

"Corndog to Waffles," he said, using his call sign and trying to reach Olvera. No answer. He tried Florida—Sunstroke. Got nothing. Spent a few moments cursing. Then he sighed and went back to work on the access electronics. He had half a dozen wires stripped, alligator clips rerouting power, and tiny meters providing information Harry didn't know if he could trust. Sweat ran down his face and stung his eyes. His fingers were sweating, too, as he dug around in the junction box trying to snag the blue wire.

"Come on, you scum-sucking son of a canine whore . . ."

There. Got it. Harry snipped the blue wire and all of the lights inside the control box went dark. He frowned. Were they all supposed to go out? Shouldn't the light on the circuit reroute he'd patched still be on?

He froze, listening for the sound of alarms. Sweat ran in lines down his face and his fingers were cold with tension.

Nothing.

He touched the Send button on his earbud. "Corndog to Sunstroke."

Nothing from Jim Florida.

He tapped it again. "Corndog to Waffles."

Olvera didn't answer, either.

"Oh, mannnn," whined Harry. He really hated those guys. Seriously. If ISIL ever wanted someone to publicly cut into lunchmeat, Harry could suggest a couple of names.

Harry tried the calls again. And again. Persistent nothing. That's when his annoyance began to change to something else. It wasn't yet fear, because Harry was almost always afraid. No, this was still over on the doubt side of worry. They could both be maintaining radio silence because they weren't in places secure enough for a verbal response. Which was semi-likely. Not hugely likely, but at least possible.

Harry squatted in a pool of his own indecision for another three minutes, then he thought, to hell with this crap. He wasn't going to win a commendation or leach approval from his father if he did nothing. The job was to break into the vault beneath the Széchényi Library before the exhibit went live, take photos of everything incriminating, and then get out without getting caught. The actual arrest would be made by the counterterrorism gunslingers of Hungary's Terrorelhárítási Központ. The CIA did not make those kinds of arrests on foreign soil. No, sir. There was far more political currency to be gained by handing over the collar to the locals. Career-wise, though, if he scored this on his own—without the other Stooges—then he was, on Agency terms, a made man. Harry had seen what happened to the career trajectory of those agents who scored on something like that. He wanted his own elevator up past the glass ceiling.

Maybe even make Dad proud. A faint possibility, but still a possibility. His father, after all, had saved the world three times from major bioweapon releases. Three times.

Balls.

He shifted his position to address the metal panel. It was stiff, but he managed to dig his screwdriver into a gap and lever it open enough to put the edge of his hand against it. It didn't want to move, but it did. One stubborn inch at a time. And as it opened a puff of air blew out at him.

"Nicely done," he told himself. You took your back-pats where you could find them.

Then Harry set the panel aside, removed his flashlight, and aimed the beam inside. He saw a square chamber with stone walls. It appeared to be empty except for an old metal chest, bound by straps of iron.

"Bingo," he murmured. He put the flashlight between his teeth and climbed inside.

It was at this point that the trajectory of Harry Bolt's life changed.

Completely and irrevocably.

CHAPTER TWENTY-FOUR

When I could move, I got up and used the head to clean up. The nausea eased up by slow degrees but it didn't go away. Top and Bunny sat like a pair of shivering old men. They sipped water and ate salty crackers and didn't say a word or look at anyone.

I'd already called Church while we were still in Antarctica airspace to tell him what had happened, what we'd seen, and what I did when I thought this was a genie that could not be let out of the bottle. Not sure if he agreed with me or not.

Half an hour later Church called me back and hit me with the news about Houston.

The power had gone out. Not the whole city, but enough of it. Too much of it. Planes had fallen out of the sky. Thirteen of them. Some of them crashed on runways at George Bush Intercontinental Airport. That was horrible enough. One went through the roof at Air-Sea International Logistics near Lochinvar Golf Course. One pancaked down between the Budget and Avis car rental offices off Palmetto Pines Road. And one of them hit the top floor of the Houston Airport Marriott Hotel. The jet was fully fueled and every seat was booked. There was a sales convention at the hotel. Two-thirds of the rooms were booked. We wouldn't know how many were dead. Five thousand was a conservative guess.

Five thousand people.

Gone.

How do you take news like that? What's an appropriate reaction for a loss of life so dramatic that the world itself seems to wobble as all those souls take flight on burning wings? The part of me that is a decent, ordinary human being—that aspect I called the "Modern Man"—was appalled, shocked to silence, disconnected from coherent thought. The part of me that was a killer wanted to bellow out in rage and denial because this was an attack on the tribe. The human tribe. The Killer wanted to heal hurt by causing harm. And the Cop, that part of me—the central aspect of who I was—wanted answers.

"No one has taken credit yet," said Church. "However, I spoke with Harcourt Bolton shortly before we got the news and he has been building a case to connect ISIL with the power outages that occurred earlier this year." He explained about the black marketer Ohan, about Kill Switch.

"What do we know about it? What kind of weapon is this?" I demanded. "Was it some kind of e-bomb?"

"Unknown, but unlikely," said Church. "There are no reports of any kind of explosion prior to the crashing of those planes."

"I don't understand. The power went out and then back on again? That can't happen with an EMP."

"I know. This must be something else. I've scrambled teams and they're en route. I have Jerry Spencer and the whole forensics team on a plane. Same with Frank Sessa, though there is no evidence of any kind of explosives. In short, Captain, it's too soon for us to know what happened. Something interrupted the power inside a roughly circular area around Bush airport. As far as we can tell, everything inside that zone that uses electricity was shut off. We have reports that this includes cell phones and battery-operated devices."

"Why Houston, though? What's there that they wanted to hit? What's the statement? No, wait," I said, "if this is ISIL, then that might explain it. Most of the commanders in their forces are ex-Iraqi military. George Bush launched the first Gulf War. His son launched the second. Maybe this is a statement. A revenge killing."

Church nodded, not liking the idea but agreeing with the logic. "You may be right."

"This is what happened at the NASCAR thing, isn't it? And the presidential debate?"

"So it seems."

"Which means they were, what? Test drives?"

"That would be my guess," said Church. "But, Captain, it seems to me that you experienced this yourself. In your report you said that your equipment shut down and then restarted down in the cavern."

I was silent. I'd told him that not an hour ago. So why hadn't I put two and two together?

Church was on the same tack. He asked, "How are you feeling?"

"Bad," I said. "But I'm going to divert this plane. Find me a safe runway in Houston and we'll—"

"No, Captain," said Church. "I was calling to inform you, not to put you into play."

"Why not? This is why we have a Special Projects Office."

"I'm aware of that, but you said that you and your men were exposed to some possible toxins."

I had every intention of yelling at him and demanding that he put us into play. Instead I had a coughing fit that lasted two minutes. It left me spent and weak and feeling as fragile as spun glass.

"Go home, Captain," said Church. "Let the medical team check you out. I'll keep you posted."

The connection went dead.

INTERLUDE NINE

Oscar Bell poured three fingers of scotch into a chunky tumbler and handed it to Major Corrine Sails.

"Thanks," said the major, sipping it, nodding, and taking the glass with her as she began walking slowly around the big office. There were cases of books, mostly histories of science, histories of war, histories of governments. No fiction, no autobiographies. Nothing that connected the man with other people. There were no framed photos on the walls, no family pictures on Bell's desk. No trophies of any kind. Major Sails noted all of it as she sipped her whiskey.

"Have a seat," said Bell, waving a hand toward a pair of rich leather chairs positioned in a window alcove. Outside a pair of catamarans bounced over the light chop, and farther out to sea a big trawler was heading out to the fishing grounds off Montauk Point.

"Lovely view," said Sails.

Bell nodded, accepting the comment without any visible sense of pride. She wondered if he ever took genuine pleasure in anything. Probably not. Her colleagues in the Department of Defense had warned her that he was a few degrees colder than a Vulcan. No visible warmth, no detectable personality. Not even precisely unlikeable, because there was nothing to like. Nothing really to react to.

She thought he was probably wretched in bed. A get-it-done approach to sex that was probably all about insuring progeny. No wonder he went through wives the way most people went through changes of clothes. The women were attracted to the billions, but not even the hardiest gold-digger seemed able to stay in it for the long haul. Sails couldn't blame them. Not that Bell wasn't attractive in his own way. He was lovely in photos and on TV, and when there was a camera he

131

could turn on the charm and produce a winning smile. Off camera and away from the press he was a robot.

"If they sent you," he said without preamble, "then somebody who doesn't have their head up their ass took a look at my proposal."

Sails nodded. "They did. I, in fact, did."

Bell studied her for a moment. Sails knew that the man would have had her checked out. Her work with DARPA, some of her nonmilitary published works, and maybe even her paper on the probability of interdimensional physics as a valid and emerging field of legitimate study. He was the kind of man known to be thorough. Not exactly judgmental as demanding to a very high degree. He had, at least as far as his defense projects went, a very open mind. And because Bell was a scientist as well as a contractor he generally personally vetted the people with whom he worked.

"And—?" he asked.

"As I understand it this device—this 'God Machine'—was designed by your son?"

"Yes."

"Who is thirteen."

"Yes."

"He designed this without assistance from any adult?"

Bell sipped his scotch. "Yes."

"That is remarkable."

"No kidding."

They studied each other for a moment. "Mr. Bell," she said, "I have a few very important questions."

"I figured you might."

Sails crossed her legs and smoothed her skirt. Bell did not even flick a glance at her legs. Nothing. The man really was a robot.

"I guess we need to start with the obvious," she said. "Why is it called a 'God' Machine?"

"Ask my son."

"I can't. You won't let anyone near him."

Bell shrugged. "Figure of speech. Look, cards on the table. Prospero is a very troubled boy. You've probably read his psych evals and they're all over the place. Highest IQ ever scored. So high, in fact, it calls the validity of the test into question. Kid's legitimately off the charts. That said, he's also deeply disturbed. His shrink says he's not actually on the spectrum because there are too many ways in which he doesn't fit the profile for Asperger's or autism. He doesn't fit into any slot. I can say without contradiction that he's one of a kind."

"Well, Mr. Bell, I don't know if we can actually say that, can we?"

Bell stiffened. "What's that supposed to mean?"

"Oh, come on," she said, smiling, "do you think that the Majestic program operates in a vacuum? You look surprised."

"Shit," said Bell.

She nodded. "Do you have any current affiliations with Howard Shelton?"

"No."

"But you know him."

"Knew him. We had a falling-out. The man's a psychopath."

"Maybe, but he's our psychopath."

"Cute. My answer stands. I haven't spoken to Shelton in years. Not since I agreed to adopt Prospero. And let's be clear on that, Major; Prospero is my son. That's legal."

"Does he know he's adopted?"

"He's smart," said Bell. "I'm sure he suspects. Doesn't change the fact that he's my legal son."

"An argument can be made that he is the property of the United States Department of Defense."

"Is that a fight you want to pick? Because I'll take it to the Supreme Court. That'd put a lot of dirty laundry on the public wash line."

"You signed certain papers."

"And I'd be happy to produce them for public scrutiny. *Rolling Stone* magazine would do a cover story on them, have no doubt." Bell snorted. "I invited you here to talk business and you come at me with threats? No wonder people blow whistles on you assholes."

Sails held up her hands in a placating gesture. "We're just having a conversation. Nobody's making threats."

"I fucking well am. If you try to take Prospero away from me I'll—"

"Don't," she said. "We got off on the wrong foot. Let's back up and try this again. Fair enough?"

Bell thought about it for a moment, his eyes cool and calculating. "It's your dime, Major."

"Howard Shelton," she said. "You worked with him in the past?"

"You already know I did," said Bell irritably. "I did two off-the-books contract projects for Majestic Three. A gyroscope mounting and the spherical guidance system for one of his T-craft projects. It went nowhere."

"Has he invited you into any other projects related to the T-craft?"

"No. I thought that was a dud."

She did not comment on that. Instead she asked, "Has he invited you to bid on any other projects?"

"No."

"What is your current relationship with Mr. Shelton?"

Bell almost smiled. "We stopped sending each other Christmas cards, if that's what you mean."

"Please explain."

"Why? It's a matter of record and if we're having this conversation, then you've read the transcripts. I did some work for Majestic Three and now he's using other contractors. I lost four major contracts because Shelton got fickle. It took me a while to recover from that."

"From what I can see from your corporate earnings statements, you haven't quite recovered yet."

"I'll get there. It won't be with Shelton. No way. End of story. I have nothing to do with him or M3. That whole Majestic project is a black hole into which Uncle Sam is pissing money that would be better spent elsewhere." Bell snorted. "No, Major, I have nothing to do with Shelton or his mad science games."

Sails set her scotch aside. "Tell me," she said, "does your son know who he is? Hasn't he ever wondered why he is so unlike other children his age? Hasn't he ever wondered why his intellect is so far above anyone else's?"

"He knows he's gifted," snapped Bell. "He thinks he's a freak."

"'Freak'?" she echoed. "So you haven't told him? I mean, what on Earth would he say if he ever had his DNA sequenced?"

Bell sneered. "Stop trying to intimidate me, Major. You're not formidable enough to sell it. Save it for the rubes. You're acting like you discovered something and are calling me on the carpet for it, but let's be clear—I called you. As soon as I saw what Prospero was attempting to build I brought it directly to you. Per the agreement I have with the DoD. This is me being a team player, so stop trying to scare me to death."

They sat and drank scotch for almost a full minute before Sails replied. "You live up to your reputation."

"Flattery. Nice. What's next? An offer for a blow job?" He rubbed his eyes. "Jesus, Sails, can we cut through the bullshit? I brought the God Machine to you because I know what it can do. Not what my son thinks it will do. He thinks it'll open a doorway to a different universe that will allow him to go home. Like I said, the kid's off his rocker. But in the process of developing it he hit a couple of speed bumps, and that's what I want you to pay me to develop."

"Speed bumps?"

"What he thinks are design flaws are actually a golden goddamn fleece. Two in particular."

"Yes," she said, almost purring. "A portable electrical null field generator?"

"I nicknamed it Kill Switch."

"Catchy."

"Yeah, well," said Bell. "It's truth in advertising. We both know there's nobody who has anything remotely close to this. This is a quantum jump forward in defense technology and don't pretend that it's not. If we can work out the kinks and solve the overheating problems and configure a portable version, then we win the arms race. Bang, just like that. Done. You know it and I know it. This is potentially more important than the Manhattan Project. This is a brand-new branch of science and my son created it. My son."

"My colleagues feel that anything Prospero develops is a by-product of existing military technology."

"A 'by-product'? That's what they're calling my son now? Jesus. If you're here to bully me into giving it up without an offer, then you are sadly and sorely mistaken."

"I didn't say that," she replied smoothly. "I'm being frank about what some people in my department think. I didn't say I shared their view."

Bell stood up and held out his hand. "You're empty, give me your glass." He crossed to the wet bar, poured more of the scotch, came back slowly, handed her the fresh drink, clinked against her tumbler without making a toast, and sat down. Sails considered the amber depths of the whiskey.

"Take a moment to consider everything you know about me," he said. "With everything that's probably in my file, is it your considered opinion that I am more likely to be swayed by threats and intimidation or an offer of inclusion and partnership? Go on, think that through. I have plenty of scotch and we have all afternoon."

CHAPTER TWENTY-FIVE

THE NATIONAL SZÉCHÉNYI LIBRARY
F BUILDING OF BUDA CASTLE
BUDAPEST, HUNGARY
TWO WEEKS AGO

Harry Bolt climbed into the room, removed the flashlight from between his teeth, and used the powerful little beam to sweep the room. He produced a small device from his pants pocket, thumbed it on, and held it out on the flat of his palm as he turned in a slow circle. The tiny green light did not change to yellow, which meant there were no hidden alarms and no electronics down here. There was a large hatch in the ceiling that had a heavy steel door. No doubt it was securely locked from above. That was okay. He didn't need to mess with that.

Instead he moved to the chest. It was a big, square box except for a domed lid. Three feet per side, and it sat on a platform of cinder blocks. The chest looked very old, and was made out of iron from which rust had been forcibly sanded off. The box was covered on all sides by a variety of ancient religious symbols. He recognized some of them. Crucifixes and Hamsa hands, an Egyptian ankh, a St. Benedict medal, a Seal of Solomon, an ancient Roman word-square, a mezuzah, a Turkish evil eye—and others that he did not recognize. His first reaction was to smile at the mumbo jumbo because Harry did not believe in very much, but then a cold shiver suddenly rippled through his body and his heart began to flutter. He looked around. The underground chamber was small and filled with shadows that his meager flashlight could not dispel. Harry suddenly felt very alone down there. And very scared.

"You're an idiot," he told himself, but his words seemed unnaturally loud. Alarmingly so, and he hushed himself as if someone was listening. As if maybe the box itself was listening. That thought wormed its way through his brain and, try as he might, Harry could not mock it into silence.

He made himself focus on the task at hand. Heavy iron bands held the chest shut and these converged at the hasp, from which hung a remarkable, heavy, old-fashioned padlock. More of the strange symbols were carved onto every square inch of the lock. He bent to peer at the lock, and then nodded. This was better; this nudged him back into his comfort zone. He was mediocre with electronics but he loved to pick locks. His father had hired a locksmith—and former professional thief—to give him lessons. That was a birthday present when Harry was eleven. His dad was like that. His father was never off the clock. He was Bolton, Harcourt Bolton, all the damn time. Even at Thanksgiving. Even on Christmas morning when Harry was a kid. Giving a complete professional forensic evidence collection kit when he was ten. Wrapped by the maid, no doubt. Another year it was a professional disguise and makeup kit under the tree. Always stuff like that.

Most of the time Harry hated his father for trying to turn his son into a clone. But as he removed the leather toolkit from his pocket down there in the dark, he was cool with it. He stepped up to the chest, studied the lock for a moment, then selected a tension wrench from the kit. He inserted it into the bottom of the keyhole and applied slight pressure, then he slipped a pick into the top of the lock and gave very slight torque to the wrench as he scrubbed his pick back and forth. He felt one of the pins move. Nice. He repeated this until all of the pins had shifted, though he was surprised to find that there were double the normal number of them and each moved with rusty reluctance. But Harry had a deft hand and after six minutes of patient work the lock clicked open.

"Easy-peasy, Mrs. Wheezy." It was a nonsense thing the locksmith had said every time he opened a lock, and Harry had picked it up.

Harry gingerly removed the lock from the hasp and set it aside, then very carefully lifted the lid. The lock and the lid were absurdly heavy, almost as if they were made of lead instead of steel, but when he raised the lid he saw that the underside gleamed with gold and green. Copper. Or an alloy of both. Harry fished in his mind for what he'd learned of metallurgy from the locksmith—who insisted that his pupil understand all of the materials he might encounter. The name came swimming up out of his memories. *Molybdochalkos.* He grinned at himself for remembering that.

Then, as he looked inside the chest, his grin faded. He expected to find a false top, maybe with some actual ancient relics on it, with the real booty below—IDs and debit cards and maybe some weapons.

Instead he saw a book. That's it. Nothing else. A book. It was big, two feet long and eighteen inches wide. At least seven inches thick, and it, too, was sealed by metal bands. Six of them running laterally and two more going up and over. Each one was fastened with a smaller but no less sturdy padlock. The bands were covered by a different kind of engraving than had been used on the chest. Instead of the holy symbols of protection, the bands and the book they surrounded were covered by monsters. Prancing goats with too many heads, writhing squids, demon faces with hundreds of eyes, shapeless mounds with too many mouths and worms for hair.

Harry flinched away. It hurt his mind to look at those symbols, and in his creeped-out imagination, they seemed to move. Or to tremble in anticipation of moving. He licked his lips, which had gone totally dry. His tongue felt like old leather and his heart was punching the inside of his chest.

"This is bullshit," he told himself.

The room threw echoes back at him that distorted his words into meaningless and sinister mutterings. He forced himself to focus on the rust-pitted locks on the metal bands. When he touched them they felt strangely warm. It was more like touching skin rather than metal. Harry recoiled. He did not like any of this. Not one bit. He closed his tool kit and put it into his pocket, closed the chest, reset the lock, and moved over to the small hatch through which he'd entered.

Except . . .

Except that he did not do any of that.

His eyes seemed to glaze and when he blinked them clear he was sitting on the floor with his back to the wall, his legs stretched out before him, and the big book resting heavily on his thighs.

Harry said, "What—?"

He had no memory at all of how that happened.

His eyes watered and Harry blinked again.

And he was no longer in the chamber. Now he stood in the entrance foyer to the museum. Again there was no memory of having climbed out through the hatch or of making his way up here. It was as if he had stepped out of his own mind and left his body to run on autopilot.

Except that wasn't it. And he knew it. He could feel something shift inside of him. *In his mind.* In a moment of absolute mind-numbing terror Harry Bolt realized that he was not alone inside his own head. There was someone else in there. He flung the book away and ran screaming from the building.

Only he didn't.

He *wanted* to. He saw himself doing that.

But he did not.

Harry stared at the book. He no longer held it but he clearly had not thrown it away. It lay on the floor at his feet.

It lay in a wide, dark lake of blood. A puddle of it that seemed to cover the whole floor. There were islands in that lake. Lumps. Red and torn. Covered with the last shreds of clothing. The gray and black of the library's security patrol.

The all-black of the same kinds of clothes that Harry wore. Soft, nonreflective, nonbinding black.

Roy Olvera.

Jim Florida.

Their eyes stared at him with sightless astonishment; their mouths hung open as if frozen that way as they screamed their last screams. The bodies were . . .

Gone. No. Not gone. The islands in that lake of blood wore the same kinds of equipment. Parts of it. What was left of it. All of it crisscrossed with knife wounds and punctured with the red dots of bullet wounds.

Harry stared for three full seconds.

Then he screamed.

INTERLUDE TEN

Oscar Bell watched the major as she walked out to her car. Bell leaned against the doorframe and watched her drive off. He was four scotches in and felt more of it than he showed.

Songbirds sang in the trees and overhead a gull whose breast was flawlessly white sailed on the breeze, heading out to sea. Bell stepped down into the yard and strolled across the grass toward the backyard. The expensive play set that had been erected when Prospero was four was still there, cleaned by the yardman but as pristine as the day it was assembled. Prospero had never used it. Not once. Bell took his cell phone out of his pocket and sat down on the saddle of the center of three swings.

His first call was to Dr. Greene. After a quick exchange of meaningless pleasantries, Bell asked, "You mentioned something to me last year and I wanted to clarify it. You said that Prospero had atypical creative drives. Do you remember? You said that there was a definite correlation between his mood and the quality of his creative output. What did you call it? The tortured artist syndrome?"

"That was an off-the-cuff label," said Greene. "The formal description is—"

"Save the jargon. Explain it to me. Layman's terms."

"Well," said Greene, "it's a phenomenon that has been observed in certain cases, particularly with people who have demonstrated artistic abilities coupled with savantism. In short, when Prospero is happy he develops a kind of creative lassitude. He doesn't draw, he doesn't write, and he doesn't even go into the laboratory you made for him in the playroom. In other children freedom from stress sparks creativity. With Prospero there is a paradoxical effect. When he is feeling stressed, or has been in a fight with one of the other boys, or, um, has had, um, difficulties with you, then he is significantly more creative in all aspects. Most notably with his scientific pursuits. That is where his truest passion lies, and I suppose we can theorize that research comforts him. Or, perhaps, it empowers him in times when he feels disempowered. There is a theory that Vincent van Gogh experienced the same kind of thing, hence the nickname of the 'tortured artist syndrome.' It's not an official label, as I said."

"Okay," said Bell, "I get it. Put that in writing. All of the clinical support that you can find on it. I want a thorough report and I want it in seventy-two hours."

He disconnected before Greene could protest or ask questions.

Bell used his heels to move the swing slowly forward and back.

His second call was to Gunther Stark, commandant of the Ballard Military Boarding School in Poland, Maine.

When that call was ended Bell sat on the swing for nearly an hour. Waiting for his son to come home from school. He sat there, slowly moving back and forth on the relic from a childhood that had never really happened.

Bell tried to hate himself for what he was about to do. He tried.

But no matter how far down he dug in the cold, hard soil of his soul, all he ever found was more darkness and more dirt.

CHAPTER TWENTY-SIX

I told Top and Bunny about Houston.

It hit them like it hit me. Sick as we were, all three of us were ready to lock and load. We sat there, hurting and trembling with impotence as we watched a live news feed on my laptop. I thought it would look bad. It looked worse. Some of the fires were still burning. The power was back on and the sky was filled with emergency helicopters. News choppers, too, even though they were being pushed back beyond a safety zone. God, how many times would we have to look at scenes like this? In America, around the world? How had terrorism become so powerful while we seemed to be dropping to our knees? Or maybe that was the wrong way to put it. How many times could we be forced to our knees and still manage to get back up?

"Funny," said Bunny bitterly, "but I always thought it would be a nuke. After nine-eleven, after Atlanta and San Francisco, I figured the next step up would be a nuclear detonation on U.S. soil. Something smuggled in by a North Korean team, maybe; or some Russian cell trying to bring back the Soviet Union. Or the Iranians. But I never figured ISIL for being able to hit us this hard at home. Never."

"Yeah, well, there's that old thing about assumptions," grumbled Top. He turned to me. "Did Mr. Church really stand us down for this?"

I nodded. "Right now this is someone else's job. CIA, State Department, every intelligence agency we have, and Bug's team. We have Jerry Spencer and Frank Sessa on the ground in Houston doing forensic evaluation, and Harcourt Bolton's doing deep background for us. We all want someone in the crosshairs, but so far no one from the Islamic Nation has stepped up to own it. The president's moving assets into play, though. If we can connect the dots to ISIL, then this will change the game."

"Third Gulf War," said Top.

"Jesus Christ," murmured Bunny.

I got up and went into the head for a while because my lower intestines wanted to crawl out of my ass. I sat there on the can and put my face in my hands.

All those people. The fuse lit on another war. Where was the end to it? How could we ever hope to put the pin back into the grenade? Was it always going to be like this?

Bad thoughts for a sick man to have. Bad, bad thoughts.

I went back and dropped onto a seat between Top and Bunny. For a long time we sat there, each of us shivering and sweating. Bunny looked like he was falling asleep. His eyes were glassy and unfocused. Top's brown skin had faded to a dusty gray. He met my eyes and nodded to me, conveying a truth, making an agreement. Top's like that. We can say a lot to each other without words.

Aside from the two pilots, we had six team members aboard the plane. Bird Dog and the other equipment handlers, as well as the general crew. All of them were trained as medics, but none of them were doctors. They were clustered together at the far end of the plane, looking at me looking at them. They looked worried, too.

I staggered to my feet and stumbled to the intercom on the bulkhead beside the cockpit door, identified myself, and asked to speak to the pilot.

"I can buzz you in," he said.

"Negative. Do you have active seals?"

"Yes, sir," he said crisply.

"Okay, then listen to me, Captain," I said. "I am initiating a flash-fire protocol. You are hereby ordered to seal the cabin. No one gets in. "

A pause. "Yes, sir," he said, and despite the typically bland way pilots spoke no matter what was happening, his voice had gone up a full octave.

"I do not want this plane to land in San Diego. They have a biohazard response unit at the Naval Auxiliary Landing Field on San Clemente Island. Get clearance to land us there. But call the Pier and have our big bio-containment module flown over, too. The flight crew will need to be quarantined, too. I don't know if this thing is contagious but no one is going to take chances."

"Captain Ledger," said the pilot, "what's happening back there?"

I wiped sweat from my eyes. The interior of the plane was filled with too much light and it seemed to be moving sideways.

"I really don't know," I said.

INTERLUDE ELEVEN

Oscar Bell did not enjoy writing checks as large as the one that kept Prospero out of jail, or the one that insured that his son would remain as a student and cadet at Ballard. With each zero his pen gouged deeper into the check and left deep impressions on all the checks beneath it.

He tore off the two checks and tossed them onto the desk of the school's commandant, a withered husk of an old soldier named Gunther Stark.

"He stays," Bell said flatly. He could afford the repairs, but he'd feel it. He would have to move some holdings around. Ideally he'd find a way to bill Major Sails for it, providing her group accepted his proposal.

Stark glanced down at the checks, inhaled sharply through his nose, and exhaled slowly. Like a man dealing with physical pain.

"Tell me, Mr. Bell," said the commandant, "have you spoken with your son about this?"

"Of course I have."

"Did he tell you what he was trying to accomplish?"

"He . . . may have said something. What of it?"

Stark said, "He used materials and equipment from our lab to build a small-scale particle accelerator. When it was turned on, not only did it destroy a considerable portion of the lab and the surrounding rooms—"

"And you have a check that will make it even better than it was."

"—that device also knocked out the power in the entire school."

Bell's mouth twitched. "What?"

"Oh yes. There was some kind of power surge that canceled out all power. No lights, no computers, no alarms. It even shorted out the halon fire-suppression system and knocked out the cell phones. We couldn't call the fire department."

Bell leaned forward. "Really? How long did it last?"

"What does that matter?"

"How long?"

"I don't know," said Stark, annoyed. "A minute or two."

"How much damage was there to the wiring? What about cell phones? Were the works melted?"

"No, nothing else was damaged. The cell phones and everything came back on. So did the lights, but—"

"Everything came back on?" demanded Bell. "This is important. Apart from what was damaged by the explosion, was there any other damage to any electrical device?"

Stark drummed his fingers. "We seem to be getting off the point."

"No, we're not. Answer my questions." Oscar Bell's tone did not invite further quibbling.

"No, sir," said Stark, "there was no other damage. You are not liable for further reparations."

Stark grabbed his checkbook anyway and began writing a third check. This one was large enough to make the commandant stare in slack-jawed amazement. Bell tore it off, leaned across the desk, and slapped it down in front of Stark.

"I—I don't understand, Mr. Bell," stammered the commandant.

Bell pointed a finger at the man's face. "Listen to me," he said sternly, "and hear what I say. You are going to rebuild your lab and you're going to get it done in one month. I don't want to hear any bullshit about how difficult that's going to be. One month. I'll send some of my own people to oversee it. You will also build an extension that will be dedicated to my son and his work. You hear me? That addition will be Prospero's. You'll post two guards on it around the clock. If anyone sets one foot into his lab other than Prospero, his teachers, or you, then you will answer to me. I want you to tell me you understand."

"I . . . well, yes. Of course I understand."

"I will have my people set up a limited Internet access for Prospero. It will allow him to do research and to interface with other labs. I'll arrange clearances. But understand, Stark, that Net connection passes through my own company's mainframes. Nowhere else. And Prospero will have to log on and log off. I will give him a password directly. No one else uses that network and Prospero is not to have any access to any other Internet connection. None. That is an absolute rule."

"What is this all about? If you want your son to do research of this kind, why not move him to another facility? Away from the other boys."

"Fuck the other boys. And fuck you if you're too stupid or inept to keep them away from that lab. Prospero is to have anything he needs or wants in terms of what will help him in this research."

Stark nodded. The check sat on his desk and it seemed to burn with real fire.

Bell leaned back. "I'll expect regular reports on my son's activities. I'll also send people out to inspect his lab and his work. They'll call ahead to schedule times when Prospero won't be there to interfere."

"Of course."

"If you have questions, ask them now," said Bell. "Otherwise let's get this in motion."

"There are, um . . . two things, Mr. Bell," said Stark. "The first is so unusual that I don't know if I should even mention it, but you've made it very clear since the beginning that you want to know everything concerning your son. However, this is somewhat tangential to—"

"Stop pussying around the topic and just say it."

"It's about the dreams, sir," said Stark.

Bell stopped breathing for a moment. "What dreams?"

"It was the night of the explosion. Several of the boys complained the next day that they had very strange dreams. We had the staff psychologist interview them and as far as he can determine there were two very distinct types of dreams. Or, maybe they were hallucinations somehow induced by the energetic discharge of the machine."

"Who are you quoting?" Bell said sharply.

"Oh. About the discharge? That was Professor Childers, Prospero's physics teacher. After hearing from all those boys I called a meeting with our psychologist and everyone who had any connection to what your son was working on."

"Tell me about the dreams."

"As I said, they took two forms. For most of the boys they had nightmares about some huge monsters. Big blobby things with tentacles. The psychologist has drawings if you want to see them. What's so strange about it, though, is that the boys mostly drew the same thing. Even boys who don't socialize with one another. We did interviews to see if they shared experiences, and to determine if that polluted the memories through association. But . . . no."

Bell did not comment. "And the other kind of dream?"

"That's even stranger. A few boys had those. Only six of them out of the whole school. And though the dreams were similar, they were also different. In each case the boys dreamed they were somewhere else. In other places. One was at home in his room. Another was in a poker game in what he believes is Paris, although the boy has never been to France." He ran through the others. "In each case," he concluded, "it was like they were suddenly elsewhere, seeing things they could not possibly see. One of them was able to accurately describe the inside of the Tate Museum in London, even to a description of the ticket seller. The psychologist made a call and verified the accuracy of this. Isn't that the strangest thing you ever heard?"

Oscar Bell removed a pack of cigarettes from his inner pocket, selected one, lit it with a lighter that bore the Department of Defense shield—a Christmas gift from years ago—and smoked. He did not ask permission and he tapped his ashes into a coffee cup that sat beside the NO SMOKING sign. Stark said nothing.

"I'll want everything," said Bell. "Copies of those interviews, the files on each boy, the minutes of that staff meeting."

"But, Mr. Stark, I can't do that. That is confidential information."

Bell blew a long stream of smoke over Stark's head. "You always struck me as a realist," Bell said. "Do you want to sit there and tell me that in the version of the 'real world' as you see it that I won't get that information? Or let me put it another way. You're a career soldier. An officer. You've been in combat and led men into battle. Has none of that taught you how to pick your battles?"

Stark sat in silent stillness. He did not answer, and they both knew it was answer enough.

After a long time Stark changed the subject. "I have one more, er, question regarding your son," he said. "Prospero is sometimes a difficult boy, as you are no doubt aware. He, um, acts out, and here at Ballard we have policies in place to enforce discipline and encourage proper behavior."

"Oh, for Christ's sake, don't be such a pussy. I'm not asking you to change how you treat the little shit. As long as he doesn't have bruises on his face when the human services people come for their quarterly inspection I don't give a flying fuck what you do to keep him in line.

He's always been an asshole and I have the feeling he always will be. Can't change that. Kid has some bad wiring. So, sure, if you need to kick his ass every now and then, do it. Spare the rod and spoil the child. My old man had a heavy enough hand and I turned out fine." He jabbed the air with a finger again. "But no head injuries. And nothing that will keep him out of the lab."

He stood up and Stark shot to his feet, as well.

"I think we understand each other, Commandant?" suggested Bell, his dark eyes intense. He offered his hand and when Stark took it, they shook.

Like gentlemen.

CHAPTER TWENTY-SEVEN

THE NATIONAL SZÉCHÉNYI LIBRARY
F BUILDING OF BUDA CASTLE
BUDAPEST, HUNGARY
TWO WEEKS AGO

Harry Bolt did not know that he could scream like a movie actress in a grade B slasher flick. It was not something he'd ever be proud of. Though at the moment he gave in to it as the only possible response.

He screamed his head off.

Then one second later he stopped. Because that's what you do when someone presses the cold, hard, merciless edge of a knife against your throat.

The figure came out of nowhere. One minute he was alone with the dead parts of his team and the next someone occupied the shadows to his right. Dressed in black, holding a knife to his throat.

"Shhh," she said.

Harry Bolt's body was a block of ice, but he cranked his eyes sideways to see her with his peripheral vision. Definitely a woman. Young, slim, very fit. She had long dark hair pulled back into a ponytail and flexible combat clothes that clung to her. Even in that moment Harry checked her out. That was Harry. She was built like a dancer. Tall, though, with small breasts and long limbs. She was an inch or two taller than Harry, who was five nine. Her features were foxlike, with sharply defined cheekbones, thin lips, and intense eyes. Her clothes were fitted with lots of pockets and crossbelts for weapons. A compact Micro Tavor-21 Israeli bullpup assault rifle with an extended thirty-two-round magazine was clipped to one belt. A pair of sheaths were strapped to each thigh. Both empty. One of those knives was held down at her side, the other was keeping Harry on his tippy-toes.

She said, "Who are you?"

"N-night watchman," he stammered.

The woman smiled. Very coldly. The knife pressed more deeply into his throat. "Try again. Are you with the Brotherhood?"

"The . . . who?"

She rattled off something that sounded like Latin to him. "Ordo Fratrum Claustrorum."

"I—I have no idea what you just said," he admitted.

She studied him. It was hard to tell if she believed him. Her expression seemed to be a mix of relief and disappointment.

"CIA?" she asked.

Ouch, he thought. "Wh-who are you?" he said, hoping to get a grip on this conversation.

The woman lowered the knife and stepped back.

"A friend," she said.

"What kind of friend? What agency?" He knew that she wasn't American because her accent sounded Italian.

"You won't have heard of us. It's above your pay grade." She turned him into the light so she could take a better look. Her eyebrows rose. "Wait, I know who you are. You're Harcourt Bolton's son. You're with the Hungary station."

"I—"

"You're one of the Three Stooges."

Yeah, well, that was like a kick in the nuts, though he tried not to let it show on his face.

"Who *are* you?" he asked again.

She ignored that and looked past him and he turned to follow her gaze. The heads of Olvera and Florida seemed to glare at him, their dead eyes filled with accusation. Harry's stomach did a greasy little backflip.

"I'm sorry for what happened to your friends," she said.

"Christ, did *you*—?"

"Don't be an idiot," she snapped. "Of course I didn't do that."

"Then—?"

She suddenly froze and stared beyond the blood to where the big ironbound book lay. The sight of it tore a cry from her and the knives were back in her hands as if by magic. She whirled and kicked Harry in the stomach, knocking him backward into the wall, then she was on him, the one blade back at his throat and the other pressed to the underside of his crotch. Her eyes seemed to blaze with fire.

"Did you open the book?" she demanded. "Lie to me and I will gut you like a pig."

"*No!* I didn't open it. I swear."

She bent close to look deeply into his eyes and he could almost feel her pry open his head to look inside. The moment held, stretched . . .

And then she sagged back, exhaling and removing the knives. She looked relieved but visibly shaken. "No, you did not look into that book."

"I . . . ," he began, but he had nowhere useful to go with that.

The woman sheathed one of her knives but kept the other in her hand as she walked through the blood toward the book. She knelt and used the very tip of the knife to touch it. "Such an ugly thing," she said. "You have no idea how many people have died because of it. We need to take this book out of here. The men who killed your friends are probably downstairs looking for it. They will be furious when they learn it's gone."

"Furious?" Harry pointed to the corpses. "How much madder can they get?"

She shook her head. "You have no idea. They are the Ordo Fratrum Claustrorum. The Fraternal Brothers of the Lock, sometimes known as the Brotherhood. A sacred order charged with finding and destroying books like that one."

"Personally not a fan of book burning," he said. "But I'm considering amending that policy. That thing gives me the creeps."

"It should," she said, nodding. "If you truly understood what this is you would run screaming from here."

"I might anyway."

The woman smiled at that.

"Look," said Harry, "will you at least tell me your name and who you work for? Are you with Terrorelhárítási Központ? No, you sound Italian. Are you with the Nucleo Operativo Centrale di Sicurezza, or maybe NATO?"

"Hardly. You haven't heard of my group, so don't ask. For now you can call me Violin."

Harry grunted. "Violin? That your real name?"

"Don't be naïve."

"Well . . . can you at least tell me you're one of the good guys?"

She gave him a long, strange look. "You really are an idiot, aren't you?"

"I—," he began, but this time it was another voice who cut him off. A man's voice. A sharp growl of surprise and outrage.

Harry and Violin turned as five strangers came crowding through the doorway to the inner library. They, too, were dressed in black. And they, too, carried knives. Lots of knives.

Guns, too.

The obvious leader of the group pointed to the book on the floor. Everyone looked at it. Even Harry. Then the men all raised their eyes and looked at the man and woman standing on the other side of the book. The leader pointed his knife at them. He said something in Italian that, once again, Harry couldn't translate. But he knew what it meant.

The five men howled in fury and came running forward to kill.

INTERLUDE TWELVE

BALLARD MILITARY BOARDING SCHOOL
POLAND, MAINE
WHEN PROSPERO WAS THIRTEEN

"And all of this is for me?" asked Prospero without even trying to hide the skepticism in his voice. "This lab, all this equipment. All of it?"

Commandant Stark smiled. Prospero always thought the man had a truly oily smile. He bet that if he put that face in a vise he could wring a gallon of grease from it.

"Of course, Cadet," said Stark, whose voice was icy and hard, quite at odds with his unctuous leer. "You know that your father loves you and wants only the very best for you."

"Uh-huh," said Prospero. "Right, because my father adores me. It's well known."

Stark's smile flickered but the lights stayed on. "He has gone to great expense and trouble to make sure that everything in this lab is state-of-the-art. Your father is a great man, Cadet. He is a true American and a patriot. I am proud to call him a friend."

"And does he call you a friend? Do you go out on man dates? What's it like to blow a man like dear old—"

The blow knocked the rest of the words from Prospero's mouth. Stark was old but he was not slow, and he had refined the techniques of punishment and brutality over many years. The back of the commandant's hand caught Prospero in exactly the right way to knock Prospero in nearly a full circle and detonate bombs behind his eyes. As Prospero staggered, the commandant stepped forward and clamped one hand around the boy's throat and locked the other around his scrotum. The pain was unbelievable and the force lifted Prospero onto his toes. Stark leaned so close that his lips brushed Prospero's cheek as he spoke.

"Listen to me, Cadet," hissed Stark loud enough for only the two of them to hear, "and mark me. If it were up to me I wouldn't piss on you if you were on fire. I wouldn't buy water from you if I was on fire. You are a useless, ungrateful, psychologically fractured piece of shit who isn't worth the calorie burn it would take to stomp you to death."

Prospero could not speak. The pain stole his voice and left only a tiny squeak in his throat.

"But your father is a great man and he is a patron of this academy," continued Stark. "For some reason that I simply cannot fathom he seems to care about you. If you had any idea how much money he paid to repair the damage your little stunt caused you would shit your pants. And then he paid double that to have these computers and pieces of equipment flown in from companies all around the world. There is more money in this equipment than it takes to run this academy for five motherfucking years." He gave the boy's scrotum a squeeze that tore a scream from Prospero, which Stark stifled by increasing the pressure of his choke. "Now . . . I don't know what kind of mad scientist Dr. Frankenstein bullshit he thinks you'll get up to with this stuff, but he is paying the light bill around here and that's enough for me."

Stark used his double grip to walk Prospero back and then slam him hard against the front of a massive mainframe computer. Prospero's head banged hard off the metal and fresh fireworks burst in front of his eyes.

"You will respect your father and you will goddamn well show respect for me, Cadet Bell. You can have all the access you want to this lab and these machines, and your father even secured positions for four research assistants who have advanced degrees in physics and engineering. Imagine that, responsible adults who are here to work with you and jump when you yell 'frog.' But let us be crystal clear, Cadet. You will never again speak ill of your father and you will never—ever—disrespect me again. Your father does not want you marked, boy, but believe me when I say that there are things I can do to you—things I would enjoy doing to you—that would leave no marks at all. Not a one."

Another squeeze, this time with a sideways twist. Prospero begged him to stop, but the words were again squeezed to silence by the stricture on his throat. The edges of the room began growing dark and indistinct.

"This is my school, my house, Cadet," said Stark, his spit flecking Prospero's cheek, "and while you are here you belong to me. Body."

Squeeze.

"And."

Squeeze.

"Soul."

With a grunt of effort Stark rammed him backward once more and then stepped back to allow Prospero to fall. The boy thudded down hard on elbows and knees, gagging and weeping, his forehead pressed against the floor.

CHAPTER TWENTY-EIGHT

I didn't know what to expect when we landed. I hoped we'd see the rest of Echo Team standing there. Lydia Ruiz, Montana Parker, Brian Brandon Botley, and Sam Imura. Instead we were greeted by a bunch of marshmallow men. A dozen techs and twice as many armed SPs in white hazmat suits. The shore patrol guys all had their guns in their hands. Not pointing at us, per se, but not pointing away, either. It was a statement.

One of the marshmallow men stepped up and identified himself as the base commander. "Captain Ledger," he said crisply, "we are glad to see that you and your team are back safe and sound."

It was an unfortunate choice of words and it hung like a bad smell in the salt air. Pretty sure none of us were either safe or sound.

"Yeah," I said, "we're peachy. What's the drill here? What are your orders?"

"Sir," he said, "we need to get you off of this airstrip and into the biohazard unit." He held up a BAMS unit and the lights were flickering between red and orange.

One of his men pushed up a cart on which a heavy steel drum was positioned, its lid tilted back. We knew this drill. Everything we had went into the drum. Weapons, tech, radios, and clothes. Everything. Then the SP closed and sealed the lid and it was wheeled off toward the back of the biohazard unit. Another tech hosed us down with some kind of chemical that smelled like ass and tasted like shit. We stood there buck naked in a hot breeze, shivering as if the Antarctic winds had followed us. They handed us blankets and we wrapped them around our shoulders, achieving neither modesty nor warmth.

"Thank you for cooperating," said the officer. "I know this is difficult."

Top mumbled something very foul about the man's mother, but halfway through it his eyes rolled up and he fell. Bunny caught him and lifted Top's limp body. Bunny is enormously strong, but he was also sick. I put a hand on his shoulder to steady him. His skin was as hot as a furnace. Doctors and orderlies in heavy-duty white rushed to help us. Accepting the burden of Top Sims, guiding Bunny and me into the chamber, catching us when we fell.

INTERLUDE THIRTEEN

"Major Sails," said Bell, smiling like a barracuda as his guest came striding across the carpet, hand extended. They shook and he waved her to a seat. "Scotch?"

"Do you have bourbon?" said Sails.

"No. Can't stand the stuff. I have thirty-year-old single malt."

"That's fine, thanks."

He filled two glasses and handed one to her, then he sat on the edge of the desk, choosing the position so that he was set higher than her, making Sails look up as they spoke. Bell was aware that she knew the trick, but knowing it and not being affected by it were worlds apart.

"So, do we have something to toast?" he asked. "Or are you here to threaten me some more?"

Sails raised her glass. "A toast, definitely."

They clinked and drank. "I like the sound of that. Tell me."

"Before I do," she said, "I heard that your son had a bit of an accident at his boarding school. Something about an explosion?"

"What of it?"

"He's been continuing to work on his God Machine?"

"Of course."

"Good," she said. "Was he hurt?"

"No. He remote fired the machine from another room. Kid's crazy but he's not stupid."

"An expensive failure," she said.

"Is there a point to this? Do you want to use that to bust my balls on the dollar amount of my bid?"

"I don't, actually. I was just noting it."

"What I think you're doing, Major," he said bluntly, "is reminding me that you know where Prospero is and that you're keeping an eye on him. And I'm okay with that as long as you keep your hands off of him."

"We have no intention of interfering with his research," Sails assured him. "My concern, if you want to know, is that he remains safe during the, um . . . more turbulent stages of his research."

"Like I said, he's not stupid."

Sails air-toasted him on that. "My superiors took particular notice of the power blackout that seemed to coincide with the incident at the school. All of Poland, Maine, went dark."

"Isn't that interesting as hell?"

"It is. Sadly, one of the local merchants passed away, did you hear that? It seems his pacemaker suddenly stopped working. It happened during the blackout, and local authorities are baffled. I heard they're blaming it on sunspots."

Bell laughed. "Sunspots? Nice spin. Anyone buying it?"

"We may have seeded that to the local press," she said, making it sound offhand. "Sunspots are known to have unusually powerful effects on electrical conductivity."

"Yeah, how about that?"

Sails set her glass down and reached into her purse to produce a crisp envelope with a sturdy seal. Bell inspected it, arching an eyebrow at the seal. It was a red circle with an infinity symbol. No eagle, no name, no wording. Bell felt his heart quicken. He had heard of this group but had never once come this close to it.

"This isn't what I expected," he said.

"Open it."

He did. The letter was on heavy stationery, the kind rarely used in this digital age. A single sheet. The text was brief and to the point. He was being officially advised that his proposal had been accepted pending his signing nondisclosure agreements and taking certain oaths. Upon completion of those steps half of the proposed and agreed-upon price would be transferred to his account. Upon delivery of a working machine the other half would be deposited. There were notes about bonuses based on early-delivery dates, and penalties for exceeding the deadline. That part was commonplace and there were usually workarounds and compromises to be made.

What interested him most was the name at the bottom of the letter.

It was neither a military nor bureaucratic name. The letter was signed by a scientist.

Someone Bell already knew.

Someone Bell used to be related to. He looked up.

"What's this bullshit?"

"It's not bullshit," said Sails.

"This is from Mark Erskine."

"Yes."

"Is this a joke? He's my fucking ex-brother-in-law."

"Yes. And he's Prospero's uncle."

Bell looked at the name again. "How is he involved in this? He's not in the Department of Defense and he's not with DARPA. He didn't even know what DARPA was when I mentioned it to him."

Sails smiled. "Believe me when I tell you that Dr. Erskine is very familiar with DARPA and with many aspects of advanced research for the Department of Defense. What you might call off-the-record departments."

"I don't believe you. . . ." Bell stopped. "Wait. Are you telling me that Erskine is with Majestic?"

Sails smiled. "We call our division Gateway."

"Son of a bitch!" swore Bell. He flung the letter at her but Sails plucked it out of the air and folded it neatly.

"Mr. Bell," she said, "do you honestly think we would not have eyes on children like Prospero?"

"Children like him? What do you mean by that?"

She spread her hands. "Prospero may have many unique and very attractive qualities—as we both know—but he is hardly as alone in the world as he thinks he is."

"Jesus Christ."

Sails stood up so that she was eye to eye with him. "Let's stop the dance, Mr. Bell. May I call you Oscar?"

"Sure. Whatever."

"I'm Corrine," she said. "The truth is that we recognize that you have been able to find the formula for getting Prospero to work up to his greatest potential. 'Tortured artist syndrome'? That's amazing. That report from Dr. Greene started fires all through my department. And while I can't say that I am comfortable with some of your methods, the results speak for themselves. I'm here to congratulate you and to present our offer. You made it. You're in." She paused. "You won,

Mr. Bell. Be happy. Dr. Erskine is very excited about the God Machine. He is already making plans to build a full-scale version of it at a secure location we have set aside. More on that after you've been sworn in. Erskine thinks that the meltdown problems can't be solved when working on scale versions. It's too hard to observe the electrodynamics. So he'll build a fully functional device, and if—no, when—we solve the power sequencing problems and reach field implementation, you will very likely go down in history as the man who prevented the next world war. Together we could actually save the world. How would that feel, Mr. Bell?" She smiled and held out her glass. "Care to toast to that?"

"Save the world?" he echoed. "Fuck the world."

But he clinked his glass with hers.

CHAPTER TWENTY-NINE

NAVAL AUXILIARY LANDING FIELD
SAN CLEMENTE ISLAND
68 NAUTICAL MILES WEST OF SAN DIEGO
AUGUST 20, 11:26 P.M.

They put me in a small medical bay that wasn't much bigger than a porta-potty. Everything was white and sterile and scary as hell. Doctors and nurses came in wearing hazmat suits, trailing wires and hoses. They took every sample that it is possible to take from a human being, and they did it all very fast. Desperately fast, which was not at all reassuring. They asked me a lot of questions but the more I talked, the more truthfully I answered them, the stranger the looks they gave me. Soon they weren't even meeting my eyes.

My fever spiked and then dropped sharply. Did that a couple of times. Each time it spiked I saw the numbers on the machines. First time was 100 degrees. Second time was 101.4. My heart was racing. My joints hurt and my glands felt like hot rocks under my chin. Sweat poured down my body. They had me on IVs but I think all of it flowed out of my pores. The lights began getting brighter, sounds became tinny and shrill.

"What's wrong with me?" I asked, desperate for something to cling to.

"We're doing everything we can," someone told me. Or maybe everyone told me that. Not an answer. Even a bad answer is less scary than that.

Then another doctor entered the room. Same hazmat suit as the others, but the face behind the plastic was one that I absolutely wanted to see. Needed to see. It was the face of a man who always seemed to have answers for me.

"Rudy!" I cried, reaching for him, but he stood in the doorway and would not approach within touching distance. Rudy Sanchez looks and even sounds like Raúl Juliá from the old *Addams Family* movies. A rich baritone voice, intelligent eyes that were filled with wisdom, and a manner of quiet confidence that usually put the pin back into the grenade when I was, psychologically speaking, ready to blow.

But not now. He stood in the doorway, wrapped in the highest-level protective gear in the catalog, and studied me with eyes that were filled with pity, and concern, and fear.

"Rudy—?"

"Cowboy," he said quietly, "the medical team here is doing everything they can."

It scared me even more to hear him spout a company line like that. When the doctors say that it is never—ever—a good thing.

"How are Top and Bunny?"

"We're trying to understand this," said Rudy. "Joe, please, you have to tell me exactly what happened down there."

"I already told them, goddamn it."

"Tell me. Please . . ."

So I did. I told him every bit of it. Not sure if there was anything that I hadn't already shared with Church and the other doctors, but I went over it again. Saying it to Rudy, though, helped steady me. At least a bit. He listens with every molecule of his body. He doesn't miss things and he does not judge. He listens, he disseminates, he works through it, and he understands. Usually. As I spoke I saw the doubt grow in his eyes. And the fear.

"Fuck, Rude," I growled, "it's all on the cameras. Check them. Pull the memory cards from the telemetry units on our suits. Upload the memory from the BAMS units. It's all there. Everything. The video cameras on our helmets. Look at it, Rudy. Look at it and . . . and . . ."

I could hear my voice fracture and falter. I could feel my tongue growing thick, muffling my speech, making it hard to breathe.

Hard to think.

Hard to . . .

The fever came back all at once. It was like someone doused me with gasoline and threw a match. It came at me like a blowtorch, like a flamethrower.

I remember trying to tell Rudy that I was in trouble. I remember reaching for him, and I remember seeing the fear turn to panic in his eyes.

I remember falling.

The floor opened a big, black mouth and I fell into that. Somewhere behind me, above me, elsewhere, I could hear the doctors yelling, nurses yelling, machines yelling. Then there was a long electronic scream. I knew that sound. Knew it too well.

Rudy screamed, too. At least I think he did.

Those screams followed me all the way down into the dark.

CHAPTER THIRTY

THE NATIONAL SZÉCHÉNYI LIBRARY
F BUILDING OF BUDA CASTLE
BUDAPEST, HUNGARY
TWO WEEKS AGO

Harry Bolt yelled and backpedaled as he went for his gun.

He stepped into a puddle of blood, his foot shot straight out in front of him, and he went down hard on his ass. Violin leapt over his falling body and he caught a momentary glare of complete disapproval on her pretty face. He saw light flash from the edges of her knives and then she was among the men.

Shots rang out, but Harry did not see Violin stagger or fall. How she evaded the bullets was something he would never understand. Never. Lying on the floor and watching her was like sitting in a movie theater and watching Black Widow or Wonder Woman. It was surreal. She moved too fast, twisted like a dancer, reacted with perfect timing.

It was beautiful.

And it was absolutely terrifying.

Because of the knives.

The men were good. Harry had to give them props. He knew that if it was him in that fight he'd be as dead as Olvera and Florida. Deader, if that was possible. They were brutal and they fought like a well-oiled machine. Practiced, experienced in killing together, merciless.

Violin should have died.

Five to one. Five big, muscular, powerful, and expert killers against a single woman who was at best half the weight and muscle mass of the smallest of them. They should have ripped her apart.

Except that's not what happened.

As Harry lay there in the puddle of blood, stunned, his pistol forgotten in his hand, he saw the impossible unfold before him.

Violin moved with a coordination that bordered on the supernatural. She danced. That was it, he realized; her fighting style flowed like lovely choreography. She stepped, turned, swept, ducked, leapt, twirled, bent, lunged, dodged, and flowed like honey. Like mercury. Like light.

The air around her was filled with rubies.

That's how it looked to Harry.

Rubies.

Bright droplets that glowed with heat as they flew.

The men yelled, and growled, and bellowed, and screamed, and cried out for their mothers.

As she cut them to pieces.

Not with the brutality that they had used on Olvera, Florida, and the library guards. No. If murder could have an aspect of beauty, if the act of killing could become an art form, then this was what he was seeing.

Pieces of them fell.

And they fell, and even in their deaths they seemed to swoon to the ground like danseurs whose moment of dramatic demise was demanded by the music, by the narrative of the dance.

One of the men danced backward. The leader. He parried her cut and reeled away, bleeding but not mortally wounded. He flung down his knife and reached for the Tanfoglio pistol in his shoulder holster, and for a moment Violin was engaged with two other men. It was in that single moment that Harry realized that Violin, despite everything, might lose this fight. That she might die.

The man raised the pistol.

And Harry fired his gun.

He emptied his entire magazine at him. He carried a Sig Sauer P220 with a seven-round flush magazine. All seven rounds punched through the air. The distance was nearly point blank.

The leader of the killers wheeled around and stared.

Harry stared back.

Not one of his goddamn bullets had gone anywhere near him. They'd struck the wall, the door, and two rounds had gone through into the main hall.

Harry Bolt was a lousy shot. Always had been.

The man gave him a quizzical look. A kind of battlefield "are you serious" look. Nearly a smile. Then he raised his gun toward Harry.

Violin whirled and cut his hand off at the wrist. She checked the swing and slashed him across the throat. All in the space of a frenzied heartbeat.

The leader dropped to his knees only a second before the other two men pirouetted away from the angel of destruction, took sloppy wandering steps, and fell.

The room became a tableau.

Like a superwoman in an action movie, Violin stood with both hands held out, almost crucified against the reality of what she had just done. Her knives dripped red; her body was splash-painted with red. All around her were the men who should have ripped her apart. A faint wisp of gun smoke lingered in the air.

Harry stared up at her in awe, in shock, maybe in love.

She snapped her wrists down and the blood went flying from the oiled blades. She reversed the knives and slid them into the thigh sheaths.

All in a moment.

All in a dream.

Yeah. Harry Bolt was in love.

She looked down at him, at the slide that was locked back on his gun. "You're not only an idiot," she said. "You're a useless idiot."

Outside there was the sound of sirens. Someone had heard the gunshots. Or maybe they heard the screams. Violin bent and pulled the black shirt off of the dead leader and then carefully but quickly wrapped it around the book.

"Get up or go to jail," she snapped. "Whatever you're going to do, do it now."

With the book clutched to her chest, she whirled once more and dashed for the front door.

Harry Bolt staggered to his feet and, because he had no idea what else to do, ran to catch up.

Harry did not look back and therefore did not see the dark SUV pull up outside the library. He did not see the six men in dark suits, white shirts, and dark ties enter the library. He did not see them hurry back out only a few seconds later.

Because Harry did not see any of this he did not pay much attention to the fact that he was leaving a trail of bloody footprints behind as he ran.

He did not see the six men begin to follow those prints.

Harry Bolt, after all, was not a very good spy.

JONATHAN MABERRY

CHAPTER THIRTY-ONE

Junie Flynn was asleep, lost in a dream of strange creatures that blossomed like flowers from twisted trees, then broke off and went flapping on gossamer wings. The landscape was filled with discordant images of intense beauty and ferocious ugliness, and in her dreams Junie was one of the newly hatched creatures who flew over forests of living plants, along beaches of jagged glass sands that ran beside oceans of boiling mercury. When she cried out, her voice was a piercing shriek that sounded like the dying wail of a wounded seabird. Or like a child who was lost and knew she would never again be found.

It was a dreadful dream and this was the third consecutive night she'd had it.

That was how sleep was for her. Her dreams were seldom about Joe or their life here in California. She rarely dreamed of things that had happened during the day, or of the incidental mundanities of life. Her dreams flowed like a river between fantastical and nightmarish.

As did her life.

She seldom shared those dreams with Joe and never with anyone else.

Never.

On those nights when she woke shivering and bathed in fear-sweat, Joe calmed her and comforted her, and from the soothing things he said it was clear he thought that her sleep had been troubled by the cancer she had beat two years ago, or the baby she had lost when an assassin's bullet destroyed her uterus. Or of the things she had witnessed while coasting the edges of the violent world of the DMS.

But that wasn't it.

That was never it.

Her dreams took her to strange worlds that Joe would never understand. Junie thought she did, though. After all, her DNA was so complicated and it belonged, at least in part, to other worlds than this one.

Was that where her dreams took her? she wondered. Did this fractured and surreal landscape exist in some other place, and were images of it somehow stored in her cells?

She hoped not, because it was a dreadful, dreadful place.

If that was true, though, then she found it strange that she never saw people in those other worlds. Not once.

Or, maybe it was that the creatures who lived there did not fit any definition of "people" that her senses would recognize. There were plenty of creatures here. Bizarre forms that seemed to change shape the moment she looked away from then, as if it was a game for them to hide from her through transformation. Flesh—if flesh it was—flowed and shifted and assumed improbable forms. Some of them were devilishly similar to things that triggered recognition but did so imperfectly. It was like trying to read a book written in Rorschach inkblots. Other forms were simply devilish in their own right, and when the creatures were in these forms they looked up at her as she flew overhead and they smiled with mouths that were filled with row upon row of teeth.

Tonight, though, the dream changed and in doing so found a new level of strangeness. A new level of horror.

This time she saw a human form running naked along the beach.

A man.

The soles of his feet were shredded from the jagged glass sand and there were awful gashes on his knees and palms from times when he fell. His body was crisscrossed with scratches from plants that reached for him and claws that sought him with pernicious delight.

He ran and ran.

Despite the pain, he ran.

Despite the damage, he ran.

Junie flew above him and tried to call out his name, tried to tell him where to go to escape the things that bit and the things that tore. But her voice was a wail and she had no words.

She could not speak his name even though it screamed inside her mind.

Joe.

Her lover ran from shambling, twisting, metamorphosing beasts that chased. But he also ran toward a great, gray storm cloud that hung strangely low over the horizon.

Except that it wasn't a storm cloud.

No. It was something far more dangerous. Something far worse.

Joe ran in a blind panic toward it, and the cloud—that shapeless mass—lifted itself from the horizon and rose into the sky. Silent, powerful, indifferent to gravity, acknowledging no physical laws at all. It rolled backward, exposing a face. Eyes that burned with black fire and a snarling mouth wreathed by wriggling tentacles.

As it turned its face upon the world, every single creature below, from the shape-shifting monsters to the sentient trees, screamed out in a language that did not belong in this or any world.

She screamed herself awake.

INTERLUDE FOURTEEN

Dr. Greene was not expecting visitors and it was too late for clients. His secretary and nurse had already gone home and the office was locked. He liked working into the evening because the quiet gave him time to reflect on his day's sessions and dictate case notes. His iPad was snugged into the speaker dock and Miles Davis was blowing soft, sad, complex jazz and blues at him.

When the door to his inner office opened, Greene yelled in shock. A high, sharp, almost feminine sound. He half jumped up but succeeded only in shoving his chair back so that it struck the wall hard enough to knock a framed certificate from its hook.

Two men stepped into the office. One was black, the other was white. They were both in their middle thirties. Tall, fit-looking, and wearing identical black suits, white shirts, black ties. Both of them had wires behind their ears.

Neither of them was smiling.

"Who the hell are—?" began Greene, his anger shooting up to match the level of his shock. But the black man silenced him by placing a finger to his own lips in the kind of shushing gesture an adult might use on a child.

The white man raised his hand and pointed a gun at Greene. Or, at least some kind of gunlike weapon. It had a handle and trigger, but instead of a barrel there was a blunt snub of an end with no opening, and around it were four steel prongs that curved inward so that the metal balls on the end nearly touched.

"Dr. Michael Greene," said the man with the gun. It was a plain, uninflected statement, not a question.

"Who . . . who are you?" gasped Greene, his voice subdued as much

172

from the shushing finger as the strange weapon. "How did you get in here?"

"Dr. Greene," said the black man, lowering his hand, "we need you to turn over to us all of the materials you have on one of your patients."

Greene bristled. "That's absurd. Are you with the government? Let me see your identification. Let me see a warrant."

The white man and the black man said nothing, did nothing except stare at him. They both had brown eyes that were as flat and uninformative as the painted eyes of mannequins.

"Doctor-patient confidentiality is—"

And that was as far as he got.

The black man suddenly raised his foot and kicked the side of the desk. Greene's office furniture was all made from heavy hardwood, seasoned and sturdy, with steel reinforcements and a dark cherrywood glaze. The desk weighed nearly 350 pounds. So when it shot backward, propelled by that single kick, the desk struck Greene with shocking force. The desk's legs were buried deep in the carpet, without casters or wheels, and yet that kick moved it like it was made from balsa. The footwell engulfed Greene's knees, but the desktop crunched into his gut so forcefully that it snapped the doctor forward with such speed that he had no chance to get his hands up to protect his face. His nose, chin, and forehead slammed down. Pain exploded in his head and blood splashed outward to form a rude Rorschach pattern on the open file folder for one of his newest teen patients.

Greene rebounded from the desk and sagged into his chair, bleeding and dazed. The lights in the room seemed to flare to white-hot brightness, but that was only in Greene's head because immediately darkness seemed to cover him like a blanket.

Then the desk was gone. Through a haze of blood and stars, Greene saw the black man grab the corner of the desk and yank it out and then shove it sideways. Both men closed on the sprawled doctor. The prongs of the gun dug into the soft palate under his chin. The men leaned close. He could smell their breath. It was like smelling the heated breath of a pair of predator cats. Foul and fetid.

"Dr. Greene," said the black man in a voice that was somehow more frightening than the violence for its softness and lack of emotion, "you will give us all of your files— hardcopy, digital recordings, and computer files—on one of your patients. You will do it now and you will hold nothing back. If you have any duplicates of this information you will tell us where it is and how we can obtain it. You will not hide anything from us. And when we are finished with this transaction, you will never speak of this to anyone. You won't mention it. You will not tell the police, your family, your rabbi, or your friends. You will tell no one. If you need medical assistance, you will tell the doctors that you tripped and fell. They will believe you because you will want to be very convincing. If you fail to comply with us now, or discuss this incident with anyone later, we will kill you, your wife, your children, your parents, and both of your sisters. Do you understand me, Dr. Greene? No, do not nod. Tell me that you understand. Tell me that you are willing to comply with all of these requests. Assure me that you will obey every rule we have set forth."

Blood ran down the back of Greene's nose, filling his throat, making him gag and choke. The pressure of the prongs eased so that he could turn his head and spit blood onto the carpet. He coughed and spat again. Fireworks seemed to detonate all around him and he was nauseous and dizzy.

"Dr. Greene," said the white man, "my associate has asked for your compliance." He placed the prongs against the top of Greene's left knee. "You do not need either of your legs in order to assist us. A legless man can still direct us to the information we request. So can a man with one hand and one eye."

His voice never rose beyond a soft, conversational tone.

Greene began to weep. But he also began to nod.

"Don't," he begged. "Please . . . don't."

"Will you cooperate, Dr. Greene?" asked the black man.

"Y-yes!"

"Will you obey all of the rules we have agreed upon?"

"Yes."

"Good. And you will hold nothing back? You will give us every bit of information, every record, every copy of tests, and all case notes on this patient?"

"Yes." Greene was trying not to sob. Failing. Bleeding. Losing himself into this moment. "Which . . . which patient?"

The pressure of the strange gun left his knee.

The black man said, "Give us everything you have on the patient coded in your case notes as number three-three-six-P-eight-one."

Greene stopped breathing for a moment and stared at them, and in that moment he knew what this was about.

"Give us everything you have on Prospero Bell," said the white man.

CHAPTER THIRTY-TWO

NOWHERE

I don't know where I was. Or if I was anywhere.

I've always wondered what happens to our minds when we die. People talk about seeing their life flash before them. That happened to me, but not in the right way.

It wasn't my life I saw.

It was the people in my life.

I saw Junie. My lady, my best friend, the love of my life.

She was in our living room in our condo in Del Mar. I watched her drop the phone and slide off the couch onto the floor. She was screaming.

Screaming.

I could hear the voice on the other end of the phone.

Rudy Sanchez.

Junie's screams drowned him out. Drowned out the world.

Ghost was there. My big white shepherd. Fierce combat dog, veteran of many of this world's killing fields. He came to her, whining, his tail drooping, pressing his muzzle against her as she curled into a ball, knees up and arms wrapped around her head.

A man came rushing down the hall. Slim, young, scarred, familiar. Alexander Chismer. Known as Toys. Her close friend. My former enemy and now a kind of ally. A man who had saved the lives of Junie and Circe and maybe a good portion of the world. He still held the hand towel with which he was drying off. He hadn't even dropped it when she screamed.

"Junie!" he yelled, and vaulted the couch rather than run around it. He dropped down beside her and pulled her into his arms. Like a friend, like a brother. "What is it, love? What's happened? Jesus Christ, tell me what happened?"

She kept screaming a single word.

"No!"

Over and over again. Ghost howled every time she did.

No.

Or maybe it wasn't "no." Maybe it was a name, something that sounded similar.

Joe.

When someone screams like that it's hard to tell.

I heard a sound. No, sounds.

"He's coding, damn it."

Another voice. A stranger's voice.

"Charging . . . charging . . . clear . . ."

And then my mind and my body and my soul were filled with hot light.

I stood on a hill that swept down toward a mansion that had been built to imitate an English manor house, though I knew I was in America. Somewhere.

The house was burning.

Bodies littered the lawn.

I saw Ghost. His white fur was splashed with blood and he was limping badly. Some of the bodies down there were dressed in the unmarked black battle-dress uniforms that we wear when the DMS goes on a job. The clothing was badly torn. The bodies inside had been ripped up by shrapnel and gunfire.

Suddenly there was a man standing next to me. Tall, strong. Familiar in a way I couldn't quite place. He wore the same thing as me. Exactly. Even down to the bloody bandage wrapped around my upper arm.

His face, though . . .

Even though he was three feet away I couldn't see his face. It was blurred, indistinct, like the face of someone who moved at the wrong time when a photo was being snapped.

He spoke to me.

"Did you honestly think you'd win, Joe?"

I tried to speak, to tell him that of course we'd win. That I would win. But the only thing that came out of my mouth was a torrent of dark blood.

He stood there and laughed as I sank down and died.

I felt a needle go into my chest.

And I was somewhere else.

I stood in a darkened room. Another living room. Sea air blew through the window and cold moonlight traced the edges of another man and woman who huddled together in their grief. A big dog whined and howled.

Not Junie, though. Not Toys. Not Ghost.

Dr. Circe O'Tree-Sanchez sat on the couch and held the weeping form of her husband, Rudy. Their dog, the monstrous wolfhound Banshee, sat by the window and howled at the moon. In a bassinet ten feet from them a baby slept through it all.

Circe said, "I'm sorry, my love. I'm so sorry."

I tried to say something. I couldn't let this moment stand. The script was wrong and the actors were all reading the wrong lines. I yelled at them. Rudy and Circe did not héar me. Could not. Of course they couldn't.

But Banshee . . .

The big dog stopped howling and turned her head toward me. Toward where I thought I stood. Or hovered. Or whatever a dead man does.

Banshee's eyes met mine.

She *saw* me.

They say that dogs—some dogs—can see things in the unseen world. Junie tells me that kind of thing all the time. Dogs can see spirits. And ghosts.

Banshee could see me.

Me.

I screamed.

And a voice said, "Hit him again."

"Charging . . . charging . . . clear!"

I blinked and it was bright daylight.

Mr. Church stood in the shadows thrown by a huge old oak tree. Autumn leaves blew gently across the tops of the autumn grass and between the rows of headstones. In the trees, birds sang songs of leaving and of farewell; the songs they sing before they all fly away because winter is coming.

The cemetery was quiet and still green. Church wore a topcoat and he had one gloved hand in his pocket. The other held the hand of a tall, stern-faced woman who wore a ruby red cloth coat and a broad-brimmed gray hat.

Lilith. She looked older than I remembered. Not much, just a little. Not Church, though. He never seems to change. His face was hard, though, without trace of humor or hope.

They stood looking down at a gravestone. I didn't need to read the name on it to know what I was seeing. They did not speak for a long time and I thought they wouldn't. Then Church broke the silence.

"I did not see this coming," he said. "I should have. This is my fault."

"How many times will you be betrayed before you realize that you should never trust anyone? You believe in people, St. Germaine. That will always get you hurt. It always has."

"This war is to protect people."

"We'll never agree on that," she said.

Church looked at her. "What can we agree on?"

"The war is the war," she said softly. "No matter how many of our family we have to bury, we still have to fight."

Church drew in a breath, sighed, nodded.

Then he stiffened and turned, his eyes searching the graveyard as if he'd heard something.

"What is it?" asked Lilith, releasing his hand and reaching under her coat, half-drawing a concealed pistol.

Church said nothing. His roving eyes stopped and fixed on one point.

He looked directly at me.

Like Banshee, I think he could see me.

But how? What did that mean? What does something like that mean about a person? How could any ordinary person see me?

I was dead, after all. I was dead and time had passed. The grass on my grave looked old.

White-hot light blasted me out of that moment.

I saw Bug in his office. The threadbare goatee he'd been trying to grow these last few months was now a full beard. Scraggly and unkempt. Like the rest of him. Bug was a small guy, thin and nerdy, but that had changed. Now he was a skeleton, a stick figure. Gaunt, with hollow cheeks and dark smudges under his eyes. His hair was badly brushed and his nails were bitten down to raw flesh.

He was at his console in the MindReader clean room. Except it wasn't clean. His desk was a mess, littered with pizza boxes and plastic plates on which half-eaten food was going bad. Cans of Red Bull and empty coffee cups were everywhere. Amid the detritus was a framed picture of his mother, murdered by the Seven Kings. There was a picture tacked to a wall-mounted corkboard. Grace Courtland, my former lover and a victim of the Jakobys. That corkboard was crammed with photos, many of them overlapping like a pile of dead leaves. I saw my old teammates John Smith and Khalid Shaheed. I saw Colonel Samson Riggs and Sergeant Gus Dietrich. I saw so many of the people I'd known and fought alongside. The people I helped bury.

And there, in one corner, was my own face.

And Top Sims and Bunny.

Lydia Ruiz was there, too. And Sam Imura.

All of us.

All of the dead.

I wanted to yell at Bug, to tell him that Lydia and Sam and a lot of the others weren't dead, that he was wrong.

But he wasn't wrong. This was Bug but this wasn't now. This was what the world was going to do. To us and to Bug. There was none of the innocence left in his face. All of the joy of life had been bled out of his eyes and all that remained was fear and hate.

So much fear. So much hate.

If the world could destroy someone like Bug, if the things that bad people do could erase the powerful innocence of a person like him, then what hope was there for anyone else?

I wanted to say something to him, to warn him to step back from the abyss, to find an anchor for his hope. To continue being alive while he was alive. But I wasn't Jacob Marley and this wasn't a Christmas story with a happy ending.

Blast. The bright heat.

Again.

I saw something else, something that shifted my brain into another gear without bothering to use the clutch.

It was me.

In bed. Hooked up to fifty kinds of weird machines that beeped and pinged and insisted that I was still alive. Some kind of alive. Not the good kind. I looked thinner, wasted, smaller, deader.

But not dead.

I was in an oxygen tent and there was a man with me. He wore a hazmat suit, but I could see his face. I knew him.

Dr. William Hu.

He sat in a chair beside my bed, bent forward as he read through a thick stack of medical test reports. His face was drawn but his eyes were intense. The floor around him was littered with papers.

"No," he said, and flung a file folder away. He read through the next one, growled the same thing. "No."

It went soaring across the room.

"No.

"No.

"Goddamn it, fucking no."

He was alone and I was sleeping. Or in a coma. But somehow I knew he was talking to both of us. He flung down another report.

"Don't you goddamn die on me, Ledger. Don't you do it. I won't let you die, you son of a bitch."

I watched him search for answers. I watched Dr. Hu fight for me. As if my life actually mattered to him. Maybe it did. I can't stand the guy. Never could. He hates me, too. So not once have I ever wondered how deep that animosity ran.

Perspective is every bit as sharp a knife as assumptions are dull.

"Shit," he snarled. "No, no, no."

Blast.

I was elsewhere.

And somewhere else again. And somewhere else after that.

Was this the same thing that happened back under the ice when I was in the bedroom of the cottage shared by Bunny and Lydia? Was I walking through someone else's life again? Is that what the dead do? Is a haunting some kind of perverse peeping Tom show that never ends?

I saw the man with the blurry face several more times. Nearby. At a distance.

And I realized that I'd seen him once before. When I was awake. When I was alive.

Down in the ice. Down in the frozen cavern of Gateway. He'd

been there, ducking out of sight right as everything started going to hell.

Who was he?

What was he?

Blast.

Elsewhere.

This time I didn't know where I was.

For a moment I thought I was back inside the cave down in the Antarctic. It was a cave and it was huge, but . . .

It was hot. Geothermal heat. I could see steam rise from vents off to my right. Huge columns rose twisting toward a ceiling that was so vast it was lost in shadows. Every once in a while static lightning flashed within that smoke, and in the strobe bursts of light I saw things.

There was a machine. The same one we saw in the ancient city. A massive ring of steel and copper and glittering jewels.

Except it wasn't the same. This one was even bigger. Two or three times the size. Monstrous. And it was glowing. It was alive.

I thought about that word. *Alive.* Felt it. Tasted it. Knew it to be true. The machine was actually alive. It pulsed. Throbbed. Breathed. Lived.

But that was only part of what I saw. As troubling and frightening as that machine was, it paled almost to insignificance by what hung in the air above it. I'd glimpsed it before, but now I saw it. It was titanic. It stood there, miles high, dominating the sky. More powerful than the tortured landscape of the fuming vents of superheated steam.

It was a thing. A creature. Maybe a god. I don't know and even though I was already dead and insubstantial, I knew this monster could hurt me. It could consume me. Its legs were like towers, like skyscrapers, and the body was vaguely humanoid. But the head . . . Jesus Christ. The face was covered by thousands of wriggling feelers that knotted and twisted like gigantic gray-green worms. Long worms surrounded its mouth. But . . . no, they weren't worms, they were more like tentacles, but each one was bigger than the largest arm of the greatest squid or octopus that ever lived. The creature tore at the air with scaly claws that looked like they could slash through plate steel, and behind it, stretching out from its back, were leather wings.

That's what I saw standing above the machine. A god from some drug-induced nightmare universe.

I hoped.

I prayed. I screamed. I begged the world to make this thing nothing more than a fantasy of a dying mind. Or a dead man's nightmare.

The godlike creature threw back its head and from that mouth, hidden by those writhing tentacles, came a roar so impossibly loud that it shattered the ground on which it stood. I saw vast pillars of lava leap up and then everything was covered with smoke and fire.

The flames wrapped around me, around my ghost, and burned me down to nothing.

INTERLUDE FIFTEEN

BELL FAMILY ESTATE
MONTAUK ISLAND, NEW YORK
WHEN PROSPERO WAS SEVENTEEN

"Christ, Corrine," gasped Bell as soon as she entered his study, "you look like shit. What happened?"

"I need a drink first, Oscar. Bourbon. Hit me hard." She sank into a chair and held out a hand, grunting her thanks as he gave her a tumbler he'd filled with four fingers of Pappy Van Winkle. It wasn't his usual drink, being more of a scotch man, but Sails had brought the bottle on one of her previous trips. She preferred the rougher taste of bourbon to the smooth burn of single malt. Sails took a huge gulp, forced it down, gagged, coughed, and nodded her thanks.

Bell set the bottle down on the edge of his desk and pulled a chair close to hers. Sails looked like she'd aged ten years; she was grainy and pale, with dark smudges under her eyes and a nervous twitch in her hands. She took another substantial mouthful.

"That fucking machine," she said.

"What about it? Was there an explosion or something? I told Prospero he needs to make that regulator work or—"

"No," she said, shaking her head. "It's not that. I mean . . . maybe it's that, too. But this was . . . this was . . ."

And she began to cry.

Oscar Bell came out of his chair, pulled her out of hers, and held her close. It pissed him off that he had fallen in love with her, that they were in love with each other. That was inconvenient and it went against one of his strictest rules: never let sentiment interfere with business. But, it had happened, and now it was a fact. He loved this cold, vicious, brilliant monster and she loved him.

He held her close and let her cry it out, let her cry herself to the point where she could find her voice again. It took a while. It required more of the bourbon, and by the time she was calmer and they were seated together on the big sofa by the fireplace, her voice was thick from weeping and slurry with alcohol.

She spoke and he listened.

"It's the God Machine," she said. "I hate that godforsaken thing. . . ."

The Gateway team, led by Marcus Erskine, had built two scale models of Prospero's machine. Each one had cost upwards of forty million dollars. The first one, Bell knew, had been a spectacular failure that had exploded seconds after it was turned on. Five technicians had been killed, eleven others injured, and the lab destroyed. It was almost exactly the same thing that had happened at Ballard Academy when Prospero had fired his first prototype.

The first Gateway test had yielded other effects, as well. It generated an electrical nullification field—one of the "side effects" that irritated Prospero—that was far more powerful than anticipated. It was so strong that it blanked out power on half the continent. The Russian and Chinese research stations had gone dark for an hour and when they came back online there was a massive exchange of furious communication with Moscow and Beijing. Diplomats had to scramble to keep everyone from going to a high state of combat readiness. Not that America ever accepted blame for it. They claimed to have been victims, too. Luckily there had been some sunspot activity and in the end everyone blamed that. It was the "Kill Switch" Oscar Bell had promised, but it was still uncontrollable.

That was bad, but it was fixable. Erskine had anticipated some kind of problem along these lines, though not as massive. The null field was the golden egg at the end of this hunt. A controllable, predictable, reproducible electrical null field was the whole point of Gateway. Erskine had been putting increasing pressure on Bell to obtain the last component for safe management of the device—the crystal firing regulator—but so far even though Prospero now had three of the Unlearnable Truths he had failed to discover exactly what that was. Prospero said that it was a numerical code for passing the God Machine's power through transformers attached to each of several large gemstones, but there were thousands of possible patterns, and experimentation to try and crack the code had resulted in damage ranging from explosions to true electromagnetic pulses that fried the machines at Gateway. It was becoming cost prohibitive to do anything more than keep the God Machine in idle mode, and the whole program was millions over budget. Erskine and his superiors were looking to hang the blame on Oscar, and there had been thinly veiled threats about consequences. Bell could lose the contract and there was an outside chance that if it all failed Gateway would require Bell to pay penalties to the government. That would ruin him. Bell had coerced Stark and his staff at Ballard to turn the screws on Prospero and he'd railed at Mr. Priest to find the rest of the books. He was bleeding money.

And now Sails was here, talking about how much she hated the God Machine.

Oscar Bell wanted to scream.

"What's the problem?" he asked cautiously.

"Side effects," she said.

"What are you talking about? This whole thing is about exploiting the side effects. The whole Kill Switch project is a fucking side effect."

"No," she said. "Not that. It's the dreams. Those terrible dreams . . ."

Bell's heart nearly jumped into his throat. Memories of what Stark had told him after Prospero's machine blew up the first lab at Ballard. Oscar had never shared that part of the God Machine with Sails. Until now he'd thought it was only tied to that one test. "What dreams . . . ?"

"It started that night," said Sails. "Bad dreams. Jesus, Oscar . . ."

She told him about a problem that was not reported at first, and not taken seriously even after people started talking about it. Everyone put it down to stress and grief over the disaster. It was only after the second machine was fired that Dr. Erskine and his staff started paying attention to those dreams. And to their effects. The second machine ran for three weeks before failing. The Gateway scientists had done a lot of work on the sequencing of the power regulators, and though they were far from perfect, they seemed to allow the God Machine to run in idle mode, at 5 percent capacity.

The night of that first day erupted into screams.

"Why?" demanded Bell. "What was happening?"

That night several members of the staff reported extremely strange and unusually vivid dreams. It took the base psychologists nearly a week to put together a cohesive story and even longer to cross-check it. The upshot was that during the time the energy from the God Machine was active in low idle, several staff members claimed to have been inside the dreams of their friends and coworkers, and two of them swore that they had been home. One in Saratoga Springs and the other in Cheyenne. During those dreams they were able to see things at those locations with incredible clarity, and one of them remembered what was on TV. When this was checked out, the substance of those observations matched reality with eerie precision.

So far they determined that one in eleven people tended to have dreams while the machine was idling. However, two in fifteen had the kinds of vivid dreams where they appeared to have "traveled" to other locations and witnessed events there.

At first Sails couldn't believe it. No one could. Until they had no choice. The machine was left idling for a week, and during that time several members of the team, including Erskine, went "dreamwalking," as it came to be called. Occasionally their dreaming selves roamed far away from Gateway, but more often inside the dreaming minds—or even the wide-awake minds—of other people at the base. Everyone was rattled. Sails could understand that. Everyone down there had secrets. Everyone who worked in that program had made compromises and decisions that perhaps they did not care to have scrutinized.

One industrial spy was outed and was shipped off to a black site for fun and games. One of the soldiers was discovered to have committed two rapes of women during his time in Afghanistan. One of the women was a local, the other was a female soldier. The rapist was scheduled to return home for court-martial but was found outside in the snow with his ankles and wrists tied. It was seventy below.

Paranoia ran high at Gateway. People began taking sleeping pills, which seemed to work pretty well as a block against invasion. Unfortunately the quality of work product dropped. The pills were banned; everyone's locker was searched.

The suicides didn't start for nearly a month.

Bell kept his face bland. He'd heard of this sort of thing before. At Ballard after Prospero's machine blew up, and elsewhere. Howard Shelton of Majestic Three had said that they were working on something like this for the DIA, the Defense Intelligence Agency. That line of experimentation was labeled Project Stargate and had ultimately failed. It was subsequently handed off to the CIA for evaluation and then terminated.

Bell thought about his son, and about Prospero's complex genetics and parentage, if that word could even apply. Prospero was born in one of the M3 labs. The connection couldn't be coincidental. That offended logic.

"This dream stuff is real?" asked Bell, careful to keep his excitement out of his voice.

"Yes," she said. She sipped more of the bourbon and set the glass down. "They've been doing exhaustive tests."

"Have you done this? Dreamwalking, I mean."

Her eyes slid away. She said, "They sent someone down to interview everyone at Gateway."

"Who?"

"Someone from the CIA," she said.

"Christ. Have they reopened Stargate?"

Sails's head whipped around and her eyes flared with suspicion and shock. "What? How do you even know about that?"

"I don't know much," he lied. "Howard Shelton's people were working on it before the project was terminated."

"Oscar . . . has anything like this ever happened with Prospero?"

"Of course not," he lied. "I would have told you about that."

She narrowed her eyes. "Don't lie to me."

"I'm not."

It took a while for the doubt to drain away from her eyes. Then she sagged back against the cushions. "I'm afraid to sleep," she said.

"Because you're afraid of dreamwalking?"

She shook her head slowly. "Because there are so many places you never want to go."

"What do you mean?"

Without turning, Corrine Sails said, *"Ph'nglui mglw'nafh Cthulhu R'lyeh wgah'nagl fhtagn."*

Which is when Oscar Bell woke up.

He was in his bed. Alone. In a silent house.

He stretched out a hand to the other side of the bed, but the sheets were smooth and cool, the pillow undented.

Bell got up and went through every bedroom on that floor, opening doors, looking for her. Calling her name. Then yelling it. He called the guard at the front gate and asked when Corrine Sails left.

"Left, sir?" asked the guard. "I don't understand. I can check my logbook, but I'm pretty sure Major Sails hasn't been here for three or four weeks. Do you want me to—?"

Bell hung up. He pulled on a robe and ran downstairs to his office. The fire had burned down to a few orange coals. The couch was empty.

However, the bottle of Pappy Van Winkle stood on the edge of his desk. There were two glasses on the tables on either side of the couch. His, drained down to a last sip.

Hers. Filled nearly to the brim with four fingers.

Untouched.

Oscar Bell stood there for a long, long time.

In the morning he called Commander Stark at Ballard and told him that he was upping the budget for Prospero's lab.

"Sir," said Stark, "your son seems to have found a comfortable niche, even made a friend. He isn't spending as much time as he used to in the lab."

"Listen to me, you stupid motherfucker," said Bell in a nearly inhuman tone, "I'm not paying you to make my son comfortable. I don't want him fucking comfortable. I want him in that goddamn lab. I don't care what it takes, I don't care what you have to do, but you get him in there. You do it today. And if his productivity ever drops again, if I don't hear about a jump in his productivity, then I will come down there and rip your fucking lungs out. Do you hear me, Stark? Am I making myself crystal clear?"

"Y-yes . . ."

"Yes . . . what?"

"Yes, sir."

Bell slammed down the phone. The glass of bourbon was still where he'd found it. Bell went over to the couch, sat down, picked up the glass, and stared into its depths.

CHAPTER THIRTY-THREE

ARKLIGHT SAFE HOUSE
UNDISCLOSED LOCATION
BUDAPEST, HUNGARY
TWO WEEKS AGO

Harry Bolt caught up to Violin half a block from the library and dogged her heels as she ran down a side street, zigged and zagged through alleys and courtyards, followed her into hotels and out through different exits. When there were people around the woman slowed to a very casual and convincing stroll. She took Harry's arm as if they were old friends or lovers and she laughed as if he'd said something clever. Once, when a police car was passing, Violin took his face in both hands and kissed him with such fierce intensity that when they were clear and began walking again he had a large and very inconvenient erection.

After fifteen minutes of random changes of direction, Violin stopped by a parked two-year-old Ford Modeo, produced a key, unlocked the car, and when they were both belted in she drove away at a sedate speed.

"Where are we going?" he asked.

"Shut up," she said. Twenty silent minutes later, when they were at the very fringes of a middle-income residential district, Violin pulled into a garage beside a pleasant two-story home. The house was furnished and clean, but empty. Violin brought the book with her and went upstairs with it, leaving behind an order for him to sit down on the couch and touch nothing. He obeyed.

She came back fifteen minutes later without the book. She had cleaned herself up and changed out of her black clothes. Now she wore a soft crimson wool sweater over charcoal slacks. No shoes. Her long dark hair was still wet and hung loose down her back.

She carried a pistol in her hand. "There is a guest bathroom through there," she said, pointing to a hall that ran between living room and kitchen. "There's some clothes in a closet. Don't take long."

"But—"

She sat down with the pistol on her thigh. Violin didn't say anything else.

Harry went into the guest bathroom, checked it for bugs and cameras and found nothing. The window was block glass and could not be opened. He peed, then got undressed and started the shower. While he waited for the water mix to adjust, he stared at his face in the mirror. He was not a bad-looking man, he decided. Like a slightly chubby Matt Damon. Not actually fat, but not built for the kind of things he'd had to do tonight. Not built for running, that was for sure.

He saw that his thighs, buttocks, and back were stained dark with red from the pool of blood he'd fallen into. Olvera and Florida's blood. Harry's stomach did a few backflips and he thought he would hurl. He didn't.

When the nausea ebbed, he climbed into the shower and dialed up the heat to see if he could boil this all out of his brain and off his skin. Even though his skin glowed pink and spotless when he toweled off, he knew that there were some things that can't be scrubbed away. He folded the towel and looked through the closets for something to wear.

He found a pair of bright yellow bike shorts and a concert T-shirt advertising the 2012 This Is Desolation Tour for the Hungarian heavy metal band Shell Beach. The shorts and the shirt were one size too small. He studied himself in the mirror and decided that he looked like a black and yellow sausage.

When he returned to the living room, Violin was tapping away on a small laptop. She looked up with her stern face.

And burst out laughing.

"Bite me," Harry mumbled as he crawled onto the couch, his face burning. He snatched up a decorative pillow and placed it over his lap.

Violin dabbed at a tear at the corner of her eye. "I'm sorry, Mr. Bolt, but I know your father and I suppose I'm guilty of being unfair to you by expecting you to be like him."

He frowned, uncertain as to whether that was a compliment or a slam. Either way he didn't like it. "You know my dad? How? Have you been on a case with him?"

There was a flicker of something in her expression. Distaste? That's how it looked to Harry. "Harcourt Bolton is an intense individual. He is a hero of your country."

"Yeah, he's the cat's balls."

Violin frowned. "I do not know that expression."

"Doesn't matter. He's not here and I am, even if that's a disappointment. Can we focus on what just happened instead of who I'm not living up to?"

She shrugged. "Certainly, let's do that. Tell me what you know."

"Um . . . ," he began, and suddenly realized that he was in a conversation with someone who, at best, was an agent of a foreign power. Even if her government and his agency were allies, that seldom formed an invitation to be chatty. She nodded, clearly aware of the speed bump he'd just hit.

"Then let me tell you what my people found out," she said. "You are hunting a black marketer named Ohan who you believe is smuggling a portable EMP weapon called Kill Switch into the United States on behalf of ISIL. How am I doing so far?"

"Go on," he said in a voice that cracked only a little.

"Your intelligence," she said, leaning on the word hard enough to make it bend, "is faulty. But not entirely. The materials Ohan is shipping do, in fact, originate with ISIL. But these are not, as we've seen, materials to support new ISIL recruits in the States."

"So it's what? The Islamic State Book-of-the-Month Club?"

She laughed. "You know, you remind me of a friend of mine. Another American agent."

"Oh, and is he a figure of fun, too?"

"Hardly. He is the single most dangerous man I have ever met."

This time she leaned on the word "man," as if the fact that this guy was dangerous did not mean that he was the most dangerous *person*. After what Harry had seen back at the library, he was willing to bet that whoever was at the top of her list had two X chromosomes. Fair enough. Harry considered himself a progressive modern male. He was the last guy to try and prove that men always had to be tougher than women. He knew better.

"Who killed my team? Was that ISIL? Because none of them looked Middle Eastern to me."

"They are not. They had nothing to do with the shipment. They do not work for either the black marketer or for the ISIL team involved in this project. In fact they were there to make sure that shipment was never delivered."

"Yeah, but who are they?"

"I told you who they were."

"Right, something about a bunch of locksmiths who burn books for fun. I don't know what that means."

"The Fraternal Brothers of the Lock," she said. "The Ordo Fratrum Claustrorum. They were a kill team sent by the church to destroy that book."

"Whose church?"

"The Catholic Church, of course."

"Why 'of course'? Last I heard the Catholics weren't sending kill teams out."

She snorted. "You don't know much about the world, do you, Mr. Bolt?"

"It's Harry . . . and what do you mean?"

"The church is a political organization as well as a religious one. It is ancient and very powerful and the Vatican has many rooms. Many 'cells.' Not even the pope knows a tenth of what goes on inside the church."

"So these guys are, what? Militant censors?"

"A bit more than that, Mr. Bolt. The agenda of the Brotherhood runs very deep," she said. "It is their belief that certain books contain more than heretical or blasphemous writing. They believe—truly believe—that these books have actual power."

"Power? Like what kind of power? Are we talking magic here?"

She pursed her lips. "'Magic' is an imprecise word, Harry. It suggests the supernatural, and my people do not agree. This is not a world of ghosts and goblins. Not in the way most people think. Think of it more like science. What most people consider to be supernatural is actually an aspect, or perhaps many aspects, of science that has not yet been properly studied, measured, or named. Are you familiar with science at all? The belief among certain quantum physicists that there are other dimensions? Possibly many others?"

"I may have read something. Saw a few specials on Discovery Channel."

She made a mouth of mild disapproval. "You do realize that science and technology are the major stakes in all important espionage, don't you? This is the twenty-first century, Harry. The key battles of our age will be fought in cyberspace and in labs."

"Fine, and when you're done blowing Neil DeGrasse Tyson maybe you can explain what the frak you're talking about."

She laughed. "You really do remind me of my friend. A shorter, dumpier, less intelligent, and less attractive version of him."

"Hilarious."

Then he saw the laughter in her eyes and realized she was actually making a joke rather than directly mocking him. It pulled a small, faint smile from him.

"That book," she said, "was removed from a temple in Syria. One of the many archaeological sites where treasured artifacts have been stored or placed on display for the benefit of humanity. ISIL has gotten a lot of press because of the destruction they've leveled on those sites. Not merely UNESCO sites, but mosques, temples, shrines, great ruins, and more."

"I'm sure that sucks to someone who gives a wet fart, but so what?"

"So some of those sites have a second purpose," said Violin. "Some of them have been used to store dangerous objects for many years. Often the staff is seeded with soldiers or special clerics ordained for the purpose of protecting the world from the objects they guard."

"You're shitting me," said Harry. "This is a joke, right?"

"It's not. The world is larger, stranger, and darker than most people know. There are wars being fought on all levels, and many of them are very old wars in which blood has been shed for hundreds, even thousands of years. Maintaining the security over those items is critical, but the power of ISIL is so great that they have been able to overwhelm the guardians. The Brotherhood was quick to act and they sent teams into the field to try and reclaim these objects."

"If this stuff is so dangerous, why not let ISIL just destroy them?" asked Harry, then he added, "And I can't believe I'm building a case for those fucktards to do even more damage."

"If these were ordinary books," said Violin, "then the Brotherhood might have done just that. However, these books are *not* ordinary and it is possible, even likely, that an attempt to destroy them would result in a catastrophic release."

"A release of what?"

She shook her head. "I . . . don't know. There are so many different opinions on the subject because no one has ever opened some of those books. Not in many hundreds of years. In many cases the books themselves, the materials used to make them, and the inscribed metals that bind them were carefully constructed to contain the knowledge, to confine the power."

"This is nuts," said Harry. "We're talking about books. I mean, c'mon, I read explosive thrillers but it doesn't mean they actually blow up. You tell me this isn't magic but then you tell me this crap?"

Before she could answer, the front door exploded inward.

CHAPTER THIRTY-FOUR

Alexander Chismer—known as Toys to everyone who knew him—poured more wine into Junie Flynn's glass, considered, added more. Then he refilled his own. The wine bottle was nearly as empty as its two predecessors and they were both well over the line into being drunk. They drank. She cried a little and he held her. They talked off and on. Sometimes they even laughed.

The TV was on but the sound was muted. On the screen a trio of thirty-something real estate brokers were backstabbing each other in pantomime as they fought for multimillion-dollar listings of Southern California properties. Toys had turned it on because the men were pretty, but he had no interest in the show. He had even less interest in the god-awful Enya music she had on an apparently endless playlist. He endured it, though, and the middling wine. At least in terms of the latter there was a lot of it.

Apart from the TV the only lights were a few votive candles and the starlight visible through the open French windows. The music was low enough so that the soft, rolling whoosh of the waves was not drowned out. Tibetan temple incense perfumed the air, and that was okay. Toys had bought that for Junie at a shop in Encinitas.

"I wish somebody would call," said Junie. Toys figured it was the tenth time she'd said it.

"They can't," he told her. As he had before. "You know the drill with these spy chaps. Everything is hush-hush and need to know, and sweetie, we do not need to know."

"I do, damn it," she said, too loudly and with an emphatic swing of her glass that sloshed good Riesling on the couch. She yelped, lunged for it as if she could catch the spilled wine, and slid right off the sofa. She landed with a thump that spilled more of the wine.

Toys plucked the glass from her hand. "Oh, you silly cow, you are shitfaced, aren't you?"

Junie looked down at the mess and began to cry.

Toys set his glass on the coffee table and joined her on the floor, wrapping a wiry arm around her and pulling her close until she laid her head on his chest.

"Oh, my little Junebug," he said. "You are going to be a right mess tomorrow, you know that? Joe will come home and you'll be tits up on the carpet. Very exciting."

She punched his chest, and a snort of laughter bubbled out through the sobs.

"You're snorting now," he said, arching his eyebrows. "You've now become actual American trailer trash. Congratulations."

"You are a total bitch," she said as she pushed back from him. Junie swiped at her tears.

"You didn't expect me to slog all the way over here to braid your hair and have a pillow fight, did you?"

"Bitch," she repeated.

"Drunken sow," he said.

They had some more wine.

Ghost was curled up asleep in his big dog bed in the corner behind the dining room table and as they laughed, and drank, and wept, the dog twitched and grunted softly. His legs moved as shadows flitted through his dreaming dog mind.

Then Ghost snapped awake and sat up, looking around at the room, at the people, and then through the window at the night. He sniffed the air and whined softly. He got up and walked over to the French doors, paused for a moment to sniff again, taking in the scents on the night air, then he went out onto the balcony. Toys and Junie did not notice any of this, nor did they see Ghost stand up on his hind legs with his front paws on the edge of the wrought-iron rail. They did not know he was even awake until the dog raised his muzzle to the sky and let loose with a howl that was high, plaintive, sad, and entirely wolflike.

INTERLUDE SIXTEEN

Mr. Priest declined the offer of a scotch.

"Sit," said Bell, and they both settled into comfortable leather chairs. It was late and the estate was quiet. Most of the servants had gone for the day except for the live-ins, and they had been told to stay in their wing of the house. That part of the house did not have a view of the driveway.

"Where's Dr. Greene?" asked Bell. "Should I start looking for an obituary?"

Priest did not smile. "No, sir. He's alive and well."

"Where?"

"He owns property in Washington state. He's living in a Winnebago. You might be interested to know that he removed the tires and has it resting on blocks. He bought enough supplies to last him for months."

"Does he know you know this?"

"No," said Priest. "Nor does he know that we're tracking his purchases and Internet usage. He drives to several local towns to use the free Wi-Fi. He's visiting conspiracy theory Web sites. A lot of them. And he's e-mailing some of the people who run those sites. He's spoken to George Noory, Whitley Strieber, Junie Flynn, and several others. UFOs, alien races, secret societies, and government cover-ups."

Bell grunted.

"He's also been doing a lot of research on the various books that comprise the Unlearnable Truths. He's bought copies of some, but alas, they are fictionalized or pseudo-nonfiction. He's nowhere near obtaining a real one, of course," said Priest. "I've made copies of all of his Net searches and obtained duplicates of every book he's purchased or checked out of a library. I sent a complete report to your Drop Box account."

"Good."

"Our Dr. Greene seems to think he's dropped off the grid."

"Have you figured out who it was who came to his office and scared him off?"

"Yes and no," admitted Priest. "That they are Closers is unquestioned."

"Closers? Really? So they're working for Howard Shelton or someone at Majestic Three?"

"The man I had watching Dr. Greene's office followed them to a military airbase in New Jersey. It is my understanding that the Majestic program no longer uses military transport for its operatives."

"No, they don't."

"Perhaps they are working for Gateway," said Priest. "I know you are in business with them, but surely you don't trust them. Who else would want the case files about your son?"

Bell nodded. "Yeah, dammit. That's what I've been thinking, too. When you told me about Greene I figured Gateway was trying to do an end run around me. They're having some problems with their machine."

"So you led me to understand. I wonder, though, why they haven't simply taken Prospero."

"I have a whole military academy keeping an eye on him."

Priest said nothing, but his skepticism was there to be read in his bland smile.

"Okay, okay," growled Bell, "I'll have Stark add more people."

"If you like, sir, I can have some of my people keep an eye from a distance. Watch the watchers, as it were, yes? If anyone makes a move on Ballard we will make a move on them."

"What if they send Closers?"

Priest shrugged. "My people are second to none. They were trained by my brother."

"Your brother? I didn't know you had a brother."

"We are not that close, but you know how family is. Besides, Rafael has found religion. He has convinced himself that his employer's mother is a goddess and he worships the very ground on which she walks."

"And yet you think he is fit to train top mercenaries?"

Priest laughed. A rarity for him. "No one is better at turning men into murderous fanatics than Rafael. No one. He calls his elite opera-tives 'Kingsmen,' and they are as dangerous as anyone you would ever hope to meet. Or, to not meet."

"Good. Put them on it."

"There is a cost element."

"I know," said Bell. "Whatever it takes. But do not let any of those Closers come anywhere near my son. You understand me?"

"Perfectly." Priest cocked his head to one side. "Out of curiosity, sir, why is Dr. Greene even in the picture? With what he knows I would think it would be more useful to close that particular door."

"Not yet. He's the only person my son will open up to. Him and a kid at his school. Leviticus King. A juvenile delinquent with rich parents."

"Anyone we should look into?"

"I don't think so. The commandant of the school is keeping an eye on them, but it looks like they bonded out of need. King has been keeping the school bullies at arm's length, and my son is providing him with some recreational party favors. I make sure Prospero has access to a few things. It helps him unwind after sessions in the lab. Kid blows a few joints, then goes back in next day, drops some speed, and he's raring to go."

Priest nodded, then changed the subject. "You already have the first of the Unlearnable Truths, *The Book of Eibon*. Has it been useful?"

"Prospero nearly creamed his jeans when he got it. But then two days later he freaked out when he said it only had some of what he needed. He needs all of them to solve the sequencing problems."

"Correct me if I'm wrong," said Priest, "but your son is a physicist, yes? These books deal with magic and ancient belief systems. Other worlds and strange gods. I'm not sure I understand how they will help Prospero solve a mechanical problem with his machine. I ask only because it might help me determine if there are other books, or per-haps more contemporary books that might be of greater value."

Bell considered, nodded. "Prospero believes that this God Machine of his is not something new and he doesn't think it's even his original idea."

"I do not—"

"The kid thinks that this is sacred knowledge given to a special few by what he called the Ancient Ones. Yeah, I know how it sounds, but it's not the nuttiest stuff I've heard. I mean, go read the Book of Mormon or the handbook of Scientology before you judge. Fuck, read Ezekiel and all that Old Testament shit."

Priest held up his hands. "No judgment, just curiosity."

"Okay, okay. This ancient knowledge is kind of a test. Solving it accomplishes two things. It proves that you belong to the race of people from wherever these fruitcake Ancient Ones are from. Not another world, not somewhere out in space, but in another dimension, follow me? Good. The other thing you accomplish is to build a doorway that will take you home. Or, that's what Prospero thinks. He believes that the knowledge of how to build the machine is encoded in his DNA. That it is there as a kind of race memory for those of his species."

"Sacred knowledge," suggested Priest.

"I suppose that's as good a term as any. It's sacred to Prospero. The kid believes this shit with his whole heart. Always has," said Bell. "Just like he believes that these Unlearnable Truths were written by people who are either from the same race as the Ancient Gods, or who recorded what they learned from people who are. I think a little of both. Now we get to the tricky part. The science of the God Machine is amazing. I told you some of it. Absolutely brilliant. But there are some flaws in the system, and my people tell me that the flaws look deliberate. Like fail-safes."

"What are they safeguarding?"

"Use by the unenlightened," said Bell. "Prospero's words. He said that they were put there so that only a true believer could solve them. He said that other people like him have built God Machines before and that they were able to go home. Funny thing is I did some research on it and the kid may be on to something. There's a really good chance that Nikola Tesla built one. It fits, too, because right after that there was a rash of people who had some of the known side effects. Unusual kinds of dreams, visions of fantastic places. Almost a one hundred percent chance the entire surrealism art movement started because of the effect of the 'god wave.' That's Prospero's name for the energetic discharge of the machine when it's in idle mode. Are you following any of this?"

"I am following all of it, Mr. Bell," said Priest. "And it's very useful. It corresponds to some of what I've discovered while researching provenance of the Unlearnable Truths. And I think I can add to what you know. You say that the surrealism movement in Europe was a possible side effect? I'm almost certain that Mr. Tesla may have built two

God Machines, the second one being here in the United States. The sudden and dramatic explosion of a very specific kind of dark fiction and fantastical art in the twenties and thirties is not only similar to the surrealist movement; those stories are where we see mentions of these books."

Bell considered that. "That fits. I'm more than halfway sure the Russians tried to build one in Poliske in Ukraine. A full-sized one, too. That's probably why Chernobyl blew up. And the Nazis almost certainly did. Their Thule Society, those freaks. God knows that might explain a lot. For all I know the Ark of the Covenant might have been one. At this point I'm keeping an open mind. So, this isn't new, Mr. Priest. It's a matter of Prospero being the only person we know of who is able to build one now. He can't finish it, though, without a code hidden in certain passages and spells in those goddamn books. So, crazy as it sounds, we need to get the rest of them for him."

"Some of them may have been destroyed," said Priest.

"I don't want to hear that. Maybe there are copies. Find out."

"This is getting expensive, Mr. Bell."

Bell gulped some scotch. "No kidding."

"I have to ask . . . but is it worth it?"

"Christ," said Bell, "I hope so."

CHAPTER THIRTY-FIVE

The force of the blast plucked Harry Bolt off the carpet and slammed him into the wall. He rebounded and fell hard, his head ringing with the blast, eyes stinging with smoke, and flesh screaming from where a dozen splinters had stabbed him. Violin was on her knees, face twisted in pain, one hand clamped around a splinter as thick as a pencil that was buried in her chest above her left breast. Red blood boiled out around the wound and ran over her fingers.

Harry looked up to see glowing red lines bobbing through the pall as dark figures clogged the shattered doorway.

"Move!" he bellowed as he launched himself from the floor and tackled Violin as the first barrage of bullets ripped through the smoky air. They fell together, but she pushed herself away and with her free hand swept her pistol from its holster. As the first of the men entered the room, she shot him in the face.

Harry clawed his own gun free and rose to a kneeling position, bringing the gun up in both hands, and fired. The doorway was packed with men. Missing was impossible, even for Harry. He aimed for center mass on the next man in line, missed but hit him in the shoulder. The impact spun the man, jerking him backward toward the shooter behind him. It caused a chain-reaction collision as the men behind bumped into the man he'd shot.

The smoke eddied as the men pushed through, and Harry saw that these were not the Brotherhood. They were dressed differently, in dark suits with white shirts and sunglasses. They looked like Secret Service men, though that was impossible. Some kind of government goon squad. If that was the case, then they might be official agents and not actual murderous bad guys. That thought stalled him because he did not want to murder Hungarian cops.

Violin had no such qualms.

Even with a chunk of wood buried in her chest, she rose and fired, attacking them as they tried to untangle themselves. She went for headshots only, and pressed her attack because Harry's poor aim had created a momentary advantage.

There were five men in the entrance.

She killed them all.

Ten shots, two into each man.

They died.

All of them died.

Harry knelt there, horrified and dumbfounded, his gun nearly forgotten in his hands. Violin ran outside and then came hurrying back.

"The street is clear but there may be more," she barked. "Be ready to move."

Without waiting for him to reply she ran upstairs and returned seconds later with an oversized suitcase. Harry knew what had to be inside it. He could almost feel the cold power of that damn book.

She also had a medical kit tucked under her arm and let it fall in front of Harry. "Grab that," she said, pain flickering across her face. "We'll need it. Come on."

She paused long enough to scoop up her small laptop and tuck it into an oversized pocket on her left pants leg. Then she ran from the house.

Harry Bolt stood up slowly, blinking from the smoke, his ears still ringing.

"What . . . ?" he asked the room. But there were only dead men to answer.

Then he heard a thump from the rear of the house. The crack of wood, the crash of breaking glass. There were more of them.

He turned and ran.

CHAPTER THIRTY-SIX

SCRIPPS MEMORIAL HOSPITAL LA JOLLA
9888 GENESEE AVENUE
LA JOLLA, CALIFORNIA
SEPTEMBER 5, 11:41 A.M.

How do you know if you're asleep and dreaming that you're awake or if you're actually awake? After all the things I'd seen and felt, all the places I'd been, I did not know.

Maybe it was the pain that woke me. I became gradually aware of a leaden heaviness in my limbs and a pervasive ache that went all the way to the bone. In dreams I'd felt pain, but it was always big pain. The sear of flames, the white-hot burn of a knife across flesh, or the volcano heat of a bullet buried deep in my skin. Those were phantom pains or distortions of remembered pain.

This felt real.

It was not as intense, but it did not flash on and off like dream pain.

I hurt. My body was wrong and the pain owned me. It weighed me down like chains even as my senses came awake.

I opened my eyes, surprised that I had been asleep and not dead. Really surprised, actually. I was surprised I still had eyes to open.

The room was different.

It wasn't the little biohazard cubicle. It wasn't an intensive care unit, either. This was bigger. Less threatening, less dire. More normal.

If "normal" was a word I could ever apply with any accuracy to my life anymore.

It was a hospital room. A real hospital, too. It had the look, the smell.

I lay there and tried to understand what was going on.

Where was I?

What was left of me?

And . . . what were those things I saw? Was I able to go somewhere else, or were they simply bad dreams?

How does one tell?

Well . . . you ask.

I turned my head and saw that I was not alone.

A woman was curled into a leather chair positioned beside my bed. She had a blanket pulled around her, covering her to the nose. Her eyes were closed and for a long time I lay there and watched her breathe, watched her sleep. Saw the spill of curly blond hair rise with her chest, saw the down-sweep of lashes against the sun-freckled cheeks. Saw the woman I loved more than any person on this planet.

Junie.

I didn't want to wake her. She looked so peaceful and if she woke, would it be to the news that I was, in fact, dying?

Or would waking release her from the dread of believing I was already gone?

Such questions to fill the mind of a man who thought he was dead and in hell. Actual filled-with-monsters hell.

I rolled onto my side as far as tubes and wires would allow. There was no muscle tone left as far as I could tell and even that simple action was like bench-pressing a Volvo. But it brought me marginally closer to her. I reached over to her, lightly—so, so lightly—touched her hair. Whispered her name.

"Junie . . ."

Her eyelids fluttered.

And opened.

Junie looked at me with fear, with wonder.

With joy. She flung off the blanket and surged up from the chair, bending over me with equal parts passion and need and care. Being gentle with me, as if I was a fragile and easily breakable thing. Which I was.

I was almost nothing.

But I was alive.

We were alive.

And this was definitely not hell.

CHAPTER THIRTY-SEVEN

SCRIPPS MEMORIAL HOSPITAL LA JOLLA
9888 GENESEE AVENUE
LA JOLLA, CALIFORNIA
SEPTEMBER 5, 3:52 P.M.

I kept falling asleep and waking up. Kept dreaming wild dreams in between. Sometimes it seemed to me that I was dreaming even though I was awake. Or thought I was. The room stayed the same, though. There were flowers on the table and half a dozen get-well cards taped to the walls.

The hard lines of what was happening and what I thought was happening had grown fuzzy while I slept, and it was almost as if my long sleep was reluctant to let me go.

"It's okay, honey," said Junie. "Don't force it. Don't fight it."

When I looked at her, she was not Junie. She was a corpse, withered and burned. The shadowy man with the blurred face stood beside her chair. The only part of his face I could see was his mouth. He was smiling, smiling. Big white teeth.

"You're a self-righteous thug, Ledger. I'm going to take it all away from you. Everything you have, everything you love. All of it."

"Who are you?" I croaked.

He reached up and dug his fingers into the gray swirl of nothingness that was his face and slowly peeled it off, revealing it to be a mask.

The face beneath the mask was my own.

I screamed.

And woke up.

"It's okay, Joe," said Junie. Again. Exactly the same way, except this time when I looked at her she was alive and whole, and she was alone.

I blinked and I was alone. Her chair was empty and the light falling through the window was gray.

"Please." Not sure whom I was talking to or what I was asking for.

There are times, when my inner psychological parasites are at their worst, that I wonder if any of my life is real. Maybe I never survived the trauma of my teen years, when my girlfriend Helen and I were attacked by a gang. I was beaten nearly to death and she was brutalized in other ways. Maybe I never lived past that day. Maybe this is all some kind of purgatory. Or maybe my body survived but my mind snapped. There's a lot of evidence for that; I could build a case. After all, the things I've seen and done since possess the qualities of nightmares. Zombies, vampires, mad scientists, secret societies, clones, genetic freaks. Has the world gone mad or was I batshit crazy? Or some combination of both? Doubt of that kind is a terrible thing. It holds a match to the high explosives of paranoia and then everything you believe in, everything you trust, goes boom.

"It's okay, Joe," said Junie's voice. I turned toward her once more, blinking tears from my eyes. Except it wasn't Junie. It was Rudy Sanchez.

My friend.

My shrink.

Fellow veteran of the wars. A fellow traveler on the fun-show ride that was the Department of Military Sciences and the fight against terrorism in all its many forms.

"R-Rudy . . . ?" I asked, doubting this. Doubting him.

"Good morning, Cowboy," he said.

"Am I alive?" I asked.

He smiled. "You are. And thank God for that."

I looked around. It was the same room but something was different. The flowers on the table looked older. There were more cards taped to the wall.

"Where's . . . where's Junie?"

"I sent her home to get some sleep," said Rudy. "She was completely exhausted. She's been here every day."

Every day. Not sure what that meant. Not yet.

"Top? Bunny . . . ?"

He nodded. "They made it through. Thank God for that, too. They'll be fine."

Made it through. It was meant to be comforting, but somehow it wasn't.

"The rest of the flight crew is fine, too," he added. "They didn't get it as bad."

Get it.

It.

I licked my dry lips. "What . . . happened?"

Rudy took too much time girding his loins to deliver bad news. I know him, I know his face, so there was no chance he was going to say something I wanted to hear. He pulled his chair closer. He looked haggard. Unshaven and unkempt, and Rudy was always a meticulous man. The kind of guy who would take time to trim his mustache and comb his hair before leaving a burning building. Not now, though. He looked like he'd been mugged with enthusiasm, dragged by his heels through an alley, and kicked awake by homeless people. He smelled of sour sweat and too much coffee.

"Joe," he said, laying a hand cautiously on my shoulder, "you've been in a coma. You understand that?"

"Yeah, yeah, I'm sleeping-fucking-beauty. How long?"

"Two weeks," he said.

That hit me really damn hard. Two weeks? Gone. Simply erased from my life.

I said, "Tell me."

He did. It was the flu. Not just any flu, not SARS or MERS or anything like that. This was what you might call "old school." The simple truth was that Top and Bunny and I were infected with the Spanish flu. Yeah. That one. Or at least a mutated strain of it. The disease that swept Europe, Asia, and North America in 1918 and '19. During that outbreak over five hundred million people were infected, and of those one in five died. Eighty to one hundred million people. Dead. It remains as one of the worst pandemics in human history, with only the Black Plague having verifiably killed more people.

"Jesus Christ," I said, fighting to sit up. "Didn't they cure that shit like forever ago?"

"Not exactly," said Rudy. "It ran its course but there were complications. This was the end of the First World War, whole populations were displaced, and medical services were taxed and . . ." He stopped and waved his hand. "It doesn't matter. Yes, there are vaccines available for this and other strains of avian flu; however, the particular strain that infected you and your men was, until now, unknown to science. It looked like the Spanish flu and even acted like it in laboratory tests, but there were subtle differences, including the presence of unknown forms of bacteria that somehow bonded with the virus. That presented Dr. Hu's medical team—and a great number of experts we consulted—with a genuine challenge. Not that it will give you much comfort, Joe, but books and papers will be written about it."

"Um . . . hooray?"

"You should probably buy Will Hu a beer. You've become his favorite lab rat."

I tried again to sit up, and failed. "I feel like I've been mugged by the Hulk. How bad am I?"

"Weak," he said. "Once you were out of danger they transferred you here. At Mr. Church's request they began some muscle massage, passive movement, and a few other therapies to slow the rate of muscle atrophy. You're going to have to take it very slow, though, and be very careful. You'll need a lot of rest and a lot of physical therapy."

"Fuck that. I want to get the hell out of here. Right now."

"You'd fall on your face."

"Then get me a wheelchair and a protein shake. Come on, Rude, I need to talk to Church. Houston—"

"Houston is a tragedy, Joe, but it's being handled. I'm sure Mr. Church will fill you in."

"Good. He can do that at my office. Where are my pants?"

"You wouldn't make it to the door. You'll need time, therapy, and some medicines before you're fit to walk."

"Don't bet on it." I swung my legs out of bed and went to stand up. The room took a half spin and I could feel myself falling backward. When I woke up Rudy was eating a fish taco off of a paper plate. It was full dark outside.

"Did you have a good rest?" he asked, dabbing at sauce on his mustache.

"Fuck you," I said.

He smiled and took another bite.

"For a doctor you're not a very nice man," I told him.

"You are incorrect. I am well known for my courteous bedside manner."

I wanted to say something smartass. Nothing came to mind. I tried to blink my eyes clear.

The room was empty.

Rudy was gone.

CHAPTER THIRTY-EIGHT

Harry Bolt knew how to steal a car. It was one of the things he did very well. He found a Volvo that looked old enough not to have an alarm, jimmied the door, and hot-wired it. Violin slid into the passenger seat with the suitcase tucked into the footwell behind her. Her clothes were smudged with soot and they glistened with blood. Some of it was hers.

"We need to get you to a hospital," he said.

Her look could have peeled layers of metal off a tank. "Don't be a child."

"But—"

"Drive. Look for a tail, can you do that?"

"Sure, but—"

"Then go. No destination. Don't get us pulled over and don't draw attention."

"Where are we going?"

She ignored him and removed her small laptop and opened it. She did not hit any keys, but instead spoke to it. "Authorize Arklight field protocol five."

The monitor flashed several times and then settled on a screen saver with the smiling face of the *Mona Lisa*. Harry nearly sideswiped a car looking at it.

"Pay attention," snapped Violin.

The *Mona Lisa* spoke. "Oracle welcomes you."

"Oracle," said Violin, "I am in company. Friendly. Not family. Confirm."

"Confirmed. All secure data is shielded."

Violin then switched to a language that Harry did not recognize even one word of. It sounded a little like Italian, but then most European languages sounded a little like Italian to Harry, and he could not speak Italian. Harry drove aimlessly, constantly checking the traffic patterns. If they were being followed he could not spot it, and he did not think so. Beside him, the strange woman's tone became sharper, more agitated, and she said some other words he didn't know but that he was positive were curses. They had that quality.

"Pull over," she barked. When he pulled to the curb she turned the screen to him. The *Mona Lisa* was gone and now there was a diagram of a hand with splayed fingers. "Place your hand here."

"Why?"

"Do it." It was not a request, though not exactly a threat, either, but he took it that way and placed his hand on the screen. A scanner bar lit up and ran from top to bottom, mapping his palm and fingerprints. Suddenly Harry's driver's license, passport information, and birth certificate popped up in different windows on the screen.

"Hey!"

"Drive," she said, and this time gave him directions. She spoke once more in the strange language to the computer and then signed off. He caught glances of her out of the corner of his eye. She sat there, chewing her lip, looking troubled.

"You want to tell me who the heck you are, what the heck is going on, and where the heck we're going?"

"I have bad news," she said.

"Really? Why spoil such a great day?"

"Your team is dead."

"I know that. Both of them were—"

"No," she said, cutting him off. "Your station office. There was a fire. Everyone is dead."

Harry screeched to a halt in the middle of the street. Horns blared at him.

"What?" he bellowed.

"*Drive the car,*" she hissed. "You're going to draw attention."

He started driving, but he felt like he was in another world. Dazed and confused. "What happened?" he asked softly. "Was it those Brotherhood assholes?"

"No. Closers, I think," she said. "Oracle gave me the story from the news services. Authorities suspect a gas explosion of some kind. The entire building went up." She paused. "I'm sorry."

Harry nodded and wiped tears from his eyes. "I hated those guys."

"The Closers?"

"No, the guys at the office. Total bunch of dickheads." Tears ran down his cheeks. Then he bristled as her words finished processing in his shocked brain. "Wait . . . whoa, hold on just a damn second. Closers? *Closers?* How the hell are Closers involved in this crap?"

"Do you know who the Closers are?"

"I'm in the fricking CIA, of course I know who they are. Men in freaking black who used to work for Howard Shelton and those ass-pirates at Majestic Three."

"What is an ass-pirate?" she asked.

"Doesn't matter," he said. "What matters is why there are even still Closers anymore. I thought the DMS chopped them all up. How are they back and why did they target my station? And why did they try to kill us?"

Violin stared out the window for a moment, then turned and looked over the seat at the suitcase. "We are in a lot of trouble."

Harry just rolled his eyes.

"The Ordo Fratrum Claustrorum—the Brotherhood—are bad enough. They are dangerous but they're few. I can handle them, but—"

"I saw. You did pretty good against those Closers, too. Where'd you learn to fight like that?"

"My mother taught me."

"Geez. I bet you cleaned your room when you were a kid."

She studied him. "When I was a little girl my room was a filthy cell in an underground prison. My mother had to kill a dozen men to get me out."

Harry blinked at her. "Is that a joke?"

"I wish it were."

"Holy . . ."

"It's in the past where it belongs," she said. "Right now we are in deeper trouble than I thought. If these are Closers, then they will have resources we can't match. Not the two of us, and you have no station left to help us. The Closers will have people inside your embassy and in local police."

"I can make some calls. My dad knows—"

"We cannot trust anyone on your side of this, Harry. Not even your father. If the Closers are after you, then they will have people on him, tapping his phones, hacking his computers. Reach out to him and they will backtrack to you. It's what I would do."

Harry swallowed. "You have to be wrong about that. If we go directly to the American ambassador, he'll give us a marine detail and—"

Violin shook her head. "You know so little about your own profession, Harry. How is that possible for someone who works as a spy? How did you even become a spy?"

"Nepotism and bad choices," he suggested.

Violin gave him a faint smile. "We need to get this book into the hands of someone who can protect it."

"Your mother, maybe?" he asked.

"No. She is in the field and out of touch."

"How about my dad? Nobody's going to take anything away from him."

Violin thought about it. "Maybe. But first we need to get out of the country without being spotted. That won't be easy and it won't be quick. We will have to use some back routes that I know about. This is one of those times when slow is safer than fast."

"Before we do this," asked Harry, "tell me why the Closers, if that's who they are, would want an old magic book? Majestic was all about some kind of UFO bullcrap, from what I heard. Howard Shelton was into the arms race, not voodoo."

"It's not voodoo and it's not magic," she said. "It's science."

"Science? That book's a couple of hundred years old at least."

"Older than that."

"Then how's that going to be useful to some black budget government agency trying to build weapons of war?"

Violin shook her head. "You clearly don't know anything about war, Harry Bolt. Now . . . drive."

INTERLUDE SEVENTEEN

BALLARD MILITARY BOARDING SCHOOL
POLAND, MAINE
WHEN PROSPERO WAS SEVENTEEN

They sat in the dark and talked. They were unalike in almost every way. Prospero Bell was very tall, thin, pale, blond, with piercing blue eyes and a full and sensual mouth. His cheeks and nose were dappled with freckles that had paled in captivity but not fled with boyhood.

His friend—his only friend in the whole world—was completely different. Shorter, bulkier, with hard muscles and a deep tan. Hair that was as black and glossy as crow feathers, and a hairline that plunged down his forehead in a dagger-point widow's peak. A saturnine face, thin lips, and eyes as dark as midnight. His given name was Leviticus Kingsley Grant, but he called himself Leviticus King. Like Prospero, Leviticus hated his father, and unlike his friend he had gone a step farther and forsworn the use of the family name.

They had met in "re-training," which was the Ballard academy's soft-soap nickname for the punishment room. Both boys had given up keeping track of the number of times they had been beaten, or made to kneel on grains of rice, or forced to stand barefoot on the hard rims of metal barrels hour after hour. None of these tortures were ever reported to their parents, and both boys knew that if they tried to report them, their fathers would not care and the punishments would likely intensify. It was a locked system, a no-win scenario until they were eighteen. And even then Prospero did not believe they would escape. Paperwork was already on file to induct them into the military, and though conscription was technically illegal, all the right hands had been greased. They would go into the army and any attempts to escape that machine would result in federal prison. It was a trap and they were fully aware that they were not the first sons of rich men to be sacrificed on the altar of expediency and offered up to the gods of profit. Nor were they the first blue blood embarrassments to be hidden away from public scrutiny and paparazzi cameras. Not by a long shot. Some of the older boys and instructors bragged of having gone through these tortures themselves and having "seen the light" in the process.

The light.

Seeing the light was a big thing at Ballard. It was all about seeing the light, the light, seeing the goddamn light.

Which is why Prospero and Leviticus sat in the darkness.

They had a couple of joints King had stolen from the locker of one of the grounds crew, and the marijuana was laced with chemicals Prospero cooked up in his lab. They were edging toward being nicely baked. Getting high helped. Anything that sanded the edges off the world helped.

Prospero took a long hit off the joint, elbowed King lightly, and handed it to him. He held the smoke until they were both ready to burst and then they blew the smoke into the cold furnace behind them. It was summer and the big iron beast was off, and this late at night no one would see the smoke rising from the chimney many floors above them. This was a practiced routine, one they'd thought through and knew was safe.

"Evil is just a word," said Prospero, picking up the thread of their meandering conversation. "It doesn't mean anything."

"Yeah," said King. "That's the part I don't get. You're saying there's no such thing as evil?"

"No, I'm saying it's the wrong word to use. It's too broad, too easy."

King took a hit and passed the joint. "How is 'evil' easy?"

"Because it's not a real thing," said Prospero. "Think about it. You and I use the word the wrong way. We call our dads evil. We call the sergeants and the cadet trustees evil because of the things they do to us, but are they actually evil?"

King took another deep hit. "Yeah, I'm half-gone, man, so you're going to have to explain that to me. Because they seem pretty goddamn evil to me."

"Maybe," said Prospero. "Okay, context. As a society we call people like Charlie Manson evil. We call serial killers evil, and we call Hitler evil. But at the same time people use that word to describe everything from cancer to a natural disaster."

"Okay, some of that I get," said King. "People calling cancer evil is stupid."

"It's imprecise," corrected Prospero. "The word loses its meaning when it's applied to anything natural."

"Okay, sure. So?"

"Go the next step. We use it to describe moral crimes."

"Like mass murders."

"Sure, like mass murders, but then you have to step back and look at the nature of morality. Killing a dozen people and cutting out their hearts is wrong because the current set of laws in America says it's wrong, right?"

King blinked in confusion and then got the point. He nodded.

"But go back through history and you'll understand where I'm going with this. Take ancient Egypt," said Prospero, warming to his topic. "It was a common and accepted practice for the retainers of a pharaoh to be sacrificed in order for wealthy nobles and pharaohs to enjoy the same kind of lifestyle after death that they had during their lifetime."

"Harsh," said King. "But I get what you're saying. It was okay back then. Okay for the pharaohs, I mean. I don't think the staff was all that jazzed about it."

"Probably not," agreed Prospero, "but the culture did not take their opinions into consideration. What the rulers did was culturally acceptable and therefore not evil. Same thing for the Aztecs."

"Yeah, those cats loved cutting hearts out. An Aztec? Shit, he'd cut out a heart just for shits and giggles. No big thing to them."

"Not evil to them," said Prospero, nodding. "Even though it's exactly the same action as other kinds of ritual killing."

King took a hit and passed the joint back. "So . . . you're saying that serial killers aren't evil because they believe that what they're doing is correct as they see things?"

Prospero patted him on the thigh. "Yes. A lot of them are in their own headspace. For some it's damage from their upbringing, for some it's bad brain chemistry. Whatever. The point is that the act of killing is not evil to them."

His friend was silent for a moment, looking deep into the shadows around them. In a quiet, almost cautious voice he said, "They still hide their crimes, though. They do a lot of stuff not to get caught. They know they're breaking laws."

"Which only shows that they have cunning, and in some cases intelligence. They know that there are people around them who believe in an entirely different set of laws, or a different moral code, or even a different religious viewpoint. Knowing that, and understanding that these people feel that theirs is the only valid viewpoint and that they are willing to impose those rules and the accompanying punishment on anyone who doesn't share those views is common. That happens all the time. Salem witch trials. The way the Puritans persecuted the Quakers. The way whites treated the blacks—and still do. Persecution and violent enforcement of a self-created set of rules does not make the persecutors 'good' any more than it accurately defines the rule breakers as evil. If it did, then the Founding Fathers would be considered 'evil' because they violently rebelled against the rule and laws of England. But nobody here calls their killings 'murders' and they don't label them as evil."

"Where are you going with this, man, 'cause you're harshing my buzz."

"First, I'm trying to establish that evil is not really a religious concept. It's entirely secular."

"Why? Because religion is for shit? Because the whole 'God' thing is total bullshit?"

"No," said Prospero quickly. "I'm not saying that at all. We're not talking about the existence of God. Or gods. Or anything like that. We're talking about evil as a cultural concept. As I see it—and history supports this view—evil exists as a label used by one side in an unequal dispute over behavior."

King smoked and thought about that. "What about Nazis?"

"If they'd won the war and conquered the world," said Prospero, "the widely accepted belief—or at least the dominant social policy—would be that their actions—things like the Final Solution—were a means to an end, and that end was the unification of the world. They might even have ended war and future historians might have looked back on them with admiration."

"They killed all those Jews and Polacks and Gypsies and shit."

"Sure, but then they lost the war. The winners, the Allies, became the dominant social group, and in their view, the Nazis were evil. This isn't new. Rome was corrupt, but because there is more well-documented Roman history, the historians who wrote the history books talk about the 'sack of Rome' as if it was an evil act by barbarians. You get where I'm coming from?"

"Sure," said King. "But so what?"

"So," said Prospero after a very long toke and an even longer withhold, "so why should we—the two of us—have to accept being the school's bad boys? Why do we have to accept being the black sheep of our families? Why do we have to feel guilty whenever we get caught doing things?" He paused, watching the smoke swirl and tangle like the tentacles of some amorphous sea creature. "And why do we have to feel that we're sick, or mentally imbalanced, or socially fractured just because the school therapists tell us we are?"

"Well, dude," said King with a laugh, "let's face it—we're not normal. They busted me for setting cats on fire. I had to pretend I was sorry, but you know I'm not. And they don't get it that I like cats. I really do. I wouldn't burn them if I didn't. It felt so right. Hell, it was right. They're just too stupid to get it."

Prospero turned to him, his face lit by the glowing coal of the joint. "That is exactly my point. It is right for you. It isn't evil for you. It's not even wrong for you. You understand what happens when something that's alive burns. You can see into that fire and you know."

Leviticus King sat up and looked at him. He wasn't smiling anymore, and even the glaze in his eyes seemed to harden. "Yes."

"When I tell you about the things I see in my dreams, you don't make fun of me."

"Nope."

"Why not?" asked Prospero.

"Because that's your stuff. It's in your head. It belongs to you."

Prospero nodded. He wanted to hug King, but this wasn't that kind of moment. "You know what those things in my dreams tell me, right? You know what they want me to do. What I must do . . . right?"

"Yeah, man, I know."

"If I did them . . . would you think I was wrong?"

King took a moment with that. Then, very carefully, said, "Not if you did it because it was right. For you, I mean." Then he stopped, paused as if listening to a thought, and he smiled, too. "Oh. That's what you mean by all this good and evil shit. If you believe it, then it's not evil. Even if someone else thinks it is."

Prospero gripped his friend's arm with both hands. "Yes!"

"Wait, wait," said King quickly, "there's something else, isn't there? If you believe this stuff—"

"And I do," swore Prospero. "You know that I do. I have to."

"—then what your old man did . . . that was evil. He took the God Machine away from you. He—what's the word? Sinned? He sinned against your beliefs. And he made it worse by taking something from your, um, church, and selling it to the fucking Department of Defense. Shit. And he keeps you in here so you keep working on new stuff, and he knows that you have to because it's part of what you believe. That you have to keep working on the God Machine project."

"Yes," said Prospero.

"So he's exploiting you and pretty much pissing on your religion and waving his dick at your god. And he's doing it to make money. From your perspective that makes him evil as shit."

"Yes."

"And we both know he's leaning on Stark to make you keep working in the lab. He's turned you into a slave. That's some evil shit right there."

"Yes," said Prospero again.

King nodded. "Same goes for my dad when he beat the shit out of me after I torched my middle school. I was doing something important and he didn't see it. Or couldn't see it. Or whatever. He hurt me because he doesn't share the same perspective. He sinned against me."

"Yes."

"So, what we're saying here," continued King, working through it slowly but definitely getting there, "is that they are sinners and by our personal standards they're evil."

"Yes," said Prospero once more. "And history shows that anyone has the right to create a new moral, societal, or religious code as long as they have the power to enforce it."

"Which we don't have," sighed King.

Prospero laughed. "That's because we've been in here rotting. It's because even we've half believed that we're the freaks and they're the righteous ones."

"I'm not sure I ever really believed that."

"Sure you did. So did I," said Prospero. "If we truly believed all along that we had been sinned against and that whatever gods we each pray to empowered and sanctified us, and demanded of us that we assert our rights . . . then nothing would have stopped us from breaking out of here."

"Dude," said King, "this place is a military academy. They have armed guards. Soldiers. There's no way we'd ever get out of here without killing someone."

He laughed as he said it. But the laughter faded when Prospero did not join in. After almost a full minute, Prospero Bell said, "And that is the next thing we have to talk about."

CHAPTER THIRTY-NINE

SCRIPPS MEMORIAL HOSPITAL LA JOLLA
9888 GENESEE AVENUE
LA JOLLA, CALIFORNIA
SEPTEMBER 6, 9:15 A.M.

I slept and the nightmares came back.

This time I was there in my hospital bed, feeling sick and strange, staring at the darkness on the other side of the room's single window. There were orange sodium vapor lights in the parking lot and they painted the undersides of a row of palm trees in Halloween colors. The palm fronds looked like the talons at the end of black arms.

It was an odd dream because it felt exactly like being awake, and I couldn't figure any way to tell if I actually was awake or if this was truly a dream. Ever since I'd been hit by the blast of air from that machine there seemed to be no way to pin certainty about anything to the wall.

When my door opened and Rudy Sanchez stepped into the room, I felt immediately relieved and reassured. If anyone could help me through this and guide me back to solid ground, it was Rudy. Stable, reliable, practical, wise Rudy.

He came over to the side of my bed and smiled down at me. He wore a summer-weight suit and a Jerry Garcia tie I'd bought him for his last birthday. He leaned on his walking stick, the silver wolf head newly polished and gleaming.

"Joe," he said.

"Hey, Rude. I had a weird night," I said. "I keep thinking I'm dreaming. It's freaking me out."

Rudy raised his cane and laid the heavy silver head over one shoulder as he studied me. "Do you think you're dreaming now?"

"I . . . I thought I was. I mean, until you came in."

"But now you believe you're awake?"

"God, I hope so." I laughed. "I can't tell which way's up."

222

He nodded. "That makes sense. It takes at least minimal intelligence to understand what's happening."

I grinned. Rudy seldom makes jokes at my expense, but he got in a good one every once in a while.

"I am awake, though," I asked him. "Right?"

He canted his head to one side, appraising me. "Do you know why things went wrong down at Gateway?"

"I—"

"It's because the Deacon sent the wrong man down there," said Rudy. "He should have sent the best, but instead he sent you."

"What—?"

"Instead he sent his pet thug."

I sat up, frowning, not understanding what was happening here. "Hey . . . Rude . . . what the hell—?"

And Rudy Sanchez swung his cane at my head.

CHAPTER FORTY

He swung hard and fast but it was the surprise that nearly got me killed.

"Rudy—*no!*"

I flung a hand up to save my face, but I was slow and the heavy lump of silver punched into my hand and slammed it back against my face. He growled like a dog and whipped the cane back and chopped down again. I bashed it aside and rolled away from him as he tried for a third hit. The cane chunked into the pillow hard enough to make the bed jump, but this time I was out of range, rolling off the far side, dropping down, trying to land on my feet, failing, falling hard. His shoes clacked on the linoleum as he raced around the end of the bed. I grabbed the corner of the wheeled bedside table and shoved it toward him, jolting him so that his next swing missed, too. But it was a near thing. The cane whistled down past my ear and thumped against the edge of the mattress.

"Rudy!" I yelled. "Stop it. What the fuck are you doing?"

Rudy laughed. A brutal, vicious laugh. It was his face, his voice, but that laugh did not belong to my friend. And it occurred to me that his accent was wrong. American without the cultured edge of the Mexico City in which he was raised.

"You're a piece of shit, Ledger," he said, spitting the words as he fought to push the cart out of the way so he could get to me.

I was so weak, so clumsy, that I couldn't rise to fight him. My knees wouldn't hold me and I collapsed down as I tried to rise, but I used the momentum of that to kick out and ram the table into his thighs. He staggered back and then grabbed at the lip of the table to wrench it out of his way.

Was this a nightmare? If so, then I was free to act, to fight, to destroy this distorted version of my best friend.

Or was it real and was Rudy the victim of some kind of psychic fracture? Had he been doped? And . . . how could I save myself without hurting him?

I yelled for help as loud as I could.

The table went crashing onto its side as Rudy forced himself past it to get to me. The cane rose again and this time I had nowhere else to go. There wasn't enough clearance for me to roll under the cumbersome hospital bed. I was in a narrow chute formed by the bed and the wall, with the night table behind me and nothing to use as a shield.

"Fucking die!" bellowed Rudy as he brought the cane down again.

What choice did I have?

Really, what choice?

The heavy silver wolf flashed toward me, driven by Rudy's strength and his rage. And I kicked him in his bad leg.

I kicked him hard.

There was a sound like a gunshot. Brittle, huge, terrible.

His leg buckled backward, folding in a sickening way. The cane cracked me on the bunched muscles of my shoulder. Rudy fell, his face twisted—not with the agony he had to feel, but with hate. Raw, unfiltered hate. He crashed against the window, striking the heavy glass with one elbow and the side of his head. I rose up to one knee and tore the cane out of his hand, flung it across the room, tried to catch him as he fell.

Rudy lunged forward and tried to bite me.

Bite. Me.

His teeth snapped shut an inch from my Adam's apple as I reeled backward.

"Stop it," I begged. He punched me in the chest, the ribs, the face. He grabbed my hair and tried to pull me toward his snapping white teeth.

I ducked forward, dropping my chin, and head-butted him, smashing his nose, hearing the cartilage snap, feeling blood burst against my skin. Rudy sagged backward and I whipped a flat palm across his jaw that snapped his head around. His eyes flared once as the extreme angle stretched his brain stem and short-circuited the electrical conduction from brain to body. It happens to boxers and martial artists. It happens with whiplash victims. It's happened to me.

His body slumped immediately, sagging atop me in a boneless sprawl. I caught him, wrapped my arms around him, hugged him to me to prevent him from forcing this fight any further.

But he was done.

Out.

We lay there in a strange, bloody, awful embrace while I screamed for someone to come help us. I begged to wake up.

But I was already awake.

This was a nightmare but it was not a dream.

CHAPTER FORTY-ONE

Rudy and I were players in a midnight circus. He was a trained tiger who'd slipped his leash. I was a clown. None of it was real, none of it was funny.

The nurses and orderlies came running. It was probably only seconds since the fight started, but it seemed like hours. They swarmed into the room, yelling, demanding answers as if I had any. They stabilized Rudy with a neck brace and four of them gingerly lifted him onto a gurney to wheel him down to emergency. I was helped up and back into bed, but then a hospital cop came in and stood there with one hand on his sidearm as a frightened intern tried to make sense of my story. Then the doctors came with harsher questions. Then more cops showed up.

I had no answers that made any sense and it was abundantly clear that no one believed a word I said. The cops wanted to put me in four-point restraints. I told them to contact someone at my office. They produced a set of handcuffs and decided that, at the very least, I should be cuffed to the bed rails. I made it clear that I would shove those cuffs up someone's ass so far they'd chip molars on the way out. Two of the cops drew Tasers and it took the direct intervention of the hospital administrator to keep my room from turning into an MMA pay-per-view brawl.

Then Sam Imura arrived.

He is the sniper on Echo Team and one of my most reliable operators. Cool, calm, intelligent, and authoritative. He flashed impressive credentials that identified him as a special agent of the National Security Agency. He isn't, but the DMS doesn't have badges. We're allowed to borrow what we need.

Sam is a hard guy to stare down. He looks every bit like one of his Samurai ancestors—and that's no joke, the Imuras were Samurai going back nine hundred years. He had that flat stare that lets you know nothing about him except that he was in charge. Sam also brought two junior DMS security people with him and positioned them outside my door. Another two were sent down to the emergency room to keep an eye on Rudy.

When we were finally alone, Sam turned to me and his poker face dropped like a brick. "What," he said, "in the hell happened?"

I told him.

He called it in to Mr. Church, explained it, then handed the phone to me. I went through it again. Church said next to nothing and I couldn't tell whether he believed me or not. Rudy is, after all, Church's son-in-law and the father of the big man's only grandson. So, there's that.

"Keep me posted," said Church, and disconnected the call. I stared numbly at the phone, then handed it to Sam.

"That was helpful," I said.

Sam pulled a chair close to the bed and sat there while we picked through it moment by moment. Even after careful, considered analysis it made no frigging sense. Then he left for almost an hour. When he came back he resumed his seat. His poker face was back in place.

"How's Rudy?" I asked.

He took so long in answering it was clear he didn't want to tell me, but I pressed him. "You broke his leg, shattered his nose, and sprained his neck. He's in surgery."

I closed my eyes. "Has anyone called Circe?"

"No. Mr. Church doesn't want her to know until we have some answers." He sat back and folded his hands on his lap. "Do we have any answers, Boss? You come up with anything while I was out?"

"Not a goddamned thing."

We sat with that for a while.

"Poor Rudy," he said.

"Yeah," I said.

It was a long night.

JONATHAN MABERRY

INTERLUDE EIGHTEEN

BALLARD MILITARY BOARDING SCHOOL
POLAND, MAINE
WHEN PROSPERO WAS SEVENTEEN

Prospero's birthday was tomorrow. He would be eighteen, and by law that would mean he should be able to walk out of Ballard without Commander Stark or any of his goon squad saying a word.

Should.

Not would.

Stark had made it very clear that he would not be leaving Ballard anytime soon.

"Sorry," replied Prospero, "but in sixteen hours your tenure as my keeper ends. If you want to get in a few last cheap shots, go right ahead. And tomorrow, when I take possession of my trust fund, I will bring ten kinds of lawsuits down on your head. And I'll be filing legal charges for child abuse, physical abuse, assault and battery, and a few dozen other things. If you think my father will step to your defense, then you are sadly mistaken. I'll have you and the rest of the Ballard Neanderthals in prison within a week, see if I don't."

Stark, however, kept smiling. They were in the commander's office. Alone, though there were two sergeants outside, ready to step in if needed.

"Tell me, Prospero," said Stark, "aren't you even a little curious as to why I am not shivering with fear right now?"

"I already know. It's because you're too stupid to know when you're beat. I'm holding all the aces, motherfucker."

"Such language," said Stark. "However, I like a challenge. You have aces, you say? Hmm, let me see what kind of hand I can play." The commander opened the top drawer of his desk and removed a folded sheet of paper. He waggled it between his fingers for a moment, then handed it across to Prospero. "Read it."

Prospero hesitated, not liking this at all. But he plucked the letter away and opened it. He read it through. Then read it again. His hands were shaking by the time he finished the second pass.

"This is bullshit," he said, slapping it down on the desk. "No way this is legal."

"And yet it is," said Stark pleasantly. "Signed by two psychiatrists and countersigned by the judge."

"What doctors? I haven't had any fucking psychiatric evaluations."

"No?" said Stark with mock alarm. "But it says so right here, right above where it says that Judge Bernstein has remanded you to my custody until further notice."

Prospero shot to his feet. "No! I'm leaving tomorrow and you can't stop me. This is bullshit. This is my asshole father and you involved in criminal conspiracy."

"This," said Stark, reaching to take the paper back, "is legal."

Prospero sat there, frozen, unable to think. "Why . . . ?"

"Ah, a fair question. Let me tell you how this works," said Stark. "And understand, this comes straight from your father, so if you need to hate someone, hate him. He has been remarkably frank with me because, you see, he trusts me. He knows that I can get results. Your father is very generous with people who are able to get him what he needs."

"My . . . research . . . ," whispered the boy.

"Of course. From what I gather, your father obtained something very important from you a few years ago. The God Machine, I believe it's called. That made him very happy. You were sent to me, however, because you tried to sabotage his work and punish him for taking your little toy. Even though as your father he had every right to anything of yours. Every right."

"No," said Prospero, but Stark ignored him.

"Your father needed you to be somewhere safe. In a place where you could continue your little science projects, but well away from him. He loves your mind, Cadet, but I fear he does not love you. So sad. Understandable, of course, because apart from your knack for science you are a psychotic, worthless pile of cold shit."

"Go to hell," said Prospero, but without emphasis. He felt like he was dying inside.

"As long as you continued to do research, your father was happy with the arrangement. But then you had to go and screw up the arrangement. Maybe it's true that genius has a short shelf life, or maybe you just don't have what it takes to be a superstar, but you seem to have peaked. Your father has become more and more disenchanted with the work you've done. He's even gone so far as to speculate that you might be deliberately sabotaging your own progress so you'd burn off your last few months until you turned eighteen. And then you'd be out of here, thumbing your nose at your father and all of your friends here at Ballard."

Prospero said nothing. They both knew it was true.

Stark nodded, however. "You are not, as it turns out, as smart as you seem to think you are. No, Mr. Bell, not by a long mile." He tapped the sheet of paper. "This is proof. Bet you didn't see that coming, did you, my young Einstein? Bet you never even considered that there was a card we could play that would trump anything in your hand. Oooo, it must sting to be out-thought by the Neanderthals. Now, the way this works is that you will continue your research but you will light a fire under your own ass. You will no longer drag your feet, and you will produce whatever it is your father wants. You will do this as quickly as humanly possible and you will make sure that everything you do is exactly to your father's specs. He will have his people test it. Then, and only then, will he consider having the doctors and the judge reexamine your court-mandated commitment." Stark leaned forward. "Screw with me, Cadet, or make me look bad in front of your father, and I can promise you that there are things we can do to you that will make you believe that you are not in a nice, comfortable military academy but are, in fact, in one of the inner rings of hell itself. Have I made myself absolutely clear?"

That's when Prospero bolted from the room, blew past the two sergeants, and tried to lock himself inside his lab. He hadn't even managed to inflict any significant damage to the mainframe when the sergeants broke through the door and fell on him.

He barely remembered the beating.

All he knew was that Stark and the two sergeants seemed to enjoy it. He did not remember when it ended. Maybe they got tired. He had no recollection of how he got out of the lab. There was a tiny fragment of a memory of being dragged.

His next fully conscious moment was the water.

Shower water falling on the side of his face, and a familiar voice saying, "Jesus," over and over again. Which was strange because that wasn't his name. Or even the name of his god.

Darkness again.

The sound of dripping water found him in the dark. He was wet, he knew that much. But there was something around him keeping him warm. A towel. Several towels.

Prospero was afraid to open his eyes. He'd never been beaten this badly before. Never. Not by his father and not by anyone at Ballard. This time, though, they'd kept at it. Hitting him with telephone books because that wouldn't leave marks. The damage was all shock wave, all internal. Slapping his testicles with loose hands. No bruises there, either. Just pain and sickness.

Other stuff. His rectum hurt again. Another kick? Something worse? There were sadists among the sergeants. Artists at pain and humiliation.

It felt to Prospero like all of it had been done. Like Stark and his Gestapo no longer cared what they did.

It took a long time before the lights came back on inside his head. He was not in the infirmary, not in a local hospital. He was in one of the big communal showers. Fully dressed, soaked, wrapped in those towels.

"Jeezz-us," said a voice. "I thought I was going to lose you for a while. You look like shit."

Prospero turned his head very slowly and carefully. The lights were low and the locker room was empty except for him and Leviticus King. The other boy sat cross-legged on the floor beside him, elbows propped on his knees, the neck of a Coke bottle dangling from between his index and forefinger.

"How . . . how bad is it?" asked Prospero, his voice thick with pain and shock.

"Your face is still pretty, if that matters," said King.

"It hurts," moaned Prospero. "You got anything?"

King held out the Coke bottle. "It's high octane."

He helped Prospero sit up and steadied the bottle while his friend sipped. Prospero gagged at first. It had to be at least three-quarters vodka. But he took a breath and took a second sip. And then a couple of gulps.

King sat back and took a pull, too.

"El Comandante told me that you won't be leaving us tomorrow," he said. "I think he had a boner when he said it. Your dad must have written him another check."

Prospero nodded.

They passed the bottle back and forth.

King sipped some booze. "What exactly is the God Machine anyway? You said it was some kind of EMP thing?"

"That's only part of it. It's not an EMP, it's a null field. It interrupts electrical conductivity above a certain level. Anything stronger than the central nervous system of a person. Machines."

"He already has that, though. I mean . . . isn't that what he took when you were a kid?"

Prospero nodded again. He felt like something was broken inside and could not tell if that was true or not. It felt like he was dying.

"He stole a prototype. It was the best I could do at the time, but it wasn't right. I've . . . learned so much since then."

"And—?"

"And it doesn't work. There is a brief null field when you switch it on, but the core processors melt down. It's useless. I've been working on fixing it, and I've been giving him bits and pieces of it. What I really need are the last of the Unlearnable Truths. There's a code hidden in some of the books. I think I've figured out how to find it, but I don't have all the right books."

"A code for what?"

"It's complicated."

"Tell me anyway," said King.

Prospero wiped a trickle of blood from his ear. "The God Machine is built like a particle accelerator, only instead of colliding particles it superaccelerates them to open a doorway."

"To—?"

"Another world," said Prospero. "If I'm right, then maybe to an infinite number of other worlds."

"You lost me. You talking like Mars and Jupiter and shit?"

"No. I said it wrong. Imagine that there are an infinite number of worlds. Each is almost identical to Earth except in one little way. Like in one world I have blue eyes instead of green. Like that. Some of the differences would be so subtle that you could never tell. You might never see where the difference is. But some would be radically different because of cause and effect. If the asteroid that wiped out the dinosaurs had hit another chunk of space rock first it might have broken up and been smaller, which wouldn't have killed all the dino-saurs. Or it might have been bigger and destroyed the world. Or it could have hit later in the day and because of planetary rotation hit a different part of the world. You see how many possibilities there are? It's chaos theory applied to interdimensional physics." Prospero took a ragged breath. Talking was helping him regain control. His knowl-edge was the level place on which he could find balance. "Now, imag-ine the possibilities. If we can access all these worlds, we can find worlds where, for whatever reason, humans never evolved. Those worlds would have no pollution and all of the natural resources would be untouched. You could mine them for minerals or you could move there. Or just let humanity expand outward through an infinite num-ber of worlds."

"Wow. And that's what your dad wants?"

"I wish. Right now he wants to use the side effects. The null field and some other stuff. I don't know that he even believes in the omni-verse."

"But you do?"

"Yes. I think I came from one of those other worlds. Somehow. I don't know how. But I believe it. And I think my god is not the god of this world, but the god of some other universe, and I can feel him calling me home."

King took a sip, thought about it, took another, and handed the bottle back. "That is some deep, deep shit."

"I know. It's the fundamental belief in my personal faith."

"Um. Sure. So what's the problem? Why not just finish the ma-chine you built here and go the fuck home?"

"I wish. The problem is that in order for the God Machine to cycle high enough to open the door, the power has to be very precisely regulated through a network of crystals. Gemstones."

"Like the ones you have to check out of Stark's office every morning."

"Yes. But having the gems doesn't solve the problem. The sequence of channeling power through the crystals is the key. There is only one way to do it to allow the God Machine to cycle up to full power. Use the wrong sequence and as soon as you rev above a low idle there are cata-strophic errors."

King grinned. "Like when you blew the ass off this place?"

"Like that, yes."

"Have you figured it out? Do you know the sequence and are just keeping it from your old man?" asked King. "I mean . . . have you actually solved it?"

Prospero turned and took a long, hard look at his friend. "Why are you asking me this?" Fear suddenly leapt up in Prospero's heart. "Oh my God . . . please don't tell me you're in on it. . . ."

"In on . . . ?" Then King stopped and smiled. "You think I'm a snitch for Stark? You think I'm a snitch for your dad?"

Prospero was too frightened to say anything. He felt lost. Totally lost. He wished he still had the stone carving of his god, but Stark had taken that from him on his first day at Ballard.

King nodded. "Yeah, I can see how shit-scared you are right now. You're paranoid as fuck and I don't blame you. Your dad—your own dad—sold you out and he's keeping you here as a slave. That's some rough shit. And you're a cash cow for Stark. Your dad must be shoveling gold at him." King shimmied closer. "Now, you listen to me, man, and you listen good. I don't give a high-flying shit about much. I hate my family and I hate everyone in this shit hole of a place. I'd burn it to the ground if I had somewhere else to go, and yeah, that's fucked up because I don't have anywhere else to go. You want to know how many times I laid in my bunk and thought of killing myself? I could do it, too. There are a lot of ways to do it right and I know them all. Here's the thing, though; you want to know why I haven't hopped the night train? You want to know the only goddamn reason I'm still alive and still want to be alive?"

He leaned forward and poked Prospero in the chest.

"You. Laugh if you want to. Make fun of me, or do whatever, but it's true. You are the only friend I've ever had. That's sad, too. Cry me a river, but there it is. Since you came here it's been you and me. I don't like anyone else and I sure as shit don't trust anyone else. You and me, Prospero. A couple of rejects kicked to the curb by everyone who is supposed to give a damn. Sad, sad story. Someone should make a movie. Girls would cry buckets."

He poked him again.

"Now, you want to start thinking I'm with them? Really? Me? Holy fuck, Prospero, you want to go and do that to me?"

There were tears in King's eyes.

"You're my brother," he said, almost snarling the words. "You're the only one who ever gave a shit about me and you're the only one I ever or will ever give a shit about. We live out in the storm lands, man.

Don't cut me loose now. Don't let me drown. Fuck . . . I'd die for you." He caved forward and pressed his forehead against Prospero's. "I'd fucking die for you."

It took a lot for Prospero to move, or to want to move, but he did. He lifted his aching arms and wrapped them around the weeping boy's shoulders. He held him.

And it occurred to him that he had never held anyone like this before. Not even his mother.

King kept repeating what he'd said.

"I'd die for you."

After a long, long time, Prospero whispered something to him. A statement and a question. A counter to King's promise.

"I don't want you to die for me," he said. "But would you kill for me?"

CHAPTER FORTY-TWO

SCRIPPS MEMORIAL HOSPITAL LA JOLLA
9888 GENESEE AVENUE
LA JOLLA, CALIFORNIA
SEPTEMBER 7, 7:41 A.M.

The following morning Sam told me that Rudy was stable and resting. Church had arranged for the top orthopedic surgeon in California to fly in and do the repair work, but the prognosis was that Rudy would likely need more work later. Sam said that he heard them talking about a total knee replacement. That was the leg Rudy had smashed in a helicopter crash a couple of years ago. A replacement was inevitable, so they'd schedule it as soon as his other injuries were healed.

The neck sprain was bad because neck sprains are always bad, and they were keeping him heavily sedated while they assessed it. His nose was a mess and he'd probably need to get some work done on that, too. I felt absolutely horrible. Rudy was my best friend. He was a gentle person and a far better man than I'll ever be. No one had a clue as to why he'd gone crazy. Sam said that the blood tests they'd taken all came out negative. We were waiting on results of a CT scan and other tests.

Except for Sam, I was not allowed to have any other visitors. The DMS lawyers had to earn their retainers by keeping me from being arrested. You know the expression "cluster-fuck"? Yeah, well this is pretty much going to be the gold standard example of that henceforth.

I tried to pump Sam for news about Gateway, but he parried my questions by claiming ignorance—which was probably bullshit—and by saying that Mr. Church planned to debrief me personally. That meant that he was probably told to play dumb, and you can't trick information out of Sam Imura.

The only good news was that they decided to let me go home. Or, maybe it was that they were happy to get rid of me. I'm a terrible patient. Lots of bitching, yelling, threats, escape attempts. I don't make life easy for anyone and the staff seemed happy as hell to wheel me down to the front door. Pretty sure the orderly thought long and hard about shoving my wheelchair into traffic.

Junie was there, waiting for me at the curb. She came running to grab me, hold me, damn near squeeze the life out of me, showering my face with dozens of small kisses, tears in her eyes. Ghost was with her and he barked very loudly and bounded around like a puppy until I gave him a big hug and a kiss on his furry head. From the haunted look in Junie's eyes I could tell that she knew some of what had happened. Maybe not the Gateway stuff, but about the flu and about Rudy. I heard her whisper to Sam and heard him tell her that Rudy was stable.

"Stable" is a nice word but it's often used as a lie, a comfort pill.

Sam drove me home, with Junie holding me in the back of a DMS SUV and Ghost staring at me from the front shotgun seat. At home, I had to lean on Junie and Sam to make it from car to elevator and elevator to bed. After Sam left I used a cane left over from a previous injury to thump my way onto the balcony. The Pacific was a gorgeous blue and there were spouts from whales migrating north. Seagulls and pelicans floated on the breeze. Junie made coffee and kept feeding me high-protein foods. I'd lost weight and energy and she was doing her level best to fatten me up and bring me back to life.

It was working, too. I felt better as the day went on and by the following day the cane went back into the closet. Let me clarify that . . . I felt physically better but my head and my heart still hurt.

Rudy. Damn it.

The tough part was trying to fill in the blanks of everything that had happened while I was out. And a lot had happened. I got some of it from Junie, and Sam had doled out a few thin slices of news, and some of it came from my secretary, Lydia-Rose, who kept calling every five minutes to make sure I hadn't wasted away and died.

Top and Bunny were okay. Both of them had come out of it sooner than me. Bunny was back in the gym as soon as he could walk, and when the physical therapists asked him to do ten reps he did twenty. He'd already put back a lot of the weight he lost. Lydia was taking very good care of him. Bunny and Lydia had maintained a relationship for years that was technically against DMS protocols. But since I'm his boss and I broke that same fraternization rule within two weeks of signing on I was not about to throw stones. Top and I gave him a big-brother chat once, and he told us to go fuck ourselves, so there was that. Since moving to San Diego he and Lydia had bought a cottage on the beach in Encinitas. Cute little place. Never would have figured Bunny for having a green thumb, but he does the gardening. He taught Lydia how to surf and she taught him how to dance. Love, baby. It keeps the old world spinning.

Top was another matter. He's not as young as Bunny. He was almost ten years older than me and I was eight years older than Bunny. None of those had been easy years for Top. He'd been marked by our war. Marked by bullet and blade, fang and claw. And now by disease. He was back to work at the Pier, but on light duty.

I kept trying to get Church on the line but he was always busy. Lydia-Rose and Sam had both been evasive about why. Something was going on and they had clearly been instructed not to tell me. Maybe it was because Church didn't want to overload me before I was well enough. Or maybe not. I learned that he was at the Pier, and so I informed Junie that I was going into work the next day.

We had a big fight about that. Shouting, throwing of things. Some tears. Some very careful make-up sex.

In the morning she gave me the car keys she'd hidden. Along with a paper sack filled with protein bars, vitamins, and lots of other healthy crap. She made me swear, hand to God, that I wouldn't toss it in the Dumpster in the parking garage.

That night, while we were lying there, naked and sweaty and entwined, I found out that Junie was dealing with problems other than her drowsy and frequently irritable boyfriend. Someone had broken into FreeTech, the company she runs. Church set the company up and hired her to run it, and mostly she takes some of the less lethal technologies the DMS confiscates from the bad guys and mad scientists we fight and then repurposes them for humanitarian aid around the world. Funny how there are useful side effects even from evil science. Crazy old world. In any case, when Church sent me to San Diego to open the Pier, he moved the headquarters of that company out here, as well. Junie now has seven hundred employees in forty-six countries, but only a handful of them know the source of these radical technologies.

Junie told me that two nights ago—the night I woke up—two of her most trusted employees, a scientist and a lieutenant who was second in command of FreeTech security, brought big canvas laundry carts up from the basement, loaded them up with computers and reams of technical papers, and rolled them out of the building at around three in the morning. The two thieves had since vanished.

"What did they get?" I asked.

"A lot of research," she said, "but nothing we don't have backups for. It's just so scary that they came in at all. Why would someone steal that stuff?"

"Anything from the Majestic program?"

She shrugged. "Sure, a lot of our stuff originated there, but none of it's labeled 'Majestic.' There are no direct links to the overall program or to M3. All we have in our records are the things we're doing with that tech."

"Don't you have some of the Majestic stuff on your computer?"

"Well, of course I do, but my computer is always with me. I never leave it at the office unless I lock it in the safe. Same with Toys."

I grunted. Toys—aka Alexander Chismer—is a former career criminal, terrorist, and enabler of terrorists who has inexplicably become Mr. Church's pet project. Church is apparently convinced that even someone with as many crimes on his soul as Toys can find genuine redemption. It makes me wonder why Church cares. I once suggested to Rudy that Church has so much blood on his own hands from things he did in the years before he started the DMS that maybe he needs proof that redemption is possible. Rudy offered no comment. He's Church's therapist, too.

In any case, Toys was put in charge of an obscene amount of money and charged with the task of making sure that it was used for the betterment of mankind. The money was stolen from Hugo Vox and the Seven Kings. How Church obtained it and why he risked giving it to Toys is beyond me. On the other hand, I have seen Toys in several situations where he could have done the easy thing or the wrong thing and instead he chose to put his life on the line to try and accomplish the right thing. Last year he saved the lives of Junie, Circe, and Circe's unborn baby. So, right now I have a no-murder policy in place for Toys. It is subject to change.

He is the financier beyond FreeTech and is Junie's confidant in that enterprise. He's one of the very few people who have access to some of the information once contained in the Majestic Black Book.

"Where does Toys keep his data?"

"He has a laptop he brings home with him, but it's one of the Xeno-mancer units built by Bug. Totally secure. And he has to contact Bug to get access whenever he logs on. It wasn't at FreeTech that night," Junie said. "So really, they didn't get much that they could use." She laughed. "It's weird, but I'd uploaded my old podcasts once when I was upgrading my computer. I backed up everything to my office hard drive and never deleted that part of it. I . . . well, I listen to them sometimes. Those were copied, too. How weird is that?"

When I met Junie she was running a very popular conspiracy theory podcast. UFOs, secret societies, hidden agendas, shadow governments. Like that. Nonsense stuff . . . except that all of it was true. Junie was born into the Majestic program and raised by foster parents who worked for Majestic Three. She knew whereof she spoke.

"What's Church doing about it?"

"He put some people on it, but as far as I know they haven't found anything yet. I'm just glad no one was there to get hurt," said Junie, but she had tears in her eyes. "I just can't understand why they'd do something like this. I know them both. We're friends. They don't have criminal records, there's never been a complaint about them, and I've certainly never had to reprimand either of them. It makes no sense at all."

We talked it through but there was nowhere to go with it. Like everything else in my life lately it was an inexplicable mystery.

Around midnight I got a call from Sam to say that Rudy was awake and lucid, but that he did not remember anything about what hap-pened. Nothing. His last memory had been of driving to the hospital to see me.

"Did you talk to him?" I asked.

"I did. He's deeply troubled by what happened," said Sam. "I'll stay here at the hospital until they transfer him to a private room. The big man told Circe what's going on and she's sitting with Rudy now."

"Look, Sam," I said, "when you see Rudy next . . . tell him how sorry I am. Please. Let him know."

Sam sighed. "Cap, you want to know what Rudy told me tonight? He asked how you were doing and told me to tell you that he's sorry. He said that he sends his love."

We were silent for a long time.

"Jesus Christ," I said.

"I know." Sam hung up and I clung to Junie for a long time as my heart broke and broke.

In the morning, I got dressed without help and over breakfast I caught up on the news. No one had yet stepped up to take responsibility for the disaster in Houston. Even the most radical right and left pundits had begun to question whether this was, after all, a terrorist attack. There was no evidence of any kind of explosion, no strange devices found at the scene. All they could find was wreckage and dead bodies.

I didn't buy it, though. No way in hell. Houston was only the most recent bizarre and destructive power failure.

Well, just call me paranoid. And you know that old line from *Catch-22*. Just because you're paranoid doesn't mean they aren't after you.

The next morning I drove to the Pier.

I still felt like crap, but it was time to get back to work.

CHAPTER FORTY-THREE

Junie wanted to drive, but I insisted that it was no longer beyond me. And I was right. This morning I'd come awake with real energy. The high-protein diet, the massages, the meditation, the good loving with an astounding woman—all of that did wonders for me. I felt alive again. And with the vigor came anger and a fiery determination to figure out what the hell was going on.

I arrived at the Pier with Ghost as my wingman. Wing-mutt. Whatever. We hit the Starbucks drive-through. Venti Pike for me, couple of egg and sausage sandwiches for the fur-monster. Like old times.

The Special Projects Office is a big building built onto the end of an old amusement pier, hence its nickname. Our engineers dug into the bedrock under the seabed, too, so we had plenty of room for offices, labs, a massive fitness center, an even bigger training hall, storage, a garage, and more. I'd moved some of my most trusted staff out here from my old shop, the Warehouse, in Baltimore. We had 209 people working at the Pier and I'd been dreading a welcome-back party of some kind. I was wrong, though. The place was empty except for a few of the support staff.

My secretary, Lydia-Rose, met me at the front door, fists on hips, glaring at me. She's short, very curvy, very energetic, with lots of wavy black hair and the brightest smile in Southern California. Normally. She wasn't smiling now and as I got out of the car she was wagging a stern finger at me.

"You should still be in bed," she snapped.

"Happy to see you, too," I said, and kissed her check. Then her scowl melted away and she gave me a hug that nearly snapped my spine. Lydia-Rose's hugs straddle the fine line between hugging and mugging.

"I was so worried!" she cried as I disentangled myself from her with considerable effort.

"Where's Church?"

"In the big conference room. But he's in a mood. Maybe you should rest first."

"Maybe I'll take a buddy nap with the boss."

She gave me one of those looks, like she wasn't sure if I was joking. Or nuts.

The conference room was empty when I came in, but it was set with pitchers of water, coffee, tea, and two plates of cookies. A plate of Oreos and animal crackers on the near side of the table, and a plate of vanilla wafers on the other.

I looked at the cookies, then heard the door open behind me. "I sense a disturbance in the force."

"Yes," said a voice, and I turned to see Mr. Church.

Church is a big and blocky man, somewhere well north of sixty but looking like age didn't matter much to him. Dark hair going gray, eyes mostly hidden behind tinted glasses, and he wore very thin black silk gloves. All the time. His hands had been badly damaged during the drone thing a few months back. Company rumor says that they did some kind of radical procedures on him, and from what I can see he has full use of them, but he always wears the gloves now. Bunny has a pool going that Church has some kind of cyborg Darth Vader hands under the silk. I don't know if I agree. Maybe it's just that he has one flicker of vanity and doesn't want to show scars. I've asked Rudy about it, but he declined to answer. Rudy's more of a grown-up than the rest of us and prefers not to speculate about someone else's pain.

Church did not offer to shake hands, because he doesn't do that anymore. But he did something he'd never done before. He placed a hand on my shoulder.

"It's good to have you back, Captain," he said. He squeezed my shoulder once and then walked around to the far side of the table, pausing briefly to scratch Ghost's head. Ghost wagged at him, too.

I asked, "Rudy?"

"Resting," said Church. "However, if you're looking for an explanation as to what happened at the hospital . . . we don't have one. I've had three top psychologists interview him and I sat with him myself this morning."

"Sam said he doesn't remember what happened."

"That's not entirely true. Dr. Sanchez remembers almost everything, but he said it was like remembering a dream. He said that he was aware of what he was doing but he described it as watching events on TV. There was no direct connection to his actions."

"So what are we talking here? Is he possessed? Is he going to spit green soup and levitate now?"

Church did not smile. No reason to. "I have reached out to a number of experts—friends in various industries. They are flying in from all over the globe. We will get to the bottom of this."

I touched his arm. "Look, Rudy is my best friend. He's a better man than either of us. We need to help him."

Church nodded. "We do and we are. Now, please, sit. We have much to catch up on and time is not our friend."

"Is it ever?"

"Sadly, no."

I sat down and poured myself a cup of coffee, added milk but no sugar. It occurred to me that I hadn't seen Brick Anderson, Church's personal aide and bodyguard, and I commented on it.

"He's picking up my cat," said Church.

I waited, expecting there to be more. A punch line maybe. When he did not offer further explanation I said, "Um . . . cat? As in pet?"

"Yes," he said flatly. "Why do you sound so surprised? People own pets."

"You don't."

"I do, actually."

"Let me guess," I said, "it's a white-haired cat and you've decided to name it Blofeld."

Church selected a vanilla wafer from the tray, broke it in half, and nibbled one piece. "No," he said.

"Well, what is—?"

Before I could finish the question the door opened and in walked Brick with a plastic pet carrier. Brick is roughly the size of Nebraska. He used to be a top field operator before he lost a leg in combat. His new one is ultra-high-tech and hard to spot beneath his clothes. Church always takes care of his people. Actually, a lot of the DMS support staff is made up of former field agents who fell in battle but did not fall off of Church's radar. Family is family.

Brick is special, though, and we all knew it. Church trusts few people, and even among his inner circle there's almost no one who he shares his personal life with. When Church's former aide, Gus Dietrich, was killed during the Majestic Black Book case, Brick stepped up to fill that gap. He is a very smart but very quiet man, and he is fiercely loyal to Church. He is valet, butler, driver, confidant, and bodyguard. A friend, too. He has his own apartment in Church's house and his clearance level is actually higher than mine.

Brick smiled at me. "It lives."

"Kind of."

We shook hands, and I watched as he set the pet carrier on the table and opened the door. The cat that emerged was big and blocky like his owner, with smoky blue-gray fur and eyes as dark and round as ripe pumpkins. He had small ears that bent forward, and walked on short, strong legs. I recognized the breed, a Scottish Fold.

"Bastion," said Church.

The cat walked across the table and I offered my hand for him to sniff. He did, then looked away with typical feline disinterest. I was noted but not deemed worthy of further interaction. My own cat, Cobbler, seldom treats me with any more enthusiasm, and I feed that little bastard. Ghost would walk through fire for me. So, on the whole I've become a dog person.

Ghost watched the cat with undisguised contempt. He's not a cat person, either. Bastion eventually settled onto the chair beside Church.

Brick said, "Got a call from Circe. She is not happy that you have Rudy in quarantine. She said that you are due for dinner tonight because someone has to eat the lamb chops she bought for her husband, and she doesn't want to hear any excuses about the world coming to an end. Her words. Oh, and she said to bring wine. Something that goes with lamb chops."

"You told her that there is a grave national crisis and that I don't have time to socialize?"

Brick grinned. "Sure. Want to hear exactly what she said to that?"

Church sighed. "No, I believe I do not."

"She said she wants you to bring a complete copy of Rudy's medical file. Nothing left out. I'll get one, so we're good there."

"Will you please pick up the wine, too?"

"Already did," he said. "Got a couple bottles of the 2009 Bodegas A. Fernández Tinto Pesquera."

Church nodded. "Very good choice. Thank you."

To Brick, I said, "Wine? Isn't Circe breast-feeding?"

Brick gave me an ironic smile. "I'll tell you what she told me, and I quote, 'I have a week's worth of breast milk in the fridge and a husband in intensive care. If I want to get hammered, then anyone who tries to stop me is going to get a bullet in the kneecap.' Unquote. And for the record, Joe, I don't think she was joking."

I exchanged a look with Church. He clearly didn't think she was joking, either.

"Enjoy your lamb chops," I said to him.

Church never uses foul language, but the look he gave me probably burned off five years of my life.

Brick left, chuckling and shaking his head. Church ate more of his cookie. The cat watched him and I watched the cat.

"So . . . cat," I said, shifting back to safer ground. "Never figured you as a cat person."

He shrugged. "Bastion was a gift from a friend."

"Oh?"

"Lilith."

"Oh," I said, putting a totally different inflection on it. It brought to mind that dream fragment I had of the two of them standing by my tombstone. Holding hands. Lilith was a mysterious woman with a horror show of a past who escaped a particularly brutal kind of sex slavery to form a female intelligence network called the Mothers of the Fallen. She also spearheaded Arklight, the militant arm of that group. She was one of those women who seem to exude power and at the same time be untouched by time. Spooky but beautiful in a harsh Queen of the Damned sort of way. Her daughter, who I knew only by the code name of Violin, was a former lover of mine. Violin is an occasional ally and a trusted friend. Lilith, not so much. The memory of the dream fragment I had of Church and Lilith at my grave went skittering across the front of my brain like nails on a blackboard.

Church said, "Lilith is apparently of the opinion that I am best suited to relationships requiring minimal emotional give and take."

"Ah," I said.

Despite the long history Church clearly had with Lilith, there was also a lot of animosity there. Far as I can tell it's mostly on her part, but that's a guess. I don't know the details. Even so, Lilith seemed to have genuine feelings for Church's daughter, Circe, who was a new mother. Lilith was also one of a select few who knew that Circe was Church's daughter. Circe was, as far as I knew, Church's only living blood relative. Bad guys had killed the big man's wife and other daughter, so he kept Circe close but also kept their relationship a secret. I've seen what happens to people who have tried to leak that secret, and to people who have tried to hurt Circe and her baby. If I wasn't a manly man, those memories would probably give me nightmares. As it is, being in fact a manly man, I have a great collection of top-notch bourbons that can insure dreamless sleep. Just saying.

Church said, "Bastion was her second choice. I declined the first."

"Which was?"

"A *Reduvius personatus.* An unpleasant insect more commonly known as an 'assassin bug.'"

I winced.

"She sent Aunt Sallie a mated pair of hissing cockroaches for Christmas."

"Wow." I cut a look at Bastion. "So this is, what? Her mellowing? Or does the cat have a poisonous sting?"

Church took a moment with that. "I reminded Lilith that I frequently visit my grandson. Even Lilith had some boundaries."

"Ah," I said again.

He finished his cookie and took another from the tray. I sipped some of my coffee, which had begun to cool.

Church looked at me and said, "A lot has happened while you were ill."

"No kidding. A lot's happened since I woke up. But . . . seriously, Boss, is it as bad as it seems?"

"No," he said. "It's a great deal worse."

CHAPTER FORTY-FOUR

HOME OF NATHAN CROSS
1912 MIDDLETON STREET
MADISON, WISCONSIN
SEPTEMBER 8, 6:30 A.M.

Nate Cross left his house at exactly 6:30 in the morning. He went through the kitchen door into the garage, unlocked his car, slid behind the wheel, and started the engine. It was while he was buckling his belt that he saw the dashboard clock change to 6:31.

He punched the button for the garage door, put the car in gear, and as the door rolled up to let the rich morning sunlight in, he drove onto the street. He lived near the end of a cul-de-sac that was shaded by elm trees most of the year and kept green by pines in the winter. A lawn care team was unloading its truck to do the first round of leaf removal. Nate nodded to the crew foreman, who was a kid from the neighborhood.

At the corner, Nate turned onto County Highway MS, heading for the on-ramp to West Beltline Highway. The commute was an easy one, especially this early. It was why he left the same time every day. There was a window that he could use to beat the rush-hour traffic.

It took him only sixteen minutes to get to his place of employment, Bristol-Hermann Laboratories. He drove through the two security checkpoints, swiping his card at one and letting the guard examine it at the other. The guard did that every day even though he knew Nate and had been to parties at his house. Nate parked in the underground lot, in his usual spot, locked his car, and used his keycard again to gain access to the elevator. He got out on the fifth floor and had to swipe his card twice more to gain access to the cluster of offices reserved for his team and then to enter his own lab. Throughout a normal day he would swipe that card over two dozen times. Anytime he left the lab, when he went from one office suite to another, when he went to the cold room, when he used the elevator to go down to the cafeteria. Lots of swipes, lots of security steps, lots of electronics watchdogging Nate and everyone else at Bristol-Hermann Laboratories in Madison, Wisconsin. Today was no different from any other day in any other week or month in the eleven years he'd worked there.

He was mindful of the security steps and occasionally found them tiresome, but he never tried to do an end run around them. No one there did. It wasn't the kind of place where an employee would have that kind of thought. Security was, as all the signs and posters in the building said, everyone's responsibility. Even if there weren't cameras watching and guards everywhere, the nature of the work kept everyone on their feet.

At 7:43 Nate went down to the cafeteria. He had his silver coffee thermos with him, as he usually did. The cafeteria was empty but Nate could smell the rich aroma of fresh coffee as soon as he walked inside. He crossed to the two big silver urns that stood on a table against the far wall. Above the urns was a big flat-screen TV. The reporter from the local ABC affiliate was giving a stock roundup from the previous day's trading. The DOW was down thirteen points but the NASDAQ had closed high. Apple was up, too, and the S&P 500 was trading in the same solid flow as it had for a week. Nate glanced at it as he slowly unscrewed his thermos, then he stepped up to the first urn. He removed the lid and sniffed the billowing steam. Colombian. Very nice. Without pausing or looking at the security cameras, Nate reached up and poured half of the contents of his thermos into the urn. He replaced the lid and repeated this with the decaf. Then he screwed the lid back on, filled his thermos with hot water, dropped in a teabag, and went back upstairs to his office, where he sat at his desk and logged on to the company intranet. He spent the next hour reviewing test results from yesterday's field tests.

Nate Cross was not a scientist but he understood quite a lot about various areas of science. Viral outbreaks, flu epidemics, and bioweapons. His job at Bristol was to coordinate the flow of information from various agencies, process disease samples flown in from outbreak sites around the world, and assign technicians to process and analyze each sample to determine the strain. His reports would then be prioritized and sent to his direct supervisor, who would in turn share the information with the Centers for Disease Control and the National Institutes of Health, as well as more than a dozen government agencies. Many of those reports would be forwarded to corresponding agencies around the world, including the World Health Organization. His work product helped keep the global disease response network functioning. If there was a outbreak of tuberculosis in a village in Uganda, Nate Cross processed the samples. If a new strain of mumps presented in the fishing villages in the poorer sections of Ireland, Nate was in the loop. That was his job.

He also worked with the processing of samples of weaponized diseases, which was one of the reasons security at his company was so tight. Aerosol anthrax, samples of the old Lucifer 113 Russian Cold War bioweapon, the airborne Ebola that had very nearly been launched on a cruise ship a few years ago—Nate handled those samples, as well. He collected and registered them and made sure they were forwarded to the agencies responsible for both antibiological warfare research and disposal of unwanted bulk amounts.

Nate was good at his job and although from a distance his job looked terribly exciting and dangerous, it was actually rather tedious and bland. Samples arrived in heavily sealed containers and were transported by federal agents. Security, when it functions at a prime level, does not allow for excitement.

After he was finished in the cafeteria, Nate returned to his office and began reading e-mails and filling out the stack of paperwork in his in-box.

He only stopped when the screaming started.

He sat back in his desk and stared at the wall. Listening to the sounds. The shouts, the weeping, the shrieks. Then, later, alarms. And finally, gunfire.

At 9:19 he got up from his desk, closed his laptop, opened his office door, and walked out into the hall. His assistant, Miriam, was standing by her desk, eyes wide, her clothes torn, her scalp glistening red in places where she'd torn out handfuls of her hair. If she recognized him it did not register on her face.

Down the hall, one of the junior lab technicians was slowly removing his clothes, folding each piece, and placing them on a neat little stack. He'd begun with his shoes and now wore only a shirt and tie. His penis was fully erect and he was singing an old Backstreet Boys song. His lab partner, a short Indian woman, lay sprawled at his feet with half a dozen pens and pencils buried in her eye sockets. She still breathed, but shallowly, and her body twitched and shuddered, heels rapping an artless tattoo on the carpet.

Nate Cross walked past them, and past a dozen other employees. Some alive, some dead. One of them was on fire, seated at her desk, flesh melting, hair blazing, eyes wild. When she opened her mouth, flames rushed in.

The fire alarms went off and a moment later the sprinklers kicked in, twitching and pulsing as they sprayed water over everything. Nate ignored it as he walked the length of the building to the office of the senior virologist, Dr. Shaw.

Dr. Shaw had swept everything off of her desk and was copulating madly with a male temp half her age. Her hands were locked around the temp's throat and as she screamed herself into an orgasm she crushed his windpipe. The temp had made absolutely no attempt to resist her.

Nate watched a moment. Dr. Shaw was wrinkled and fat and ugly. He picked up a wooden chair, hefted it, and very quietly and efficiently beat her to death. Then he took her keycard, which provided access to parts of the building that were off-limits to anyone but the most senior research staff. He took the stairs down to the high-security floor, using the keycard at every point, entered the lab, and went to the hot room. The lab staff was gone, but there were splashes of blood, broken equipment, feces, and torn pieces of lab coats everywhere. Nate used Dr. Shaw's keycard to open the hot room.

When he left the building five minutes later, the fire companies and police cars were screaming into the parking lot. Nate walked to his car, opened the trunk, removed a commercial Blade 350 QX3AP quadcopter drone that he had bought from Ace Hardware, opened a small metal container that he'd installed where a camera was usually affixed, placed sixty-five vials inside the container, sealed it, started the drone, and let it fly.

A policeman saw it rise and came running over, yelling, his gun already in his hand. Nate Cross watched the drone go up and then saw the shift in vector as the drone's controls were taken over by someone else. The drone rose and turned and vanished into the morning sky as the police officer wrestled Nate to the ground.

INTERLUDE NINETEEN

The heat from the burning building chased them all the way to the fence.

The two of them were flash-burned, dazed, caught off guard by the intensity of the blast. The school itself was dark, though, except for the fire. The God Machine had consumed the lights, the power, the alarms.

Despite the pain of the burns, King and Prospero laughed as they ran.

Behind them there were shouts. Yells. The deep-throated barks of the pursuing dogs.

When they reached the wall, King pushed Prospero up, steadied him, helped him climb, shoved him over into the bushes on the other side.

King was nearly to the top himself when he lost his footing. His sneaker slipped out of the toehold in the chain link. King wailed as he plunged backward.

The sound he made as he fell was horrible. Like a wet stick breaking.

"No!" screamed Prospero as he lunged toward the fence to climb back.

The dogs were coming. Four of them. Big shepherds racing far ahead of the guards.

"R—run . . . ," gasped King. He flapped one arm to wave Prospero away. "Go . . ."

Then his arm and head fell backward as the dogs swarmed in.

Prospero screamed.

And screamed.

And he ran.
The gates opened.
The dogs ran so much faster.
But the fire ran faster still.

CHAPTER FORTY-FIVE

THE PIER
DMS SPECIAL PROJECTS OFFICE
SAN DIEGO, CALIFORNIA
SEPTEMBER 8, 8:05 A.M.

"Give it to me without the candy coating," I said.

Church frowned. "You've been gravely ill, Captain. How sure are you that jumping back in is the best call?"

My answer was a glare that boiled a few degrees above nuclear.

"Fair enough. Where would you like to start?" he asked. "Gateway?"

"No, Houston. How many of our teams are on the ground? Where are we with the investigation? I want to head out there as soon as we're done here."

Church shook his head. "It's under investigation. No one has taken credit, though ISIL is at the top of the list of likely suspects. The president convened a special task force that is currently being headed up by Harcourt Bolton. We are assisting as needed."

I shot to my feet. "Whoa, wait a goddamn minute . . . we're *assisting*? Since when are we anyone's water boys? I mean, even for Bolton."

"It's fair to say that POTUS is less enthusiastic about the DMS than I'd like."

"Why? Because of Gateway? I already told you I made a judgment call and—"

"No, Captain, Gateway is significant, but a number of our recent cases have had unfortunate outcomes."

I slumped down into my chair. "First I'm hearing about it."

"It's been a busy week while you've been out of it." Church tapped crumbs off his cookie. "I don't much subscribe to 'luck,' but this has had the earmarks of a losing streak. Gateway is just one of several instances of coming out on the wrong side of a critical play."

I held up my hand. "Oh, really? And how exactly is Gateway an example of us dropping the ball? All that weird stuff that happened down there? Those clones or whatever they were? That machine? And the city? You saw the videos, man, you saw the photos, you have all of our field telemetry. What do *you* think was going on down there?"

"Captain," he said slowly, "there was absolutely nothing stored on any of your cameras. There was no telemetry from the body cams. There is not one shred of evidence to support what you claim to have witnessed."

I stared at him in open-mouthed shock. "What the hell are you talking about? We documented everything. Everything."

"It appears," said Church, "that all of the data has been wiped."

"Wiped? No," I said, rebelling at the thought. "No, no, *no*. No way. How's that even possible?"

"I had your verbal report following your departure from Gateway," he said. "Since their recovery, First Sergeant Sims and Master Sergeant Rabbit have prepared extensive and detailed after-action reports. All three of you said there was a power outage of some kind, so it's possible, however unlikely, that this is our culprit."

"It hit us like an EMP," I said, searching my memories. "Knocked everything out, even the flashlights. But then the electronics rebooted without signs of damage. Doesn't that ring a bell? You want to tell me the president doesn't think that's somehow connected to Houston? Or the NASCAR thing? Or the damn presidential debate?"

"He does, in fact, think those events are connected," said Church. "However, we have no proof of any kind that it is the same technology Dr. Erskine was working on at Gateway. Bug has not been able to find any records explaining what the Kill Switch project was."

"Oh, for Christ's sake," I bellowed as I leapt to my feet, "it was called fucking Kill Switch!"

Church waited for me to sit down. I did. "First things first. I had our tech team go over all of your equipment and it is in working order, so that rules out an EMP. Dr. Hu's electronics team is working up some theories on how this might have happened. He has been following a few promising leads and his report is pending. So, let's table that part of it for now. For the moment we are left without photographic or telemetric reference. There is nothing, in fact, beyond your own testimony."

I closed my eyes.

"If this is too much for you, Captain, I can have someone take you home," said Church, gesturing toward the door.

"Don't," I warned him, and he nodded. We both knew that too much time had already passed. We had to get somewhere with this. I drank the tepid coffee and poured a fresh cup. "Okay, okay, then tell me what you think. Do you believe my account of what happened down there?"

"I have no way of knowing what to believe."

"You can trust my word, for a start."

"This isn't a matter of trust, Captain. I believe that you are telling the truth as you know it. The same goes for your men. I do not now, nor have I at any time, believed you were lying to me. However, all three of you were exposed to a virus and other biological and chemical agents that have yet to be identified. You were also struck by some kind of energy wave from the machine you discovered. There is no way to theorize on how these things may have affected your perceptions. The lack of corroborating information did not wash well with the president." He paused and sighed. "The subsequent failure of several other missions by DMS teams hasn't helped."

"What's that supposed to mean? What failures?"

He briefly explained some of what had happened, and hearing it was like getting hit by a series of very hard punches.

Broadway Team had gone after Somali pirates who were doing some contract work for an ISIL group out of Nigeria. The pirates were planting limpet mines on ships. Broadway went after them in what should have been an easy hunt-and-kill mission. Instead they got lost at sea and wrecked their Zodiac on a sandbar. Two bombs went off and two ships went down.

Then Scorpion and Rattlesnake Teams signed on with an ATF squad to rip down a cartel that was using drug mules to smuggle military drone parts to a radical militia crew in San Antonio. One of the shooters from Rattlesnake accidentally discharged his weapon at exactly the wrong moment. The result? Nine dead, including three ATF agents. Sure, they got some of the bad guys, too, but not all of them. The drones made it to San Antonio and the FBI had to step in and stop the militia men from blowing up the Alamo.

In Florida the Tiger Shark Team commander, Glory Price, apparently lost her mind in the middle of an operation. She turned her gun on her team, killing two and wounding four before finally shooting herself in the heart. Glory was a friend of mine and that was hard to hear. Damned hard.

In Washington state Wolfpack Team fumbled a mission and let a semi loaded with stolen military ordnance slip right through their fingers. Within two days terrorist kill teams were firing rocket-propelled grenades at civilian targets in Seattle.

Like that.

It was insane. In all, out of the last seventeen DMS missions, there were only two that were successfully completed. The others failed in whole or part, and we were burying a lot of our friends. This is what had happened while I slept. It was so much. Too much. I sagged back against my chair, too heartsick to even throw something at Church to make him stop, but he told me all of it. Every case, every failure, every civilian death, every death or serious injury incurred.

I wanted to laugh this off with a snarky comment and defuse it and make it go away. I wanted to dismiss it as another one of my bad dreams. But you can't do that. Not when it's this real.

I gradually became aware that Church was staring at me with great intensity.

"What?" I asked, my tone belligerent and defensive.

"You have no comment? No observation?"

"What the hell do you expect me to say? I was in a coma and—"

"Stop," he said, holding up a hand. "Don't do that. Don't make me reevaluate the decision to allow you to come back to work."

"What are you talking about?"

Church laced his gloved fingers together and said one word. A name. He said, "Rudy."

And then I got it. He saw me get it.

I said, "Glory . . . ?"

"Something is happening, Captain. People we trust are acting in irrational and unpredictable ways. We don't know why and we certainly don't know how. I had asked Dr. Sanchez to study the recent reports to see if he could identify any pattern of behavior. Sadly he wasn't able to complete that report. When possible I've had Dr. Hu perform a variety of medical tests on our people, including blood work from Glory Price and some of the others. So far there is nothing, no causation, no presence of chemicals or brain damage. We're testing for parasites and other biological agents that might be affecting behavior. So far . . . nothing."

JONATHAN MABERRY

We sat there and stared bleakly at each other across miles of hurt and confusion.

When I could talk, I said, "Six of those cases . . . they were against ISIL?"

"Six confirmed, with three others as possibles."

"Since when are they players on this kind of scale?"

"Times have changed," said Church. "They've stepped up their game by embracing other kinds of weapons. Our allies in the global counterterrorism community—notably Barrier in the UK—have been tracking ISIL involvement in computer hacking, the sale and transport of bioweapons, and even multiple attempts to obtain nuclear weapons. And they've been forming dangerous alliances with small and large extremist groups in Saudi Arabia, Syria, Lebanon, Yemen, and elsewhere. They've even buried their differences with al-Qaeda. They are growing at an exponential rate."

"How? I mean, how are they getting that kind of traction so damn fast?"

"Unknown. Aunt Sallie's analysis suggests that they have managed to either place their people in our intelligence services or they've turned some of our people. Ours and our allies. They have made a series of strategic moves that have been so successful that we have to accept that they have people inside. Nothing else can explain it. They've avoided traps, vacated before carefully guided drone strikes, and surged into areas of weakness, and they've done this over and over again. They are, in fact, winning this war." It looked like it hurt Church to say that. "And the DMS is not contributing to a response in any useful way. In fact, as the president has taken pains to point out to me on a daily basis, we are functioning at such a low level of effectiveness that we are helping our enemies. It is not unlikely that our charter may be revoked."

"Can he do that?"

"He is the president."

"*Will* he do it?"

"If this trend continues to slide downward, then yes." He looked away. "Perhaps he should."

I have never once heard Church say something like that. It scared the hell out of me. I expected my inner Killer to wake up and begin roaring for blood. He didn't. For whatever reason that part of me was sleeping. Nice fucking timing.

I shook my head. "How could all this happen that fast?"

"It had to have been in motion for a long time," said Church. "To have planted enough agents inside our intelligence services to do this much damage and provide that much information to our enemies speaks to a massive campaign. Something on the scale of the Seven Kings."

I jerked upright. "*Is* it them? Are they never going to lie down and die?"

Church stroked Bastion's silky fur. "No, Captain, I don't think there's anything left of the Kings. This is not them. This is almost certainly ISIL, and we are witnessing an evolution of that organization. Somehow they have put together a network of spies that rivals or exceeds anything we have ever encountered."

I sat there, numb, uncertain how to even think let alone sure of what to do.

"I hate to kick you when you're down, Captain," said Church, clearly meaning to, "but there's more. The president has officially given the power outage case to the CIA. It's theirs and we are out except as intelligence support and some minor logistics."

"Why would he do that? The Agency is a dinosaur. Even if we've dropped the ball a few times, we still have the best overall record for success in cases like this. We even beat Harcourt Bolton's clearance record. So how the hell does the CIA get put into play and we're making coffee for them?"

"The decision was made by the White House."

I slapped my palm on the table so hard it made Bastion and Ghost jump. "It's a bad damn decision."

"It's worse than that, Captain," said Church. "Harcourt Bolton has been asked to step in as 'special director' for the duration of this crisis."

"Special director of what?"

"Of the DMS. He is codirector with me and is now personally running the Special Projects Office."

CHAPTER FORTY-SIX

First Sergeant Bradley Sims stepped out of the Expedition and stood looking up at the high-rise. He wore a plain dark blue suit, white shirt, quiet tie. He was aware, however, that he did not look like a businessman. He looked like what he was. Or, at least something like what he was. The people who passed on the street cut looks at him and then looked quickly away, some looking guilty or nervous. Or hostile. Same reactions from men who looked like him and who wore suits like that. Cop, they thought. Local or federal, but definitely cop. Which was close enough to the mark. Special operators sometimes did a few of the things cops did. They made arrests. They took down bad people. Top had taken down some very bad people over the years. A few went to jail. Some went to black sites from which they did not return. And a fair few went into the ground.

The badge in his pocket gave him authority but it was a lie. He did not work for the FBI and never had. Nor did he work for the NSA, the Secret Service, the Supreme Court police, the Housing Authority, the Drug Enforcement Agency, the Border Patrol, the Department of Alcohol, Tobacco and Firearms, or the U.S. Marshals Service, but he had badges and credentials for each in the glove compartment of his Explorer. Just as he had papers proving that he held both noncommissioned and officer rank in every branch of the United States Armed Forces as well as those of Canada, Mexico, Great Britain, and France. He could have a working set of credentials for virtually any police or military organization in the world with a phone call.

The Department of Military Sciences, however, had neither badges nor ID cards. They did not officially exist except by a charter, the details of which were outlined in a sealed executive order.

But he knew he looked like a cop. Nobody on the street smiled at him, which was fine, because Top wasn't in a sunny mood. The job down in Antarctica had done him some harm. Not physically, and not where it showed, but he could feel it. The fear was there and he caught glimpses of it when he looked in the mirror. There was a slight tremble of the hand, a hesitation in the step that was never there before. Not even after the Red Knights and the Majestic Black Book cases. Not even after the horrors he'd seen in the tunnels beneath the Dragon Factory.

No, all of that was science. Weird science, sure. Bad science, no doubt. But those horrors had been the end results of physics and medicine, genetics and chemistry, structural engineering and radical surgery. At the end of the day—and there had been some very bad days for Top and his colleagues—everything they'd encountered could be mapped out, dissected, dismantled, and explained.

The things that had happened in the Gateway lab could not be.

Not yet.

And now the DMS was falling apart. Instead of providing stable ground for him and Bunny to stand on, the ship was canting down into the watery deep. Top had lost friends on some of the other teams. Other friends were under investigation for mishandling of their cases. A few were probably going to jail.

It was all falling apart and Top felt the timbers splitting inside his head and heart.

Top glanced over his shoulder. Bunny was still seated behind the wheel, hands in his lap, eyes staring at who knew what. Memories? Possibilities? He certainly wasn't looking at anything on the street. It hurt Top. And it did not help one bit that Top understood what was going on in the young man's head and heart.

Even so, this was a job and it needed getting done, so he rapped lightly on the side window. Bunny flinched. A rare and ugly thing for him. Bunny was a good kid but he was tough as iron and, in Top's experience, did not have much "give up" in him.

Unless now he did.

It was hard to say.

It was bad to think about.

Bunny rubbed his eyes, took a deep breath, and blew out his cheeks as he exhaled.

Top tapped on the window. "Come on, Farm Boy, they ain't paying us to be tourists."

Bunny got out of the car, closed the door and locked it, buttoned his jacket so the breeze wouldn't blow it open to show his shoulder holster. He came around the front of the Expedition and stood beside Top. Now the crowds on the street tended to cross to the other side. The ones that didn't parted like a river around a rock. Top looked up at Bunny.

"You good to go?"

"Yeah, I guess," Bunny said, and took a step toward the building.

Top shifted around to block his way. "'I guess'? What kind of horseshit is that? I asked you a straight question. Are you good to go?"

Bunny straightened. He was nearly six seven and had massive arms and shoulders. Blond hair and blue eyes and a dark tan that made his white teeth seem to glow. Top had seen Bunny pick grown men up and hurl them like sacks of potatoes. He'd seen him throw himself into a crowd and batter half a dozen other men down to the ground. He'd walked side by side with him through a hundred vicious fire-fights. As he searched Bunny's eyes he looked for that man. The one who anchored Echo Team with muscle and heart.

And Top could see the moment when Bunny became aware of what was going on, when he understood the conversation they were both having with unspoken words.

Bunny took another big breath, and exhaled slowly. "I'm good," he said.

Top studied him a moment longer, then nodded. "Me, too," he lied.

They turned and went to the back of the car to remove one briefcase and a metal equipment case. Top took the briefcase and Bunny hefted the equipment. They walked into the building, flashed their FBI credentials at the guard, and took the elevator to the sixteenth floor. Neither said a word.

Their job was a simple one. The only tenant of the sixteenth floor was the office and private laboratory of Dr. Raoul San Pedro. The office had been shut up except for a twice-monthly cleaner who dusted the furniture. Following the incident in Antarctica, the office had been officially sealed by the FBI and a police detail had been assigned to guard the door pending resolution and disposition of San Pedro's effects. Top had a federal order in his pocket that would allow him and Bunny to enter the premises and remove anything that might be of use. The order was vague in detailing what they were looking for, but sweeping in the authority it afforded them. The tools in the bag Bunny carried were to help them locate hidden electronics or a safe, and if a safe existed they had what they needed to open it.

Except that isn't what happened, because as soon as they stepped off of the elevator the whole routine pattern of the job changed.

There was no cop in the hall.

There was only blood.

"Shit," gasped Bunny as he dropped the heavy case and went for his gun. Top beat him to the draw.

The hall was empty. They pivoted to cover it, up and down, but aside from the elevator there was only a janitor's closet, the fire stairs, and the double door to San Pedro's office.

The closet door stood open, the supplies spilled out onto the floor in a tangle of mops, brooms, an overturned wheeled bucket, burst bottles of cleaning fluid, ruptured cans of spray polish, and a roll of black plastic trash bags that was twisted across the floor like the shed skin of some dark snake.

Bunny immediately ran down to the other end of the hall to check the fire stairs while Top crouched and kept his weapon trained on the doors to the lab. One door was closed, the other was ajar. When Bunny returned, shaking his head to indicate that the stairs were clear, Top nodded to the open office door. There was a clear handprint painted in bright red. A line of blood ran slowly down from it. The two men exchanged a brief, knowing glance. Blood is thick and clots quickly. For it still to be wet enough to crawl down the door meant that this was new.

It meant that this was still happening.

Top gave a curt nod and Bunny immediately shifted to flank the door. There were a few different ways to play this. Go in high and low and shoot the first thing that didn't look kosher. Go in fast and quiet and let the situation dictate what happened next. Or stay in the relative safety of the hall, identify themselves as federal officers, and demand that whoever was in there lay down their weapons and cooperate with the arrest.

Those were all methods Top and Bunny had used many times.

Sometimes a situation was so thoroughly in motion that they didn't get to call the play.

Like now.

The door opened and a man stood there. A medium-tall white man dressed almost identically to them. He held a weapon in his left hand. Not a Glock like Bunny or a Sig Sauer like Top.

This was a stubby pistol with three converging metal spikes at the business end. No open barrel. Not even something to fire flachettes like a Taser. It was not that kind of weapon, and both DMS agents recognized it at once. It terrified them both as much as it made them furious.

"Federal officers. Drop your weapon!" yelled Bunny, his own pointed center mass at the man. "Do it now or I will kill you."

The man smiled at them.

He pulled the trigger of his strange little gun.

It made an odd little sound.

TOK!

The air shimmered and the wall behind Top and Bunny exploded.

INTERLUDE TWENTY

Prospero wondered what it would be like to die.

It was coming.

He didn't fear the pain. His body felt like it was wrapped in barbed wire. Those dogs . . . their teeth . . .

God.

They kept biting even while he was stabbing them to death.

Damn dogs.

It hurt so bad.

The fires, though . . . that had been worse. Smart as he was, it never occurred to him that running uphill from a burning building was a stupid idea. The winds were blowing steadily from the south and the lawn burned, then the shrubs, and then the trees. Prospero could have outrun it if not for the damn dogs.

Was it a blessing that it had started to rain? Was that a gift from his god? Or was that a punishment, extinguishing the flames so that he could suffer longer?

He did not know and that lack of knowledge screamed in his head.

Now he crawled through the grass and left a trail that glistened like the mucus of a great slug. The slime looked black in the moonlight and was only red when another part of the building collapsed and sent a pillar of fire into the air.

Prospero prayed to his god.

He prayed to the dreaming god who slept beneath the waves.

He begged his god to wake, to stretch out a mighty hand and bring him home. God wouldn't need a machine to do that. It was only the small, the weak, and the helpless ones like Prospero who needed a doorway. Gods didn't need anything.

He prayed for salvation. He prayed that God or one of his servants would answer his prayers.

"Please," he begged as he crawled.

In the woods behind him the sergeants began yelling. They'd found the dogs.

They would be coming soon.

Prospero crawled faster.

Then he heard a sound and froze. Not behind him. This was a soft noise as a foot stepped down on the thick grass. Prospero's heart sank as he raised his head and looked up, looked ahead.

There, between him and the road, was a pair of heavy old willows, one leaning left, the other leaning right, each one pulled into ogre shapes by their age and ponderous weight. Beyond them was the black ribbon of the road.

And there, idling with its lights off, was a car. The driver's door was open.

Prospero held his breath and tried not to make a sound. Was this one of the sergeants come up the side road to head him off? What would happen? Would it be more kicks, or more of the cattle prods? Would it be a knife or a bullet?

The knife Prospero had brought with him from the school was back there somewhere, stuck in the second dog's throat, wedged into bone.

There was a second soft noise and a piece of shadow detached itself from the black trunk of the left-hand tree. It moved forward, becoming man shaped. Was there a gun in his hand?

The figure came and stood over him.

"Prospero," he said. A quiet voice. Cultured. Foreign?

The boy raised a bloody hand, half to ward off a blow and half to beg for help.

"Please . . . ," gasped the dying boy.

"Prospero," said the man. Sure now. Prospero could see the flash of a smile. Bright white teeth. Then the figure squatted down and lifted him as easily as if he weighed nothing. No grunt of effort. Nothing.

The boy clutched the man's dark shirt. "Did he send you? Are you one of his angels?"

The man just smiled and carried the boy to the car.

CHAPTER FORTY-SEVEN

So, yeah, kick me while I'm down. Kick me, stomp on me, park your car on me.

Church said nothing as it all sank in. I mean, on one hand, hooray. Bolton is the real deal. All those wins he racked up in the field, all of the deep and crucial intel he's obtained since then. Still my hero, but at that exact moment I would have gladly chopped him into cat treats and fed him to Church's cat.

"Well," I said, "I'm back now. It's going to get pretty chummy if we're both trying to squeeze our asses into my chair."

"It won't come to that. Harcourt has been very considerate of our feelings," Church said dryly. "He's using one of the spare offices and has said, many times, that he will work with us. He didn't ask for this assignment and I believe he feels embarrassed. It's possible he even resents being put in this position."

I nodded. Nobody was winning right now. I said, "You're old friends with Bolton?"

Church took a moment. "We have worked together in a number of cases that ended satisfactorily."

"Wow, you couldn't have been less enthusiastic if you were actually asleep. Why? What have you got against Bolton?"

"Against him? Nothing."

"But—?" I prompted.

"Captain, this isn't high school. It's not required that everyone in our line of work be close friends or confidants. It is enough that Harcourt and I have found a certain rhythm for effective collaboration. He has his way of getting things done and it works for him."

There was a lot left unsaid and I could read a bit between the lines, but it wasn't the right moment for a confessional conversation. Not that I thought my chances of prying details out of Church were any good.

"For now," he said, "please understand that I am not running the ISIL investigation. That is entirely under the directorship of Harcourt Bolton. The president has asked me to finalize our official report on Gateway and then to focus on another matter."

"Which is what? Some kid stealing lunch money?"

He smiled thinly. "Gateway first."

"Sure. Fine. Let's do that. Because as we all know, a pile of rubble is far more important than the threat of a global terrorist organization." When he made no comment I resisted the temptation to roll my eyes like a Valley Girl. "Where do you want to start?" I asked quietly. Almost demurely, damn it.

"We need to understand what happened down there, and there are a few factors to consider. You described an underground city as well as some of the other elements, notably the oversized albino penguins."

"Yes."

"Are you aware that there is some precedent to some of what you described?"

I stiffened. "What are you talking about? What kind of precedent?"

Mr. Church said, "Certain elements of your account—and those of your team—parallel elements of a story that is very popular among devotees of a certain kind of pulp horror fiction. Have you ever heard of, or possibly read, the short novel *At the Mountains of Madness* by the writer Howard Phillips Lovecraft?"

"Sure, I heard of Lovecraft, but I don't read much horror. Never read that book. Was there a movie?"

"The novel was written in 1931 and published in 1936 in a pulp magazine called *Astounding Stories*. It was very popular and has been reprinted in book, e-book, and audio form many times since. Circe tells me that the story helped popularize the concept of 'ancient astronauts' as well as Antarctica's place in that cycle of myths."

I lunged at that. "Well, maybe they're not myths. We saw that city, and, let's face it, we're not exactly as skeptical of little green men in spaceships as we used to be." I gave him a hard look. "Are we?"

I wasn't making a joke.

A few years ago we in the DMS had been forced to adjust our thinking about the possibility of extraterrestrial life. We no longer had the luxury of being knee-jerk skeptics. Not anymore. Church and I both knew that our world had become substantially larger during the Majestic Black Book case. We'd stumbled onto a covert arms race between a secret cabal within our defense department called Majestic Three and their opposite numbers in China, North Korea, and Russia. They were all trying to reverse engineer exotic technologies from crashed vehicles. And by "vehicles," I'm not talking about anything with a local license plate. Start with Roswell and work from there and you'll climb into the same boat. Majestic Three, or M3 as they were more commonly known, were so far off the radar that even the DMS thought they were only some kind of pop culture conspiracy myth.

Not so much a myth, as it turned out.

The three "governors" of M3 were top-grade scientists who were preparing to launch a fleet of triangle-winged super-speed T-craft that they wanted to use to start, and win, a war with the other superpowers. They had lots of weird science culled from those crashed ships, and it gave them a real edge for a while. Echo Team went up against M3's own special ops guys, a group of—no joke—men in black. Called themselves the "Closers," and they had all sorts of nasty gadgets including these nifty little microwave pulse pistols. Not exactly rayguns but close enough.

The kicker was that the original owners of that tech—who we never got to actually see—made it clear that they wanted their toys back. Specifically they wanted the design science for the T-craft, which was all kept in a special handwritten journal. The Majestic Black Book. The governors of M3 kept that book well protected, and a lot of the hard science was recorded only in it. They didn't trust the security of computers, even those that weren't attached to landlines or Wi-Fi.

E.T. and his buddies bullied us into recovering the Black Book. We did, and the original was turned over. I wasn't there for that part of the job. I'd taken some gunshot wounds during the big, messy finale. By the time I got out of the hospital the Majestic Black Book case was over. Since then none of us have heard a peep from anyone who doesn't have "Earth" as point of origin on his passport.

Now . . . there was this crazy stuff in Antarctica.

Church sighed. "It's a troubling matter."

I laughed. "Yeah, you could say that. And you weren't attacked by a mutant penguin. Have you seen Bunny's face?"

"I have."

"Speaking of Bunny . . . where is he? Where's Top? Where's everybody?"

"Most of our teams are out on assignment. You can talk over the specifics with Harcourt later. As for First Sergeant Sims and Master Sergeant Rabbit, they are on light duty. I have them out collecting evidence from the offices of the scientists who were killed down at Gateway."

"They okay?"

Church made one of his rare jokes. "Shaken, not stirred."

I laughed louder than the joke deserved. Ghost woke up again, looked around, saw there was nothing to eat or bite, farted very loudly, and went back to sleep. Church, without comment, went and opened a window. The sea air was nice. Bastion jumped off his chair, climbed up to the windowsill, and sat there watching the pelicans.

CHAPTER FORTY-EIGHT

The blast picked Bunny and Top up like the hand of a fiery giant and slammed them into the opposite wall. The force hit the man in the dark suit, too, but he was already falling, struck at the same instant by bullets fired from both DMS agents' guns. Everyone went down. The gunman toppled backward through the doorway, but Top and Bunny slammed into the wall and then crashed to the floor.

It was all very fast, very noisy, and very painful.

Top coughed and tried to blink his eyes free. His gun was gone and he began frantically slapping the floor to find it. Found it under a piece of burning wallpaper, swatted the flames away, grabbed the gun, fumbled it back into his hands. All in a wild moment while his brain tried to process what was happening. The hall was filled with choking dust and burning rubble. The heat was immense and Top shimmied away from the flames that were spreading across the far wall.

A shape rose in the gloom. Massive and hunched, and it took Top's dazed brain a second to realize that it was Bunny, staggering to his feet, his gun clutched in his fist, blood streaming down his face from between ruptured stitches.

"Motherfucker!" bellowed the young giant. "Top? Top—are you alive, you old bastard?"

"Kiss . . . ," gasped Top, "my black . . . ass."

Bunny grabbed him with his free hand and pulled Top up. The door to San Pedro's office stood open, the wood nicked and charred. Both men raised their weapons.

"That was a fucking microwave pulse pistol," growled Bunny.

"I know."

"That fucking guy was a—"

"I know."

"—fucking Closer."

"I know."

The fear was there for Top to hear in his own voice.

A Closer.

One of the elite group of trained killers who worked for the warped scientist who had developed the MPP handguns as well as a long list of other even more deadly weapons.

But Howard Shelton was dead.

His organization, Majestic Three, was gone. Torn down by the DMS. Top and Bunny had both been there when that group was ripped apart.

The Closers had been killed or arrested. Employment records from M3 had helped the DMS and the FBI track them all down. There were no Closers anymore. There was no M3 anymore. And no one had MPP pistols.

No one.

Except . . .

"Fuck me," said Bunny as he began inching toward the open door.

"No," said Top, "fuck them."

His fear was still there, but now anger was burning hotter than the flames that were eating the wall behind them.

"What's the play?" asked Bunny.

"Fuck 'em if they can't take a joke," said Top. He reached into his jacket, produced a micro-FB, flipped the arming switch with his thumb, and hurled it side-arm through the doorway.

The new generation of flash-bangs were tiny, less than a fifth the size of the M84 stun grenades used by the military. But the flash and the bang were 30 percent larger.

The explosion rocked the room and made the dividing wall shudder as if it had been rammed by a truck. The sprinklers overhead kicked on and the whole hallway was caught in a rainstorm.

"Go, go, GO!" yelled Top and they were up and running, moving around the edge of the doorway, pointing their guns, following their barrels into the room, cutting left and right, seeking targets.

The Closer who had shot at them was on the floor, his face scrunched up with pain, eyes blinking as he tried to see, his MPP held up in a two-hand grip as he fired blindly.

TOK!

TOK!

TOK!

The superheated microwave blasts tore the room apart.

Literally tore it apart. Desks and filing cabinets exploded into burning clouds of metal splinters and blazing paper. The whole doorway disintegrated into a cloud of superheated gas. Top once more felt himself lifted and thrown like a doll. He crashed into an oak desk, rebounded, and fell hard onto the floor. The world swirled around him like toilet water after a hard flush, and he fought to hang on to his gun and to his consciousness.

Bunny was somewhere on the other side of a cloud of burning dust, cursing and grunting. Top could hear the sound of a vicious fight as vague shapes moved in an awkward ballet.

The Closer got to his feet and swung the MPP toward him. His face was lined with pain from the flash-bang, and blood ran from both ears, but his eyes had cleared and there was a cruel smile on his hard mouth.

He said a single word as he raised his gun to fire.

"Sims."

Top shot him six times. Three to the chest, but that only staggered the man, and Top remembered that the Closers wore a micro-mesh undergarment that was harder to penetrate than Kevlar and whose structure nullified most of the foot-pounds of impact. The 9mm rounds drove him backward but didn't put him down.

The next three shots went into his face.

The cruel grin disintegrated into red nothingness and the rounds punched through the back of his skull, pulling streams of blood and brain matter behind them. The Closer went down and Top rolled onto his knees, sweeping around to find Bunny. Immediately he had to throw himself to one side as a figure came hurtling through the smoke toward him.

A big figure with blond hair, and for a terrible moment Top thought that it was Bunny.

But it was not.

This man was a stranger and unless Top read his autopsy report he would remain one. His head was twisted more than halfway around, and his eyes bulged with shocked awareness at how this day had ended so much differently than he expected. The big body landed hard and lay immobile.

By then Top was up and moving, running into the smoke.

He saw the third Closer and he saw Bunny.

The man saw him, too, and Top could see his eyes, could see the quick calculation of his eyes. The man knew he could not win this fight. Or maybe he did not want to roll those dice.

So he did something that Top would have thought impossible.

The man ducked under a looping right from Bunny that would have dropped a bull, grabbed the big young man by the arm and belt, picked him up, and hurled him at Top as easily as Top might have tossed a small suitcase. The man did not even grunt with the effort of lifting 240 pounds of solid muscle.

Top tried to get out of the way.

Tried.

Failed.

And went down.

By the time he and Bunny managed to untangle themselves, the Closer was gone. The office was filling with dense smoke and everything seemed to be on fire. They paused, looking around, trying to decide how to save the moment. The Closer was nowhere to be seen, and the other two were dead.

Top dragged Bunny to his feet and they ran for the elevator, but when the doors were halfway open they suddenly stopped. The lights went out, inside the car and in the hall. In fact the whole building seemed to go strangely still despite the water pulsing from the sprinklers. Then they died, too.

"Stairs," yelled Top and they blundered through the smoke to a crash-door and into a stairwell.

It was utterly black. Even the battery-operated emergency lights were dark. Far below they could hear the clatter of footsteps.

"Give a light," growled Top, but Bunny already had his powerful little penlight out. He slapped it into the clip on the underside of his gun. But the light did not flash on. There was nothing, not even the faintest glow. They stood for a moment, confused and disturbed, lit only by the trembling firelight behind them. The stairwell was like the mouth of a dragon, black and deep and treacherous.

Bunny leaned one hand on the rail. "We go down there and he's waiting . . ."

No need to finish it.

"How'd he kill all the damn lights?" asked Top. "Don't make no sense."

They saw a brief flash of daylight at the very bottom as the killer broke from the fire tower.

"Call it, Top," said Bunny.

If they had been dressed for combat they would have both been carrying nonelectric chemical flares. Below them the door swung shut and the stairwell was immediately plunged into total darkness.

"Call it in," said Top. "Let's get a BOLO out on this son of a bitch. And we need the fire department."

But, of course, their cell phones and earbuds were as dead as the lights. The fire behind them began to roar.

INTERLUDE TWENTY-ONE

Oscar Bell dreamed of her.

Or, maybe it was that she dreamed of him.

He was in his bedroom, alone in a midnight house, all the doors locked, all the alarms set. Dogs on the prowl, guards with guns. The way it always was.

Not that German shepherds and mercenaries with automatic weapons could keep them out.

No.

Nothing could keep them out.

Not unless he wore one of those ridiculous skullcaps. Jesus, he hated the thought. A grown man, a multibillionaire who owned more companies than he could count, a scientist and defense contractor, wearing a fucking aluminum foil hat. Well, technically a dome-shaped glass and crystal-lined metal alloy hat.

It blocked out most of the intrusions.

It stopped the dreamwalkers from stealing into his head and stealing his knowledge. It kept his slumbering mind from being complicit in the theft of his own technologies.

Shutting the barn door after the cows had run off, though. He was sure of it.

Not that Bell knew who exactly had been sneaking around in his head. Someone from Gateway, for sure. Some of Erskine's remote viewer spies, those fuckers.

And someone else.

Was it Prospero? Was the boy still alive? If so, what on Earth was he up to? The rumors Bell was hearing terrified and sickened him. ISIL, for Christ's sake. Selling the null field to a gang of insane murderers. How was that any kind of justice, even from Prospero's perspective?

How?

If it was true, and Oscar Bell did not have real proof.

Then there was Corrine.

She'd been in his dreams, and maybe inside his head twice now. Both times on nights when he forgot to wear the damn helmet.

Bell hated it. He was no romantic and even if he was, having someone inside his head like that was not romance. It was rape. It was a violation on a level that ran so deep that he wanted to saw open his head and scrub his brain with Lysol.

Damn the woman.

After the first time, he tried to call her, but her assistant said she was unavailable. After the tenth call Bell decided that Corrine was down at Gateway.

Last night's dream . . . well, that sealed it.

He'd become aware that he was sleeping. It was like that. You are asleep but then you realize that you're asleep. You are still inside your body but you are aware the body is sleeping.

That's how it began. And then she was there.

It was not like meeting her in the flesh. There was no flesh. It was her but it was like he could see her with some sense other than eyes. There is no word for it in the English language. "Sensed" her did not fit because there was no precise sensory input. No sight or smell, no sound or touch. But she was there and he knew it was her.

Corrine Sails. Stripped of everything. No uniform, no face. No skin or bones. No blood or breath.

Just her, whatever "she" was.

Bell knew why so many people had committed suicide. It was a nightmare encounter. Her thoughts were right there, shooting through him like electrical shocks, as if the nerve signals fired by neurons were stun guns. He had no defense against them and the power was raw and immediate. Bell wasn't sure how exactly his body was registering them. Again, there were no words for this kind of contact. It wasn't even a purely electrical connection, either. There had to be some of that, of course, or the helmets wouldn't work, but on the plane of communication there were other rules, other forces yet to be cataloged. Someone at Gateway had tried to coin the term "soul-speak" but it was too silly for the scientific and military minds to grasp.

Bell, despite his cynicism, thought it might be right.

What were souls, after all? If they existed at all, then they were some kind of energy that had no label in science. Yet. Quantum scientists would have to label them at some point, give them a properly sober Latin name, place them in a category, force them into a range, measure them and meter them.

That would come. Science wasn't there yet.

When Corrine stepped into his mind Bell was sure that the contact dragged them both into another place entirely. The soul level? Maybe.

Or another dimension.

Another world?

Another universe?

After all, the God Machine was Prospero's attempt to open a doorway that would take him to what he believed was his home. To another world, but not another planet.

To a different universe than this.

Or to a different plane of existence where words like "world" and "universe" and even "dimension" had no practical relevance.

They did not really talk to each other. Conversation is a product of organic machinery. Breath vibrating the larynx, tongue and lips forming words, the jaw hinge moving, and electrical impulses accessing memories and forming thoughts, using syntax and vocabulary. All physical things.

They had no bodies in that place.

But he heard her. Felt her. Whatever it needed to be called.

Corrine was trying to tell him something. He was sure of it.

Warn him?

Maybe. Probably.

But warn him about what? About who?

He couldn't remember what frightened her, only that something did. It terrified her. It was the only clear thing Bell could remember when he woke up.

However, he woke up naked, on the balcony where they often stood after making love. Except he stood on the stone rail, his toes over the edge, his body swaying as if trying to leap.

It took a lot of scotch to stop the shakes.

He did not know why he crawled under his desk with a gun.

All he knew is that after that night, he never went to sleep without that goddamn helmet.

CHAPTER FORTY-NINE

"The Gateway matter has presented us with a number of complications," said Mr. Church. "Particularly in the matter of reliable information. Most of the records are unavailable to us through our usual channels, and that includes MindReader. We know that the project was initiated fifteen years ago and the focus of the research being conducted at Gateway has changed many times. We know that Dr. Marcus Erskine was the head of the research and development team down there, and that they were working on several projects that, on the surface, appear to be unrelated."

"That's all we have?"

Church removed a folder from his briefcase and slid it across the table to me. "This is something Bug dug up for us from very deep in the records of the black operations file attached to Gateway. It's a fragment of a project proposal paper written thirteen years ago by Dr. Erskine."

I read it hungrily, needing answers. Unfortunately most of it was scientific mumbo jumbo that shot way over my head. However, there were footnotes and annotations in the distinctive scrawl of Hu's handwriting and Bug's juvenile scribble. The story this all told was bizarre. Erskine hadn't gone down there with one purpose in mind. Gateway was one of those cluster projects where several ultra-top-secret research programs were being conducted under one roof, with Erskine as overall director. Unfortunately each project had a code name. Kill Switch was the easiest to understand—a weapon that interrupted power. But also referenced—without useful explanations—were projects labeled "Dreamwalking," "Dreamshield," "God Machine," "Freefall," and "Unlearnable Truths."

Church was petting his cat and looked way too much like a James Bond villain. Even the gloves creeped me out.

"This is all we have?" I demanded.

"It's a piece of what was clearly a larger document. Bug said that most of it was scrubbed from the Net and this is part of an editing memo that he was able to salvage. The text is suggestive of certain kinds of projects that surface every once in a while. Psychic phenomena, esoteric espionage, thought projection."

"Thought projection? You mean mind control?"

"Possibly," he said. "I've put out some feelers for information on any project related to that, with a bias on anything that might explain what happened to Glory Price and Dr. Sanchez."

I sipped my coffee, realized it had grown cold, and splashed some warm into the cup. "Mind control . . . ? Is that even a real science?"

Church said, "There are a lot of radical projects in the various levels of R and D. Some are improbable, most hit walls and are proven to be unsound, some are merely unlikely, a few stretch credulity to the breaking point. But every now and then we advance the more arcane branches of science by an interesting inch or two."

I drained my cup and set it down. "We didn't get close enough to assess the process down at Gateway. And without our body cams and telemetry we got bupkes. Do you have anything else?"

"That was all Bug found. I asked him to dig deeper but so far he hasn't found anything of use."

"What about that QC thingie? I thought our new quantum computer could find anything."

"Bug hasn't fully integrated that science into MindReader," Church said quietly. "He has been readjusting."

I nodded glumly. Several months ago I'd recovered a prototype of a truly practical quantum computer. Normally Bug would have freaked out about it and danced the Snoopy dance, but the guys who owned that tech had made some vicious attacks against us, targeting our families in order to cripple the DMS. Bug's mother was killed by a small drone packed with explosives. Her murder nearly killed Bug, though in a different way. It took Church a lot to get him to even agree to come back to work. Since then Bug sounds and acts like his old self, but I think a lot of it's game face. My dad, Church's daughter Circe—who was pregnant at the time—and other innocents were also targeted. Rudy was attacked and Aunt Sallie nearly died. If Bug needed time to get up and running, then I wouldn't be the guy standing over him with a whip.

That said, I kind of wanted to stand over him with a whip because I fucking well needed to understand what happened in Antarctica. When, of course, I could actually stand.

I sighed. Very audibly, and Church gave a small, sympathetic nod.

"I'm not sure the QC would help," he said. "Even if we had all of the MindReader upgrades finished we still might be looking for something that does not exist on any computer."

"'Verbal briefing only,'" I quoted, and he nodded. "So what are we thinking about all this?"

"That is still a work in progress, Captain. We need a lot more information. Currently the pieces don't seem to fit together in any way I find comfortable."

"Well, join the damn club, Boss." I rubbed my tired eyes. "So, are we both thinking the same thing? That our friends from outside the neighborhood are the ones who built that city?"

"Ah," he said wistfully, "if there were only something left to study, then perhaps we could answer that question."

"You think I shouldn't have called in an air strike?"

"I wasn't there, Captain, and I try not to Monday-morning quarterback my officers. The call was made and that's that. Even if it was the same call I would have made, it still leaves me with regret that we can't explore that city."

"Yeah. Sorry I didn't pick you up a travel brochure, but I was in the moment."

"Apparently so. Unless we can identify and interrogate any surviving persons involved, we may never know what most of these programs are, or were," said Church. "Excavating the site is pointless. Have you seen the satellite pictures? Cartographers around the world will have to redraw their maps of Antarctica. To say that the president would very much like to have you skinned alive is not an understatement. He used those exact words."

"Nice to be admired for one's accomplishments."

Church gave me a sour look.

I said, "Well, okay, maybe I was going off the deep end when I tried to order a nuke—thanks for running interference on that one— but the rest? Yeah. You didn't see what we saw. Maybe it was us hallucinating, but I don't think so, which means the strikes I ordered kept whatever it was from getting out. Or . . . if it was some kind of psychic warfare, then this is on them for playing us. Either way, I stand by my call."

"Have you heard me say otherwise?"

"Yeah, well . . ." I stopped and changed the subject. "So . . . what does Bolton make of this? Does he think I'm crazy, too?"

"Harcourt has been very sympathetic to your recent troubles. He has also tried several times to intervene with the president. The fact that our charter has not been terminated is largely due to him."

"Ah. But what does he think about all of this?"

Church took a moment with that. "He was not involved in the Majestic affair, but he's been briefed on it. He knows that we are dealing with some extraordinary matters."

"You're dancing around it, Boss," I said. "He doesn't believe what Top, Bunny, and I saw down there, does he?"

Church picked up a cookie, looked at it, then set it down without taking a bite. "He has expressed some concern that, with a lack of evidence, we should all avoid jumping to conclusions."

"Sigh," I said. I got up and stretched my aching muscles and began pacing the room, feeling restless and angry.

"Harcourt is working the Kill Switch angle," said Church. "Portable directed-energy weapons, particularly jammers and EMP-type devices, are the next hot technology. The science of miniaturization is catching up to both military and terrorist needs for man-portable weapons of that kind. They are very attractive to terrorist groups because of the relatively low cost and ease of transport."

"Houston," I said. "That's ISIL, right? I mean that's what we all think?"

"It's a high probability, but they are being coy about taking credit because of the obvious global political and military backlash."

"Sure, if we knew it was them, then everyone would go on a witch hunt for them. A lot of civilians would get killed in the process, though."

"Regrettably, yes, but that witch hunt would happen. Nothing could stop it."

I squatted down to pet Ghost while I thought it through. "Houston was big," I said slowly, "but it wasn't enough. It was a stupid risk because of what you just said."

"But—?" he said, gesturing to encourage me to follow my thought.

"But, I think there's another shoe about to drop. Houston was a punch but it wasn't a knockdown punch. Not even close. Same for the racetrack and the debate. They were jabs, but somewhere there's a big overhand right coming. Whatever it's going to be, the Kill Switch thing is going to set it up."

"Agreed."

I straightened. "What about nuclear power plants? What would happen if they hit one of those with the Kill Switch device?"

"We looked at that," Church said. "If this was twenty or thirty years ago, then they would have had a real chance at causing a catastrophic nuclear event. But the safeguards built into all domestic nuclear power plants wouldn't permit it. Older systems were based on the SCRAM method that inserts chemicals into the reactor to effectively negate the reaction and cool down the rods. The SCRAM systems were electronically and mechanically based, and Kill Switch would have been effective against them. However, the newer systems are classified as passive designs, but these still require batteries if AC power is lost. The problem ISIL would face is that the emergency diesel generators on the current designs can be manually started. They use air-start motors. And the control rods are held out by electromagnets, so in the event of a power loss, gravity would let them drop into place, thus preventing overheating and meltdown."

"Well, that's a goddamn relief."

"It is," he agreed, "but it's not an answer to our question. What is their play?"

We knocked theories back and forth but it was all speculation. I was just about to get up and go find Harcourt Bolton—half-sure I wanted to fawn on him because he's my hero and half-sure I wanted to put two in the back of his head for invading my home turf—when Church's phone rang. I swear sometimes you can tell it's going to be bad news from the way the phone rings.

This was one of those times.

Church's phone rang and he took the call and he stiffened with new tension. "Thank you, First Sergeant. Come back here as soon as you are able."

He disconnected the call and told me about Top and Bunny.

INTERLUDE TWENTY-TWO

Oscar Bell set the phone down.

The sun was behind the trees and it threw somber brown shadows through the window. The sound of birds in the trees was wrong; they sounded like rude people talking in church. The house was still. Empty of children for years now, empty of wives old and new, empty of everyone except the live-in staff who knew not to make noise and not to be seen. The mansion was so big these days. Once, the sixteen bedrooms and eighteen baths, the formal and casual dining rooms, the kitchens, the sitting rooms and libraries and offices had all felt alive. Vibrant.

That was then.

It was different now and Bell could feel the change.

He could hear it. On evenings like these the wind came whispering off the ocean and found cracks in the walls and gaps in the windows, and it howled at him.

Like ghosts.

He wondered if one of those ghosts belonged to Prospero.

Was the boy dead? Or was he alive somewhere in the world, hating him, as Bell knew he deserved to be hated?

Was he even on this world?

Bell had no idea.

Such a loss.

He wondered about Prospero's mother. Surrogate or not, she had loved the boy as much as a fractured mind like hers could love. As much as a broken heart like hers could love. When she killed herself it was an act of murder and it stole something from this place. From Bell, too. Even from him.

And now Corrine.

Gone.

"Suicide" is such a clinical word but it was safer than the truth. It was a buffer from the details.

Erskine had told him, though. He'd been happy to, the cold-hearted son of a bitch. He'd used the details like a knife to stab him.

"The silly bitch took off all her clothes and went walking out in the snow," Erskine had said. "She'd shit herself, of course. But that was before she went outside. Stupid cow."

Erskine had to know that Bell and Corrine were sleeping together. He was like that. He knew. And he had the God Machine. He had those dreamers.

Sadistic sick fuck of a bastard.

Telling him about Corrine was the knife, but it wasn't the point of the call.

"The project is a failure, Oscar," said Erskine. "After a careful review we can only conclude that you were aware of the unreliability of the machine. That you knew about the instability and chose not to inform us is nonfeasance. That you were informed by Major Sails of problems at our facility related to the device and still chose not to provide information is malfeasance. You have grossly violated the terms of our agreement and you are in further violation of the spirit as well as the word of the understanding between you and the Department of Defense. Our attorneys are filing actions against you and I have no doubt we will recover all fees paid to you and receive a judgment of penalties for damages."

The words battered Bell, driving him down into his chair and almost onto the floor.

"Marcus . . . why are you doing this? We're family, for Christ's sake!"

"Family?" Erskine burst out laughing. "Even after all this you really don't understand how the world works, Oscar."

That had been the end of the call.

After that it was the lawyers and the process servers. The federal agents who came to seize the property and all his holdings. The bank officers who told him that his assets had been frozen. The IRS account managers who called to schedule audits.

It all came tumbling down.

Down, down, down.

And yet through all of it all he could do was think of Corrine Sails. That mind. That devious, lovely mind.

Gone.

His own mind, always cruel, conjured memories for him. The taste of the side of her throat. The feel of her nipples as they grew hard between his lips. The heat of her when he slipped inside. The sounds she made when she came. Guttural, primal. Ringing now in his ears.

Those memories were like knives to him.

Those memories were like swords.

There wasn't enough scotch in all of Long Island to drown them away.

It was a terrible, terrible thing to realize that love is in the heart only after the heart itself is too badly broken to contain it.

CHAPTER FIFTY

Top and Bunny wouldn't be back to the Pier for an hour, so I stumbled down to the office that had been commandeered by Harcourt Bolton. His secretary—one of his people, not one of mine—told me that he was out of the building. I left a request for a meeting when he got back.

"You're Captain Ledger?" said the receptionist, a busty Nordic blonde with big plastic boobs, collagen lips, and merciless eyes. The name on her desk placard said MUFFY. There are so many jokes I might have made had it been a different day. "You used to run this place, as I understand."

I wanted to yap at her like a kicked dog and tell her that I *still* ran the Pier, but I didn't have the energy for a losing fight. Instead I slunk away with Ghost in tow.

On the elevator I looked down at him. "We are not having a good day, kiddo."

He wagged his tail at me. So I gave him a dog cookie.

My office was where I left it, and I was thankful I hadn't actually been evicted from the building. Small comforts are better than none.

"Can I get you anything?" Lydia-Rose asked after giving me a thorough up-and-down appraisal.

"Coffee."

"Weren't you finishing a big Starbucks when you got here?"

"Yes."

"Did you have any of the coffee I put in the conference room?"

"Maybe."

"Don't you think you've had too much already? Your hands are shaking."

"Three things," I told her. "First, there's no such thing as too much coffee. Second, caffeine has nothing to do with my jitters. And third, there's no such thing as too much coffee."

She sighed and went over to the big Mr. Coffee and began making a fresh pot. I heard her say several things in back-alley Spanish that questioned my sanity, my parentage, and my personal hygiene. I went inside and slammed the door.

After a couple of tries I managed to get Bug on the line for a video-conference. When his face filled my laptop screen I saw that he was still trying to grow a goatee. A recent style choice that wasn't working out all that well. Bug's in his late twenties but puberty hasn't completely unpacked its suitcase in his genes. His brown face was dusted with about nine black hairs.

"Looking good," I told him.

"Oh . . . bite me," he said. He wore a baggy gray sweatshirt with UNIVERSITY OF WAKANDA stenciled on the chest. "How are you doing, Joe?"

"I've had better incarnations," I admitted.

"Should you even be at work?"

"Considering the day I'm having so far," I said, "I'm thinking about returning to the hospital and asking if they can put me back into a coma."

"Ouch. Hey, that whole thing down in Antarctica was weird," he said. "Freaky."

"You think?"

"No, I mean I'm genuinely freaked. I'm into the whole Cthulhu Mythos thing and—"

"The what?"

"Didn't Mr. Church tell you about the book, *At the Mountains of Madness*?"

"Only a little about the author. H. P. Lovecraft, right?"

"You ever read his stuff?"

"A few short stories maybe."

"Okay, short version is that Lovecraft created a kind of fantasy backstory to his horror stories. Gods, alien races, monsters, other dimensions. Like that. His stories were self-referential. You see, there's this race of ancient space beings called the Great Old Ones who used to rule the Earth. They lost control of the world over time and some of them left and others went to sleep. One of the biggest and baddest of these gods is Cthulhu, and he's asleep in the undersea city of R'lyeh. A lot of the stories deal with people who stumble onto a cult who worship one of the monsters, or in some cases have managed to interbreed with them or their even more monstrous servants, or they catch a glimpse of one and go totally gaga nuts. In the stories these creatures either live in places here on Earth that are so remote no one ever goes there—except the poor dumb son of a bitch of a protagonist—or they exist in a parallel dimension. Sometimes Lovecraft kind of confused the two. You're just lucky you didn't run into any *shoggoths* down there."

"What a *shoggoth*? Or do I even want to know?"

"Not really. The *shoggoths* are this race of shapeshifting monsters created by another race of ancient creatures called the Elder Things."

"Not the Great Old Ones?"

"No. It's complicated, I know. The Elder Things were more like space travelers who settled on Earth a billion years ago. They built huge cities, and believe me, Joe, I've been losing sleep ever since I heard how you guys described the city you saw. It fits."

I said nothing, trying to let it sink in. Trying to decide what I believed. What I could allow myself to believe.

"This whole cycle of stories is the Cthulhu Mythos," Bug said. "Lovecraft invited his writer friends to tell their own Cthulhu stories. A lot of them did. A whole lot. People still do. There are thousands of Cthulhu stories, and a lot of them are actually better than the stuff Lovecraft wrote. Even Stephen King. You can see the influence everywhere. You know those Hellboy movies you like so much? That's inspired by Cthulhu. But, between you and me, Lovecraft was a misogynistic, racist jerk who couldn't write dialogue worth a darn."

"Useful to know," I said. "But, kid, I'm pretty sure I don't believe any of this shit."

"You were in the city, Joe. Bunny got his face eaten off by a giant penguin, and Erskine got funding to develop a whole line of psychic weapons. Want to hear a wild theory, Joe?" asked Bug, leaning close to the screen as if afraid of being overheard.

"No," I said weakly, "I really don't."

"I'm kind of thinking it's real. Or some of it, anyway. Like I said, I've read all of this stuff and there have been people over the years who've suggested that Lovecraft wasn't so much making this up as having visions. They did a History Channel special once about how the artists from the surrealism movement believed they were painting images from other worlds they traveled to in dreams. And Erskine had programs called 'Dreamwalking' and 'Dreamshield.' I'm just saying. There was something down there, and between you and me, I'm really glad you called in an air strike. Imagine what would have happened if terrorists or even a foreign power got their hands on these kinds of weapons?"

I looked around my office for something to drink, but there was no booze. Someone had even swiped all the beers from my fridge. Maybe they thought I was never going to come out of the coma. Inhuman bastards. Ghost came over and leaned against me. To comfort me or maybe to receive some for himself. I ran my fingers through his thick fur. "Bug," I said, "you're hitting me with all this, but where does it take us? What do I do with it?"

He shook his head and it was clear my question punched him in the gut. He sagged and looked lost. "Oh, man . . . I really don't know. I just look stuff up. You're the field guy." He tried on a smile but it didn't fit well. "Everything's gotten weird lately, you know? All those screwed-up missions. We've faced some big things before, but nothing like this. We took down the Seven Kings, we busted up the Jakobys and Majestic Three and the Red Knights, but man . . . what's happened to us? We dropped the ball on so many jobs they're not letting us anywhere near the ISIL thing. And the Gateway stuff is past tense. That place is gone. Are we just spinning our wheels? God, I never felt so lost before."

Bug and I studied each other through the digital magic of the teleconference screen, saying nothing for a long time. Then he cleared his throat.

"You ought to talk to Junie, she's into a lot of this weird stuff."

"I know, but I'll have to get clearance from Church. In the meantime, all we can do is work on this. So let's work it. What have you dug up on Erskine?"

Bug tapped a few keys and scanned the data. "A lot and not much. Erskine was rich and well connected. His whole family is made up mostly of industrialists and defense contractors. They've been making all kinds of dangerous toys for the government going back to the Civil War. They were heavily into Pittsburgh steel before that went south, then they moved into advanced R and D."

"Doing what kind of research?"

"You name it. Radar and sonar systems. *Anti*-radar and sonar systems. Control systems for tanks and fighters. Aerodynamics for stealth aircraft. New hull designs for attack and missile subs. Composite materials for fighter craft hulls. Erskine had a couple of dozen subsidiary companies, but he directly oversaw the electronics division."

"Particle accelerators?"

"Not Erskine, but his partner, Raoul San Pedro, worked on some of that. He was down at Gateway, so I guess he's dead. Pretty much everyone on Erskine's team was there."

"San Pedro? Isn't that the guy whose office Top and Bunny were at today?"

From Bug's expression it was clear that he knew about the encounter with the Closers. "San Pedro worked on several accelerators. His great-grandfather worked on the nine-inch cyclotron at UC Berkeley back in the early thirties, and contributed to the eleven-, twenty-seven-, and thirty-seven-inch versions. His grandfather helped build Berkeley's Isochronous cyclotron in 1950. And his dad is on the patent for the super proton synchrotron they built at CERN."

"Uh-huh," I said, barely following. "Bunch of brainiacs, got it. What about the machine we saw down at Gateway? *Was* that an accelerator?"

"I did image comparisons of the drawings you, Top, and Bunny made of the one you saw at Gateway and that thing you saw *looked* like a hadron collider, but it wasn't exactly the same. Maybe that's because your sketches are kind of, well, sketchy. Anyway, I talked to a bunch of eggheads and the thing nobody understands so far is that the one down there was built more like a tunnel that curved down into the earth, right? It wasn't a circular loop?"

"No, unless it was unfinished."

"Still wouldn't make sense. You wouldn't build one at that angle. These things are circular with no sharp bend, and never upright. And they are massive. We're talking thousands of tons of material, and they build them flat so gravity doesn't warp the structure. That's how they get the particles up to speed, by running them in a circle as close to the speed of light as you can manage, and then you collide them with particles going in the opposite direction. The machine you saw isn't configured for that. You said that the one down there blew air at you?"

"Real damn hard. That's how we all got sick."

He shook his head. "Yeah, that's not making any kind of sense."

"If it's not an accelerator, then what was it?"

"Beats the crap out of me, Joe. And so far it's beating the crap out of everyone I talk to."

"Other than Erskine and San Pedro, who else are we looking at?"

He leaned close and dropped his voice again. "Look, Joe, I, um, *might* have looked into Mr. Bolton's computer records. A bit. You know?"

"Why? Has he done something naughty?"

"What? Bolton? God, no. It's just that he has a higher clearance than Mr. Church right now. At least as far as the Kill Switch thing goes. But . . . well, I guess I got nosy."

"I ought to hit you with a rolled-up newspaper," I said. "Did you find anything?"

"Not sure. Mr. Church showed you the stuff I got before, right? The black budget report? Did you see the mention of a project called the God Machine? Well, I don't know what it is, but there were two names in a footnote. One marked with an 'I,' which means inventor, and one with a 'D' for developer. Both had the same last names and I think I know who they are. The inventor is P. Bell, and that's got to be that weirdo Prospero Bell."

"Who?"

"Son of Oscar Bell? He's the other name, the developer. O. Bell."

"Again I say, who?"

"Oscar Bell is Erskine's brother-in-law. Or he was. He was married to Erskine's sister. She's dead, though."

"There was no Oscar Bell on the personnel list at Gateway."

"Uh-uh. Oscar's a private defense contractor. Or he used to be. His company went bankrupt a few years ago and he started drinking. After that he fell off the public radar. I'm running a deep background on him to see if he's anywhere."

"What about the son?"

"Oh, man, that's a really sad story," said Bug. "Prospero was this genius kid that was supposed to be smarter than Stephen Hawking. Super-freak intelligence. Way off the scale. Incredible inventor, though. Published papers on particle physics and quantum theory when he was a teenager, and from what I can tell from the people I've talked to, Prospero was as crazy as he was smart. Some of his theories are groundbreaking and other scientists have been trying to catch up because it's apparently going to open all sorts of new doors in research. Other stuff he came up with was nutty. But Prospero also had a lot of emotional problems. His dad sent him to a military boarding school to try and straighten him out, and even paid to have a state-of-the-art lab built for him. But that backfired. First he blew up the lab, and then a couple of years later he set fire to the whole school and tried to break out."

"Tried? What happened to him?"

"Died in the fire. Him and a friend."

"So how's his name on a black budget request for Gateway?"

"From the dates on the report, the God Machine is apparently something Prospero came up with when he was still a teenager. From the way I'm reading this, his father took the design, whatever it was, and sold it to the government. At first they paid him for it, and those are pretty big numbers; but then something happened and they took it away from him and sued him to recover the monies paid. That's what broke him."

I chewed on that for a moment. "Jesus, Bug, this is the first solid lead we have. Do whatever you have to do to find this guy."

"Sure, but like I said, you should talk to Junie."

"Why?"

"Remember that conspiracy theory podcast she used to do when you guys first met? I used to listen to it all the time. She had Oscar Bell on her show once. If anyone knows where he is, it'll probably be her."

CHAPTER FIFTY-ONE

I picked up the phone to call Junie but before I could even push a button it rang and it was she.

"How are you?" she asked.

"Wishing I was still in a coma," I joked. She didn't think that was funny. "Look, baby, any chance you can drop what you're doing and come to the Pier? Mr. Church and I have a few things we need to talk to you about."

"Is it urgent?"

"Depends. I can hear a helicopter. Where are you?"

"About to fly inland. There's an environmental engineer I need to see. Linda Higdon. She has a water reclamation process that might work with something we've been developing here at FreeTech. Linda's going to be at a testing facility out by the Salton Sea but only for the rest of the day and then she's on a flight to Kenya. I've been trying to arrange this for months. If her process is compatible, we could maybe reclaim five million gallons a day once it's up and running. Think about what that would mean to the farmers who are being crushed by the drought."

"That's actually kind of amazing," I said, not joking.

"Do you need me to cancel with her, or—?"

I could tell she wanted me to say no, so I said no. The DMS was warming the bench right now, and even the stuff Church and I were banging back and forth was by-product. It's not like the president was letting us do our jobs. Damn it.

"No, it's good. Go talk to your scientist. Will you be home tonight?"

"Yes, but late. If you don't feel like you can be alone, go over to Sam's place. He has a guest room."

"It's all good," I assured her. "I have plenty of people to hold my hand."

She paused. "I hate to do this. You've only just come home."

"I love you, too. Go save the world."

And she was gone.

CHAPTER FIFTY-TWO

SCRIPPS MEMORIAL HOSPITAL LA JOLLA
9888 GENESEE AVENUE
LA JOLLA, CALIFORNIA
SEPTEMBER 8, 3:47 P.M.

Top and Bunny were still at the crime scene, Bolton wasn't back yet, Church was on the phone being yelled at by the president, and I didn't have any beer in my fridge. So I checked out, leaving a request for Lydia-Rose to call me the second Top and Bunny got back.

With Ghost trotting beside me I got into my car and went to visit Rudy.

And immediately wished I hadn't. Rudy looked small and shrunken, paled to a ghost, wrapped like a mummy. He had bandages over his face with a metal brace to hold his nose in shape. He wore a soft cervical collar. His leg was hung from straps and framed by a postsurgical sling. The broken nose had given him two black eyes.

His wife, Circe, had been very reluctant to let me in. Even though it had been Rudy who attacked me, she seemed to regard me as a thug who had attacked and brutalized her husband. Mind you, she didn't actually call me a thug. That was the word Rudy had used and it hung in my head.

Thug. Weird, but the shadowy figure in my dreams had called me that, too.

It took some time and a lot of promises, but Circe agreed to let me in. She sat on the far side of the bed, holding one of Rudy's hands in both of hers. Circe is a beautiful woman with masses of curly hair and olive skin. A fierce and uncompromising intelligence glittered in her dark eyes. I was godfather to her son but in that moment I was the man who crippled her husband. I sat across from her and held Rudy's other hand. The room was silent for a long time. It wasn't a chatty moment, and it was maybe forty minutes or an hour before I felt Rudy's hand twitch. His fingers curled to grasp mine. He was weak but there was a desperate strength in those fingers. I got to my feet and leaned over him.

"Hey," I said gently, "hey, brother . . ."

Rudy has one real eye and one glass. Another souvenir of violence that came his way during our time at the DMS. Another unfair mark on a good and decent man. Both eyes look real, and I swear both were filled with a pain born of the awareness of what had happened.

"I'm sorry," I said. "God, Rudy, I'm so sorry."

He started to shake his head, then winced as the bruised muscles and tendons in his neck protested. He hissed. A tear gathered in the corner of his good eye and fell down past his cheek and ear before melting into the foam of the cervical collar.

"J-Joe . . . ," he breathed, his voice weak and faint.

"I'm here, Rudy."

"Joe . . . that . . . that wasn't me. . . ."

"I know, Rude, it's all—"

"No," he said with more force. Circe stood up and he saw her, his eyes ticking back and forth between us. "No . . . that was not *me*."

"I know," I said.

It wasn't him, of that I was certain. But who—or what—was it?

The pain of his injuries—physical and psychic—began to scream at him. Circe called the nurse and they added something to his IV and Rudy went down into darkness. Like a coward, like a fool who knows nothing, I left him there and went out into the bright sunshine of a day whose rules I had utterly failed to grasp.

CHAPTER FIFTY-THREE

"Why did you do it?"

Senior DMS field agent Captain Allison Craft asked the question for the fiftieth time. Maybe the hundredth. She'd lost count. The man in the chair, Mr. Nathan Cross, said the same thing he'd said each of those times.

"I don't know."

They were in an interview room at the Central District building. Captain Craft, topkick of Rimfire Team, the DMS field office in Milwaukee, had commandeered the room and the prisoner. Craft had flashed Homeland credentials and Aunt Sallie had cleared the red tape. The police, who were seldom generous when it came to sharing their prisoners or yielding jurisdiction, seemed happy to let this case go up the food chain. There were seventeen dead at Bristol Labs, and virtually everyone else employed there was either in the hospital—many critical—or in cells. Only a few had escaped without going crazy. Jerry Spencer, the DMS forensics chief, had brought in his team and it was clear that a powerful hallucinogen had been introduced to the staff, likely through the coffee and tea urns. Tests were being conducted, but the nature of the drugs used to cause the outbreak held less critical importance than what Cross had stolen from the lab and sent flying off on a drone.

The drone had been found two miles away in a field near the entrance to the highway. There was nothing in the metal container bolted to its undercarriage.

"Why did you do this?" demanded Craft, who was both scared and frustrated.

Nate Cross sat there, shocked, horrified, tears and snot running down his face, skin blanched white, cuffed hands trembling with a palsy born of realization of what he had done.

"God . . . God . . . ," he said, his words tumbling out, lips shiny with spit, ". . . I don't know, I don't know, I don't know. . . ."

He could describe some of what had happened, and Craft was confused because the man seemed to want to help. He was desperate to help, but there were huge gaps in his memory.

"It was like I was watching it," said Cross. "Like it wasn't me. I could feel it . . . see it. All of it. But it wasn't me doing it. I swear to God."

"You're going to have to do a whole lot better than that," snarled Craft. "Do you want to see the video again? Do you want to see what you did? I'll show it to you again."

"No!" he wailed, and he looked from her to Davis, her partner, and back again. Sobbing, pleading, begging them to believe what he was saying. "Please, God . . . it wasn't me. I swear to God Jesus it wasn't me."

Craft's phone rang. She glanced at the display. "Auntie," she said.

"Go ahead," said Davis. "I got this."

Craft stepped out into the hall to take the call. "He's holding to it," she said into the phone. "We've been at it for hours and he hasn't budged. And, I don't think he's feeding us a line. Something happened to him and—"

"Listen to me, girl," said Aunt Sallie in a voice that could blister paint, "you put on your big girl panties and go get me some answers. I'm going to call you back in one hour and I want to hear something useful, do you hear me, sweetcheeks?"

"I—"

The line went dead.

"Bitch," breathed Craft, resisting the urge to drop her phone and stomp on it. The interview room door was closed and she stood for a moment glaring at it, willing the situation inside to be different than what she'd left a moment ago. She took a breath, squared her shoulders, and reached for the knob.

That was when she heard the gunshot.

Through the door it was a muffled *pok*.

"*Oh, shit*," she cried and tore the door open, drawing her own gun, fearing what had happened. Fearing that Cross had somehow gotten free and . . .

She froze in the doorway. Nathan Cross sat there with his head thrown back, mouth open, eyes staring up at the ceiling. There was a small black hole above the bridge of his nose. Behind him the wall was splashed with bright red that was speckled with bits of gray and knots of hair.

Phil Davis stood beside Cross's chair, his Sig Sauer in his hand.

"Jesus Christ, Phil . . . *what have you done?*"

Davis turned to her and smiled. "Sorry, Phil's not here at the moment," he said. And he shot Allison Craft twice in the face.

He was still smiling when he put the hot barrel under his own chin and blew the top of his head off.

CHAPTER FIFTY-FOUR

I'd left my car with the valet people with orders to keep the engine running and air-conditioning up high. Ghost sat in the front passenger seat, head erect, brown eyes watching me, and there was a weird spark of suspicion in his eyes. He even bent to sniff me when I slid behind the wheel. He made a noncommittal *huff* sound.

"The fuck's with you?" I demanded.

Ghost flinched back from the severity of my tone and I immediately felt bad. The dog was scared and confused. Maybe it was the smell of the hospital. Maybe it was the stink of my own fear and shame. Either way I had no reason to bark at him. So I twisted in my seat and bent close to press my forehead against his. We do that. Junie calls it a mind kiss. For me it's a pure animal thing, a communication between members of the same pack. Only this time Ghost pulled back. He turned and looked out the window as if I wasn't there. Or, as if he was looking for his real pack leader. I stroked his fur but he did not respond at all. It made me strangely sad and disconnected. I put the car in gear, pulled out of the parking lot, and began heading back to the Pier.

I was on Mission Bay Drive behind an old De Soto woody with surfboards on the roof and stickers all over the back from great beaches all over the world. I could see a pair of shaggy blond heads in the front, broad brown shoulders—one set bare, one in a dark tank top. An old Del Shannon tune floated back at me from their open windows. "My Little Runaway." Ah, it must be great to have nothing to do and be able to surf the waves, work on your tan, romp with the sun bunnies, hoist cold ones with your crew, and listen to that old-time rock and roll That's what sunny Southern California days are made for. If you have troubles, go drown them in the big blue Pacific. Feed your worries to the fish.

The red light turned green and the small convoy—the surfer boys and me—started up. Road speed was forty and we'd just gotten to thirty-five when the driver suddenly stamped hard on the brakes. I was two car lengths back and I have fast reflexes, but the front of my Explorer still chunked into the back of the De Soto. Not hard enough to deploy the airbags but hard enough to hurl me against the seat belt with enough force to snap my teeth shut and half the breath to be punched out of my lungs. Ghost went flying forward, slamming heavily into the glove compartment and then crashing down into the footwell. He yelped and barked and then began to growl as he scrambled to claw his way back onto the seat.

I threw the car into park, and sat there, neck hurting and head swimming.

Through the window I could see the two surfer jocks open their doors and step out. One wore bright blue trunks and woven hemp sandals, no shirt. The other had a threadbare SURF SAN DIEGO tank top over khaki shorts and flip-flops. Ghost was leaning forward, nose pressed to the windshield, muzzle wrinkled, teeth bared. I was so pissed that I was tempted to let the dog go use his teeth to teach these stoners some manners. Instead I clicked my tongue a couple of times to give him the code for standing down. He continued to growl, so I poked his shoulder with a stiff forefinger.

"Ghost, settle."

He turned toward me, teeth still bared, and growled again. At me.

My anger turned to a deep and sudden apprehension.

"Ghost," I said, forcing my voice to be firm, commanding, but calm, "*settle.*"

We stared at each other for five long seconds. The look in Ghost's eyes was hostile, feral. His six titanium teeth—replacements after a fight with Red Knights in Iran—glittered like daggers. I love my dog, and my heart was hammering at the thought that this moment might twist its way down into something weird and bad.

Then I saw doubt flicker in those familiar brown eyes. His muzzle trembled, the lips dropping to cover those teeth.

"Ghost," I said, "settle."

The tension drained slowly from his muscular shoulders and neck and he sagged back, looking confused and even a little scared by what had happened between us. He whimpered softly and thumped his tail. I reached slowly over to him and he pressed his head into my palm. I wanted to pull him close, hug him, fix whatever was wrong between us.

I never got the chance.

There was a heavy thud on the outside of my door, hard enough to rock the car on its springs. I whipped around to see Blue Shorts cock his leg for a second kick. Ghost snapped back into combat mode, rising, snapping out a warning bark.

Tank Top kicked the window on Ghost's side of the car. It was a powerful kick that sent a crack running from side to side. It sent Ghost into a frenzy, barking loud enough to burst my eardrums and throwing his body against the glass.

So I thought, fuck it.

I jerked the door open. Ghost whirled and I gave him a command. "Roll down."

It was our code for taking someone down but not killing them. He shot past me with a look of wild animal joy in his dark eyes. He shot past Blue Shorts and there was a howl—human, I think—as Ghost launched himself at Tank Top.

Blue Shorts tried to deck me as I got out of the car. He kicked the door, trying to smash my leg, but I jammed it with the heel of my palm, then shoved it open as I got out. He swung a heavy right hook punch at my face, and he put his whole body into it, trying to drop me with a single blow. Even weak and wasted I slap-parried the hit and drilled a single-knuckle punch into the flat meat of his left pectoral. It staggered him, but not as much as it should have. He was muscular and his chest was beefy, but he wasn't made of stone. That punch should have hurt him, but he shook it off and waded into me with a series of fast lefts and rights, swinging wide but not wild, trying to get torque into his hits so they'd do real damage.

There are a lot of ways to manage a fight. If I thought this clown was a real bad guy, a killer, I'd have put him down in about two seconds. If you're an expert, killing is easier than controlling. Thing was, though, I didn't know why he was attacking me. He was dressed for the beach and he looked like an overgrown beach bum. A professional might have dressed like this for surprise but in such a case there would be a gun in play by now. He was just wailing on me. Maybe he was high, maybe he was nuts. I danced backward, tucking my chin, using shoulders and elbows and palms to keep him from doing real damage, and all the time I was yelling at him to get him to stop, to tell me what was going on. He said nothing. His eyes were glazed, almost unfocused, and there was very little expression on his face.

Suddenly an icy hand clamped around my heart. It was exactly the same kind of expression that had been in Rudy's eyes.

Exactly the same.

Shit.

Ghost had the other guy down, and I could hear growls but no screams. That wasn't good. All around me cars were stopping and people were gathering, watching, yelling, demanding to know what was going on.

Blue Shorts slipped a nice one past my guard and tagged me solidly in the short ribs, driving the air out of my lungs in a deep whoosh. The Killer inside my soul roared and I could feel his bloodlust, his murderous desires trying to batter aside my conscious control. God, if he took over this fight, then surfer boy here was going to die in a quick and ugly way.

I jumped backward out of range of his next punch, and away from my own ability to reach out with a killing blow.

And then the Killer was gone.

There was a sudden immense silence inside my head. The red rage was gone as soon as it had appeared. The other aspects of myself, the Modern Man and the Cop, were jarred into silence, too.

The next punch nearly took my head off.

I heard someone yell, "Hey—*watch*!"

I got a hand up just in time, but the blow was packed with everything Blue Shorts had. It crashed into my forearm and sent me reeling sideways into a parked car. I rebounded and he hit me with a straight right hand to the chest that stalled me into a statue. It was like having a mining machine bore a hole straight through my sternum and out through my backbone. Then Blue Shorts closed in to smash me with an elbow across the face.

I fell against him to jam the blow and because I had nothing else. Not in that instant. I was bigger and heavier than him and my sagging weight drove us both backward like a boxer clinching with a better fighter while trying to catch a little air. Lights were exploding inside my head and I knew that I was maybe one hit away from going down.

So I used the clumsy embrace to slam him against the fender of my car. As we hit I drove my knee into his crotch, head-butted him, and then grabbed his hair and jerked his head down as I brought my knee up again. It mashed him. His nose and lips split and the power went out of his knees. Gasping and dazed, I shoved myself back from him and took him down with a sloppy foot-sweep. He landed hard and badly and lay there, curling into a fetal ball.

I staggered back and had to lean on the car to walk around it, afraid of what I was going to find on the other side. Tank Top was down and bloody, but Ghost had been in more control of his fight than I had. His guy was chopped up a bit, but not in any way that wouldn't heal. Tank Top would be fine after some stitches, some cosmetic surgery, and a lot of physical therapy. He got off lucky, because although Ghost is a loveable goof most of the time he is by nature and training a killer. He has a lot of experience in the hunt and in the kill.

I got some flex-cuffs out of my car and bound both men and then leaned like a sloppy drunk against the door and called the police and the Pier.

CHAPTER FIFTY-FIVE

The EMTs took the surfer boys away and I wasted time filling out police reports. By the time I got back to the Pier I could feel each separate place where I'd been hit, and I hurt. A lot.

I went over it with Church, with the duty officer, with Lydia-Rose, with the DMS attorneys. The story did not vary and it did not make sense. Was this a mugging? Was it some kind of drug-induced road rage? Neither of the surfers had a record more serious than parking tickets. Neither had any political ties of any significant kind.

So . . . what was this?

I thought of Rudy and Glory Price and wondered it if was possible for there to be such a thing as a plague of random violence. Normally that would be the kind of question I'd ask Rudy.

Damn it.

I went into my office bathroom and splashed some cold water on my face and wondered who the hell the old guy was who looked back at me from the mirror. Thin, sallow, with bags under his eyes and a shifty expression. I wouldn't trust that face if I was seated next to him on the bus.

"Well," I told him, "are you a lot of fun to be around."

He told me to go fuck myself.

My phone rang and I hurried back to take the call. It was Church and I could hear the whine of a helicopter behind him. An echo of that reached me through my window and it was clear he was on the roof helipad.

"Where are you going?" I asked.

"Airport," he said. "I'm going to Madison."

He told me about the incident at Bristol-Hermann Laboratories, and the subsequent murder-suicide at the police station. Captain Allison Craft and her partner were dead. So was the only suspect who could explain what happened.

"What did they get away with?" I asked.

He said, "That lab processes rare strains, mutated strains, and weaponized strains of highly infectious diseases. The perpetrator stole samples of several of the most virulent diseases currently in existence. And, Captain . . . one of them is SX-56."

I nearly slid out of my chair. The room was suddenly too bright, the edges of everything too sharply defined. It felt like I was surrounded by things that could cut me.

SX-56.

"Jesus Christ . . . ," I breathed. I've faced all kinds of monsters, but it's not the ones with fangs and claws that scare me. Not really. It's the ones too small to hit, too small to shoot. Viruses.

SX-56 was a hypervirulent strain of smallpox. The disease has been killing people since at least 10,000 BC. They found traces of it on the mummy of Pharaoh Ramses V. At the end of the eighteenth century it was killing four hundred thousand people each year in Europe alone. It ravaged the skin, caused blindness in many of its victims, and even though it was lethal to everyone, it was particularly aggressive in kids, killing 80 percent of those infected. Conservative global estimates of people killed by smallpox in the early to mid-twentieth century? Maybe five hundred million.

Be with that number for a moment. Let it bite you deep enough to bleed.

Even during the height of the Cold War, the United States and the Soviet Union worked together to produce vaccines that stopped the disease in its tracks. The global eradication of smallpox was declared December 9, 1979. The monster was dead. We'd won.

Except that we didn't.

Samples of the smallpox virus existed in labs, in viral storage facilities, and in government bioweapons research centers. Yeah . . . the kinds of labs that are illegal according to all international treaties. But Russia has them, so does China, and every other major power.

So do we.

A few years ago new cases of smallpox began cropping up. Mutant strains that were resistant to the vaccines. They struck and they went away. Over and over again. The press lauded the World Health

Organization doctors who descended on the outbreak sites and prevented the spread, and yes, those guys are actual superheroes. But here's the thing . . . those outbreaks were deliberate and careful experiments conducted by terrorist groups. It was a pattern I've seen too often. I shut down a few of these labs, and in such cases I tended to be moderately harsh. Scorched earth harsh.

The latest and deadliest strain of smallpox was SX-56, developed in Russia by a team officially labeled as "rogues." I knew better. Everyone in my line of work knew better. They were no more rogue than the Ghost Net hackers who were officially disavowed by the Chinese government.

SX-56 is a monster. There's nothing scarier. It's on a par with *seif al din* and Lucifer 113. Yeah, that kind of scary. It is an ultra-quick-onset weaponized pathogen. Because the virus has a simple gene structure it doesn't need much incubation time. Unlike anthrax, there's no specific drug, antibiotic, or antiviral medicine that can treat people who have it. You get it and you die. If you're an adult you might live long enough to see your children die first. It is an immensely cruel weapon. I knew that research samples of it existed at the CDC, the National Institutes for Health, the FDA, and even in labs affiliated with Homeland Security. The lack of tighter regulations is one of the reasons I never get a good night's sleep.

And Nathan Cross stole it and sent it off strapped to a fucking drone.

Holy God. Is the entire world insane? I mean, really . . . tell me that we're not all out of our son of a bitching minds.

"What the hell is happening?" I demanded. "Why are people going crazy?"

"I don't know," said Church. "I'm afraid many of the answers are buried down at Gateway."

He hadn't meant it to hurt, but it hurt.

It really killed.

CHAPTER FIFTY-SIX

Here's another fine example of the world kicking me when I'm down.

The smallpox case was taken away from us before Church had even made it to the airport. Gone. Bam. Done. Handed over to the CIA. Brick called to tell me. He didn't say so, but I had the feeling that Church was not in any mood to tell me himself. Church has iron control but no one can take that many punches in a row. They were on their way back to the Pier.

You can sit there and gape in shock or you can do something. I yelled at Bug and at Dr. Hu to get me some actionable information. Bug already had his whole team on it, and he didn't seem to care any more than I did that this wasn't our case. Hu, who usually entertains himself by insulting me, had a different take today.

He said, "Believe me, Ledger, I am going to make sense of this. I am not going to be ass-raped by the fucking CIA."

Then he hung up. I wanted to pat him on the back.

After that, I began tearing through the reports of the DMS failures, looking for patterns and trying to build a case out of scant information. No, let me correct that. It wasn't that we had insufficient information, we actually had a lot of it, but so far it didn't make much sense. The Cop part of my brain was offended by that. I needed answers and I needed logic. I'm occasionally an idiot, I'll accept that, but at the end of the day I am a trained investigator who needs things to make sense. You see, people don't understand the cop mind. They think we like puzzles. We absolutely do not. We like order. We attack mysteries in order to put disparate pieces back into their proper place. We don't enjoy the process. It's the end result that matters. Order out of chaos. It's not entertainment, it's who we are.

So the core of this thing seemed to originate at Gateway and the projects Erskine was running. Using what few resources I had, I began to make a list of the things I knew and to draw inferences from them.

Point one, the God Machine. It looked mostly but not entirely like a hadron collider. It had a hatch or opening. Air passed in and out of it. What was it? I had no idea because I lacked enough information.

Point two. Kill Switch. It was a directed-energy weapon that appeared to be able to temporarily interrupt electrical fields. It was nonlethal. Top, Bunny, and I had been exposed to it down at Gateway. People in Houston, at the NASCAR track, and at the debate had all been exposed to it. It stopped everything from digital watches to cell phones to engines. According to the reports it also stopped pacemakers. However, it did not short-circuit the central nervous system of living beings. There were no animal deaths. Not even birds or insects. I called Dr. Hu back and asked him about that. He told me that it was scientifically impossible. He sounded offended by that, too. And he hung up on me again.

Point three. Dreamwalking. The name was suggestive. Could it be some kind of mind control or psychic possession? A week ago I would have laughed at that idea. Now it scared me. I sent another request to Bug to get me any information on known research into mind control or manipulation using mechanical, chemical, or electrical means. As an afterthought I told him to check out research into psychic control.

"Joe," he said, "Mr. Church already has us working on that."

Interesting.

Point four. Freefall. So far we hadn't come up with anything on that. Not a word or a whisper.

Point five. Dreamshield. What was that? A defense against whatever kind of weapon Dreamwalking was? No way to know for sure, but my gut said yes.

Lydia-Rose tapped on my door and leaned in. She does that. Leans. Not sure why she doesn't actually step into the doorway or come inside. Leaning does it for her. A head, one shoulder, one boob, and a smile.

"Joe—? You have a visitor."

The door opened and he was standing right there.

Him. The guy that every shooter, every spy, every special operator in the United States intelligence and covert military services pretty much thinks is a god. Our god. Specifically the messiah of the clandestine trade.

Harcourt Bolton, Senior.

CIA superspy. A guy who's closed more top-level cases than I've had cold beers. A man who has saved the world so often that we should consider adding a fifth face to Mount Rushmore. Like that, and maybe double that.

Ever since Church had told me that the president appointed Bolton as codirector of the DMS I'd been privately trying to hate him. But that was for shit as soon as the man walked into my office. I instantly stood up and very nearly saluted. He was tall and handsome in a sixtyish Kevin Costner way. Powerfully built, but built for speed, built for action. Am I gushing? You bet you. I was a fanboy and this was Captain America. This was Batman.

"Mr. Ledger," I said, hurrying around the desk and offering my hand. "I'm Captain Bolton."

His smile was warm, amused, and patient. He shook my hand—and, yes, his grip was firm and dry—and he made no comment as what I'd said caught up to my stripped-gear brain.

"Um, I mean I'm . . ."

"Call me Harcourt, Captain," he said. "May I call you Joe? It's a pleasure to finally meet you. I've been following your career with great interest. The Deacon was right to rely on you as his right hand. You put my record for big-ticket saves to shame. I'm honored to shake your hand."

It is entirely possible I said, "Eeeep." Not sure, but let's not rule it out.

It was in that moment that I became incredibly aware that my office was a mess, with a cluttered desk, stacks of folders everywhere, an open box of half-pawed-over doughnuts on the credenza, and the stale odor of overworked idiot perfuming the air. I wanted to tuck in my shirt and check to see if my fingernails were clean.

"And who's this?" said Bolton, nodding to Ghost. "That's a handsome dog. Combat trained, I expect. A beautiful example of the breed."

He held out his hand to be sniffed. Ghost took his scent but then backed away, ears flattened, eyes narrowed. He even started to growl.

"Stop it," I snarled, and Ghost jerked backward from me.

"No, no, it's okay," said Bolton easily. "I was petting Bastion and your dog probably smells that."

I ordered Ghost to lie down. He obeyed, but it took me three tries. That was embarrassing, too, but Bolton did not comment on it. Too classy a guy for that.

"So sorry to intrude on you without a call," said Bolton, "but with everything going on . . . well, you understand. Do you have time for a quick catch-up chat?"

"Oh, geez, I've got no manners at all. Please, come in." I swept files from a leather guest chair and very nearly pushed him into it. "Rose, bring coffee and—"

"Tea for me, if that's okay," said Bolton.

"Tea. Sure. We have tea. Rose, do we have tea? Get some tea. Right now. Milk and cookies, too. And send someone out for pastries."

"Just tea," said Bolton, smiling, trying not to be too openly amused by my circus clown performance. I tried to straighten my desk without looking like I was straightening my desk. I opened a drawer and put my old coffee cup and the ham sandwich I was about to eat into it. Sadly, I wouldn't find that sandwich for days. Then I sat down.

Yes, I am fully aware that I was acting like a moron. No, like a Trekkie who suddenly found himself in an elevator with Captain Kirk. I don't actually have many heroes, but when I go bromance I go full bromance.

Bolton sat back and crossed his legs. He did it with great elegance. Very nice suit, polished shoes with rubber soles made to look like leather. Great for walking quietly while still looking nonchalant. Those shoes jumped onto my Christmas wish list.

Yeah, I said it. I coveted the man's shoes.

Bolton said, "The Deacon tells me you've been working the Gateway case. Where are you with that?"

And suddenly I was back in the real world. I laid my hands flat, fingers splayed, on the files that still covered most of my desk. "This," I said, "is a grade-A prime example of a clusterfuck. Pardon my French."

"I've heard the word before, Captain. And as I work for Uncle Sam I've had cause to use it more times than I can count." He paused, looking briefly uncomfortable. "Let's get this out into the open right from the start, okay? I didn't ask for this post. Being director of the Special Projects Office. I think this is the president taking a cheap shot at the Deacon. I think it shows a remarkable lack of faith in an organization that has done more measureable good for this country than anyone else. Including the CIA, and that's my home team. And I am embarrassed to have to act as your boss. That's wrong."

I said nothing.

"Between you and me and the wallpaper, Captain, this is your shop and this is your op. You call the shots. I'll be happy to file reports to mollify POTUS, but I'm not going to come in and piss in your yard and pretend I'm the dog with the biggest dick. Are we clear on that?"

"Thanks," I said. "That means a lot. More than I can express."

We shook hands. But I sagged back, feeling how weak and sick I still was.

"I heard you got beat up," he said, nodding to my bruises.

"It worked out in my favor," I told him. "But thinking about it hurts my head."

He nodded. "Another case like what happened with your friend Dr. Sanchez?"

"Yes. If you have any suggestions or theories I am all ears."

"Sadly, no. This is a strange case."

"Strange doesn't begin to cover it. This started off weird and got weirder."

Bolton said, "You mean the *Mountains of Madness* and the connection to pulp horror writers? I know, it's maddening. However, the reference to the God Machine in what your man, Bug, found . . . ? I think I might have something useful on that."

"What?" I cried, nearly leaping over the desk at him.

"It's not much, but it's something I caught wind of ten, twelve years ago. I was working an industrial espionage case that involved one of the tangential players from Gateway."

"Our case," I corrected, and he winced.

"Okay. Our case. The espionage thing involved Oscar Bell, who used to be married to Marcus Erskine's sister. Bell's files had been hacked and I recovered them because he was working on several important defense contracts. I, ah, may have *peeked* into Bell's private files."

"Naughty, naughty."

"I know," he said with a straight face, "I'm so ashamed."

"And—?"

"And that's where I first saw mention of the God Machine. Bug probably told you that it was a bit of weird science cooked up by Bell's son, Prospero. Brilliant kid, incredible IQ , but quite mad, I'm afraid. Died in a fire, I understand. Anyway, from what little I read, the God Machine was designed to facilitate interdimensional travel. And I'm pretty damn sure that's what Erskine was building down there. I think that's what you and your team saw. And," he said, "I'm equally sure that's why Erskine called his project 'Gateway.'"

CHAPTER FIFTY-SEVEN

"Interdimensional travel?" I asked. "Okay, we're now having a conversation in which interdimensional travel is a thing. Sure. Why not? My day hasn't been nearly weird enough. But seriously . . . why? What's the appeal, I mean in terms of Washington bean counters and Defense Department paranoids?"

Bolton shrugged. "It was sold to the government as a source of cheap, renewable energy and endless raw materials."

"How so?"

He launched into an explanation of the omniverse theory and how, if such a theory could be proved, it might mean that there are an infinite number of worlds like ours which could be mined for fossil fuels, minerals, clean water, and so on.

"And you believe this?" I asked, smiling.

"I didn't used to," he said, "but then I read your after-action report. Something weird happened down there. Something very weird that you and your team—three intelligent, experienced agents and trained observers—could not explain. Something our current science can't explain. And we know for a fact that Bell and Erskine were tied to a project to explore this. Someone in government believed in it enough to fund it. So . . . sure, I'm keeping an open mind." He paused. "That said, if such a technology exists and infinite worlds do, in fact, exist, this whole process is in its absolute infancy. There is no chance in hell they are going to get it right without a lot of things going badly wrong. The fact that the Russian, Chinese, and American stations down in Antarctica all went dark at the same time is suggestive. Maybe they opened a doorway and something bad came out."

"Something like what?"

His eyes drilled into me. "You said you saw something that looked like a giant monster. Maybe what you saw was some kind of animal. Something from one of those other worlds."

I said nothing.

"And consider this," Bolton added. "You were exposed to a strain of the Spanish flu that is unknown to science. Unknown to *our* science. I asked Dr. Hu about that and floated the theory that this could have been a virus from an adjacent dimension."

"How'd he take it?"

Bolton laughed. "He threw me out of his lab."

"Yeah."

"He's a dick," said Bolton.

"He is." I loved it that Harcourt Bolton despised the same cretinous jackass that I did. Made me feel special.

"Tell me, Joe," he said, amusement twinkling in his eyes, "are you buying anything I'm saying? Does this give us a working theory?"

"My considered opinion," I admitted, "is that it beats the shit out of me."

He blew out his cheeks and rubbed his eyes. "I'm right there with you, Joe. I've been chewing on the God Machine concept for years now, ever since I recovered Bell's files . . . and now there's the Gateway incident. Quite frankly I don't know what to believe. Over the last twenty years I've seen science twisted into new shapes that I don't recognize. Makes me almost long for the days when the worst thing we had to deal with were Soviet spies smuggling nuclear secrets and plans for the stealth bomber. Now this stuff? Joe, I'm more than half-glad I'm too old to go out into the field anymore. I sure as hell don't envy what you went through down at Gateway."

I said, "Has anyone ever actually proven that alternate universes exist?"

"Oh, hell no. In quantum physics, in superstring theory, they've gone pretty far in making a case for additional dimensions beyond the common ones we know. But they're mathematical constructs at this point. And that's an attempt to understand complex quantum dimensionality. No one's crossed the line and done the math to build a credible case for other universes." He paused. "Except maybe Prospero Bell."

"And Marcus Erskine believed in it enough to get a gazillion dollars' worth of covert funding."

We sat there and stared at each other.

"Shit," I said.

"Shit," he agreed.

CHAPTER FIFTY-EIGHT

Late in the evening on a hot September night.

Bunch of us sitting around on the back deck of the Pier. Top and Bunny were back and the rest of Echo Team had returned from the make-work assignments they'd been sent out on. We talked about the Closers, about the fight at San Pedro's office, about Gateway, about Rudy, and about the surfers. We talked and talked and we got exactly nowhere. Junie wasn't home yet and I really wanted to pick her brain about Prospero Bell, but she was out of cell phone range.

So we sat and let the day burn its way into night.

Bunny was sprawled on a lounge chair, shorts, no shirt, a Padres cap pulled low to throw shadows over the line of six stiches. Lydia sat next to him in a bikini top and cut-off military camo pants. Montana Parker, Brian Botley, and Sam Imura were all in civvies. Top was in sweats and I was wearing one of my most obnoxious Hawaiian shirts—fluorescent toucans and bright blue howler monkeys doing a line dance. Every flat surface was littered with empty beer bottles. An impressive number of them.

Or, seen from our viewpoint, not nearly enough of them.

There was no moon and the sky above us was filled with cold little diamond chips that bathed us in blue-white light. Beneath the Pier the endless waves slapped against the pilings and washed against the beach. The surf roar sounded like faint and distant crowds of people talking, talking, talking, and saying nothing.

Echo Team, there to save the world.

This was the first time we had all been together in weeks.

"Got to go home," I said for the fifth or sixth time. No one responded. Ghost didn't twitch. Sam opened a fresh pair of Stone IPAs and handed one to me. We didn't toast. You do that when you want to remember something.

A bit later Bunny asked, "Is this it, then? Is the DMS going down the crapper?"

I shook my head. Not to deny that possibility, but because I didn't know.

"How the hell have we managed to drop the ball this many times?" asked Montana.

"I know," grumped Brian. "When did we become the guys who mess up?"

"Dreamwalking," I said, putting it out there.

"Which means what?" asked Montana.

"Don't mean nothing," growled Top. "Some voodoo bullshit."

We drank.

Bunny grunted. "At least we stopped whatever the hell was going on down there under the ice."

We drank some more. The world turned.

"Even so," said Montana after a while, "you guys pretty much blew a hole in the map."

Bunny took a long pull on his beer and studied her down the barrel of his bottle. "You weren't there."

"No," she said, "I was not."

"Kind of glad I wasn't there, either," said Brian.

Everyone nodded. Everyone drank.

"Wish we were in on that Kill Switch thing," said Lydia. "Feels wrong to be watching from the sidelines."

Far out there over the black horizon a piece of ancient space iron scratched a streak against the darkness. It seemed to last longer than most shooting stars and we all watched it.

No one said a word.

Not about the star.

Not about anything. For a long time.

It was Sam who finally broke the silence. Making a statement that was also a question.

"So," he said slowly, "penguins?"

No one said anything for a long, long time.

I think it was Top who started laughing. A quiet trembling of the shoulders, and for a crazy moment I thought he was crying. Then, as he shook his head I saw the gleam of white teeth in the starlight. A moment later Bunny burst out with a donkey bray of a laugh.

Then we were all laughing.

Even if we didn't think it was funny at all.

CHAPTER FIFTY-NINE

I was dead on my feet and was in the parking lot, reaching for my car key, when my cell rang. Church. I leaned against the fender of my replacement Explorer and wondered what would get me in more trouble—throwing the phone against the wall real damn hard or finding out what Church wanted to tell me. Ghost gave me a "don't do it" look.

I did it.

"Just for once," I said instead of a hello, "tell me something I want to hear."

"Would it change the complexion of your day if I told you we had a lead?"

"On what? On who's hiring ex–SpecOps shooters?"

Church made a sound that might have been a laugh. "Maybe we can turn this around."

"How?" And I surprised myself by really wanting to know.

"Aunt Sallie sent a team to Washington armed with federal warrants."

"How'd she get those? I thought we didn't have any friends left in Washington."

"She asked nicely," said Church in a way that suggested that Aunt Sallie did not, in fact, ask nicely. Auntie looks like Whoopi Goldberg but her personality is closer to Jack Bauer from *24*, with a little Charlie Manson thrown in to make her more personable. It is very difficult to summon enough courage to say no to her.

"What are the warrants for?"

"Majestic," said Church, "and anything related to Gateway, Dr. Erskine, and Oscar Bell. The first two came up dry. We probably have all of the Majestic records that exist under that label. As for

Gateway, Bug keeps hitting walls. But Bell was married to Erskine's sister and there is a real chance we can establish collusion because Erskine was working for the DoD when he bought Bell's God Machine project. A federal judge agreed and Auntie's team has obtained several dozen boxes of paper records. They've done spot-scanning of the paperwork and so far none of it is on the Net or in the computer records of the DoD or DARPA."

"Ah," I said, getting it now. "They kept it all on paper to keep it away from us. Shit, that's smart."

"We have those records now. Auntie flew twenty-five analysts down to D.C. to join the retrieval team. Bug sent Nikki and Yoda, too. We have every available eye reading and scanning those records. They'll work through the night and with any luck we'll have some leads by noon tomorrow."

"Jesus, I hope you're right."

Church said, "Captain . . . Joe . . . I want you to have some faith."

"In what?"

"In me," he said. "In the DMS. I know things look bleak, and I certainly share your frustration for feeling like we're closed out of the important cases—"

"We are. I'm a damn soldier, and so far the most I've done is beat up my best friend and a couple of surfer boys."

"You're not a soldier," he said quietly.

"What?"

"I didn't hire you to be a soldier," said Church. "Or have you forgotten? When I recruited you it was because you were a detective, an investigator. You're a cop, Captain Ledger. That's what you are and that's what you do. The combat, the warfare, the killing . . . those are unfortunate side effects of our job. Of your job. They are not your defining characteristics. You are tearing yourself apart for the wrong reason. You want to get back into the war, I get that. I do. However, we aren't being called to fight. Not at this moment. We are being called to make sense of this, to find answers, to build a case."

I said nothing, but damn if I didn't feel every single one of the punches he'd slipped under my guard.

"This is what I need you to do," he said. "Go home and get some sleep. Get plenty of it. Then report to work tomorrow and take over this investigation. I am telling you this as your boss and as your friend.

You need to stop being a bystander. You need to refuse to be marginalized. You need to be the cop that you are. You need to solve this."

The phone went dead in my hand.

I put it in my pocket and walked over to the parking garage window. It looked directly out over the surf. How long did I stand there watching the waves crash down on the sand?

Maybe five minutes. Maybe ten.

There are times I'm afraid of Mr. Church. There are times I hate him. Right at that moment, though, I'd have walked through fire for him.

I looked out at the tumbling waves, listened to the hiss as the frothy bubbles popped, watched starlight glisten on the wet sand.

Then I went home and went to bed.

CHAPTER SIXTY

In the morning I got up and kissed a sleepy Junie who had gotten in late and didn't look like she was quite ready to face the day. I showered hot enough to boil all of the sickness, indolence, and self-pity off my skin, then I shaved, dressed in jeans and one of my more sedate Hawaiian shirts—this one had tropical fish on it—put down bowls of glop for Ghost and Cobbler, washed down a fistful of vitamins with my first cup of coffee of the day, and then set off to work.

On the way I called Bug, who was East Coast time and was already up and at the Hangar.

"You have anything for me?" I asked.

"Yeah-h-h-h-h," he said, but he stretched the word out so long that it sounded like he wasn't sure what it was he had. "You won't believe how much stuff we got. We're talking seventy-one file boxes, each one crammed with stuff. That's something like three hundred thousand pieces of paper. Auntie had them bring it all back here and we're using the high-speed bulk scanners. But that's just scanning. Then everything has to be processed through MindReader and—"

"Bug," I said, cutting him off, "I don't care. Tell me if you actually got something."

"Yes," he said. "Maybe."

"Try harder than that."

"Well, first, we got a slight hit on one of the Gateway projects. Freefall. It's vague and it seems to be tied into the Kill Switch thing. Our best guess so far is that it's some experimental way of knocking down drones, but really, that's all we have on it so far. The good news is that we have a line on four previous addresses for Oscar Bell."

"That's something. I'll send someone to run that down. What else?"

"Okay, first, Oscar Bell is dead. Murder-suicide. After the DoD sued him he went totally bankrupt and broke. The IRS froze every penny of his assets and he lost his house and everything else he owned. And he drank, too. He apparently went crazy and killed three people at a diner in some Podunk town in Washington state, then turned the gun on himself."

"Why didn't MindReader pick that up?" I asked.

"Not sure. We have a copy of what looks like the original hand-written police report and another that looks like it was printed out, probably at the police station where it was filed. But when I checked with the local police department they have nothing at all in their computers. Nothing in hardcopy, either. I'll send you what I have."

"Okay. What else?"

"Some of this is freaking me out because one of the other file boxes contained an inventory list of restricted documents. But get this, Joe, I'm not talking like military top-secret stuff. I'm talking Catholic church sort of restricted."

"Not following you. What kind of stuff are we talking about? Holy Grail? Ark of the Covenant? Jesus' birth certificate?"

"It was in Latin," said Bug. "Index Librorum Prohibitorum. I had to look it up. It means 'List of Prohibited Books.'"

"Okay. So . . . ?"

"So, I called Circe because this is her sort of thing, and she said there were two of these lists. One was stuff that was against church policy or critical or like that. *Pascal* by Voltaire, *Monarchia* by Dante Alighieri, Casanova's memoirs. Like that. Naughty stuff. But when I read some of the titles on the inventory sheet she said that none of them were on that list. She thinks that list is one that was supposed to be a big church secret. Circe knows about it because . . . well, she's Circe. She knows that kind of stuff. She told me that there was a group of these psycho monks who used to go around taking these books away from people and sometimes killing them. Like if the Inquisition and the library police had a cranky kid. She called it the Ordo Frat-rum Claustrorum. Anyway, here's the really freaky stuff. Half the books on the list are ancient books of magic and alchemy. The Greek *Magical Papyri*, *Arbatel de Magia Veterum*, the *Pseudomonarchia Dae-donum*, *The Black Pullet*, *Ars Almade*, which is book four of the *Lesser Keys of Solomon*, *The Ripley Scroll*, *The Book of Soyga*, an Icelandic book called the *Galdabok*, and—here's one you'll recognize—the Voynich manuscript."

Yeah, I recognized that one, all right. It's a weird fifteenth-century text written in an unknown language and kept at the Beinecke Rare Book and Manuscript Library at Yale University. Experts had tried for centuries to decode it, and even doubted that the language was real. Circe cracked the code, though, with the help of some additional pages we found. As it turned out, the language was that of the Upierczi, a race of very bad people living in caves beneath the Arabian sands. The Upierczi are genetic offshoots, a splinter line of evolution that showed how perverse science can be. They are the reason we have legends about vampires.

"There's more," said Bug. "Those books were only half the list. There was a separate part of the list preceded by a long list of warnings and prayers about how the world will end if these books are ever read or even opened. Really wild stuff."

"I've found extreme religious orders, as a rule, are prone toward general nuttiness," I said.

"No, this is worse than that," said Bug, "and this is where we run right into the whole *Mountains of Madness*–Elder Gods stuff."

I nearly sideswiped a kid on a bike. "Shit," I said. "Tell me."

"In those books by H. P. Lovecraft and some of the other writers—August Derleth, Robert E. Howard, Henry Kuttner, and like that—there's a bunch of books of ancient dark magic. You heard of the *Necronomicon?*"

"In movies, sure."

"Right, those were movies based on, or inspired by, Lovecraft's Cthulhu Mythos."

"What about it?"

"The *Necronomicon* is on this list," said Bug. "Actually . . . almost all of those books are. Joe . . . I don't think they're fake. I think all of this is real."

CHAPTER SIXTY-ONE

The things Bug told me about those creepy old books gnawed at my nerves all the way into work. How could they not? But I tried to put them into perspective with what Bolton and Bug had both said yesterday. Maybe it really was a matter of many of the things we believed to be supernatural were actually unclassified aspects of very real science. After all, in my years with the DMS I'd encountered the Upierczi, who were the flesh-and-bone basis for vampire beliefs. And I'd been on a case in the small town of Pine Deep in Pennsylvania where I'd taken down a genetics lab that was trying to create a kind of supersoldier based on another genetic anomaly—lycanthropy. Did this explain all of the stories of werewolves and vampires around the world? Maybe not, but it made the darkness at the edge of town less of a place of magic and more of an area of mystery. The Cop part of me wanted rational answers, and to achieve that I needed a lot more information than I had.

I got to the Pier as fast as I could.

A sleepy Junie called me at ten and I asked her if she could come in, explaining that Church and I wanted to ask her some questions. She said to give her an hour. When Junie arrived she looked apprehensive.

"You're being very mysterious," she said.

"It's been that kind of week."

"You've only been back to work less than two days."

"Tell me about it," I said as I opened the door to the conference room. Church was in the same chair but in a different suit, looking fresh and rested. He stood up and gestured to a chair.

"Ms. Flynn," he said, "thank you for coming in. Please sit. I apologize for the inconvenience but I believe that when you hear what we have to say, you'll understand."

As she sat she glanced from Church to me and back again. "Is this about ISIL?"

"Why do you ask?"

"It's all over the news. That's all anyone's talking about. The power outages. Everyone thinks Houston was because of them."

"I am going to share some information with you," began Church, "that is of a highly confidential nature."

She nodded. Church has never asked people to sign nondisclosure agreements. If he doesn't trust someone he doesn't tell them anything. And Junie was family.

"There are a number of things we want to share with you, and some of them may be unpleasant," said Church. "I don't think you'd thank us for sugar-coating it, so let's start with the one that most affects you. We believe the Majestic program may still be active."

Her face went dead pale beneath her spray of sun freckles, and she put a hand to her throat. "No . . . oh, God, are you sure?"

"Sure enough."

We took turns laying it out for her. I started with the Closers who attacked Top and Bunny at Dr. San Pedro's office. Church told her about the extreme cult of secrecy built around Gateway and how it was hidden in almost the same way as Majestic Three. We told her one of the things Aunt Sallie had learned last night, that the late Oscar Bell had worked on projects for Howard Shelton. Those ties, plus the exotic nature of the Gateway project.

As we laid it out, Junie's shock was replaced by a critical intensity. Her body became less rigid but her eyes were as sharp as a hawk's. She is not an ordinary person by any stretch. She has very high intelligence and an eidetic memory—she cannot forget anything she's learned. Makes it really fucking hard to have an argument with her. Trust me on this.

During our info dump, Harcourt Bolton came in, exchanged silent greetings with Junie, and sat to Church's right. Bastion jumped into the man's lap and began cleaning himself. Pretty sure that did not endear either him or Bolton to Ghost, who gave them both the evil eye.

For Bolton's benefit, Church even filled in some of Junie's background, after first assuring her that Mr. Super Spy was there on the orders of the president and that all information shared in that room was confidential. I could tell Junie didn't like it, and there was a damn good reason.

I'd met Junie when the DMS was looking for the Majestic Black Book. At first I thought she was nothing more than a smart and pretty lady who was half airy-fairy hippie and half conspiracy theory podcaster. Even split of both. She'd talked about the Black Book and Majestic Three on her podcast, so I went to see how she knew about them and to see how much of it was, in fact, conspiracy theory bullshit. Turns out . . . not much at all. Majestic Three had been building advanced weapons of war, including a new generation of ultrasophisticated stealth aircraft, using technologies recovered from crashed vehicles. They had also recovered some biological materials from those wrecks. Nothing alive, but they managed to sequence the DNA. Let's just say that the DNA was exotic. M3 ultimately discovered that in order to use the technology of these vehicles they had to include an element of that DNA into the mix. That was a big problem for a long time, but they solved it by genetically grafting the alien DNA to human embryos, creating true hybrids. They raised thousands of them in groups called hives. Most of the hybrids died off. A flaw in the DNA made them exceptionally prone to diseases, particularly brain and bone cancer.

When I met Junie she was battling brain cancer.

Yeah. Run with that and you'll get into the right end zone. Not a comfortable place to be. Does that mean she has antennae or any of that stuff? No. Her DNA is more than 85 percent human. But along with the cancer—which she's beaten twice now—she got an exceptionally high IQ, perfect recall, and higher than normal aptitude in science, mathematics, engineering, and other related sciences. She had been in one of the last batches of hive kids, and in order to breed more socially adept children, M3 seeded many of those kids into foster homes. Most of the foster parents were employees of M3 or in some way associated with it. Howard was the mastermind behind this whole thing. He's dead and, hopefully, burning somewhere. Sick bastard.

"And that brings us to the God Machine," said Church. At that point he turned it over to Bolton, who told Junie what he'd told me. I have to admit, she took it better than I had and she asked smarter questions.

She glanced around at each of us. "You realize that this is not a new theory, right?"

"Please explain," said Church and Bolton at the same time.

"The God Machine, it's been around for a long time," said Junie. "I mean, a device that can open a doorway between our world and another, that's not a new concept. It's a scientific twist on the conjuring circle. And, please bear in mind, I said 'circle.' It's always been a circular doorway. Nearly every culture has some version of it. Nikola Tesla was working on something like this, maybe exactly this. There's a story that's been floating around the conspiracy theory world for over a century about Tesla building an interdimensional doorway at his laboratory at Wardenclyffe Tower in Shoreham, New York. According to the story, he was approached by a very rich old man who paid him to build a machine called an Orpheus Gate. The description matches the God Machine, even down to the gemstones, which, according to the story, were somehow used to regulate the power. Tesla told a colleague sometime later that he built two of them. The first one vanished as soon as it was turned on, and it blew out all of the power in the entire region."

"Well, well," said Bolton.

"Orpheus Gate," murmured Church, nodding. "I've heard of that, but I did not make the connection. I should have. Apparently we've all been off our game."

Bolton nodded. "Agreed. None of us are at our best right now."

Junie picked up her story. "When the Orpheus Gate was activated there was some kind of intense energetic discharge—something he called a 'God Wave.' It knocked Tesla out and he was sick for weeks afterward. He had a high fever and hallucinated badly."

"If there's any more precise description of his symptoms," I said, "I'd like to share it with Dr. Hu. Maybe match it against the symptoms of what Top, Bunny, and I had. After all, we got sick after an energetic discharge from the Gateway machine."

Church nodded and asked Junie to continue.

"The whole experience shook Tesla's confidence," she said, cutting me a quick look, "and it changed him. That was when he started shifting his focus from sustainable energy and communication systems to weapons of war. Death rays and that sort of thing. Some historians say that he went mad, and maybe we know why."

"'Mad' is a relative term," observed Bolton.

"There's more," said Junie. "In 1918 a constable in a small fishing town in Spain reported that a strange machine appeared in a farmer's

JONATHAN MABERRY

barn. Actually he said that it looked like it exploded through the side of the barn. He found a naked old man near the machine who claimed that he was a traveler who was trying to find his way home. The constable got sick shortly after that, and so did everyone in the town. That's where the first cases of the Spanish flu were reported."

Well, yeah, that hit us all like a cruise missile. Junie looked around at our stricken faces.

"What?" she asked.

"Ms. Flynn," said Church, "did anyone tell you what kind of virus Captain Ledger and his men were affected by?"

"No. Just that it was a rare mutation of the flu."

"Yeah," I said. "The Spanish flu."

CHAPTER SIXTY-TWO

Church immediately called Dr. Hu and Bug and brought them up to speed, and ordered them to run down this information. Almost immediately Bug came back with hits. Even for MindReader, a Net search required the right keywords. The hits he got were not on the "God Machine" but on the "Orpheus Gate."

He even found pictures.

"On the screen," I told him and Bug sent them to the big flat screen on the wall. We stared, dumbfounded. It had been there all along but we were looking for it the wrong way.

The Orpheus Gate. Orpheus descended into hell to rescue his love.

"What is hell anyway," mused Junie, "but a name for another dimension that's inhospitable to life as we know it? Couldn't that just as easily be another dimension, another version of the world rather than something supernatural?"

No one told her she was crazy. Incredulity was a boat that had already sailed, caught fire, hit an iceberg, and sank. Even Hu, who tended not to believe in much of anything, wasn't trying to knock this down anymore. Want to know why?

There was a photo, a crisp black-and-white, of a bunch of stern-looking men standing in front of the same goddamn machine I'd seen down in the Antarctic. Same thing. The guy who stood in the center of the front row was shorter than the others, with black hair and a Charlie Chaplin mustache. We could see him very clearly because the Nazis always did take good pictures. The accompanying caption told us that we were seeing Hitler inspecting the development of a new weapon being designed by top scientists of the Thule Society.

A second photograph was in color and was grainy and poorly framed, suggesting that whoever took it hadn't been allowed to snap that shot. It was of an underground chamber filled with clunky old computers of the kind used in Europe in the 1980s. The photo showed workers installing small dark objects into a panel. Gemstones. The photograph was taken at an underground lab in the Ukrainian town of Poliske. Just a few miles from Chernobyl.

And there were other images, photos of worse quality and even some crude sketches by people who claimed to have seen such a device or worked on it while employed either by the government or a defense contractor.

"Guys," said Bug, "I am ringing all sorts of bells here. Seriously. Orpheus Gate? Yeah, there's a whole bunch of stuff. Let me put some people on this and I'll get back to you with the bullet points."

Dr. Hu stared gloomily at us from a window in the big screen. "Let me study the data."

His window vanished and we stared at each other.

Junie was thoughtful for a moment, then asked, "You said that this project was under the directorship of Marcus Erskine, right? I know that name. He's been in the conspiracy theory rumor mill for a while. Back when I was making my list of possible governors of M3, Erskine was always in my top twenty. His sister, Lyssa, was married to Oscar Bell. She was nice but Oscar was a total shit. I think he's the reason she committed suicide. Poor girl. She never should have married him."

"Bug told me Bell was on your podcast once."

"Whoa, wait," interrupted Bolton, looking completely thrown, "you *knew* Oscar Bell?"

"Personally?" said Junie. "Not really. I knew Lyssa through the conspiracy community. She was a regular caller on my podcast."

"And Bell was a guest?" asked Bolton.

"No. He called in once. I didn't like him very much."

"Please tell us about it," said Mr. Church.

She nodded. "I was interviewing a man Oscar used to know. Oscar called in, clearly drunk, and laid into my guest. Accusing him of lying and distorting the truth. He accused him of having driven Oscar's son, Prospero, to suicide, and then he accused him of keeping his son as a prisoner. Oscar was irrational and contradictory. It really upset my guest, and when Oscar threatened to find him and kill him I ended the interview. I was furious because we were really getting somewhere. We were talking about this amazing dream diary one of his patients had kept, and how the things in it were clear proof that other worlds exist and are accessible."

Harcourt Bolton leaned forward. "Who was that man? Who was your guest?"

"Dr. Michael Greene. He used to be a psychiatrist in the Hamptons but he closed his practice, sold his house, and went into hiding after he was threatened by men in black. Closers."

My pulse jumped. "Whoa, whoa, wait a second. His name was Michael Greene? You're sure?"

"Positive. Why?"

"Because," I said, "last night Bug found a police report that Oscar Bell walked into a diner in Washington state and killed the only three people in the place. A waitress, the cook, and Dr. Michael Greene. Then he killed himself."

She stared at me. "Oh my God."

Mr. Church removed a folder from his briefcase and placed it on the table, drummed his fingers on the closed cover for a moment, and then slid it across to Junie. However, he kept his hand there to keep the folder closed.

"Do you know who Prospero Bell is?"

"Yes, of course," she said. "He was Oscar and Lyssa Bell's son. He was Dr. Greene's patient."

"Have you ever seen a picture of Prospero?"

"No."

"You're sure?" asked Bolton.

I said, "Junie has total recall."

"Why do you ask?" Junie said to Church.

He nudged the folder an inch closer to her. "Because so much of this centers around Prospero, I asked Bug to get me a complete workup This is a photograph taken while he was a cadet at Ballard Academy in Poland, Maine."

There was something about the way he said this that made Junie hesitate. I hadn't seen the photo yet, either, so I leaned against her as she opened it. I felt her body go rigid, her muscles tense as soon as she saw the picture. It was a high-res color photo of a seventeen-year-old boy in a military school uniform. Blond wavy hair, blue eyes, a splash of freckles across his cheeks.

He was male and he was twenty years younger, but in every other respect he looked like an almost identical twin of Junie Flynn.

CHAPTER SIXTY-THREE

Harcourt Bolton looked at the photo and then at Junie. A deep frown line appeared between his brows. "I don't understand. Did I miss something? Is Prospero Bell related to you? Was he your brother?"

Junie picked up the photo and stared at it for a long, long time. A tear broke and rolled down her freckled cheek. "Oh God," she murmured. "There's another one out there. . . ."

"Another . . . what?" asked Bolton.

She touched the face of Prospero Bell. "I—I think he's like *me*," she said in a ghostly whisper. Her skin was dead pale beneath her freckles and there were ghosts of old memories haunting her eyes. "I think he was another hybrid. Another hive child."

Church looked like Church always does. The man could be on fire and he wouldn't twitch. He ate a cookie, though, and I'm almost positive there's some kind of subliminal code when he chooses to do that. Bolton, on the other hand, looked like he wanted to jump out of his skin. He almost looked like he was going to leap across the table and kiss Junie.

"Miss Flynn—may I call you Junie? Yes? Great . . . Junie, can you tell me exactly *what* Dr. Greene said about Prospero?"

"First off, understand two things," she replied, "first is that Greene never named him. He referred to him as Patient X. I made the connection only after Oscar Bell accidentally outed his son when he called in to attack Greene. Second, the interview was cut short when Oscar Bell actually threatened Greene."

"Okay, but what did he *say*?" repeated Bolton.

She told us a story that was equal parts fantastic, tragic, and horrible.

About a genius boy who never believed he was entirely human and who found comfort only in two things. His dreams and science. Prospero said that the idea for his escape machine—that was how Greene referred to it—came to him in dreams. He said that its design was somehow encoded in the parts of his DNA that were not human. In order to find his way home—or to the place he truly believed was his home—Prospero began building versions of a device. A doorway. A gateway. The God Machine.

When Oscar Bell realized the potential for the machine, he took the first prototype away from him and sold it to the military as a new weapon of war. The thing was that the prototype was far from complete and it malfunctioned constantly. But it was those malfunctions that were the basis of the contract the kid's father sold to the Department of Defense.

"Did he explain the nature of those side effects?" asked Bolton. He seemed very excited by this and was even sweating a little. I guess we all were.

"In general. Dr. Greene was not a physicist," she said. "And also the Closers took all of his case notes. He had to rebuild everything in his files from memory. But . . . sure, he said that there were two of these 'faults' that Oscar sold to the government. One sounds like what's happening around the country, like what happened in Houston, though I don't understand how ISIL could have gotten their hands on it."

She described the first fault for us. When the machine was first turned on there was something like a reverse power surge. All machinery around the machine—but not including the machine itself—would stop working. This included batteries. It only affected nonorganic electrical conduction. It did not shut down the central nervous system of people inside that nullification field cast by the machine.

"That's Kill Switch," I said, slapping the table. "There's no way it's not."

"Agreed," said Church, and even Bolton nodded.

"This means that we know what they were doing at Gateway, and it means that the ISIL attacks are our case. Boom," I said. "Get the president on the phone."

Bolton patted the air with a calming gesture. "Slow down, Joe. This is still theory. We can't prove any of this."

I started to say something loud and nasty, but Junie touched my arm. "Let me tell the rest of it, honey," she said.

"Do we need to hear more?" asked Bolton. "Kill Switch is the thing we need to be afraid of and it's what we need to stop. My guess is that Erskine was using it to create a weapon to be used against drones. Don't forget, they had a project in the works called Freefall."

"And we'll pursue that," said Church, "but for now let's hear the rest of what Ms. Flynn has to share."

Bolton looked annoyed and impatient. I could sympathize. I wanted to jump right on this. If ISIL had a directed-energy weapon that could knock down our drones, then it would cut our combat effectiveness down by one hell of a lot. I started to say something but caught Church watching me. He gave me a tiny shake of his head.

Junie said, "Dr. Greene said that one of the other faults of the machine was that while it was in idle mode some people—not most, just a small percentage—experienced two distinct types of unusually vivid dreams. The largest majority of those affected had dreams in which they saw monsters and alien landscapes and images that can best be described as psychedelic. Surreal. The boy told the doctor that he believed these people were actually traveling to those worlds, that the energetic discharge transported their consciousness through the dimensional barriers so that what they saw were beings and locations that existed in other worlds than ours. Greene said that the boy was convinced that the entire surrealism art movement was brought into being because certain people had been touched, in one way or another, by this energy. They had journeyed to other worlds in their dreams and then tried to capture what they'd seen in their paintings. Salvador Dalí, Max Ernst . . . artists like that. Greene said that the boy told him that there was a whole group of writers who had been similarly influenced."

"Let me guess . . . H. P. Lovecraft and his crew?"

She frowned. "How did you know that?"

"We've been chasing pieces of this," said Church. "Continue, please."

"Well," she said slowly, "even though Greene lost contact with the boy and had to flee the Closers, he never let go of this. He did a lot of very quiet research. He thinks the energetic discharge may have been what drove Hitler mad. And he thought that these same kind of dreams might have been what kicked off the psychedelic movement

JONATHAN MABERRY

of the sixties. People who'd had those dreams who were using drugs to find their way back to that other world."

"I don't see how this is useful to us," said Bolton. "It's interesting as a cultural phenomenon, but it doesn't seem like it poses a threat. The Kill Switch is our primary concern."

She looked at Bolton for a long, thoughtful moment. "You're with the CIA?"

He hesitated, then nodded.

"I'm surprised you don't already know about this stuff."

"What do you mean?"

"Remote viewing," she said. "Project Stargate?"

"I'm not sure I follow," he said.

"It was a program started by the Defense Intelligence Agency."

"Wait," I said, "I'm lost. Wasn't *Stargate* an old TV show?"

"This is different," said Church. "Project Stargate was a clandestine research project."

He gave us the lowdown. The Stargate project had been a covert line of research based primarily at Fort Meade in Maryland and overseen by the Defense Intelligence Agency and SRI International, a defense contractor. The goal of Stargate had been to determine the authenticity and potential of psychic phenomena. The officer in charge of it was Lieutenant Frederick Atwater, known as "Skip" to his friends. Skip was an aide to Major General Albert Stubblebine. According to DIA and CIA legend, Skip was a "psychic headhunter" for the project, searching for candidates who scored high on the ESP evaluations. People whose abilities might open the door to the first generation of psychic spies.

The project was high concept and, had it worked, it would have changed the nature of espionage. Imagine it. A psychic spy was, according to Stargate, an operative who would not need to physically visit an enemy location or foreign country, but who would instead be able to project his consciousness there and remotely view the enemy, view their installations, overhear conversations, and so on. It was an outlandish idea that everyone took seriously, and the United States was far from being the only nation actively involved in this research. The Russians had gone farthest with it and had spent millions trying to not only get inside the heads of enemy agents and scientists, but to hijack them, to psychically control their actions. It was like carjacking someone's mind.

Scary stuff. Considering that I have at least three people inside my head at any given time, I knew the terror of ceding control. I was a different person when the Modern Man or the Killer was in the driver's seat.

Junie said, "The DIA handed the Stargate program to the CIA."

"And the Agency canned it," said Bolton, dismissing it with a wave of his hand. "It was nonsense and it didn't work."

He told us that the Agency officially concluded that ESP was not provable, any results were not reproducible, and it was all, essentially, a waste of time and money. If the Russians got anywhere with their program, which was nicknamed "Remote Control," it didn't keep the Soviet Union from collapsing. Bolton said that everyone dropped their research on it. A book, *The Men Who Stare at Goats*, was written about it, published in 2004 and made into a George Clooney movie in 2009. Neither the book nor film actually mentioned Stargate, though conspiracy theories abounded. From the military intelligence perspective, however, it was a failure and it was dumped.

"And yet," said Junie, "Prospero Bell told his therapist that this kind of thing was a side effect of this machine. This God Machine or Orpheus Gate, or whatever we need to call it."

"Sorry," said Bolton, "I'll buy the electrical null field, because we're seeing that in play. But psychic projection and psychic possession is too far-out, even for me."

I turned and studied him. "Then how do you explain what happened with Rudy Sanchez, Captain Craft, Glory Price, and a lot of other people? How do you explain the two surfer boys who attacked me yesterday? No offense, Harcourt, but are you going to sit there and tell me that you'll believe in interdimensional travel, electrical null fields, and this God Machine and *not* the psychic projection stuff? I mean, come on, Erskine had a project division coded *Dreamwalking*. What the hell else could it have been?"

He gave me a tolerant smile. "For the record, Joe, I never said that I believed that the God Machine did anything more than disrupt electricity. I certainly don't think we're dealing with cross-dimensional travel, and I'm sorry, but psychic warfare was researched ad nauseam and all they discovered was a way to squander a whole lot of taxpayer dollars. No . . . I'll buy a lot, but that doesn't work for me."

He stood up, smiled and glanced around, then gave another shake of his head.

"Junie," he said, "you are a remarkable woman and you've brought us some incredibly valuable information, but we need to stay focused. Now, if you'll all excuse me, I need to get on the phone to the president. I have to try and convince him that the DMS hasn't lost a step getting to first base and you, Captain Ledger, have to be taken off the bench."

He left behind a big and very pregnant silence. Church sat for a moment considering the door that Bolton had closed behind him as he left. He slowly ate a Nilla wafer and made no comment about Bolton's parting remarks.

Something occurred to me and I dug a sheet of paper out of our case notes and placed it in front of Junie. "Bug said that there was a list of ancient books among the papers of one of the Gateway team. He ran it by Circe and she said that it was part of something called the Index Librorum Prohibitorum."

"Oh, sure, the Pauline Index. What about it?"

I told her about the inclusion of the supposed fictional works by H. P. Lovecraft and the others.

"Oh," she said, "you're talking about the Unlearnable Truths."

Church stiffened. "How is it you know that phrase?"

Junie shrugged. "That's what Dr. Greene called those books. When Oscar Bell called, one of the things he ranted about was how he'd ruined himself by trying to find those books."

"Did he say why he wanted them?" asked Church, and maybe there was some actual human emotion in his voice. Some real excitement.

"Prospero seemed to believe that these books contained some kind of mathematical code that would help make his machine run correctly. And by 'correctly' he meant that it would open the door to his world. The conversation never got farther than that—that's when Oscar Bell started making threats and it all fell apart." She touched Prospero's photo. "I heard rumors that there were experiments with certain cell lines. Not clones exactly, but what they called 'birth pairs.' Until now I never knew if that was true." A tear rolled down her cheek. "Now I know. God . . . Prospero Bell was my brother."

We sat there in silence for a while, each of us deep in speculation as to what this all meant. Then two things happened that changed the course of the day. Maybe the course of the world.

A call came in on Church's private line. He didn't put it on speaker, so I only heard his half of it. "Violin," he said, "it's good to hear from you. Your mother said that you've been off the radar for quite a while. She was concerned." He listened. Listened some more. Then he said, "You should have called me. I would have been able to bring you in. No, I don't care what your mother has been telling you about us. The DMS is not falling apart." He shot me a look that dared me to contradict him. I mimed zipping my mouth shut. To Violin he said, "Where are you now? Very well. Go to the Hangar. Aunt Sallie will arrange transport here." He paused. "I'm sorry, who did you say you were with? *Really?* That is very, very interesting. Yes, bring him along. I would be extremely interested to meet him, too. Fly safe and don't worry. Bring the item with you."

He said something else to her in the language of Upierczi, which is also the private language of Arklight and the Mothers of the Fallen. Church probably doesn't know that I've managed to sort out a lot of that language. I'm very talented with languages.

What he said was, "Be safe, sweetheart."

He said it the way a father might. Yeah. So . . . there's that. Which is confusing, since both Lilith and Violin told me her father was Grigor, the so-called King of Thorns, head of the Upierczi. I'd killed Grigor in the tunnels under an Iranian power station. How, then, did that explain Church's connection to Violin? An adopted daughter? I don't know and I doubt he'd tell me under torture.

When the call was done Church stared into the middle distance for a long time. When his eyes came back into focus he looked at Junie.

"As you overheard," he began slowly, "that was Violin. She has been on the run from two competing groups of operators. One is a religious order I've run into once or twice over the years. The Ordo Fratrum Claustrorum."

"I've heard of them," Junie said. "There are a lot of stories about them. The conspiracy rumor mill is rife with them. They're supposed to be pretty scary."

"They are," said Church. "The Brotherhood, as they're also known, is very real and highly dangerous. But they're only half the problem. The other team that has been chasing Violin are Closers."

"Why?"

"Because," he said, "Violin has obtained one of the books from that list. *De Vermis Mysteriis.* The—"

"*The Mysteries of the Worm*," said Junie. "That's one of the books Lovecraft mentioned in his stories. It's . . . real, isn't it?"

Church nodded gravely. "So it would appear. Violin has had a great deal of trouble getting it out of Europe. The Closers and the Brotherhood have been very aggressive, and she and her partner have had to go to ground to keep themselves and the book safe."

"Her partner?" I asked.

"Yes," said Church slowly, "she has partnered with a young CIA field agent formerly of the Hungarian station. His name is Harry Bolt."

I shook my head. "Don't know him."

"You know his father," said Church. "Harry shortened his name some time ago. His birth name is Harcourt Bolton, Junior."

PART THREE
LIGHTS OUT

•————•

*Deep into that darkness peering, long I stood there
wondering, fearing,
Doubting, dreaming dreams no mortal ever
dared to dream before;
But the silence was unbroken, and the darkness
gave no token. . . .
—Edgar Allan Poe
"The Raven"*

CHAPTER SIXTY-FOUR

THE PIER
DMS SPECIAL PROJECTS OFFICE
SAN DIEGO, CALIFORNIA
SEPTEMBER 8, 1:19 P.M.

Junie Flynn stepped onto the elevator, pushed the button for the parking garage, and was tugging her cell phone out of her pocket to make a call when someone yelled for her to hold the car. A hand shot between the doors and the rubber buffers bounced back from the wrist of Harcourt Bolton.

"You're fast," she said as he stepped inside.

"Old but not dead yet," he said, grinning and puffing a little from having run down the hall.

"Parking lot?" she asked.

"Yes. Been a long day and we old duffers need to take naps or we fall asleep in meetings."

"It's only a little after one."

"I was up all night," he said, and reinforced it with a yawn that made his jaws creak. "God, excuse me."

They got off in the parking garage, but Bolton touched her arm before they went their separate ways. "I've heard a lot about you, Junie. You're quite an impressive woman. You've overcome so much. You've dealt with hardships and obstacles that would have crippled most people, and yet here you stand. A radiant woman of intellect and power. Compassion, too. FreeTech is a testament to good intentions."

Junie was surprised. "You know about FreeTech?"

"Mr. Church tells me that your company is repurposing many of the technologies Joe took away from Howard Shelton's Majestic group."

"I'm surprised he told you."

Bolton's smile was rueful. "The Deacon and I go way back. I won't

349

lie and say we've always been friends, more like friendly rivals, but we play for the same team. We both want to save the world from itself."

"I suppose that's how we all feel."

"Not all of us," he said, his smile dimming. "I heard that your offices were robbed. Such a frightening invasion. Thieves these days wouldn't bat an eye about hurting someone. There are so many bad people in the world. So many people who have darkness in their hearts. So many people who want to turn out the lights on everyone else."

"Yes," she said. "And it hurts me to see how often they win."

"You think they're winning?"

"Don't you?" she asked, surprised. "With what ISIS or ISIL or whatever they're calling it now is doing? With what those people down at Gateway tried to do?" She shook her head. "It shows how sick the world is."

"Sickness can be cured," said Bolton. "And bad people can be redeemed."

"Sometimes, I suppose."

"Look at your own company. As I understand it you are taking technologies that could do unimaginable harm and are using them to save lives. And, if you want to talk about redemption, I hear that Alexander Chismer—or should I call him Toys?—is one of your employees. Or is he more than that? He has unusually high DMS-approved security clearance for a person who, by all accounts, should be serving multiple life sentences for murder, terrorism, and a laundry list of other crimes. If you have been able to reform someone like him, then perhaps there is hope for us all."

"How do you know so much about Toys?"

"You ask how and not *what* I know?" Bolton chuckled. "Come now, Junie, don't forget who I am. I'm a spy, don't forget."

Junie took a small step back from him. "I don't think I want to talk about Toys or FreeTech," she said. "I have to go."

He began to reach for her and caught himself. "God, I didn't mean to spook you, Junie. Truly I did not. I'm trying to tell you how much I admire what you're doing."

"I really have to go," she said. "It was a pleasure to meet you."

She backed a couple of steps away and then turned and hurried over to her car. When she got in and locked the doors, Junie turned to see him still standing there. Watching her as she started the car and drove away.

JONATHAN MABERRY

CHAPTER SIXTY-FIVE

CATAMARAN RESORT HOTEL AND SPA
3999 MISSION BOULEVARD
SAN DIEGO, CALIFORNIA
SEPTEMBER 8, 9:01 P.M.

He lived like a monk in paradise.

The resort was gorgeous, with sculptured gardens in which stands of green bamboo framed ponds of brightly colored koi. Parrots in lovely ornate cages chattered to one another, and ducks waddled in and out of a series of lazy streams that were also home to turtles and bullfrogs. Totem poles hand-carved in Bali seemed to encourage meditation in the gardens. And guests could wander beneath the cool canopy of leaves formed by over a hundred species of palm trees, with a thousand species of flowers and plants filling the air with a subtle olio of fragrances.

The Polynesian-themed hotel had over three hundred guest rooms and suites, each with a private balcony or patio. One wall of them looked out over the blue perfection of Mission Bay. From the top floors on the other side the guests could see the deeper blue of the vast Pacific.

The sad young man sat on a beach chair outside one of the ground-floor garden apartments. His was the least ostentatious of the rooms and it had the least enchanting view. That was fine with him. It was remote and it was quiet. The fact that he owned the hotel was something no one at the Catamaran knew. The staff knew that he was a permanent resident—the only such person at the place—and they mutually assumed that he was a relative of the owners.

He wasn't. He had no relatives anywhere. They were all dead. So were most of his friends.

He wished he was, too, and though suicide was always easy enough to engineer, it was never an option for him. Some of the residents of purgatory took their penance seriously. He certainly did.

Living at the resort offered him solitude when he wanted it. Tourists were notoriously clannish in places like this. There were very few of the raucous party types there, and the rest of the guests seemed to sense that they would not find a companion for idle chatter in the unsmiling young man. They were correct in that. He was never rude, but he seldom gave more than one-word answers. The only conversation he ever sought was with the resort's five parrots, Bianchi, Chadwick, Cornell, Mercer, and Scooter. They never asked complicated questions and he found them to be agreeable company even in his darkest moods.

He also had a cat.

Or, perhaps it was more true to say that the cat had adopted him.

On a chilly April night the gray-and-black tabby had come in through his open French window, jumped up on his bed, and gone to sleep without comment. The young man allowed it. After all, who was he to tell a cat where he could or could not sleep?

After a week of sharing his room, his bed, and his meals with the cat it was clear it had no intention of leaving. It was also clear that it had once been a well-cared-for housecat but had now fallen on very hard times. It was scruffy, underfed, and badly scarred from claw and tooth. No collar or tag. Only after the man received a couple of flea-bites did he scoop him up and take him to an animal hospital. The cat was given a thorough examination, received all the proper shots, had a chip inserted under its skin, was washed and groomed. When the woman at the desk asked him what the cat's name was, the young man considered for a moment, and finally said, "Job."

And Job he was.

Job and the young man kept company with one another. The cat liked being petted, so the man petted him. The cat liked grilled fish instead of cat food, and so the man requested that from the kitchen. The cat didn't like to use the cat box inside the apartment, so the man put one on his deck. It was the cat's life, after all, and the man had no desire to impose his will on it. Every once in a while, in the darkest hours of the night, the cat would allow the young man to wrap his arms around the small furry body. If it minded the salty tears that fell on its head, it did not complain.

That was how it was for the cat named Job and the man who had been born as Alexander Chismer but was never called that except by

Mr. Church. Everyone else called him Toys. He hated that nickname because it reminded him of his sins. He never told anyone that he hated it, though. He knew that some of them—Junie Flynn, Dr. Circe O'Tree-Sanchez, Helmut Deacon, and a few others—used it with affection. That was hurtful in its way, though he accepted it as a necessary part of the comprehensive plan of his punishment. The damned do not have the right to complain.

Toys and Job lived quietly. Sometimes Job decided that he wanted to accompany Toys when he went to work. He accepted a collar and leash and walked right at Toys's heel. In the car Job slept in a soft cat bed. At the office, he had his own carpet-covered perch that had several levels and allowed him to perch like a vulture up near the ceiling. From that vantage point he could look down at the people with whom Toys worked, and he could keep an eye on the monstrous gray Irish wolfhound that was always with Circe. Once in a while Junie would bring Joe Ledger's cat, Cobbler, into the office. The two cats invariably ignored each other, though Job allowed the marmalade tabby to sit on one of the lower levels of his perch.

Toys did not love many things in this world, but came to love Job in a way that was unsullied and uncomplicated. They accepted each other on their own terms and without judgment.

Perhaps there was some cosmic message or lesson in the fact that it was the cat that saved his life.

Toys was asleep, slumped in a rattan chair with his feet propped on the edge of the bed. The TV was on but the Netflix movie he'd been watching had long since ended, to be replaced by a bland information screen. The cat was asleep on his lap, stretched across the tops of his thighs. The hotel grounds were quiet except for crickets.

Then suddenly Job was awake. The cat stood up, hissing, his claws flexing to stab into Toys's leg.

"Ow, bloody hell!" cried Toys as he came suddenly and painfully awake. He shot to his feet. "What the hell are you playing at, you little bugger?"

Then Toys understood.

The French door had been opened and in the pale glow from the TV he could see figures inside his room. Four of them, and they'd all turned toward him when he'd cried out.

They were dressed in black suits, with white shirts and dark ties.

Each of them held a small flashlight. One was bent over the chair on which Toys had placed his briefcase. Two others were hunched down over his laptop. The fourth was by the door, acting as a lookout.

They stared at Toys, and he gaped at them.

The cat hissed again.

The figure by the chair said only two words.

"Kill him."

CHAPTER SIXTY-SIX

Mr. Church locked the conference room door and walked over to the big windows. The San Diego night was huge and starless. Bastion meowed softly and Church bent to pick him up and stood with the cat tucked into the crook of his left arm while he stroked him with his gloved fingertips.

After a few minutes of silent contemplation, Church lowered the cat gently to a chair, picked up his cell phone, engaged the twenty-eight-bit encryption scrambler, and made a long-distance call. It rang five times before it was answered.

"St. Germaine," said Lilith. She sounded winded.

"Are you all right?"

"I'm fine. I'm on a job." In the background he could hear the faint but unmistakable sound of a voice raised in sudden agony. The scream rose and rose and then died away. It was a male voice, and there was a quality of weariness in the scream, as if this was not the first time he had been made to cry out.

"Does this have anything to do with what happened to Violin?"

"It might."

"Lilith . . ."

"The Ordo Fratrum Claustrorum tried to kill my daughter. I want to know why. Do you expect me to sit at home and knit comforters?"

There was another scream. Briefer, but more intense.

"Have you learned anything?" asked Church.

"I learned that men are weak," she sneered.

"It occurs to me that you already knew that."

"It is important to reinforce one's perspective," said Lilith. "Though there is also a measure of disappointment in always being right."

"Why didn't you tell me that the Brotherhood had become active again?"

"I don't remember any agreement where I tell you everything that happens in the world, St. Germaine."

Church sat on the edge of the table. Outside, on the moonlit beach, a group of teenagers were playing volleyball in the dark. On the missed shots, when the ball was lost in shadows, they collided and tripped, and they never stopped laughing. Near them a couple lay on a blanket, kissing with obvious passion. Farther up the beach a blond-haired man was helping a teenage boy—almost certainly his son—sort out his night-fishing rig. Life was happening. It was moving forward with vigor and even a measure of joy. It was clean and the moon was bright and there was a purity in the starry sky and the silver-tipped waves.

"Lilith," he said slowly, "the power outages occurring here in the States are being perpetrated by ISIL. The technology was somehow taken from a program associated with Majestic. The scientists at that program had been attempting to obtain copies of the most restricted books on the Index Librorum Prohibitorum."

There was a heavy silence at the other end of the call. No more screams. Not even the sound of her breathing.

"Are you listening to me?"

"I'm listening," said Lilith.

"You know that the DMS has been weakened."

"I heard."

"We are at a crisis point and I am asking you to tell me if there is anything you know or have heard that could help us."

Lilith said, "This matter that you are working on, does it have any-thing to do with an attempt to construct and operate an interdimen-sional gateway? An Orpheus Gate."

"It would appear so. Do you know something about it?"

"Yes," said Lilith. "I know a lot about it. This is old, old science, St. Germaine. You understand me? This is very old."

"Believe me when I tell you that I can appreciate that."

"Good. Do you know about the side effects?"

"Yes."

"Going into dreams? Traveling with just the mind?"

"Remote viewing. Yes. How do you know so much?"

There was another of the protracted screams. "People talk," she said. "If you know how to ask the right questions, and in the right way."

"Yes," he said again.

"St. Germaine . . . do you know about the Mullah of the Black Tent?"

He said, "No, I do not."

"I'm surprised," she said. "The CIA are investigating him. I wonder that they haven't told you."

"I have been cut out of several information loops. Who is this person?"

She told Church a strange story about a simple cleric from a tiny mosque in an unimportant town who had, almost overnight, become a powerful force among the fighters of the Islamic State. Lilith's Arklight team had been doing hits against ISIL for months, ever since they officially enshrined the rape of the Yazidi girls and women. Some of the ISIL fighters her sisters had taken had spoken of the Mullah as a new prophet who would lead a true global jihad. To speak of him to anyone was viewed as a sin against God, and even the slightest transgression, the most offhand mention, was punished by death. Not just of the sinner but of his family.

"That's an effective security protocol," said Church.

Lilith's laugh was ugly. "I've found that every man is willing to tell everything if you ask in the right way. One of my sisters asked the right way. Unfortunately the person we asked isn't high enough to know much."

She said that the Mullah of the Black Tent was working to unite the various factions of Islam under one banner, promising that the caliphate had a great weapon that was going to bring America to its knees. Normally such claims would be met with skepticism, hostility, or indifference, because there had always been threats like that.

"They started paying attention when there was a terrible accident at a racetrack. I think you call it NASCAR? The Mullah predicted that event and it happened exactly as he said it would. Then there was a similar event at a presidential debate. It is one thing to step up and try to claim responsibility for an event but it is entirely different when the event is predicted."

"So this prophet has insider knowledge of the impending events," said Church.

Lilith's voice became intense. "Arklight is no more at war with *true* Muslims than we are with true people of any faith, as long as religion is not used like a knife. But this Mullah is dangerous. He is perhaps the most dangerous man alive today, because when he speaks there are Shiites and Sunni who stop to listen. Not merely a few, but many, and each time one of the Mullah's predictions comes to pass his following grows."

"Thank you for telling me this, Lilith. I will put resources on it and—"

"There's more, St. Germaine," she said. "Are you listening?"

"I'm listening."

"The Mullah has made several predictions about a much bigger attack. Something so big it will bring America to its knees. Now, I know we've both heard threats of that kind before, but this is different. I did not know what it could be until my sources told me about the incident at the research laboratory. About the theft of the weaponized smallpox. SX-56, yes?"

"Yes," he said, and his voice was faint. "What have you heard?"

He heard her take a breath. "The Mullah has prophesied that the hand of God will reach down from heaven and scatter pestilence across the land of the great Satan. The faithful need only watch, and from each finger of God will fall the seeds of punishment that will wipe out a generation." She paused. "Do you understand what that means? Ten fingers, ten points of attack. Ten cities. And this pestilence has to be the SX-56."

He said nothing.

"St. Germaine," said Lilith, her voice softer now but more desperate. "You know who is most vulnerable to that disease. You know how fast it spreads. This weaponized strain is the Devil's own design. Goddamn the men who conceived it it. Be damned to the people in your government for allowing it to exist. The Mullah and his army are going to launch a plague upon ten cities and slaughter a generation of children."

Church closed his eyes. "Do you know when this will happen?"

"No. The men we interrogated did not know."

"Can you find someone who does know?"

She was quiet for a moment. "Perhaps."

"Will you?" asked Church. "I know it is a lot to ask."

"I will not do it for you," she said. "But tell me, St. Germaine, what do you think I would *not* do for those children?"

She did not wait for his answer. The line went dead.

CHAPTER SIXTY-SEVEN

CATAMARAN RESORT HOTEL AND SPA
3999 MISSION BOULEVARD
SAN DIEGO, CALIFORNIA
SEPTEMBER 8, 9:11 P.M.

It was four to one.

Toys was in pajama bottoms and a plain white undershirt. No shoes, no weapons. The four intruders had guns, Toys could see the bulges under their jackets, but they came at him barehanded. Quick, quiet, deadly, all in a rush, wanting to smash him down and shut him up before he could call for help.

Toys never shouted.

He never called for help. It didn't occur to him.

The man closest to him tried to end it with a vicious front kick to the groin.

Toys twisted and crouched, and as he did so hooked the attacking foot with the crook of his left arm and chopped down on the knee with his right elbow. The joint disintegrated and the attacker shrieked. Still holding the shattered leg, Toys rammed him backward into the others. There was an instant confusion of arms and legs as they tried to catch their friend and push him out of the way at the same time so they could kill their enemy. Toys didn't give them the chance.

He jumped at them, using a leaping hip check to drive the wounded man more solidly into the others while lashing out at the two closest masked faces. He caught them both with solid palm-heel shots because there was no room for them to dodge. They crumpled under the force of the blows and the weight of their friend, and Toys landed beside the mass, pivoted to engage the fourth man, slapped the intruder's hand away as he sought to draw a pistol, and chopped him solidly across the Adam's apple. The man reeled backward, clawing at a crushed throat, trying to gasp in even a spoonful of air and utterly failing.

Toys turned again and kicked at the closest of the others, catching him on the temple with his bare heel. Toys was thin and looked skinny in clothes, but his body was all wiry strength and he knew how to hit and how to hurt. He rechambered his foot and swung a very short, very fast heel kick at the opening of the last attacker's mask, catching the man in the left eye. Now there were three injured men on the floor, groaning and crying out in pain and surprise.

For the tiniest fragment of a moment Toys paused, not really wanting to do what had to be done. Not wanting to do what he'd already done. But behind him Job hissed once more, in mingled fear and anger, and that turned a switch in Toys's head. A veil of dark red seemed to drop over his eyes and there was a sound in his ears like green wood being pulled apart.

He did not lose himself in the moment. His mind did not go black and he never for a moment lost control of himself or what he was doing. Not once.

Nor was he lost to some savage joy. No inner darkness took hold of him or owned him.

He beat them all into silence.

He broke them apart.

All the time he was aware that his cat was watching him.

And that maybe God was watching him, too.

CHAPTER SIXTY-EIGHT

Mr. Church spent the rest of the evening on the phone, disturbing some people as they settled in for the night, getting others out of bed, catching some late owls at their desks.

He called the White House and was told that the president was not able to take his call. He called thirty-four separate members of Congress and nine high-ranking military officers. He had friends who listened, and he spoke with friends who clearly did not believe him. And he spoke to many who were afraid of even talking on the phone with him. Many of them reacted with the guarded caution people reserve for the hysterical and the insane, proof that his credibility had been eroded.

He made calls to the Centers for Disease Control, to the National Institutes of Health and FEMA. He spoke with various friends in the industry. The ones he expected to have courage and vision listened and promised to help, but it was a smaller number of allies than he expected to find.

Aunt Sallie promised to put every available resource on it, but many doors had been shut to the DMS. Walls had been built.

With great reluctance Church brought Harcourt Bolton into the loop, and his new codirector surprised him by believing in this horrific new intel. Bolton hurried back to his office to see if he could get through to the people who had rebuffed Church.

Hours burned away.

Lilith did not call back.

No one returned his calls.

CHAPTER SIXTY-NINE

It would soon be a problem of logistics. Of concealment and disposal. Of constructing explanations in case anyone heard the scuffle.

Toys was aware that there were now so many details to be handled. He was aware of it, but he didn't care.

What mattered to him was the man who sat bound and bleeding on the floor. The man's legs were wrapped with an extension cord. His wrists were tied with strips torn from Toys's undershirt. He sat in a pool of his own blood. Not too big a pool, but enough. Pain had carved his face into an inhuman mask; fear had turned that mask to stone.

Toys sat on the small, wheeled desk chair. Job perched on the edge of the bed, watching like a vulture, or a jury. Also on the bed were four very strange pistols, all identical, all with a cluster of prongs instead of gun barrels. There were also four disposable cell phones, four rolls of twenty-dollar bills totaling two hundred dollars each. And four short fixed-blade fighting knives. Good knives, too.

The moment had stretched thin, quivering like a frayed guitar string that needed only a feather-light touch to snap.

Without saying anything, Toys reached back, stroked Job's fur for a moment, then reached past him and picked up one of the knives. He weighed it in his hand, getting the feel of its size, its balance. Its potential. The blade was like many that he'd handled over the years and the bound man watched as Toys moved it in his grip, reversing the hold, learning it, making it his own. Then he bent forward and set the knife on the floor near the man's right foot.

Toys sat back in his chair, crossed his legs, and settled his bloody hands in his lap.

"You know the bloody drill, mate," he said quietly. "The whole 'there are two ways we can do this' thing, right? We both know you don't want it to be the hard way, so do us both a favor and let's skip to the part where you tell me what the bloody hell you're playing at. Why did you and these effing twats break in here, what are you looking for, and who sent you?"

The man clamped his jaws shut as if afraid that all of those answers would tumble out against his will.

Toys sighed.

"If you make me pick up that knife it's going to force us to go down some very bad roads," said Toys quietly. "If you know who I am, then maybe you know *what* I am. Is that true? Have they briefed you on me?"

The man tried not to respond, but his head nodded anyway. Just a little. Enough.

"Then why do you think that this will end any way except my way?" asked the sad young man.

The wounded man stared up at him, eyes wide, growing wider, filling with a dreadful understanding.

CHAPTER SEVENTY

"Deacon," said the president, leaning back in his chair and holding the phone to his ear, "sorry to call you so late, but I just got off the phone with Harcourt Bolton. He warned me that you wanted to talk about something earthshaking."

"Warned?" asked Mr. Church.

"A joke. Personally I thought you'd be licking your wounds and keeping a low profile."

"Is that what you thought, Mr. President? I'd have guessed that a comment of that kind would be beneath you. I will adjust my expectations henceforth."

"Now is not a good time to get high-assed with me," snapped the president. "You don't have the political currency needed to buy much goodwill. Not from this administration. I know you enjoyed a great deal of freedom with my predecessors, but times have changed. Your team in Wisconsin was supposed to find out who stole the SX-56. A simple interrogation. Instead what happened? They went crazy and killed our only suspect and then themselves. Now God only knows where it is. If it's released, then any civilian deaths are on your head. Let's be clear about that."

"That is precisely why I wanted to speak with you directly. I have received reliable intel about the SX-56."

"Sure," said the president, "we heard about some of that. It's rumor-mill garbage."

"I assure you it's not. I *need* you to act."

"You need? You? Really?" The president sighed. "You used to be the best in the business, Deacon, but times have definitely changed."

"Have they?"

"Yes, they have. I don't have skeletons in my closet," said the president, "which means you don't have any dials to turn on me. Everyone seemed to want to give you a long leash and let you do whatever you wanted to do. That's not going to happen. I've gone over the wording of your charter. It was created by an executive order and it's a stroke of my pen to cancel that charter."

"So you keep telling me," said Church.

The president made a rude noise. "Harcourt tells me that you're trying to establish a connection between the power outages and that Gateway debacle."

"We believe we have."

"Are you calling to get me to put you back in charge of that case?"

"I am. We have intelligence from a reliable source that the attacks are being directed by an ISIL leader who goes by the code name of the Mullah of the Black Tent. In the last few hours I have managed to obtain copies of two different sources, one in Central Intelligence and one in Barrier, that have mentioned this man. I can find no evidence that either report was taken seriously or that any actions were taken to pursue the investigation."

"We're looking at him," said the president.

"We as in *who*, exactly?" asked Church.

"That's none of your business. It's not your case."

"It is if the agencies looking into this are not filing reports or taking appropriate actions. Why don't we have a detailed file on this man in the shared database?"

"It's a developing case. We don't know much about him yet."

"Mr. President, would you care to wager how much information I can amass in the next twenty-four hours?"

"Let me say it again more slowly so you can catch the words," said the president. "It's. Not. Your. Case."

"I see."

The president wanted to hurl the phone out the window. "You heard me that time. Good. Is that all?"

"No. I have obtained additional evidence that may connect Gateway with the Majestic program. This evidence may also connect the Stargate project with Gateway, as well."

The president laughed. "God, you're really losing it. Why are you wasting my time with this crap?"

"Because I have reason to believe that Stargate was never shut down. I believe it was transferred internally to Majestic and from there to Gateway. And I believe the technology is being used to attack the intelligence community of this country."

"You're being paranoid."

"And you're being obstructive."

"I'm sorry . . . what did you just say?"

"Mr. President, I'm coming to you with new intelligence that, at very least, must make us reconsider our response strategy to a national crisis. We are talking about the pending release of a dangerous bioweapon on ten American cities. Even if you think I'm off my game, I can't think of a single valid reason for you to dismiss it out of hand. Why would you, of all people, risk it? And yet you do. I find it curious that your response is to dismiss and mock."

"Want to know what I find curious?" said the president sharply. "That you have the brass balls to talk to me in this manner. Perhaps I need to remind you who is commander in chief and who is a subordinate."

"I am very much aware of the Washington power structure, Mr. President."

"Are you? That may require a formal review. If you thought that by calling and insulting me you would somehow reclaim what you justifiably lost, Deacon, then you are very much mistaken. You've mismanaged the powers and authority granted you by my predecessors. If I had any doubts before about putting Harcourt in charge of the DMS, I have none now. In fact I wonder if he's not the most appropriate person to take exclusive directorship of the DMS."

Mr. Church said, "Since you are being frank with me, Mr. President—and as it seems I can't get further onto your bad side—let me be equally frank with you."

"Oh, please do. You've got a little bit of rope left."

"I will give you the benefit of the doubt that you made a decision based on your understanding of the situation as it stood prior to this conversation. I called to help you clarify your vision. We are at a crossroads, you and I. I would hate to see you take the wrong path merely because you dislike me. I would hope your integrity, political sobriety, and good judgment will keep you from making choices that could have unfortunate consequences for the nation we are both sworn to protect."

"Don't you dare threaten me, you arrogant son of a bitch," growled the president.

"That was not a threat, Mr. President, though I find it significant that you've chosen to take it as such."

The line went dead.

The president stared at the phone for a moment.

"Asshole," he muttered.

Then he bent forward, cleared the line, and made a call.

CHAPTER SEVENTY-ONE

I had high hopes for a quiet night.

I got home very late and had a nice dinner with Junie. Fish tacos and dirty rice. Then we put the dishes in the sink and moved to the balcony to watch the stars over the ocean. It had been cloudy earlier but now there were stars by the billion.

Junie was in on the case now, and I was free to share the rest of what had happened with her. I told her about Lilith calling Mr. Church with a tip about a new and very mysterious ISIL leader she called the Mullah of the Black Tent.

"I thought that case was taken away from you," she said.

"Church said he was going to talk to the president about that. Maybe he'll have some good news for me tomorrow."

She touched my face. "I know you want to get back into this, Joe, but you have to give yourself time to rest."

"I've had enough rest, thanks," I said. She didn't like that answer, but she knew how to pick her fights.

The evening rolled on toward night. We talked about Majestic and Gateway. We speculated about Prospero Bell. What was he like? Did he know about her and the other hive kids? She said that Greene seemed to suggest that maybe Prospero wasn't dead, that his death had been faked. It was only an impression, though; she had nothing to base it on. My middle-aged marmalade-and-white tabby, Cobbler, came and sprawled in my lap. Junie was still on her first glass of wine because she had no tolerance at all. I forget how many glasses of bourbon I'd put away. More than my share, but on the whole not enough. Junie wore one of my flannel shirts over a skimpy top and leggings. Her feet were propped on the rail, toes touching mine. We were drifting toward a lazy, let's-go-to-bed silence when my cell phone rang. I grunted in surprise when I saw who the caller was. He wasn't someone who called me except in very rare cases when he couldn't otherwise find Junie. Bemused, I punched the button.

"Toys," I said.

"Ledger," he said.

There was a moment of silence, which is how a lot of our conversations start. A moment to assess. I hated him for a long time, and with very good cause. Last year, when the Seven Kings—led by that monster Nicodemus—invaded a hospital in San Diego with the intention of killing Circe O'Tree—Rudy's pregnant wife and Church's daughter—Toys nearly died to protect her. In doing so he helped save Junie's life. Toys was nearly cut to ribbons by broken glass. His body is covered with scars. Afterward, when he was leaving the hospital, I told him that while I still didn't like him and would never forgive him for the crimes he'd committed, he and I were no longer at war.

"Junie's right here," I said, "hold on and—"

"No," he said. "I didn't call for her. I called for you."

"For me? Why?"

"I need your help. I just killed four people," he said.

CHAPTER SEVENTY-TWO

Toys was sitting on a deck chair outside of his room but stood as we approached. He was dressed in jeans and a Hawaiian shirt, looking exactly like a vacationing tourist unless you looked into his eyes. If eyes are the windows of the soul, then beyond those panes was a bleak and wasted landscape that was devoid of all hope.

"Are you okay?" asked Junie as she hugged him and kissed his cheek.

"I'll live." He looked at me. "Ledger."

"Toys."

No handshakes. We weren't touchy-feely with each other and probably never would be. He didn't try to pet Ghost, either, because Toys is not that stupid.

On the chair next to him was his ragged-looking cat, which eyed Ghost with such obvious disdain that the dislike between them was immediate and palpable. Ghost barely tolerates Cobbler, but his general opinion of cats is that they are chew toys. The cat on the chair probably considered all dogs to be scratching posts. Ah, love.

Toys introduced the cat as "Job," explaining that the scruffy animal had been through the wringer.

"Lot of that going around," I said.

Junie reached out a hand to Job, which he sniffed and then rubbed his head against. Ghost looked disgusted and walked over to the closed door of Toys's apartment, took a sniff, and immediately began to growl softly.

I drew my gun and nodded to the door. "Shall we?"

"You won't need that," said Toys. "All of the drama is past tense. It's not pretty, though."

"I promise I won't faint," I said as I reholstered my Sig Sauer.

He gave a half smile. "I meant that for Junie."

Junie patted his arm. "I'm pretty sure I'm unshockable at this point."

Even so, Toys shifted to stand in front of the door. "Let Joe go in. Even if you are the Iron Lady, you don't need to see that. I had to, um, encourage one of them to talk to me."

"I got this," I said, and pushed past him. The door was unlocked, the lights turned low. I stepped inside and stopped, with Ghost lingering on the threshold, a ridge of hairs standing up along his back. The entire room was a mess and there was blood everywhere. He said that he'd had to encourage one of them. I spotted who that unlucky bastard was right off. He was the one who didn't look human anymore. There was only a small patch of unbloodied rug to stand on and I went no farther in. Everything that could be read was splashed on the walls and written in the taut lines of pain etched into four dead faces. The distinctive freshly sheared copper smell of blood was masked by three burning sticks of temple incense.

The men were dressed in dark suits. On the bed were four microwave pulse pistols.

Closers.

"Ah, shit," I muttered. I squatted down beside one of them and tore open his shirt, then repeated that on the others. As I suspected, this guy and his chums weren't wearing the super-skivvies. If they had been, Toys would probably be dead. Without touching anything else I withdrew and closed the door behind me. I took a moment to breathe the fragrant night air.

"I told you," said Toys quietly.

"Tell me what happened," I said, and he went through all of it, speaking quickly and in low tones. When he got to the part where he questioned the last of the four assassins, he paused and looked down at his hands. They appeared to be very clean, the way flesh looks when it's been scrubbed with furious vigor. My own skin has had that glow a few times over the years. When Grace Courtland died in my arms it took weeks before my hands felt clean of her blood.

"They're Closers," I said.

Toys nodded. "New to it, though. They hired on a few months ago."

"Hired by who?" I asked, but then my cell rang. It was Bug.

"Kind of busy at the moment," I told him.

"Unless you're taking fire, Joe," he said, "this is more important.

I've been searching through all those papers for more on that book inventory. The Unlearnable Truths. And I think I hit gold."

"I am definitely listening," I said, holding my hand out to Junie and Toys to be quiet. "Hit me."

Bug hit me. "This kid Prospero Bell believed that there is a mathematical code hidden in the unlearnable books, right? Well, he wasn't joking. That code is there, and it tells you how to program the power flow so that the God Machine works the way it's supposed to."

"To open a dimensional gateway," I supplied, and Toys stared at me, eyebrows raised so far they nearly vanished into his hairline. Junie put a finger to her lips.

"Right," said Bug, "but it does more than that. With the sequencing code you can regulate any of the Kill Switch devices on the same network. I ran this by Bill Hu and he says that what this means is that if you made a bunch of the Kill Switches, you could position them around an area, switch it on, and everything inside is switched off. Hu thinks that they've been doing this already. Houston and the debate and like that. But Dr. San Pedro's records indicate that these smaller devices are single use. They melt down completely after a few seconds. Now, if you have the master control sequence code, those devices *won't* overheat. You can place them around, say, New York City, switch them on so that everything goes dark, switch them off again, and keep doing that as much as you like. No one has to even be there to run them. And you can keep doing it when the emergency responders get there. You can make this go from bad to worse with the flip of a switch, but only if you have the sequence code."

"Jesus Christ," I said. Sweat had begun to pop out all over my body. The implications were . . . well, staggering. I actually felt the floor tilting under me. And I immediately knew—absolutely 100 percent knew—that we hadn't seen how bad this could get. Not even close.

"You okay, Joe?" asked Bug.

"Not even a little."

"Well, it gets crazier," he said, his excitement raising his voice to a mouse squeak. "We're eighty percent sure that Gateway had a spy in Oscar Bell's organization. A guy who Bell hired to obtain the Unlearnable Truths for Prospero but was actually on the payroll for Erskine and company. He used 'Mr. Priest' as his cover name, but we were able to lift prints from reports he filed, and even though the prints were degraded we ran them through—"

"I don't need the science," I said. "Give me the damn name."

"Esteban Santoro. Joe, he's Rafael Santoro's brother."

Rafael Santoro was the chief assistant—the Conscience—to the King of Fear, Hugo Vox. Santoro was one of the most brutal, sadistic men I've ever encountered. A man who raised coercion to a dark art form. He was also the man who formed and personally trained the Kingsmen, the elite special ops fighters who worked for the Seven Kings. I'd fought the man and he'd nearly killed me. Church made the guy disappear. Not sure if he was alive or dead.

Now we had to deal with his brother.

I said, "You're going to hurt me, aren't you, Bug?"

He cleared his throat. "Esteban Santoro, or Mr. Priest, used to be one of the field operators for the Ordo Fratrum Claustrorum. And when he left them he went to work for Howard Shelton. He was a Closer."

"Shit."

"And this guy Priest apparently acquired *all* of the books on Prospero's list."

"Right, but they were destroyed along with Gateway."

"The books maybe," said Bug, "but not the scans."

I stiffened. "What scans?"

"That's what we found. Priest oversaw a complete scan of the Unlearnable Truths. It was part of their search for the sequencing code."

"Where are those scans?"

"I'm working on that now. It was outsourced to one of the contractors who worked with Erskine, but we don't know which one. Nikki thinks she'll have that figured out by this morning. Noon at the latest."

"That's incredible, Bug. You're amazing."

"No, I'm not. I'm slow. I should have figured this out before now."

"No, you're amazing. I could kiss you."

"Please don't." He paused. "But that lady who works for you . . . ? The one with all the stuffed pandas on her desk? Lydia-Rose? Maybe you could put in a good word for me . . . ?"

I laughed. "Done."

"Just so you know," said Bug, "I called this in to the Pier. Mr. Church was busy so I told Mr. Bolton. He's already working on it, too."

"Nice. Thanks!"

I disconnected the call and turned to Toys. "You were the Conscience to the King of Plagues. You knew Rafael Santoro."

He flinched and went pale. "Yes."

"The name you were about to give me when Bug called . . . was it Esteban Santoro?"

Instead of being surprised he merely looked old and sad. "Yes."

"What I don't get," said Junie, touching his arm, "is why they went after you."

"They wanted my laptop."

"Right, but why?"

Toys said, "The Closers were supposed to look for any files related to Majestic."

CHAPTER SEVENTY-THREE

I ordered a team to come and clean up for Toys. The bodies were taken away in discreet laundry hampers and everything was smoothed over with the night manager. Then I called Church to bring him up to speed.

"First Junie's office was robbed, and now they came after Toys's laptop, looking for anything connected to Majestic," I said. "Our bad guys know a lot of stuff they shouldn't know and it's pissing me off. I mean, *how* do they know?"

"That is perhaps the most important question we need to answer," said Church.

"Boss," I said, "that Project Stargate stuff. I'm beginning to think we need to take a closer look at that."

"To make a bad joke, Captain, you're reading my mind."

He hung up. My next call was to Harcourt Bolton and I woke him from a sound sleep. He was drowsy and grumpy, but he perked up when I explained why I was calling. Like Church, Bolton said that he needed to make some calls.

Junie called Christel Sparks, the former cop who now ran security for FreeTech, and gave her a rough idea of what happened at Toys's place. Christel was smart and capable, and Junie trusted her. Security would be doubled around all FreeTech facilities and senior staff.

Toys came home with us and stayed in our guest room. Job came with him, which Cobbler seemed to like and Ghost did not. The two cats sat on the balcony and looked at things only they could see in the darkness before dawn. I tried to get some sleep, but I was too wired, and barely closed my eyes. So I got up early and left Junie and Toys at home. There's good security at our place, but I called Brian

Botley and asked him to swing by and camp out until Junie went into work.

Church told me about his call from Lilith, and about the Mullah of the Black Tent. I asked him when POTUS was ordering a full-team hit on the Mullah and got punched by the news that the president did not believe Lilith's intel was real. Balls.

So, I spent the morning working my own networks and calling in favors with my friends in the other intelligence services trying to find out something—*anything*—about the stolen vials of SX-56.

But everywhere I went I hit walls, too. Friends were being cagey and evasive. Others were treating me like a leper. Or like the DMS was itself a leper colony. A few truly good friends confided that they had nothing to share because no one had a clue, and they warned me to stay out of it. Word had come down that Church and all of his people were politically toxic. We were being shut out and we were being blamed. It made me feel sick and lost. I ached to be back in a coma.

It wasn't much better when I trolled for information inside our own group. Bug's team was still wading through the papers and, after the first news, had found nothing else new. And Hu was getting absolutely nowhere with trying to understand the effects of the mind control. He'd obtained some of the old Stargate records, but they were incomplete and, as he phrased it, "as useless as hairy nipples on a velociraptor." Dr. Hu is weirdly specific.

At eleven Lydia-Rose buzzed me to say that Violin had arrived and that she was in with Mr. Church. I didn't bolt and run to the conference room, but I'd have won a speed-walking competition. Once upon a time Violin and I had something very special going on. We weren't a couple, but what we had was pretty steamy. Very intense. But then I met Junie and the course of my romantic life shifted gears and changed lanes and that's the only road I'll ever take. Not sure that's a good metaphor for falling in love, but it's what I have. Violin did not take it as stoically as she'd have liked, and for a while I was almost afraid for Junie's safety. Violin isn't often like her mother, but she has her moments.

Then an assassin went after Junie and Violin was there. Junie was hurt, though. A bullet that destroyed any chance we'll ever have of having kids. Even though Violin killed the assassin, I knew she blamed herself for what happened to Junie. It was a special kind of blood debt

JONATHAN MABERRY

that is entirely self-imposed. The way I see it, Junie is alive because Violin was there, and that's a debt *I* can never repay.

Life is so very complicated for those of us who live out in the storm lands. Maybe it's that way for normal people, too. I wouldn't know. It's been too long since I've been normal. I wouldn't even know how to breathe in that world.

So now Violin was here. She'd been on the run from killers, fighting for her life while I was in a coma. Maybe if I'd been awake there might have been some way for me to reach out, to help her come out of harm's way. An egotistical male chauvinist thought? Not as much as it sounds. It's one member of a family wishing he could have been there for his dearest sister. Ghost, a member of our pack, was right at my heels, excited because he had heard Violin's name.

I whipped the conference room door open and rushed inside. And immediately tripped over someone who was bent down in front of me. We both went tumbling and clunking down onto the floor in a comedy-act sprawl of arms and legs. I landed better than him, but also on top of him, and the back of one of my heels thumped down into his crotch.

CHAPTER SEVENTY-FOUR

No one makes an entrance as graceful as Joseph Edwin Ledger. Seriously, folks, hold the applause until after the show.

We got ourselves untangled and I reached over and grabbed a fistful of shirt from somebody I had never met and wanted to punch. "Who in the wide blue fuck are you?"

The guy was ten years younger than me, a little chunky, with a round face and bright blue eyes and a mouth that was puckered with pain. He said, *"Eeerp."* Very faintly.

I hugged Violin. Ghost jumped all over her and got kisses on his furry white head. Violin reached down and pulled the kid to his feet and helped him into a chair. He moved with the kind of delicacy men use when a brute my size heel-kicks them in the wrinklies. Too bad.

"Joseph," said Violin, "meet Harry Bolt."

"Why'd you frigging trip me?" I demanded.

It took him a moment to get his voice back and it came out as a mouse squeak. "I . . . dropped my . . . cell phone. Bent to pick it up. You . . . attacked me."

"If I'd wanted to attack you," I began, and then caught identical looks from Church and Violin and snapped my mouth shut. Violin patted the groaning stranger on the shoulder.

"Harry is with the Agency," said Church. "I believe I mentioned him earlier."

I gaped at him. "Wait . . . *you're* Harcourt Bolton, Junior?"

"Um . . . yeah. I guess?" It came out almost like a question. "I . . . um . . . prefer Harry, though. Harry Bolt."

"What, is that some kind of cool superspy name? Bolt. Harry Bolt?"

His face, already flushed with pain, burned a deeper crimson. "Pretty much the opposite."

Then a voice spoke from the open doorway. "He changed it because he doesn't want to smear the family name."

Everyone turned to see Harcourt Bolton, Senior, standing there. Tall and good-looking, powerful, cultured. Annoyed and disappointed.

"Dad!" cried Harry as he launched out of his chair and rushed to hug his father. Bolton endured the hug. That was the best thing you could say about it. Endured. Harry hugged him and Bolton gave him a single, small pat on the back, then he pushed his son away and appraised him.

"What the hell happened to you?" he asked. I know he was asking about Harry's disheveled appearance and flushed face, but there was an implication of a deeper, perhaps existential question. I caught it, and from the flicker of disapproval that pinched Violin's mouth I saw that she did, too.

Harry immediately began trying to smooth down his hair and straighten his clothes. "It's been a little crazy, Dad. Violin and I had to go dark and—"

"Your entire station was wiped out," said Bolton coldly. "Your infil team was cut to pieces, Harry. I saw photos of their severed heads and yet you don't have a scratch. How did *you* escape a team of Closers?"

He leaned a little too heavy on the word "you." As if such a thing was beyond understanding.

As I believe I'd said, I'm pretty much captain of the Harcourt Bolton fan club, but right then I wanted to punch him. He was being a dick to his kid and he was doing it in front of other professionals. Not cool.

"Your son has brought us valuable intel, Harcourt," said Mr. Church. He rose and walked around the table to stand beside Harry. He never does things by accident, so that had to make a statement. Wish I'd thought of it.

Bolton sniffed. It was a snobbish, fussy thing for him to do and I could feel some of my affection for him beginning to bleed away. He'd been kind and considerate to me, but I did not like the way he treated his son. There's a saying that in order to understand someone you need to see how they treat their children. Or maybe it was their dog. Not sure. Worked out to the same thing in this case because Bolton seemed to treat Harry like a dog that had just shit on the rug.

"What intel?" asked Bolton, directing the question to Church.

"This," said Violin. She placed a heavy suitcase on the conference table, opened it to reveal a bulky item wrapped in a thick comforter. We all crowded around to watch. Inside the comforter was a book. Very large, very old, covered in strange markings and sealed with iron bands and heavy padlocks.

"Jesus," I said, "is that what I think it is?"

It was. One of the Unlearnable Truths.

"Hate to break it to you," I said to Violin and Harry, "but Bug thinks that there are complete scans of all these books in the Gateway records. He's working on locating them now."

"Impossible," said Violin. "This book has not been opened in years."

"Let's see," I said, and bent to pick it up, but Violin caught my wrist.

"Joseph, don't," she urged. "It's dangerous."

"It's only a book."

"It's much more than that, Joseph. It has power."

"I have a vault," said Bolton. "Hell of a sturdy one. We could lock it away."

"I don't think that would be our best choice," said Church, and he surprised everyone by picking the book up. Violin and Harry gasped and stepped back. Bolton looked like he wanted to grab it out of Church's hands and maybe throw it out of the window. Church turned it over, smiling faintly. "An ocean of blood has been spilled over this."

"You shouldn't touch it with your bare hands," cautioned Violin. "My mother says—"

"Your mother is a bit more superstitious than I am," he said. "I've found that things like this only have the power you give them."

Harry Bolt shook his head. "I picked that thing up and my head went blank. Like . . . a couple of times."

"You were probably hungover from partying," said his father in a caustic and emasculating way. Harry's face went beet red.

"Please, Harcourt," said Church. To me he said, "Remind you of anything?"

"Too many things," I said. "Apparently Project Stargate wasn't a total failure. Imagine that."

"No way," said Bolton, disgusted. "I told you that Stargate was scrubbed."

Church ignored him and gave Harry an encouraging smile. "Tell me everything that happened." Tell *me,* he said. Not *us.* It was the right thing to say. After a moment's hesitation, Harry told his tale. His report was hesitant at first, but I saw him visibly shift his focus from his father's disapproving scowl to Church's encouraging smile. When he got into gear he gave a clear, concise, and surprisingly insightful report of what he and Violin had experienced.

Church nodded and placed the book on the conference table. We all clustered around, and as Church bent to examine the locks and the binding, I saw him frown. He ran his fingers over the parts of the cover not blocked by the metal bands, then he licked his fingertips and wiped at the leather. Church grunted and straightened. "Now, isn't that interesting."

"What?"

"Captain," he said to me, "you're good at this sort of thing. Do you think you could pick those locks?"

"I'm better at kicking down doors," I admitted, "but I can try."

"No!" said Violin.

"Maybe we shouldn't," said Bolton.

"I can do it," suggested Harry. We all looked at him. He produced a small leather toolkit from his pocket and opened it to show as sweet a set of lock picks as I've ever seen. "Really, I'm pretty good with locks. I opened the chest this was in."

"You opened a chest sealed by the Ordo Fratrum Claustrorum?" said Bolton, his skepticism evident and intense.

"Um . . . sure."

Church stepped back. "If Captain Ledger has no objections."

"Knock yourself out, kid," I said to Harry, clapping him on the shoulder in a way that pushed him a couple of steps toward the table. "It's all yours."

Actually I didn't want to touch the thing. If it was going to explode or open a gateway to a hell dimension or whatever, better him than me. Selfish, I know, but there it is. I'm a good guy but I never claimed to be a nice one.

Harry Bolt set himself in front of the book, selected his tools, stuck his tongue partway out of his mouth the way some people do when they're concentrating, and set to work. The kid was good, I have to give him that. He had each of the locks open in seconds.

"Easy-peasy, Mrs. Wheezy," he said. Bolton made a disgusted grunt. Violin blew Harry a little kiss. The dynamic in the room was getting kind of strange.

Church placed a flat palm on the book to prevent Harry from opening it.

"Here's the issue," said Church. "I have some experience with ancient books. Perhaps not as much as Circe O'Tree, but enough. From what you've told me, Violin, and from what your mother has said, the Brotherhood and the Closers were both after this book because it is the last of the Unlearnable Truths. All of the others, according to the inventory sheet we found among the Gateway papers, have been accounted for. They were all obtained by Gateway, and it is presumed they were destroyed along with the lab."

That earned me a few chilly looks but I managed not to fall down. That bell was already rung and couldn't be unrung.

"Apart from some aspects of their subject matter," continued Church, "one of the few things that each of those books shares is that they are all examples of anthropodermic bibliopegy."

"What the heck's that?" asked Harry, beating me to the question.

It was Violin who answered. "He means that each of those accursed books is bound in human skin."

"Okay," said Harry, "I may throw up."

"Be a man," his father said under his breath.

"This book," said Church, tapping the cover with a forefinger, "is bound in leather. Ordinary bovine leather."

Harcourt Bolton pushed past his son and peered suspiciously down at the book. "I don't understand."

"People have gone to great lengths to obtain *De Vermis Mysteriis*," said Church. He flipped open the cover and then fanned through the pages. They were all blank. "This is not it."

CHAPTER SEVENTY-FIVE

HUMPHRIES-BELMONT ELECTRONICS SOLUTIONS
THE ABSALOM FOGELMAN BUILDING
6082 CENTER DRIVE
LOS ANGELES, CALIFORNIA
SEPTEMBER 9, 9:29 A.M.

"And that, sir," said Dr. Kang, "is the long and short of it."

Across the desk from the director of the computer lab sat a man with a visitor's badge clipped to his lapel and an NSA identification card hung on a lanyard around his neck. The name on the card was Special Agent Stephen Priest.

"You're entirely confident in your computer and Net security?" asked Mr. Priest. He was slim and tall, and even in his bland black suit and plain dark tie he seemed to exude a tigerish strength. It made Kang as uncomfortable now as it had when they'd begun this tour.

Kang was certain that Mr. Priest was a very dangerous man. He had the look. His smile was warm but his eyes were cold. Very, very cold. And though he always laughed in the right places—even at Kang's lamest jokes—there was something creepy about it. As if the laughs were faked to present an air of affability instead of being genuinely good-natured.

"Our security team is second to none," said Kang. "We've worked very closely with DARPA since the beginning, and, after all, DARPA *invented* the Internet."

"Not Al Gore?" said Mr. Priest, smiling.

They shared a laugh.

"Hardly. My predecessors here at the AEL, along with their colleagues at MIT's Lincoln Lab and in our main offices in Virginia, developed the prototype military networks—ARPANET, MILNET, and then the Defense Data Network—before—"

Mr. Priest held up a hand to stop him. "Please don't take this the wrong way, Dr. Kang, but that was decades ago. I don't need a history lesson. My concern is how your research is being protected right now."

Kang took a breath and nodded. "With the Russians, Iranians, Chinese, and North Koreans working so hard to hack our systems, as well as the power grids and everything else, it's—" He paused and twirled a finger as he fished for the right word. "It's *encouraged* us to make some radical jumps forward in cybersecurity to protect our vulnerabilities. We have whole teams dedicated to protecting us against malware, worms, viruses, and targeted attacks, as well as soft-probe and no-footprint intrusions. We've built firewalls, counterintrusion software packages, alert systems, and more. We're impregnable."

"'Impregnable' is a risky word choice, Doctor," said Mr. Priest. "It smacks of hubris."

Kang felt himself stiffen. Mr. Priest had been smiling when he said it but now there was no trace of evident humor. Certainly no affability.

When Mr. Priest's visit had been arranged, Kang had made sure his people did a thorough background and authority check, and the pingbacks had come from deep inside the intelligence community. Everything had been triple verified and memos had been sent by all the right people to grant Mr. Priest an unusually high level of clearance. That meant he was allowed to ask these kinds of questions and make these kinds of statements. Even the uncomfortable ones.

Kang felt his face redden and swallowed nervously. "I can assure you, Mr. Priest, that I'm not overstating things. Our system is ultrasecure. It's updated all the time. Even our own design and cybersecurity staff have to go through special procedures in order to log on. Codes are changed randomly, we have filtering systems, self-monitoring security subroutines, and—"

Mr. Priest held up his hand again. "What's to stop a terrorist from breaking in here, putting a gun to your head, and forcing you to log on and download one of your research projects?"

"Can't happen."

"Why not?"

"Because the master control programs require typed and verbal codes, and a retina scan and thumbprint."

"All of which could be coerced from you."

"No, sir," said Kang, shaking his head. "If any of our team were under coercion we would input a false command that would appear to access the system, but which would really only access a self-limiting clone. At the same time it would send out a system-wide alert that would result in all other users being asked to verify their status. They also have fail-safe codes. If two or more users indicate that they're under duress, the fail-safes crash the network."

"Wouldn't that take crucial services offline from the defense community? If you've seen the news you know that we are in a time of national crisis."

"Under those circumstances, key individuals would have to input today's command codes. Very similar to the way missile codes are handled. The codes are sealed in snap-cases that send an alert when opened, and the codes must be input only after thumbprint, personal code, and retina scan verification."

"Cumbersome," observed Mr. Priest.

"Necessary," countered Kang. "Otherwise a coordinated terrorist attack could overwhelm the system by physical force."

Mr. Priest nodded and picked up the teacup that had remained untouched on his side of the desk. He sipped, nodded again, and set the cup down. "And you don't see any holes or soft spots in this process?"

"No. If I did they'd be fixed immediately. We have our own team of cyber-hackers whose only job is to try and crack our security. Every time they do, we use that as a guide to upgrade."

"Ah," said Mr. Priest.

"Excuse me, sir, but what does that mean?"

Mr. Priest sighed. "Please don't take this the wrong way, but I can see at least two major holes in this system. I'm rather troubled that you don't."

Kang leaned forward and rested his forearms on his desk. His nervousness was quickly being trumped by irritation and anger. "I wasn't aware that you are an expert in cybersecurity."

"I know my way around. However, I'm surprised someone with your limited skill set has been given control over so many sensitive projects."

"What is that supposed to mean? What do you know about what I do?"

Mr. Priest spread his hands. "You're an electrical engineer and a mathematician. Essentially a glorified code-breaker who also writes security system code under contract to the Department of Defense.

You work on operational systems including firing controls for missile systems, nuclear plant security regulation codes, and so on. How am I doing?"

Kang stared at him, lips parting in surprise, shocked that Mr. Priest knew all of this. And he did a very fast reevaluation of this man and his potential status in the intelligence network. He cleared his throat. "The security of this office and my teams is, naturally, of the highest concern."

"Naturally," agreed Mr. Priest. "However, I'm sure you'll agree that 'concern' is a quality of intention rather than action."

"I—" Kang stopped himself and tried again. "I would value any input you have, Mr. Priest. If it's your opinion that there are problems with our system, then please explain. Maintaining the strictest security is absolutely crucial."

"I'm delighted to hear it."

Kang nearly winced. He said, "If you wouldn't mind explaining our *faults*, as you see them. Perhaps walk me through them?"

"It would be my pleasure," said Mr. Priest. He raised his hand and pointed his index finger like a gun. "You say that under direct coercion you would input a false entry code, correct?"

Kang looked at the pointed finger. The gesture was borderline rude, but he dared not say anything. "That is correct," he said.

Mr. Priest nodded and then moved his hand slowly over to the row of framed photographs on the right side of Kang's desk. There were five pictures in unmatched frames. His wife, Mary; their wedding picture; three school photos of fifteen-year-old Ashleigh, nine-year-old Kimmie, and three-year-old Jason.

"And what if someone pointed a gun at someone you loved?" asked Mr. Priest.

Kang did not answer. Such a question, such an *action*, even in a discussion of hypotheticals, was appalling. It was incredibly rude and violative.

"Sorry, Doctor," said Mr. Priest, "I didn't hear your answer."

"This is hardly a proper—"

"Doctor, I want you to answer my question. I know the lengths I would go to to protect my brother, and he is something of a disappointment to me. By all accounts you genuinely *love* your family. So, my question stands. If there were guns pointed right this minute at the heads of your wife and each of your three very lovely children, are you going to sit there and tell me that you would still input a false code? Would you actually risk such appalling harm coming to your entire family? *Could* you stick to your protocols and let them die?"

Kang said nothing. He was far too horrified to risk saying the things that rose to his tongue. And he was also trying to determine exactly who he should report this to. National security spot checks and unscheduled evaluations were all good and well, but this interview had crossed a line. Anyone would see that.

"I'd really like an answer, Doctor," insisted Mr. Priest.

"This is ridiculous and I think we're done here."

"No, I don't think we are."

Kang stood up. "Yes, we are. If you want to file an official report, then please do so, but this discussion is closed and this interview over. If you'll excuse me, I have work to do."

Mr. Priest lowered his hand and leaned back in his chair. "Dr. Kang, if you don't sit down right now I will kneecap you."

"I'm sorry—what did you say?"

Mr. Priest opened his jacket and produced a pistol. He did not point it, but instead laid it on his lap. "Do you know what 'kneecapping' is? Can you imagine what it would feel like? A bullet punching through your knee, through bone and tissue. The shock of the entry wound, the red splatter as it exits the back of your knee, carrying pieces of tissue and nerve and tendon with it. The pain, Doctor. The searing agony."

Kang felt the blood drain from his face. "Get the fuck out of my office. *Right now.*"

"No," said Mr. Priest. His tone was mild, conversational.

"I'm calling security." Kang reached for the phone.

"Make that call, Doctor, and you'll kill your wife."

Kang froze, his fingers an inch from the phone. His heart seemed to freeze, too. The world had suddenly become surreal. When he spoke his voice was barely a whisper.

"What . . . what did you say?"

"For a smart man you are moderately slow on the uptake, Dr. Kang. Let me make it clear, and since you're likely in shock I'll use small words, yes?" Mr. Priest looked amused. "Right now, even as we're having our chat, there are four teams in play. One has been following your wife since she dropped Jason off at preschool. Another is in the preschool. A third team is at Los Angeles Elementary School, and the fourth is inside University High School. Go, Wildcats." He paused for a small laugh. "If I don't send a coded signal at the appropriate time, four bullets will be fired. Five, counting the first round I fire, which will be through your left kneecap."

Kang collapsed into his chair, landed badly, and began sliding out onto the floor.

Mr. Priest made a disgusted noise. "Show a little self-respect, Doctor. Sit up like an adult." He waited while Kang wrestled his slack and clumsy limbs into the chair. "That's better. Now, I think even taking into account the degree of shock and anxiety you're feeling right now, you can predict what's coming next, yes? Indulge me, though. Tell me, just so I know your brain hasn't actually shorted out. Why is this happening?"

It took a lot for Kang to say it, to organize it into a simple sentence, but even then it stalled as he tried to force it out. "You . . . you . . . you . . ."

"Take a breath, Doctor. That's it. Now try again."

It cost him so much. Tears sprang into his eyes. "You . . . want the nuclear reset codes to—"

"No. Try again. Think of something a bit more outré."

Kang's eyes brightened as he understood, but then he frowned. "The book code? This is about that silly book code?"

Priest smiled. "Very well done. Yes, I want the book code. I want, in fact, access to your computer here, since it has the administrative authority to access any project. Who knows what other delicious things I will find? You've done considerable work for Dr. San Pedro and Dr. Erskine, I believe? Yes? Then I want everything connected with them, no matter how small or tangential."

The tears began rolling down Kang's cheeks. "Please don't hurt my family."

"That is entirely up to you. If you do what I want, absolutely nothing will happen to them. And just to comfort you, here is how it will play out. You log me in, I do what I came here to do, then I leave. You will sit here and do absolutely nothing for one hour. You won't answer the phone, you won't make any calls, you will not touch a single key on your computer. Those are the rules, and believe me that I will know if you break any of those rules. At the end of one hour I will call you on this." Mr. Priest produced a small disposable phone and placed it in the center of Kang's desk blotter. "This is what we call a 'burner.' Untraceable. It has been configured to receive a single phone call. Once you get that call, I will tell you whether I need more time or if every-thing is all clear."

"All clear—?"

"Yes. At that point you may ring all the alarms, call the authorities, and do what you like. At that point you will also know that the teams overseeing the welfare of your family have been withdrawn."

"How . . . how . . . ?"

"How do you know you can trust me?" Mr. Priest gave a small wave with his free hand. "Trust is such a difficult thing to ask, but I insist that you trust me."

"How do I know you haven't already . . . ?" He stopped, unable to finish the sentence.

"You don't. That's the real challenge, isn't it? It's all about trust, and you have no choice at all whether to trust me." Mr. Priest reached into the side pocket of his trousers, removed a sound suppressor, and with-out hurry began screwing it onto the barrel of his gun. Kang sat there, tears rolling down his face, staring in dreadful fascination. When Mr. Priest was done he once more laid the pistol on his lap. "Shall we begin?"

CHAPTER SEVENTY-SIX

Church and Bolton got into an argument about what to do next. Bolton wanted the book tested to see if invisible ink or some other kind of concealed text had been used. Church tried to convince him it was a waste of time. Violin looked absolutely devastated, and I couldn't blame her. She'd fought and killed for this book, and she'd been hunted halfway around the world by Closers and the psychopaths from the Brotherhood. To find out that it was all for nothing crushed her. It also pissed her off. A lot.

I called Bug to try and get some news, but got nothing.

I saw Harry standing like a lost soul by the window and I went over to talk to him. "Hey," I said, "buy you a cup of coffee?"

He looked down at the coffee cup he was already holding. "I . . ."

"Just an expression, kid. C'mon, let's get some air."

With only a flicker of doubtful reluctance he followed me out of the conference room and up to the back deck that overlooks the ocean. Harry Bolt did not look like a spy. He didn't even look like the kind of spy who wasn't supposed to look like a spy. At a distance he looked like a frat boy who'd had a few too many pizza and beer nights and too few afternoons at the gym. But at closer range you could see that there were some cracks in the shallow-rich-boy-jerk façade. There was a furtiveness in the eyes that spoke to a life spent dodging sharp criticism, and a sad resignation that I've seen in kids who know that they are disappointments. Some excitement because all of this was big, and a lot of the kind of fear a passenger has on a sinking ship; the kind of person who doesn't know how to work the lifeboats and who's sure he won't make the cut for bench space on the boats being lowered into the water.

I could see all this and know it because I know people, but it wasn't something to which I could directly relate. My dad had money and my brother, Sean, and I grew up in comfort. Not millionaire comfort, but definitely upper middle class. My dad is mayor of Baltimore, working through his second term. There is a lot of love, support, and respect flowing in all directions. Our Thanksgiving and Christmas family gatherings were fun, easy, without the usual kinds of infighting I often hear about. I'd expected Harcourt Bolton, Senior, to be as good a father as he was a role model, but what I'd witnessed a few minutes ago changed all that.

We were alone on the deck and we stood for a moment watching fleets of clouds sail majestically across the endless Pacific. We'd brought fresh cups of coffee up with us and Harry sipped his, looking up and out rather than at me.

"Sorry you had to see all that," said Harry.

"Your dad was pretty rough on you."

"You have no idea." He stopped, shook his head. "Shit. Forget I said that. Everything's fine, it's all good."

I turned and leaned against the rail, standing more squarely in his peripheral vision until he finally cut a sideways look at me.

"What?" he asked cautiously.

"Can I give you a nickel's worth of free advice?" I asked. "One guy to another."

"Let me guess, something like 'man up'? Or one of those 'that which does not kill us' speeches? No offense, Captain Ledger, but I've heard a lot of those over the years. I get them all the time from my station chief. Or . . . well, I used to. He's dead now."

"Yeah, well that sucks, too. I didn't know him," I said. "I barely know you, and I only met your dad yesterday."

"And yet you want to life coach me? This should be fun." He gave me a tentative up-and-down appraisal. "My dad hates you. Did you know that?"

"Bullshit."

"Hand to God. He's been talking about you for a couple of years now." Harry nodded toward the building. "You and what you do? The Department of Military Sciences. You're the real deal. You are actual superstars in special ops and top-grade espionage. You've out-CIA'd the CIA by like . . . miles. There is no one in Washington who isn't scared to death of Mr. Church. They all think he has files on them and on the president and that's why he's still in power. Everyone knows about MindReader and how it can intrude anywhere. They're as afraid of that computer as they are of the Chinese Ghost Net and the North Korean hackers. You know what's happened since word about MindReader got out? People—here and all through the world's espionage communities—have switched back to verbal orders and paper records. That made my dad's job a shit-ton harder because he relies so much on computers to keep his Mr. Voodoo vibe going. But you, Joe, you're the real problem. You're Dad's boogeyman. You're him thirty years ago. You're what Dad hoped *I'd* be. That's why I was born. I was his career equivalent of buying a midlife crisis sports car. He found a trophy wife and got her pregnant and when she gave birth to a son my dad went to work on trying to make me into Harcourt Bolton Two Point Oh. It's all about the Bolton legacy. For thirty years he was the top spy. Not top ten or top five. The best. No one had a win record like his. Maybe Church did. He was a field operator, but all of the records of his operations have mysteriously vanished." He fake-coughed and made it sound like "MindReader." "When the DMS was formed I remember Dad going through a real shit-fit. He took it as a slap in the face that the president chartered the DMS and gave it the autonomy to pick its cases and even cherry-pick jobs away from the CIA, the FBI, the DEA, ATF, and NSA. I remember Dad saying how unfair it was. How it was a betrayal after giving America the best years of his life."

I said nothing. Pretty sure that henceforth the dictionary entry for "dumbfounded" just shows a picture of my slack-jawed face. Harry nodded, though, as if I had spoken.

"Yeah, the DMS came at the wrong time. Dad was starting to lose his swing. He may know more about being a spy than anyone, maybe even more than Mr. Church. But James Bond versus the villain's hollowed-out volcano fights aren't really for middle-aged knees and middle-aged reflexes. Dad's resentment started with the first real DMS superstar, Colonel Samson Riggs. Man oh man, Riggs came on the scene like a rocket. He *was* James Bond. Riggs worked two assignments with my dad and I'll bet if you looked real close at the after-action reports you'll see that it was Colonel Riggs who made the biggest plays. But because the DMS tends to step away from the spotlight, Dad got the commendation. You guys don't give commendations, do you?"

I shook my head.

"Of course not. Humility along with nobility," laughed Harry. "That torqued Dad's nuts even harder. Maybe you're one of his cheerleaders, so this might all be coming out of left field, and you might be thinking this is a brat kid dissing his old man, but think again. I'm a fucking disgrace as a spy. I'm done, probably. I got nothing left to lose so I might as well tell the truth. Want to know what my dad did when he got the news that Samson Riggs was killed? He opened a seven-hundred-dollar bottle of French champagne. Didn't offer me a glass. He sat in front of the fire and drank the whole thing. He never stopped smiling once."

I couldn't speak. Could barely breathe.

"And then," said Harry, "*you* come along. You even *look* like Dad. Blond-haired, blue-eyed all-American boy with a good tan and laugh lines and all that hero shit. You could play Captain America. You *are* Captain fucking America. And now Dad's older and he's not a field op anymore. He sits at a desk and has to rely on his contacts and his network to keep putting numbers on the scoreboard. And, okay, so he's making some big plays. Mr. Voodoo still has some magic, but how long can that last? He's not out in the field making *new* contacts. His network has to be getting up there, too. Soon he'll be yesterday's news and he won't be relevant and it'll absolutely kill him. It's already eating at him. He's always taking naps, and my therapist tells me that's a sign of depression. You sleep to run away. Well, Dad's taking a lot of goddamn naps, because he's scared."

"You are absolutely out of your mind," I said, finally finding my voice. "I'm just not that impressive. I'm a grunt with good aim."'

Harry Bolt laughed. A harsh, bitter laugh. "God, you don't even know, do you? You might actually *be* that humble or that focused on the prize that you don't know what people in the intelligence community are saying about you. After the Jakobys? After the Seven Kings? After Majestic? Oh, don't look surprised. The public may not know who scored those touchdowns, but the intelligence community knows. The DMS was on the clock, and in most of those big wins you were running the touchdown plays. You. Joe Ledger, superjock."

I drank most of the coffee in my cup without tasting it. "Your dad and I are friends. We respect each other."

Harry dumped his coffee over the rail. "For a guy who's supposed to be sharp you are kind of a dumbass."

He gave me a mock salute and went back inside.

I stayed out there and watched the clouds. Before, they were a gorgeous fleet of magical ships sailing across the sky. Now, like the old song said, they only blocked the sun.

CHAPTER SEVENTY-SEVEN

Mr. Priest made Dr. Kang stand in the corner like a naughty little child. He did this after Kang had gone through the complex log-in procedures, which included a phone call to the security officer to give that day's code. Then Mr. Priest had the scientist remove his cell phone and then turn to face the corner, hands deep in his pockets.

"If you turn around or speak even a single word," said Mr. Priest, "I will have one of your children shot in the stomach. You're not a field operative and have never served in combat, but I'm sure you've heard stories about the degree of pain associated with a stomach wound of that severity. It's a slow death marked by unimaginable suffering, though I'm sure you will be able to imagine everything."

Kang was too terrified to even nod.

Mr. Priest smiled. "Very well. Now do as you're told. I don't even want to hear you breathing loud. I have important work to do and need to concentrate."

Twenty minutes later Mr. Priest sat back from the keyboard and turned to Kang.

"Good lord, man, did you just piss your pants? You did. You're standing in a puddle of it." Mr. Priest shook his head in disgust. "Some people have no self-respect."

He went back to his work.

Downloading the files was time-consuming because they were so large and because there were so many of them. There were only twenty-six project files of interest to him—those for which he already had buyers—but Priest wanted to take all of the active R & D files from the last five years. That would confuse the computer forensic techs who would be assigned to determine the purpose of this theft.

To facilitate the theft he'd brought six ultrahigh-capacity external drives and the necessary cables. He also used the military intranet to transfer large portions of it, routing them to 111 dummy mailboxes he'd created over the last three years. Those e-mail addresses recoded everything and bounced them out to hundreds of other e-mail accounts around the globe. At each step the data would be coded again and again until not even a superintrusion computer like the Department of Military Science's MindReader could tag it as being what it was. Mr. Priest had spent millions to hire the very best hackers to build his network.

That data would eventually come home to Mr. Priest's private mainframes, the six Titan supercomputers he'd acquired through many removes from a friend in Russia. That computer, Zarathustra, was protected against all forms of invasion. Mr. Priest had even tested that claim by running programs filled with the kinds of keywords that would attract MindReader. After fifteen months of dangling bait in the water, Mr. Priest was convinced Zarathustra was impregnable.

He paused in his work and sniffed, wondering if Kang had gone another step down into personal degradation, but he shook his head. The man's bowels were still clutched tight. Good; that would be so unpleasant.

When the process was done, Mr. Priest removed the cables and stowed the drives back into his briefcase. Then he removed another external drive, plugged that in, and sat back, rubbing his tired eyes. The screen display on Kang's desk flashed with a status bar. The four-hundred-gigabyte Trojan horse was uploading quickly. He appreciated the speed and sophistication of Kang's computers.

Finally Mr. Priest stood, leaving that last drive in place.

He came over and stood directly behind Kang, careful, though, not to step in the puddle of urine around the man's expensive shoes.

"Listen carefully now, my friend," he said quietly. "You know the terms of our agreement. You know what will happen if you break your promises. I'm leaving now. You will sit at your desk and wait for my call. You will not touch the external drive that's plugged into your computer. If you even touch it, I'll know. I'll get a signal and so will my field teams. And you don't want that, now, do you?"

Again, Kang was too terrified to speak.

Mr. Priest patted him on the shoulder.

"Good-bye, Dr. Kang. Here's hoping the day ends well for both of us."

CHAPTER SEVENTY-EIGHT

The Mullah sat in his tent and ate chicken and lentils while the men around him argued. This was a difficult meeting. An important one, because these men had brought old hatreds with them to the Mullah's tent. These were men who had sworn death threats against others seated nearby. No one had been allowed to bring a weapon with them. Only the Mullah's men had guns. Each of the others had ten hand-picked men outside, seated on the ground under palm trees. They had been instructed to read the same key passages of the Koran and to talk only among themselves. They were told that it would be a great sin against God to break the temporary truce the Mullah had called for. The men obeyed, but they glared their hatred at the others who sat only yards away.

Inside the tent, the Mullah listened to representatives of the Taliban and al-Qaeda. There were Sunnis here seated next to Shiites. There were leaders whose tribal conflicts were numbered in centuries. It was a gathering many of these men and all the rest of the world said was impossible, even unthinkable.

The Mullah had greeted them all as brothers. Seating was arranged by lottery, with no one receiving favored placement. Even the Mullah had drawn a colored stone from a bowl to receive his place.

When he was done eating, the Mullah set aside his food, washed his hands and face. Then he led them all in a carefully chosen prayer, one that had been selected because it did not play into any sectarian ideology but simply worshiped God. When this was done, he asked permission from the group to turn on his laptop computer. They agreed, though some were very cautious and uncertain.

Akbar brought the machine and placed it on a small table beside the Mullah. The old man turned it on and brought up a news update from Houston, Texas. It showed the mountains of rubble of what had once been a hotel a few weeks ago. Towers of work lights had been erected and crews of emergency personnel were picking through the debris while the voice of a reporter said that there were still forty-seven people missing and presumed dead. Rescue workers had found parts of another thirty-two. All of the other dead had long since been removed.

"You see this?" asked the Mullah. "Do you see how much damage has been done to our enemy?"

The others nodded. Many of them eyed him with suspicion or anticipation. The Mullah smiled and placed his hand over the screen.

"I did this," he said.

There was a moment of dead silence.

Then everyone began yelling. Shouts of praise, harsh denials, accusations, and even threats. The Mullah let it all wash over him. Finally it was his calm lack of response that quieted the tent. They fell silent one by one, and he nodded to each man as they did so.

"Of course you do not believe me," he said, still smiling. "Why would you? Anyone can point to an event and say, 'I did that.' We have in the past, each in our several groups. It is a tool of fear and confusion, and they are both arrows in our quiver."

No comments, merely silence and a few nods.

"I do not ask that you believe an old man when he makes what appears to be a wild claim. I would never insult you in such a way, my brothers. It would be unseemly."

A few more nods, but the men seemed to be ready for a trick.

"It is out of my respect for each of you and for all of us in our beliefs that I do not ask for trust but instead offer proof."

One of the men spoke up at last, a Taliban warlord who had fought at times with and against the Americans and whose father had died fighting the Russians. He said, "What proof is this?"

"Before I show you, my brother, I want to explain why we have not openly declared the attack on Houston to be part of our jihad." The Mullah gazed around, fixing each man in turn with a serious, penetrating look. "Some of you are here because you are already part of our new caliphate. Others, I believe, have come because you heard the rumors. Speculations in the world media and whispers from the mouths of our own people. You have heard of the Mullah of the Black Tent. You know that I have, because of the grace and guidance of God, directed our forces toward making greater gains and also helped them evade reprisals from our enemies."

A few nods, some reluctant.

"And some of you are here because you want to know if, in fact, the army of the caliphate has done this great thing." He nodded, his smile never fading. "Now you are here and you watch an old man eat chicken and show you pretty pictures on a computer. You hear an old fool make claims and you wonder—Is this a trap? Is this a joke? Is this worth the risks you took when coming here?"

"Of course we wonder those things," said the warlord. "We are not starry-eyed children. We are men who are fighting a war, and as such we do not have time to waste on fantasies and false claims."

That caused a sudden buzz of argument, but the Mullah raised his hand to call for peace. It fell, slowly and awkwardly.

"There is a saying that one picture is worth a thousand words," said the Mullah. "So, let me show you something beautiful."

He tapped a few keys on the laptop and the image of Houston vanished to be replaced by a military base. The image wobbled but it was clear.

"This is Fort Rucker army base in Dale County, Alabama. That is in the southern part of the United States. It is home to the First Aviation Brigade under the command of Brigadier General Michael Lundy. Between military personnel, civilian employees, and families, there are five thousand people on the base. The United States Army Aviation Center of Excellence is located there. Many of the their military policies and procedures that are used against our people are developed there. This is a crucial place. A key target, but one that is unapproachable. This image is from a pigeon drone, but before you ask, the drone is not armed with explosives. It is there to give us a bird's-eye view, if you will pardon the small joke."

No one smiled.

As the bird flew, its camera's eyes showed men and women training, vehicles moving, a Chinook helicopter airlifting a large air-conditioner unit to the top of a building that was under construction.

"The people on this base feel safe," said the Mullah. "They have numbers, they have gates and guards, they have their training, and we have to accept that their training is second to none. They have advanced technology and they have so many weapons and resources. We are like peasants throwing stones." He shook his head. "But what if we could reach out and, as if with the hand of God, switch off their lights, still their engines, drop their planes from the sky, silence their communications, darken their nights? What if the great thing that happened in Houston was no fluke? What if it was us? What if this is something we could do at any time? What if we held that power?"

The warlord was the only person who seemed able to speak. "Are you saying that you could do that to a military base in their own country?"

"Yes."

"Prove it," challenged the warlord. "I will go back to my people and we will watch the news and we will see if you are a lying old fool or—"

And on the screen all of the power at Fort Rucker went out. The big Chinook suddenly jerked as the rotors died. The machine fell like a dead bird. All across the base the lights went out, the vehicles rolled to slow stops, the people turned, and looked around, and yelled. Some of them screamed. The sound of the crashing Chinook rolled like thunder across the base.

The gathered men cried out in surprise. Some of them leapt to their feet.

The Mullah sat there, smiling.

"And now we give them back a shred of hope," said the Mullah. On the screen the lights came back on. The engines started up. Sirens began to wail, and only they were loud enough to drown out the screams. "And with hope comes doubt. It is the survivors of a catastrophe who are the victims, for they have seen the face of death and they know it can take them at any time. They will never be free of the memory and the fear for the rest of their lives."

The warlord wiped spit from his mouth with a trembling hand. "This is how we will win this war. This is the sword of God."

But the Mullah shook his head. "No, my brother, this is the gun."

He reached over and tapped keys to change the image. Instead of a view of burning carnage it showed a pair of men dressed in white hazmat suits. They stood in a small, poorly equipped laboratory. As the gathered fighters watched, one of them used an oversized syringe to draw biological transport medium from a heavy vial and inject it into a small device. He repeated the process over and over again until he had emptied all of the metal vials and filled the receptacles on several dozen small but identical devices. Then he and the second man went down the line and closed the lids, forcing them down hard against the springs. As each lid closed a small magnetic lock clicked into place and a green safety light flicked on.

The metal vials were each stamped with the international biohazard symbol.

"And this, my friends," said the Mullah softly, "is the bullet."

CHAPTER SEVENTY-NINE

We sat in horrified silence, watching it all unfold on the screen.

Church and Violin, Harry Bolt and me. The death toll at Rucker was small when compared to Houston, but incalculable when measured against the destroyed lives of each of those servicemen and women.

"We interrupt our full team coverage of the tragedy at Fort Rucker," said the reporter for the NBC affiliate. "I am told that we have received a statement from the Islamic State of Iraq and the Levant. We are going to play it live. Please be cautioned that we have not had an opportunity to preview this statement."

The anchor's grim face was replaced by a good-quality video of a man in a black turban with dark eyes surrounded by wrinkled flesh. His nose and mouth were covered by a black scarf and the flag of ISIL was hung on the wall behind him.

Church hit the Record button.

"I speak to you now as the voice of jihad," he said, speaking in perfect English. "I speak to you as a mujahedeen, a soldier of God. I speak to you as the voice of the new and eternal caliphate. I speak to you now to tell you that we will no longer accept interference with our culture, our people, our nations, and our faith. You may not have our oil. You may not rape our lands. You may not, with impunity, invade our countries and slaughter our people. That time has ended. God has reached out his mighty hand and drawn the curtain to cast you into darkness. You have seen this. You have cried out in that darkness and wondered why? How? Who?" He held up a finger and wagged it back and forth, the way a teacher might scold a naughty schoolboy. "A great darkness is coming. Ten of your cities will fall into hell. There is nothing you will be able to do to stop this because it is impossible to oppose the will of God. All that you can do is fall onto your knees and pray for forgiveness. You have declared war on the lands and the people and the one true faith. You and your children will pay for your sins. Darkness will fall. Darkness will fall."

The camera lingered on his eyes for several silent seconds, and it struck me that the man looked dazed, or stoned. Or something. As he'd spoken there was no flicker in those eyes. We could see his mouth move even beneath the scarf, but the eyes were like those of a mannequin. No expression, no flaring as he made his threats. No life.

The video feed ended and the anchor came back and in contrast the gleam in his eyes was equal parts stark terror and dawning realization that this was possibly the biggest moment of his career.

Church replayed the video.

When it was over, Violin said, "The Mullah of the Black Tent. God. ISIL has owned the Houston and Rucker attacks. They've just declared open war on the United States."

"He mentioned the children," I said, my voice thick, my head filled with hornets. "Jesus Christ, Church, he has the SX-56 and he's going to use the Kill Switch to hit us with it."

CHAPTER EIGHTY

HUMPHRIES-BELMONT ELECTRONICS SOLUTIONS
THE ABSALOM FOGELMAN BUILDING
6082 CENTER DRIVE
LOS ANGELES, CALIFORNIA
SEPTEMBER 9, 1:16 P.M.

The call came fifty-eight minutes after Mr. Priest left Dr. Kang's office. During every second of those fifty-eight minutes Kang sat stock-still at his desk, his hands gripped like vises around the arms of his chair. He was too terrified to move despite the sodden stink in his trousers. The digital numbers on his desk clock had stubbornly refused to hurry through what felt like a thousand years of waiting.

When the burner rang, Kang screamed.

Very loud.

There was no one in the outer office to hear the scream. Mr. Priest had—either by luck or design—chosen a day when Kang's secretary was out sick.

The ring was not particularly loud, but it shattered the silence in Kang's office.

Kang snatched it up and then froze again, caught in the horrible indecision of wanting to hear that his family was unharmed and dreading a message to the contrary.

It rang again.

And again.

Then he began stabbing at the green button with numb and trembling fingers. Punched it on and then nearly ended the call. Finally he clumsied it to his ear.

"Yes, yes . . . are they all right? Please?"

"Dr. Kang," said the smooth, familiar voice of Mr. Priest, "I appreciate your courtesy and cooperation. You are now free to do as you please. And rest assured, your family is safe."

"You motherfucker, I'll—"

"Shhh, Doctor. You've come up from the underworld, but don't assume that you will ever be entirely in the upper world. Now is not the time to turn and look for Eurydice. She is as safe as anyone ever is in such a world as this."

The reference to the myth of Orpheus was not lost on Kang, even with so much stress burning its way through him. "Orpheus" was the code name for one of the major defense projects in the databanks he had allowed Mr. Priest to plunder. One of many.

"You promised to leave them alone," growled Kang. "You promised not to hurt them."

"And I haven't," said Mr. Priest. "Good-bye, Dr. Kang. It has been a genuine pleasure."

The line went dead.

For a terrible moment Kang did not know whom to call first. His wife or the security office.

He called his wife. She answered on the second ring. Kang almost screamed. He told her to get the kids and get out of the house, to come here to the lab, to do it right away.

Kang hung up before she could ask any questions. Then he called his control officer at the Department of Defense.

CHAPTER EIGHTY-ONE

Harcourt Bolton came hurrying into the conference room.

"Christ!" he yelled. "Did you see it? Did you see that damn thing?"

"We saw it," I said.

"I've been on the phone with the president," he gasped, breathless from running from his office. "I assured POTUS that we have local teams inbound. Jerry Spencer and his forensics people are on their way, too."

Church gave him a long, appraising look, but his only response was a small nod.

"What do you want me to do?" I asked, standing up. "Echo is ready to rock."

Bolton looked embarrassed and didn't meet my eyes. "Captain Ledger . . . Joe . . . I think I'd rather have you here for, um, tactical support."

It was awkward and clumsy. He did not come right out and say that he did not have confidence in me or in Echo Team, but it was right there burning in the air.

"If you saw the whole thing, Bolton, then you have to know they have the smallpox bioweapon. We need to move on this."

"We are," said Bolton, and he leaned a little too hard on the word "we."

"What he's trying to tell you, Captain," Church said quietly, "is that this is still not our case."

"Bullshit," I snarled. "You're using our people. *My* people. That makes it my case."

"Look, Joe," said Bolton, "I'm sorry, but the president was very clear on this. I can use DMS resources, and I'm happy to do so, but the Central Intelligence has operational control."

"Then use me as a liaison."

"I . . . can't . . . ," said Bolton. He put a hand on my shoulder. "I'm sorry, but after Gateway, POTUS doesn't want you in play on anything this sensitive."

I slapped his hand away. "This is bullshit and you know it. You're treating Gateway like it was a failure. We shut down a bioweapons program that had gone off the rails and killed the whole staff. We kept it from getting off the leash. And now we've proven that Gateway is tied to Majestic. And that they were developing a psychic spy program that Central Intelligence said wouldn't work. We've proven that there are Closers in the field trying to locate more Majestic materials. We're close to locating the sequencing code to the machine that controls the Kill Switch technology." I pointed to the screen, where they were rerunning the message from the Mullah of the Black Tent. "Maybe that master code sequence could allow us to stop this shit. Did you think of that? We're closing in on it. Us, the D-fucking-MS. Not the C-fucking-IA. We're already doing *our* jobs, Harcourt. What have you and your Agency boys done that's worth a shit? Nothing. How can you bench us now?"

Bolton's face slowly transformed from a look of embarrassed concern to a scowl of red-hot anger. He got up in my face, stepping toward me. "Who the fuck do you think you're talking to, *Captain* Ledger? I've been trying to be civil with you and the rest of the screwups around here, but quite frankly my patience is wearing thin. I've run interference for you and you want to throw it in my face? You are every bit as arrogant and pigheaded as everyone says. You think you're a superhero, don't you, Ledger? You think you're the new face of government service, the top of the game, but you know what? You're a thug who gets lucky sometimes. That's it. You got too many people inside your head and none of them have any real chance of solving this thing. So, take it from someone who actually knows what he's doing and stand *down*."

"Yeah, well, *fuck* you, old man. You may have been hot shit once upon a time, but then right around the time you started losing your swing, early humans invented the wheel and you got left behind. And—"

He shoved me.

A really good, incredibly fast two-handed shove to the chest that sent me sailing backward. I lost my footing and fell, hard and clumsy. I scrambled to my feet but Violin and Harry were already up. The kid caught her arm as she went to swing on Bolton, but then Church's voice cut through everything.

"*Enough!*" he roared.

Everyone froze.

Church came around the table, hooked a hand under my arm, and hauled me to my feet. He was not gentle about it. Then he put one hand on Harry's arm and the other on Violin's shoulder and pushed them to the side so he could face Bolton. Bolton and Church were about the same size, they looked like they were the same age, and I knew they both had years and wars behind them. Bolton stood with balled fists, ready to swing. I thought he was going to hit Church. Or try to, anyway.

In a quiet, cold voice Church said, "I think it would be in everyone's best interests if you were to go attend to your duties, Harcourt."

Bolton fixed Church with a look of pure, unfiltered contempt.

"You run a sloppy shop, Deacon. Maybe it's time you thought seriously about getting out of the game."

Church nodded. "I'll take it under advisement."

They held their ground for a long moment. Any trace of civility and affability was gone from Bolton's face. He looked at Violin and dismissed her as nothing, and his eyes swept past Harry as if the kid wasn't even there. Bolton focused on me and raised a finger to point at me. "You're done, Ledger. You're a psychopath and it was a mistake to ever give you a job here. Consider yourself relieved of duty. You and your team are to turn in your badges and weapons. Security will escort you out. If you have a lawyer, I'd call him, because we will be filing charges for negligence and wanton destruction of government property because of what you did to Gateway." He shook his head. "I can't believe I ever tried to be nice to you."

Then he turned, whipped the door open so hard it banged into the wall, and stalked out.

Violin wanted to go after him. I saw her touch one of the concealed knives she always carried. I wanted to either shoot Bolton or throw myself out of the window. Even split. Poor Harry Bolt looked like he either wanted to run away or cry. He was deeply embarrassed. He sat down on one of the chairs and looked at his hands, and said nothing. Church had a calculating look in his eyes as he walked over and sat down.

My phone rang. Bug.

"What?" I asked listlessly.

"I got something, Joe," he said, his voice charged with excitement.

CHAPTER EIGHTY-TWO

Bug laid it on us. I put him on speaker so they could all hear. Mr. Priest, aka Esteban Santoro, the Gateway book sequence decryption, the coercion. All of it.

"Wait, I'm confused. Why would this guy Priest or Santoro or whatever his name is need to steal it?" asked Harry. "Isn't he *part* of Gateway?"

"Doesn't seem like it," I said. "He's running the Closers who raided FreeTech and hit Toys's place last night. And the crew that was at San Pedro's office. If I had to guess, he got left out in the cold when everything went to shit down at Gateway. Maybe he's freelance or maybe his contract has been picked up by someone else who's now after the Kill Switch master code sequence."

"The latter would be my guess," said Church.

"Dr. Hu thinks there has to be some kind of master control unit," said Bug. "Maybe it's a full-sized God Machine like they had down at Gateway. Hu thinks the master code sequence would allow that machine to interface with all the others. That way one person would have control over a fully functional and fully regulated process."

"Who?" asked Harry. "This Mullah character?"

"I suppose," said Bug. "I mean, who else? Everyone at Gateway is dead. And I don't read this Priest guy as brains. He's muscle."

"Agreed," said Church.

"Then the code sequence is our target," I said. "We need to find Priest and get it from him, and it would be nice if he resisted arrest."

Church got up and went to a quiet corner of the room to make a call. He spoke for several minutes. When he was done he turned and stood there, lips pursed, thinking for a long moment. "I spoke with

Dr. Kang. He did not personally work on the master code sequence from the Unlearnable Books, so he put the project supervisor who did on the line. After scanning and collating the pages from each of the Unlearnable Truths, a numerical pattern did, in fact, emerge. The numbers are coordinates."

"Coordinates for targets?" I asked. "We can put teams in position and—"

Church shook his head. "They are coordinates for three stars as seen from Antarctica. The Large Magellanic Cloud, Sirius, and Alpha Centauri. If you calculate their positions, you come up with set numbers. The Large Magellanic Cloud is fifty-seven degrees altitude, azimuth one hundred ninety degrees. For Sirius you have six degrees of altitude and two hundred and sixteen degrees of azimuth. And Alpha Centauri is seventy degrees of altitude and three hundred twenty-one degrees azimuth." Church paused. "However, if we can place any stock at all in the writings of Lovecraft—and so far his work, however fantastical it may appear, seems to be our most reliable source—it indicates that the builders of that city arrived there one billion years ago. References in two of the Unlearnable Truths pin the time down to within half a million years. This changes things considerably. The Large Magellanic Cloud would be altitude sixty-three degrees and two hundred seventy-three degrees azimuth, Sirius would be fifty-two degrees altitude and one hundred thirty-five degrees azimuth, and Alpha Centauri would be thirteen degrees altitude, two hundred sixty-eight degrees azimuth. These are the local coordinates; what you would see by eye, looking up. Astronomers use a different set of coordinates to plug into our telescopes and map the sky. Right ascension and declination. These coordinates are not dependent on location, but are dependent on time. And we have those, as well." He read off the numbers. "The first set, however, matches the code lifted from the Unlearnable Truths by Dr. Kang."

"Then we have the code," gasped Violin. A great smile bloomed on her face.

"But . . . we don't know where the God Machine is," said Harry. "Jesus . . . we're screwed."

"Santoro's on the run," I said. "He knows we're going to be on his ass. If he's as smart as he's supposed to be he'll figure we'll be throwing a net and putting eyes on roads, trains, airports, boats. That's going to slow him down. Even if he slips past us, he's not going to do it fast. And then the code has to be input and his team has to coordinate with the ISIL dickheads. We might have two or three days before they hit us."

"Can we shut down all the airports?" asked Violin. "Minimize the potential damage?"

"I'll speak to the president," said Church.

"Good luck with that," I said, "but I need to run Santoro down and get that code. If he's in L.A., then I need to be there."

"My dad just grounded you," said Harry weakly.

Church picked up his phone and called Brick. "I want you to locate Director Bolton. He's in his office? You're sure? Good. Prep Captain Ledger's helo. Do it as quietly as possible. If anyone asks, it's for me and I'm heading to the airport to fly back to New York No, that's a cover. Have Bird Dog on board with a full field kit. I want it fueled and smoking in five. Contact any Echo Team members currently in the building and have them meet the captain on the roof. We're going off the reservation. Thank you, Brick."

Church turned to me. "I'll reroute ops from here to the Hangar. Bug can hack into CCTV to try and locate Priest."

I smiled, and maybe in the back of my head I heard the Killer turn over in his sleep. "You trust me to do this?"

"I never lost faith in you, Captain."

Violin said, "Wait, what about me?"

Church smiled. "I have something else I'd like you to do."

Harry Bolt looked very much like the fifth wheel he was. "Okay . . . well, what about *me*?"

I walked over to him. "A lot of that will depend on whose side you're on. Your dad seems to want to tear the DMS down. Maybe you hit the nail on the head when you said he was jealous. Whatever. He's going to drag his feet and play this wrong and a lot of people are going to die. So, ask yourself, kid, where do you think you fit?"

There were a lot of ways Harry Bolt could have played it. He was a schlub, so he could play dumb and sit it out. He was CIA, so he could side with the home team. He was Harcourt Bolton's son, so maybe blood was thicker than water.

He straightened and although he was seven or eight inches shorter than me he did his best to look me in the eye.

"My father's wrong," he said.

"So where does that put you?"

His gaze shifted from me, to Church, and then settled on Violin. She gave him the kind of smile I'd only ever seen her give to me. Once upon a time. It jolted me.

Then Harry Bolt looked at me again and held out his hand. "Good hunting, Joe."

CHAPTER EIGHTY-THREE

"There they are," whispered Bunny.

He eased away from the narrow slot in the curtains so I could take a look. We were in the marina office. Bunny, Top, and me, each of us dressed in black BDUs and balaclavas. We were the only field agents at the Pier when the call came in.

"We can take them right now," said Top. He had his Heckler & Koch HK416 in his hands, the barrel lowered, finger laid along the curve of the trigger guard. The effective range of the HK416 is four hundred yards. The cluster of men was less than fifty feet from where we crouched. If I gave the word, Top would send them to Jesus without so much as a flicker. "Say the word, Cap'n, and we can all clock out early."

There were seven men on the dock. All dressed in boating clothes, or some approximation of them. Shorts, boat shoes, Polo shirts or lightweight Windbreakers. One of them wore a Hawaiian shirt with brightly colored tropical fish on it. Sunglasses and ball caps. Looking like people who belonged among all these expensive seagoing play toys. Looking ordinary. They didn't look like Closers.

"Not until we're sure," I murmured. We were all killers, but we were soldiers, not assassins.

Dr. Kang's report was that Priest had exited the building carrying a metal briefcase in which were several portable high-capacity external drives. One with the scans of the Unlearnable Truths and the master code sequence Kang's people had interpolated from the books; and several others with lots of information related to projects owned by either Erskine or San Pedro. None of them, according to Kang, said either "Majestic" or "Gateway" on them. Nothing labeled "Kill Switch," "God Machine," or "Dreamwalking," either. We didn't know what the data was, but we damn sure didn't want it to get into the hands of whoever was behind all of this. ISIL or someone else. My guess was that it was going to be "someone else," and I was beginning to get a nasty idea of how this was all being managed.

Priest's photo had been fed into the facial recognition feeds of security cameras all over this part of California, with MindReader interpreting the data. The target used some of the most devious tricks in the evil bad guy playbook to avoid capture and make it from Los Angeles all the way down to the marina here in Oceanside. By car in good traffic that's two hours, but when you're trying not to get arrested and sent to Gitmo it can take a lot longer. In this case five and a half hours, with long heart-stopping gaps when we all thought he'd slipped the leash.

If that happened, and the Mullah or whoever was in control of Kill Switch got their hands on that control code, then America was going to experience a new Dark Age. And if our worst fears were realized, inside that darkness the SX-56 pathogen was going to spread every bit as aggressively as the Black Plague had, as the Spanish flu had. Why? Because every aspect of emergency response, from cops to doctors, depended on electricity. Shutting off the lights would give us no chance to get in front of the bioweapon. So, yeah, I almost told Top to take the shot.

Almost.

But we needed the drives and we needed to ask questions and you can't ask those questions of a corpse. I wanted a name and I was damn sure Mr. Priest—Esteban Santoro—was going to want to tell me. I planned to ask very nicely. In a manner of speaking, "nicely" being a relative term. I am not a fan of torture, but these bastards wanted to kills thousands—perhaps millions—of children. There's nothing I wouldn't do to prevent that from happening. Nothing.

I kept expecting the Killer in my soul to roar out his blood challenge. He was the ultimate protector of the innocent because to his primitive sense of survival, the young were a guarantee that the tribe would survive. You had to protect them, and I remember the things that part of me has done when the bad guys have targeted kids. Those memories will haunt me until I die. Letting those children die, though, would kill me.

We'd arrived at the dock in a boat belonging to a close friend of

Mr. Church. It was a very expensive XSR high-velocity speedboat. If this came to a sea chase we had a clear edge.

"Call the play, Boss," murmured Bunny. He had an AA-12 drum-fed shotgun. He calls it Honey Boom-Boom. Bunny is working out some issues. "Time to rock 'n' roll."

"We need him with a pulse," I said. "No one's clocking out until we get those drives, feel me?"

"Hooah," said Bunny, the disappointment clear in his voice.

"Hooah," said Top, his tone more workmanlike and philosophical.

I tapped my earbud to get the command channel. "Cowboy to Deacon."

"Go for Deacon," said the voice in my ear. Mr. Church was in one of our mobile tactical operations vehicles, with all communications routed to him rather than through the Pier. "Give me a sitrep."

"Target is acquired," I said. "Santoro plus six. We are about to make our run."

"Do you have eyes on the package?"

I began to say no, but then another man came walking along the dock with something tucked under his arm. He stopped in front of Santoro, his back to me so that what they were doing was briefly obscured. I heard a faint murmur of conversation and when he stepped aside I saw that Santoro now gripped the handle of a small waterproof black plastic case. They must have transferred the drives to something safer for boat travel.

"That is affirmative," I said. "I have eyes on the package. Repeat, I have eyes on the package."

"Copy that. Bring it home."

"Roger that," I said.

I moved away from the window and knelt on the far side of the door. Top took up station beside the door and Bunny squatted like a linebacker.

We counted down and moved.

Top opened the door quickly and we went out. I went left, Top went right, and Bunny moved straight toward the men. The gas dock was wood and concrete, with three benches, a trash can, and a long row of fuel pumps stationed at the ends of a line of finger piers. There were several boats in slips, their bumpers nudging the dock in the mild swell. A dockhand was swiping the credit card of one of Santoro's men. Nice that they were paying for the gas. Made it almost seem like they were ordinary citizens.

Almost.

We moved instantly into concealed shooting positions before the bad guys could turn and draw their weapons. We yelled real damn loud. *"Federal agents! Hands on your heads. Get down on your knees with your hands on your heads or we will kill you."*

Santoro turned toward us. Slow. Without hurry, without much surprise. His expression was on the amused side of bland, his body language calm. He gave us the kind of look you'd expect to see on someone like . . . well, on someone like me. But only when I was being fronted by a pack of cranky Cub Scouts. He looked at us as if we were expected though unwanted.

"Let me see if I can guess," he said, his voice a soft and cultured baritone. "Not FBI. Not NSA, either. So who are you? Definitely not SEALs." He nodded toward Top. "You're too old." At Bunny. "You're too big."

"And I'm too charming," I said. "Put your hands on your head, asshole, and get down on your fucking knees."

His eyes clicked toward me. "Ah," he murmured, "now I know who you are. Captain Joseph Edwin Ledger. The Deacon's pet scorpion. I believe you knew my brother. What a pleasure." He glanced again at my guys. "Top Sims and Bunny Rabbit. Your right and left hands. The two cornerstones of Echo Team. I've heard some interesting reports about you fellows."

"You read anywhere that we're known for taking bullshit? No? Then get down on your knees and keep your hands where I can see them or I will kill you."

The rest of Santoro's team was still frozen where they were, and right then they looked more like confused bystanders than a crack team of henchmen. There was a glazed look in their eyes. Not exactly blank, but *off* somehow. Like nobody was home. That sent a chill up my spine.

Santoro looked at me. His eyes were sharper than the others', more intense. On the docks and in some of the boats people were watching. Scared, surprised, and fascinated despite the presence of big men with guns.

"You can't kill us all," he said.

I shifted my aim downward, confident that I could put one through his thigh without endangering the onlookers. We had them dead to rights. We were holding every card.

It was perfect.

Absolutely perfect.

Which is when it all went wrong.

CHAPTER EIGHTY-FOUR

Bunny yelled, *"On your six!"*

I spun and had a millionth of a second's peripheral vision warning as someone swung a boat paddle at me. It was light aluminum with a plastic blade, but it hit like a Louisville Slugger. My gun went flying, hit the deck, bounced once and hit our borrowed XSR, and then dropped like a stone into the salt water. I spun and blocked a second swing, caught the oar with my other hand, snapped out a low kick, and as my heel smashed his knee to junk I saw with mingled shock and horror that my attacker was the sixty-year-old dockmaster. He screamed and collapsed against one of the pumps, clawing at the ruin of his knee.

I whirled toward Santoro, who had spun around and was running flat out for one of the boats moored to the dock. A slate-gray Picuda that was two slips down from the big XSR that we'd come in. Santoro tossed the briefcase into the boat and jumped after it.

His crew was still standing where they'd been, hands half-raised, eyes blank as zombies'.

"He's mine," I snapped, and pelted after him. But I got maybe six steps before another figure rushed out of nowhere and attacked me.

Wasn't one of Santoro's goons. Wasn't the crippled dockmaster, either.

It was a teenage girl. Fifteen, maybe sixteen, dressed in flowered shorts and a bikini top, sunglasses, and a cute straw sun hat. She had no gun, no oar, no weapon except a cell phone, but she did her level best to brain me with it.

Yeah. A kid. With a cell phone. The day had already tilted sideways and now it was sliding down the rabbit hole.

I slap-parried the swing, which was surprisingly fast and skillful for a kid, and I backhanded her across the mouth. Blood flew from her mashed lips and the force spun her halfway around, but instead of falling down dazed and weeping, she used the momentum of her turn to fire off one hell of a kick. A short, chopping side snap with the blade of her right foot. I bent my knee and took it on the big muscles of my thigh, then when she tried to rechamber for a second attack I swept her standing leg. She went down hard enough for her head to bonk on the hard surface of the dock. That turned her lights off for a moment and she fell over on her back.

I spun toward my quarry.

That's when Santoro's crew joined the fight. One moment they were statues with Top and Bunny holding guns on them, the next they swarmed at me. It was crazy. They didn't go for my men. Just me. Three of them tackled me with all the force and aggression of defensive tackles at their own five-yard line. As we crashed down I heard the roar of Bunny's shotgun. One of the men still standing was plucked off the ground as buckshot tore him to red rags. Almost in the same instant Top opened up with the HK416 and I heard the distinctive sound of hot rounds punching through living flesh.

No screams, though. Not a one. It was the same with the guys who'd piled on me. There were grunts of effort, but not a yell, not a curse. Nothing. All three of them were swinging wild, full-power punches, just like the surfer boys had done. Like Rudy had done. I wrapped my arms around my head and let them break their knuckles on my elbows and forearms. They went totally batshit, hitting each other as much as they were hitting me. Their eyes may have been dead but they fought with a frenzy that bordered on mania.

It's nearly impossible to defend against that kind of assault. Even by defending I was getting hurt, and several times those wild punches had slipped through my defensive cage of bones. One shot caught me on the side of the head hard enough to fill the air around me with fireworks. I had to get out before they beat me to death. I roared and shoved upward with my hips, then twisted hard to one side like a bucking bronco. That tilted them and their combined weight dragged them sideways, and I helped by looping four fast, tight overhand lefts into shoulder and ear and side of neck. They crashed down and I kicked my way out, pivoted on my knees and started to come up, but the closest guy lunged at me, flopping forward like a dolphin trying

　　　　　　　　　　　　　　　　　　JONATHAN MABERRY

to beach himself. He grabbed my ankle, hugged my whole foot to his chest, and tried to bite me.

Bite me.

So, yeah, I guess I lost it. You see, I've had people try to bite me before. Some living, some dead. It's how I got into the DMS in the first place. I've fought infected walkers, I've fought genetically engineered Berserkers and Red Knights. I am not a fan of things that bite. My brain went into a different gear and I fell onto my hip so I could use both feet. My gun was long gone, lost during the ambush, but I didn't need it for this. I drove my heel into the man's face, flattening his nose, breaking teeth, smashing the jaw out of shape. The pain and damage I inflicted in under two seconds should have been enough to turn him into a dazed and screaming wreck.

That's not what happened, though. Instead it seemed to galvanize him. He kept trying to bite my leg, and for one terrible moment those broken teeth clamped shut around my calf. The pain was immense. Absolutely fucking immense.

I sat up and drove my thumbs into his eyes, bursting them. His mouth opened. Not in pain, but to try for a better bite.

Jesus Christ.

I screamed at him as I clawed the rapid-release folding knife from its holster inside my right pocket. The short, wicked blade snapped into place with a flick of my wrist and then cut a red line across his throat. Blood sprayed me and the dock.

He tried one last bite, but he was fading. Finally. Fading and then gone.

I rolled away and ran on fingers and toes away from the others, aware of searing pain in my leg. No idea how bad it was. Not in terms of structural damage but in potential. Was he one of *them*? A walker, someone infected with a pathogen like *seif al din*? If so, had he broken the skin? Had his saliva gotten into the wound? Had I survived the moment only to become a zombie myself? Was this it?

As I turned to face the other men I saw everyone on the dock and it burned itself into my brain in a series of images. Not a tableau, but a collage of moving nightmare images.

Bunny was standing twenty feet from me, his big shotgun held in his hands as he fired at one of Santoro's men who lay sprawled on the ground. Bunny stood there and fired blast after blast with the twelve gauge, the buckshot tearing into dead flesh, ripping it apart, destroying all semblance of humanity. Over and over and over again. And in Bunny's eyes . . . I saw nothing. They were empty and glazed and his face was totally slack.

Nearby, Top was firing at the people along the dock.

Not the henchmen, but at *everyone*.

I saw an old woman fall.

Then a skateboarder.

"Top—*noooooo!*"

He ignored me, or didn't hear me. I saw a young couple running with their baby. The father went down with five or six bullets in his thighs. The woman and the baby vanished out of sight behind the utility shed. I'm pretty sure she was bleeding, too. No way to tell about the baby. The expression on Top's face was inhuman and his muscles stood out like he was carved out of volcanic rock. He strove against the weapon in his hands as if it fought him, as if it *wanted* to kill and he was losing the fight to stop it. The civilians on the dock and inside the boat screamed. Some of them. A few were down, clutching at red bullet wounds. Some were running away as fast as they could. The rest stood there with empty eyes and empty faces.

Between the crowd and Top was the row of boats. Santoro was untying the lines to free the Picuda. In five seconds he would be able to push off. If he got away, then whomever he worked for would have what they needed to launch a catastrophic plague. A doomsday weapon. But there were the people on the dock. Here, now. In immediate need. I was totally torn. Closer to me, the last two of his men rushed in, punching the air even though they weren't yet within range.

It was all so insane. The Killer in my head had not awakened. He was not in this fight at all. Hesitation was going to get me and everyone killed, and I knew it.

I tried to run around them, to get to Santoro despite Top's wild gunfire, but my feet felt sluggish, clumsy. I tripped and nearly fell into the two henchmen. They threw themselves at me. The knife in my hand moved, maybe more from muscle memory than conscious will. The blade reached out to the hands that reached for me, and in that rapidly diminishing space it did awful work. Fingers flew into the air, chased by lines of red rubies. Pieces of their faces fell away to reveal muscle and bones. Veins opened like hoses. Then they were falling like discarded puppets, and I was running toward the Picuda as bullets buzzed like furious bees.

How I did not get killed is something I'll never know. It wasn't the Killer at work. You couldn't call it luck, either, because no one on that dock was lucky. Not that day. If anything, my survival was the result of a perverse god who wanted more entertainment.

With a howl of animal rage I jumped into the Picuda, which had swung on its last remaining line and came thumping sideways into the dock. My leap was clumsy and mistimed, and my left shoe caught the edge of a locker, sending me crashing down hard enough to knock the knife from my hand. I saw it bounce off the corner of the small black briefcase. Santoro was on the forward bow untying the line from the cleat. The second I landed he dropped the rope, swarmed over the windscreen, and came at me with blinding speed. No weapons, but he didn't need them. He should have—even off my game with the Killer gone or dead I was still a first-chair special operator. Suddenly I was backpedaling from a flurry of short, precise, vicious, and insanely fast blows. They came in at all the wrong angles and I wasn't balanced yet for a solid response. The boat wobbled as once again I tried to hide inside a nest of forearms, elbows, and shoulders. If he'd been going for face or body hits he'd have busted his hands on my skeleton.

That's not what happened.

He was a brilliant fighter. Not good, not great. Brilliant.

He used one- and two-knuckle snaps and corkscrew punches to the nerve clusters and connective tissue on the key points of my arms. Mashing nerves, deadening muscles, exploding white-hot pain.

I can deal with pain. I *know* pain. Experience has taught me that pain can be thought through and fought through in the heat of the battle, that it can even make you stronger and faster and better. The Killer who lives inside my head feeds on pain and all it ever does is make him roar; it makes him hunger for blood.

But the Killer was still asleep. And I felt like *I* wanted to sleep. When I tried to block, my arms moved too slowly and in the wrong ways. When I tried to hit him, I was clumsy and my blows packed no power.

Santoro laughed as he slapped my feeble punches aside.

"This is for my brother, yes?"

He had the same accent as Rafael. The same cruelty in his eyes as he set about dismantling me, attacking with a savage precision that made a joke out of my counterattacks and ignored my defenses.

This wasn't about pain. It wasn't even about winning.

It was about *revenge*. About punishment.

If you know where to hit you can dismantle an opponent, you can take away his weapons and tear down his defenses and turn a formidable enemy into the Scarecrow from *The Wizard of Oz*.

That's what he did.

No one's ever done that to me before. Not since I was a kid. Sure, I've lost fights before, but no one has ever outfought me so thoroughly that I felt like a punching bag. He got inside my guard and jabbed me in the right sinus, boxed my ears, smashed the nerve clusters on both elbows, hit me in the top of the left thigh, stuck his thumb in the hollow of my throat, elbow-chopped my inner forearms, hit me over the heart with a one-two combination, and head-butted me. Then he caught me with hard knuckle shots to radial and ulnar nerves and my left arm went dead. I ducked down to try and take his next punch on my skull, hoping to break some of his hand bones with the famous Ledger hard head. But he changed a knuckle punch into a slap that felt like a donkey kick to the brain. I threw myself at him like a losing boxer would do, hugging him to stifle the flurry of hits.

Santoro pivoted as I grabbed him and he used my momentum and mass, plus the tilt of the boat, to hip throw me into the cockpit. I hit the steering wheel, the seat back, every knob and control including the little fire extinguisher tucked into the metal clamps. Hit the goddamn clamps, too.

Then he jumped on top of me, catching me in the solar plexus and floating ribs with his heels, and as I folded in half, he chop-kicked me under the chin. My whole body went limp but my consciousness hung by its fingernails on the crest of the abyss.

In the movies, fight scenes are ten minutes long. In the real world they're over in seconds. Someone wins, somebody loses.

I lost.

He beat me to the edge of consciousness.

All the way to the edge.

But . . . only to the edge.

I had nothing left and it would have been nothing for him to end me with a blow to my throat. He could have stomped me to death. He had all the cards and I was a wrecked heap.

Then I saw him straighten and his eyes went momentarily as dull as his men's had. He stared right through me, but while the eyes remained dead and expressionless his mouth curled into a joyful and terrible smile.

"Sucks to lose," he said, "doesn't it? It hurts. It's humiliating."

He backhanded me across the face. Not a killing blow. It was punctuation and it was belittling. I tried to block it, tried to turn away, but my body felt like it was made of broken stone. Too damaged, too heavy.

"You don't get to win this time, Ledger. You don't get to be the hero and you don't get to save the day."

Another slap.

"You get to lose. But here's the thing, here's the fun part," said Santoro in the voice that was not his own. "You get to *watch*. You'll be there when the lights go out. You'll be there when the screaming starts. And you'll be there as all of those children start to die. You. Joe Ledger, America's shining hero. Maybe if you're lucky they'll let you push one of the death carts. Maybe your penance will be taking all of those small, diseased bodies to the fire pits. Won't that be fun?"

Another slap.

The world winked out for a moment. Maybe it was damage or maybe it was me wanting to crawl into a hole deep inside my head and not hear any of this. To not know any of it.

Then I saw the glazed look fade from Santoro's eyes. He blinked and looked around, nodded to himself, and bent to pat me down, tear my pockets open, and basically mug me. My DMS gadgets and other items clattered to the deck. He looked down at the stuff, paused for a moment, then quickly bent to scoop something up.

Then he cut a look at me, smiled once more. "Adios, my friend. It's been a pleasure, yes?"

His accent was back in place. I saw his foot move but there was no way for me to avoid the kick. It knocked me out of the world.

CHAPTER EIGHTY-FIVE

When I forced my eyes open I was alone on the boat.

There was an engine roar to my left. My body hurt worse than I can describe but the leaden heaviness was gone, and when I dragged my bruised head and shoulders up high enough to see, I saw Esteban Santoro go roaring out of the gas dock in another boat. It was the XSR. It's not a fishing boat or a motorized play toy. The XSR is a military interceptor, a British-built super-speedboat that can hit eighty-five knots. Santoro had stolen my keys and was roaring off in the boat, taking the drives with him.

The XSR kicked up a bow wave that threw the Picuda against the dock and sent me tumbling back down into the bottom of the cockpit.

There was a crackle of gunfire and I turned to see Top and Bunny, both of them bloody, firing at the XSR.

Firing and missing.

Missing by a mile.

Like they weren't even trying to hit it.

CHAPTER EIGHTY-SIX

I staggered drunkenly to my feet, unsure of how badly I was hurt. Not giving much of a shit. The key to the Picuda was in the ignition. The goons were all dead or dying. And Santoro was getting away.

All around the dock people were screaming. A minute ago they'd been mostly staring like zombies, now they were shrieking in pain, in fear, in horror. I couldn't even count the dead and wounded. Everyone seemed to be covered with blood. Top stood there, shaking his head and blinking his eyes. He stared at the gun in his hands and then with a cry of disgust hurled it into the water. Then he slapped himself. Very fast and very hard. Again and again.

"*Stop it!*" I bellowed.

He froze, mouth open, teeth bloody, eyes filled with panic and pain.

"What did I . . . What did I . . . ?" It wasn't a statement he was able to finish. What he did lay bleeding and screaming all around him.

In the distance I could hear the wail of police sirens. Behind me was the growl of the XSR.

"Get in the boat!" I roared as I unwound the bowline.

Top lingered for a moment, still caught inside the bubble of horrified realization. Then he took a wobbly step forward. Bunny was a statue, gaping at the red inhumanity on the ground before him, the shotgun hanging limply from his right hand.

"What?" he asked. "What?"

"*Get in the fucking boat!*"

Like a couple of men woken from a drugged sleep, they came limping over.

Top jumped in and landed clumsily, hardly trying to break his fall. Bunny fell over the gunnels as I moved away from the dock. When the boat was clear I turned the wheel and hit the gas. The Picuda threw a bow wave high enough to drown the NO WAKE sign and rock every other boat at the dock.

I tried not to hear the sounds of misery and outrage that chased us from the dock. When we were clear of the dock I pointed her nose toward the water that still thrashed from the XSR's passage, opened up the throttle, and went for it.

Bunny and Top clawed their way to their feet and pulled themselves along the rails, fighting the drag as I cranked the engine higher and higher. Top managed to get into the copilot chair. His face was streaked with blood. I had to shout to be heard over the engine roar.

"What the fuck happened?" he demanded.

But we both knew. Someone had been inside our minds. Someone who had access to the Dreamwalking technology, the Stargate technology. It was the worst kind of rape because the violation forced us to become complicit in murder and mayhem.

Top put his face in his hands and his shoulders trembled as heavy sobs broke like waves on the shores of his soul.

Out on the salt the XSR was pulling ahead.

"Top, we need air support," I barked.

No answer.

"Top!"

Nothing.

I punched him hard on the shoulder. Once, twice. Finally he snarled and fended off the third punch. He glowered at me with eyes that were rimmed with red and filled with the awful awareness of things he could not undo. I think that if he still had his gun he'd have blown his own head off.

"First Sergeant Sims," I bellowed, "get your head out of your ass and get me some air support. Do it right fucking now. That is an order."

That got through to him. Don't ask me how. Years of training, maybe. Or perhaps the mind intrusion was over, the invaders abandoning the minds they had wrecked, their job done. I don't know, but Top bent instantly forward into the cockpit so the wind didn't snatch his words away and tapped his earbud. I heard him yelling to Lieutenant Flaherty at San Nicolas. Then he straightened and turned to me. "They're putting a couple Jayhawks up. Two more on deck if we need them. And I scrambled a team for cleanup back at the gas dock."

His voice broke on that last part, but I didn't say anything. Instead I punched his shoulder again. "Are you here?" I demanded. "Are you with me?"

He ran a palsied hand over his face, then nodded. "Yeah," he gasped, then took a breath and said it with more conviction. "Yes, sir. I'm with you."

I had the throttle wide open and the engine howled at us. Bunny was still sitting like a zombie except for the tears that ran down his flushed cheeks. Top turned and without preamble belted the big young man across the face. Bunny slammed into the wall, rebounded, and Top stopped him with a flat palm on the chest.

"You good, Farm Boy?"

Bunny started to say something, stopped, squeezed his eyes shut, took a breath, then looked at Top. The glaze was gone. Only pain and confusion remained. And anger. So much anger.

He turned to me as if seeing me for the first time, then he glanced at the XSR.

"Let me drive," said Bunny thickly.

"I got it," I said.

"He's getting away."

"I can drive," I snarled.

"You drive like an old lady, Boss, and you're losing him. I know boats, you don't."

He was right about both. Bunny grew up in Orange County and he knew boats. I'm from Baltimore and I've seen boats. Not the same thing. It was a comedy act getting me out of the seat and getting his bulk into it. We managed with a lot of cursing, yelling, and a few threats. Finally I was kneeling in the gap between the two seats, holding tight to the seat backs. Top was mumbling prayers to the Virgin Mary. Or maybe Buddha or Odin. Whoever the hell was on call. I was beyond the capacity for rational thought. I held on and hoped we wouldn't hit anything harder than a lazy pelican, because at that speed we were going to die.

"He's getting away," yelled Bunny for like the fifth or sixth time. If he wasn't driving I'd have kicked him overboard.

Top drew Bunny's sidearm but the range was too great. Even if we had our team sniper, Sam Imura, here, I doubt he could have tagged Santoro. Distance and moving boats made for piss-poor accuracy. Maybe Top did the same math or maybe he could not bear to discharge the weapon, but he lowered it and punched the dashboard with his other hand. Very damn hard.

The sky above us was clear. Which pissed me off. There were supposed to be two angry birds from San Nicolas up there. Helicopters with machine guns and rocket pods would have been mighty damned useful right about then.

I tapped my earbud. "Bug, where's my frigging air support?"

What I got in return was an earful of static.

"Yo, Cap'n," yelled Top, nodding to the horizon, "we got company."

Far ahead, beyond the fleeing boat, a dark bulk was skimming along only a dozen feet above the wave tops. For one moment my heart lifted as I thought that we'd managed to close the trap on Santoro after all.

A *chopper*.

Then the smug *I-got-you* smile that was forming on my face froze in place and began to crack. The sun was still high and shone down on the bird with clear light. The paint job was wrong. It was black, with no visible markings.

Beside me, Top said, "Shit."

The chopper turned and a figure leaned out of the side door with something big and nasty. There was a bloom of smoke as he fired.

The rocket-propelled grenade whipped over the waves, arching over the XSR without pausing, and then sweeping down toward us.

Bunny tried to turn, tried to evade, but it was the wrong call.

"Move!" I screamed, but Top was already in motion. He hooked an arm around Bunny and went over the side. At that speed it was like falling out of a moving car. I had a brief glimpse of them bouncing and flopping across the waves like rag dolls, then I was diving into the drink on the opposite side.

Yeah, just like falling out of a car. You can't really appreciate how hard water is until you slam into it at close to fifty miles an hour. I hit the way you're supposed to, which didn't seem to matter a damn bit. The water hit me with the fists of giants.

And one millisecond later the RPG blew the Picuda into a million pieces. The fireball shot upward and the blast shock wave whipped outward through the water. Catching us.

Punishing us.

Pushing us down into the big blue.

CHAPTER EIGHTY-SEVEN

"Let's go, let's go, let's go," yelled Lieutenant Mick Flaherty as he and his crew bent to run through the rotor wash from the big Sikorsky MH-60T Jayhawk. The pilot was already at the stick and the big General Electric gas turbines were filling the air with an urgent whine.

The normal crew of four ran with two extra men, both of them sharpshooters from the SEALs. A second crew ran toward the other helicopter. Both birds were painted with the red and white of the Coast Guard, though neither was actually attached to that service. This joint special operations group worked as extensions of the DMS Special Projects Office. They extended the reach and added extra muscle to the field teams based at the Pier and at Department Zero, the big office in Los Angeles. Most of the men and women in this unit were candidates for promotion to the DMS. Each of them had flown combat missions many times.

And all of them understood the severity of the current assignment.

Capture or kill Esteban Santoro.

Failure was not acceptable.

Flaherty slapped his people on the back as they climbed inside, then he went forward and slid into the copilot's chair, put on his headset, and twirled his finger.

"Don't take the scenic route, Duffy," he yelled.

The pilot powered up and the heavy machine lifted free of the tarmac, then it swept around in a high-climbing turn, heading toward Oceanside.

There was a sudden piercing burst of static on the radio that stabbed Duffy and Flaherty and both men flinched back from it.

"What the hell was that?" demanded the lieutenant.

But the pilot didn't answer. Instead he began yelling into the microphone.

"Power's out," he roared. "I've got a dead stick, repeat, I've got a dead stick."

The engine stopped.

Just like that.

The blades continued to whip around, pushed by their own momentum, but then they stopped, too, as the helicopter suddenly tilted down toward the earth.

Like a dead bird, it fell.

Duffy screamed as he fought to restart the engines.

Flaherty screamed as he tried to help.

Inside the chopper, all of the men screamed.

All the way down to the unforgiving ground.

None of them saw the other helos cant sideways and fall, too.

Like dead things.

Both of them.

CHAPTER EIGHTY-EIGHT

I wasn't dressed for swimming. Black battle-dress uniform, military-design cross-trainer shoes. All of it soaked and heavy and conspiring to try and drown me.

My head was ringing from the explosion and every inch of my body was bruised from the punishing collision with the water. Drowning would probably feel better. And there are times that it's tempting to let it go, to give in to the darkness. That's a battle I've been fighting for a lot of years, and more than once I've had to struggle to come up with good reasons to stay on this side of the big black. Far as I can tell there's no pain once you take that step. A little fear, sure, but it would probably go away once the lungs stopped trying to breathe and the heart stopped pushing all that blood around. Then it would be the long, slow, easy slide down into the void.

Yeah, so damned easy. And I would pretend that I didn't have those thoughts. Even while I was kicking off my shoes and fighting my way out of pants and shirt.

Even then a little voice in the back of my head kept telling me that I should let go, that it was time to stand down. To rest. It used some dirty tricks, too, telling me that I would see old friends who were long gone, and that I'd see them happy and whole. And healed. Helen and Grace. My mom. Khalid and John Smith and all of the brave men and women who'd been insane enough to follow me into battle and who fell along the way. Others, too. As I sank lower and lower into the brine I could hear them whisper to me, calling me, telling me that it was better, that it was safe.

I closed my eyes.

I almost let it happen.

Almost.

But there was another voice in my head, and it found me down in the salty, deadly darkness. A soft voice that spoke only a single word.

"No," she said.

No.

She was up there. Close. Probably in our condo in Del Mar, or in her office in La Jolla. Close. And maybe in that moment, maybe as I fell, she knew it. I could even imagine her stopping as if touched, closing her eyes as she listened to the things only she seemed able to hear. Maybe listening for my heartbeat. I don't know. She's my lover but even I don't know everything that goes on inside her. No one does, I'm sure of that. Maybe no one could. She's not like anyone else I ever met or ever expect to meet.

Junie Flynn.

"No."

It was as clear as if she whispered it in my ear.

Funny thing is, I didn't hear it as "no." Not really. I heard it as "yes."

As in, yes, stay with me. Yes, be alive.

Yes, there is a reason to keep going.

Which is really all you ever need.

One reason.

One good reason.

I kicked off my trousers, let them fall, taking my gun belt into the deep, and kicked upward. Free of the weight I shot toward the surface. It seemed like a long, long way.

It was.

When you suddenly realize you want to live, that's when the panic tries to set in. The world with all of its perils wants to make a fool out of you, it wants to cheat you of that glory of survival. It wants to steal everything from you at the moment when you understand the value of what you have, and what you have to live for.

So I kicked.

Kicked harder.

Fought my way up.

And up.

Until I broke the surface like a dying seal. Gasping, vomiting seawater, blind from the black and red fireworks that were detonating behind my eyes. Choking and coughing and trying to be alive.

Something splashed in the water and I turned, pawing the water from my eyes, expecting to see Top or Bunny come porpoising up.

It wasn't.

A double shot of spouting water vapor burst upward past me like a V-shaped geyser as something monstrous rose from the churning waves. It was simply fucking vast. Forty-five feet long if it was an inch. Gray and white mottling on slate-gray skin. Two blowholes. Barnacles crusted onto its sides.

A gray whale.

So close that as it rose to the surface the displaced water shoved me backward. I was actually close enough to see a line of stiff hairs on its upper jaws.

The impetus washed me hard into a second bulky creature.

I thrashed and spun, filled with mingled terror and wonder, to see that I'd collided with a much smaller whale. Maybe sixteen feet long with no trace of barnacles or mottling. A newborn.

A shadow fell across my face and I saw Big Mama turning toward me. Or rather toward the thing that was swimming between her and the newborn. I'm no ichthyologist but I'm pretty damn sure this was not the place I wanted to be. There was a great surface turbulence and her flukes broke from the water and rose above me. Ten feet across and more than massive enough to smash me into chum.

I dove and swam the opposite way from Big Mama and Junior. I wanted no part of maternal rage. I wanted no part of any of this. Pretty sure I was going to smash my *Free Willy* DVDs if I ever got the hell out of this.

I swam as hard as I could and didn't care which direction it was, so long as it was away from them. No idea where Top and Bunny were and, truth to tell, right now I'd have fed them to the whales if that's what it would take. The sun above me was hot but the water felt frigid and no matter how hard I swam it felt like I wasn't moving. Behind me I could hear the explosive spouting of the whales. Sounded so damn close. I knew that gray whales eat mostly crustaceans. They weren't like killer whales. But they were supposed to be very defensive. One of my friends in San Diego told me that the grays used to be called "devil fish" because of how aggressive they got when hunted. So I tried to telepathically assure Big Mama that I was the furthest thing on planet Earth to something that might want to do harm to any member of her species.

I swam.

And prayed.

And swam.

And prayed.

Until . . .

The seas grew quiet around me.

I didn't slow down. Not right away. Panic owned me.

Guess it's fair to say that I stopped swimming when I didn't die. Sounds stupid, but not in the moment. My muscles were burning with lactic acid, my lungs seared by salt water and exertion, my brains scrambled. Also, in the absence of a modern sequel to *Moby Dick*, the realities of my situation were beginning to float to the top of my brain.

We didn't catch our bad guy. Someone blew up our boat. We were fifty miles away from the nearest land. And by "we" I meant me and the voices in my head, because when I stopped and looked around at the top of each rolling swell, I didn't see another person.

Not Top. Not Bunny.

No one.

CHAPTER EIGHTY-NINE

I floated.

Drifting. Drowsing. Dreaming.

Trying not to die.

Several times I rode a swell to its highest point, cupped my hands around my mouth, and called out.

"*BUNNY!*"

"*TOP!*"

"*ECHO, ECHO!*"

Loud as I could.

The wind took my shouts and shredded them over the tops of the waves. Each time I sank down and had to fight back to the surface.

After twenty minutes, maybe more, I found a seat cushion from the Picuda. Burned, soaked, but still afloat. I snatched it and hugged it to my chest and nearly wept. Spent the next ten or fifteen minutes emotionally bonding with the cushion. It was my best friend and I loved it. We bobbed together in the salt water as I oriented myself and went through my options. The math was against me.

I was maybe forty miles west of Oceanside. Maybe less, but that's a long damn swim at the best of times. Which this wasn't. I had no idea if the tide was going in or out. Layer that on top of the fact that I'd gotten the living crap beaten out of me. Everything from mid-chest down was waterlogged and turning into a frozen prune. Everything from the chest up was broiling. No hat, no sunglasses. No food. No drinking water. What was that line from Coleridge? *Water, water everywhere, nor any drop to drink.*

I think I yelled some curses at the ocean, the water, the salt *in* the water, the waves, the sky, the puffy fucking clouds, and the universe as a whole.

Drifting, drifting.

Thinking about the man who did this to me.

Thinking about how much I wanted to kill him.

Thinking about how he'd probably killed me.

Trying to make sense of it. That he was Esteban Santoro was beyond doubt. So, how did that explain his sudden change of body language and accent? Had someone at the Dreamwalking project taken over Santoro, too?

My gut told me I was right about that, although I didn't really understand it.

The same thing had obviously happened to Top and Bunny. If they were alive, if they survived this, how would they ever be able to get past it? Someone had made them commit wholesale murder. Innocent civilians. Children. It was their hands who held those guns, their fingers on the triggers.

Living past a thing is not the same as surviving it.

I drifted.

What had happened to me? I couldn't feel the presence of anyone in my head. Not really, and remember I have some experience with sharing the real estate inside my skull. I hadn't turned my gun on the crowd and I hadn't shot myself.

So what *had* happened? What had turned me into a clumsy, ineffectual nothing in that fight? What had slowed my reflexes and turned me into a punching bag?

What indeed?

If it wasn't the psychic possession of Dreamwalking, then what was it? Until now I'd been blaming it all on the fact that the Killer aspect of me had either gone to sleep or gone away. Now I wondered.

Was he gone because someone had gone into my mind and killed him? Or, was he in some kind of psychic cage, shackled, of no use to me? And did that mean without him my usefulness as an operator was nil? Worse than nil?

The sea and the salt spray offered no answers.

I floated and tried to coax the Cop forward to analyze the details, to make sense of it the way he always makes sense of things.

I wished Top and Bunny would find me. Or me them. Where were they now? Had Top and Bunny paid for their actions by going down, down, down into the watery deep? If so, despite what had just happened, this world had lost two of its heroes. Actual heroes. The best of the best. Which means that Santoro had done what no one else had managed to do. Not walkers or berserkers, not mad scientists or ancient cults, not hired killers or soldiers of foreign flags. That rat bastard had killed Top Sims and Bunny.

I did not want to weep; I couldn't spare the moisture. But the tears came anyway. Anger followed soon, though, and its heat burned those tears to dry salt on my face.

Questions, questions everywhere and not an answer to be had.

Above me the sun fell in slow defeat over the walls of the world, dragging behind it a beggar's cloak of shameful darkness.

CHAPTER NINETY

Night.

Black and wet and cold.

The sky above me was ablaze with more stars than I could ever remember seeing. I could see the soft, pale sweep of the Milky Way. There were constellations I knew and others that in my semidelirium I believed had been created just for me. To mark the event of my death.

How's that for an ego trip?

I blame it on the beating Santoro gave me. My head felt like it cracked open and fiddler crabs had taken up residence. Not sure how many hours I was out there with only a burned seat cushion and my own questionable thoughts for company. My imagination conjured an endless string of worst-case scenarios for what Santoro was going to do with all the technology he stole. He could start a war. Or wars. He could unleash plagues. He could disrupt the power grids. He could open the door to terrorist attacks that would make what Mother Night and the Seven Kings did pale in comparison.

I could have stopped him. I should have been able to. It played out wrong. Why?

Consciousness came and went, and each time I went out of my head I went all the way out. Back into the kind of dreams I'd had after being exposed to the God Machine. The kind of dreams I had when I was in my coma.

So strange, and yet so goddamn real.

In one dream . . .

I was back on the dock, but instead of fighting Esteban Santoro I was duking it out with a man I'm sure was a complete stranger to me. I'd seen him before. He was taller and more heavily built than Santoro, but with a face that was totally obscured as if covered with smoke. He fought with superb skill, top of the line, with blood on his hands and black ice in his soul.

"You're a joke, Ledger," he told me as he smashed down my guard and pummeled my face. "Maybe you were good once upon a time, but now you're only a worthless thug."

That dream ended when he grabbed my hair and chin and snapped my neck. I heard it break and felt myself die. . . .

I woke from that to find myself in the water again.

But the water was suddenly ice cold. No, it was worse than that. The water was absolutely freezing. Insanely cold, and it stabbed into me like knives. I cried out in fear and pain, thrashing to get away from where I was, impossible as that sounds. The light had changed, too, and off in the distance I saw huge mountains rising above me. Not the green and brown coastal mountains of Southern California. Somehow, impossibly, this was a massive mountain range of solid ice.

Incredibly high, blue-white in the pale sun of some nameless day. And deep inside the ice, revealed only by some trick of the light, was a wall. Or walls. Towers, too, but in strange shapes. Gigantic cones and cubes the size of cathedrals. Towering stairs too vast and grand to have been constructed for humans to climb. And even though this was buried behind walls of ice, I could see figures move.

Shapes.

Things.

And wafting toward me over the freezing waves was a plaintive call from some animal I could not name. It cried nonsense words.

"Tekeli-li! Tekeli-li!"

Over and over and over and . . .

Something dark and mottled rose suddenly out of the water. Not a whale this time. No, this was more like a tentacle, but one that was too big to comprehend. It rose and rose, taller than a building, taller than a mountain, tearing upward through water and sky until it blotted out the sun. Ice water sluiced down its length, raining killing sleet over me.

"Tekeli-li! Tekeli-li!" came the call. Not from it, but because of it. Maybe calling to it. Begging it for something I could not, and never would, understand.

Then the tentacle fell.
Toward me.
Over me.
Smashing me down once more into the icy waters. . . .

A dream.

Only a dream. I floated now in waters that, while cold, were not the lethal waters of the arctic or Antarctic. It was dark again. The stars above me were the ones I expected to see. Needed to see. I listened for that plaintive voice and heard only the faintest of echoes.

"Tekeli-li . . . Tekeli-li . . ."

My wakefulness, though, was no more securely anchored to those waters and those stars than was my sanity. Blackness wanted me so badly, and it claimed me over and over again. There were other dreams. All strange, all violent. I wanted to dream about Junie, about being in her arms, about holding her warm body to mine, about clinging to her. But she could not find me in those dreams. Only pain and horror and strangeness knew where I was.

So I drifted and dreamed, dreamed and drifted.

A few times I heard that same strange voice again—more animal than human—crying out in an unknown language. It kept repeating Tekeli-li. And in one deep, deep dream I crawled out of the water onto a coastline that was muddy and choked with slimy weeds. The message of that voice persisted and I yelled at it to shut up, but the words that came from my own mouth were equally strange.

"Ph'nglui mglw'nafh Cthulhu R'lyeh wgah'nagl fhtagn."

And then a thousand voices rose up out of the darkness to echo those words. "Ph'nglui mglw'nafh Cthulhu R'lyeh wgah'nagl fhtagn."

Beneath me, the very mud on which I knelt began to shift as if it was the skin of something vast that had been called to wakefulness by the content of that chant. That . . . prayer.

I screamed myself out of that dream.

And then I stood in a corridor in a subbasement. Not sure how I knew that, but there was no doubt. A subbasement built years ago.

I walked along the basement, beneath rows of fluorescent lights. There were doors on both sides of the corridor, and I stopped and looked into each one.

I found laboratories with equipment I didn't understand.

I found one room filled with TV monitors and advanced computer equipment. There was a security guard sitting on a folding chair, his chin on his chest, eyes closed as he slept. He wore a comical peaked hat made from shiny aluminum foil. On a table beside him were dozens of similar hats. All made from aluminum foil. Above the table was a printed placard that read:

Playroom Security Notice
All Employees Must Wear Protective Skullcaps
During Dreamwalking Exercises.
This Means You!

I looked around. It was a room—a big room—which was lined with rows of coffins. Only they weren't really coffins. Funny things to have in a place called the Playroom. They were capsules of some kind. On a small metal stand beside each one was a miniature version of the God Machine, exact in every detail except that it was no bigger than a camp stove. The machines hummed quietly and on their faces a row of tiny gemstone chips flashed on and off in a random sequence. First the diamond, then two flashes of the ruby, then the topaz, the diamond again, the emerald. Over and over, and I stood watching, transfixed, almost hypnotized, lulled to the edge of sleep. In my mind, though, a voice that was not my own whispered, "The pattern is wrong. The more they dream this way, the greater the neurological damage. We've lost so many dreamers already."

It was the voice of Dr. Erskine. When I turned to look, though, he was not there.

Another voice spoke. One I almost recognized, but it was strangely distorted, almost mumbled. "You can't expect to look at the face of God and not go crazy. It stands to reason."

There was no one there.

But I was wrong. When I went over to one of the capsules I could see that there was a person inside. He wore pajamas. How strange was that?

I realized that he wasn't dead. The man was sleeping. He wore a metal cap with all sorts of wires attached to it, and he was sleeping an electric sleep. His face twitched and his mouth moved as if he was speaking, but there was no sound. There was another person sleeping in the next capsule, and the next. More than twenty people. All of them sleeping. And when I got to the last one I saw that the person asleep in the tube . . .

. . . was me.

Frightened, I ran from the room.

Across the hall there was another door and I ran through it.

I stopped because I smelled something bad. Like burned meat. I was in another laboratory, but this was much bigger. And stranger. There, in the gloom at the far end of the laboratory, I saw it. A God Machine. Huge, gleaming. Bigger than the one I'd seen down at Gateway. It hummed and pulsed with power.

Standing before it was a twisted shape that almost—but not quite—looked human. He wore white pajamas that were smeared with food and snot and piss and blood. His skin was wrinkled and puckered and blistered. He heard me and turned to look at me with emerald green eyes.

"You're not wearing your hat," said the man.

When he smiled his teeth were white in his burned red face.

"Who are you?" I asked.

"They killed me," he said, "but I didn't die. Now I'm going home."

And then something came whipping out of the mouth of the God Machine. Huge, twisting things with suckers and claws and spikes and . . .

. . . and . . .

I woke in the cold water.

Alone and dying. Lost and forgotten.

Terrified beyond belief.

And . . . angry.

I was so goddamn angry.

Because I knew.

Son of a bitch.

I *knew*.

It's a bitch when clarity comes so sharply but so late. In dreams we are so receptive to the truth, even when it comes to us wearing a disguise.

I knew who we were fighting.

I *knew*.

ISIL, Santoro, the Closers . . . they were like arms, like tentacles attached to the same monster. As I drifted out there I thought I knew the name of the monster. And I was going to die out here and never be able to tell anyone. I was going to float into oblivion, a useless piece of flotsam drifting out on the tide. And because I was too slow to understand, everyone I loved and everything I cared about was going to die when darkness fell. All of those children would scream in the darkness and I wouldn't be able to do a thing to save them.

CHAPTER NINETY-ONE

There was a sound in the darkness.

Not a weird cry or my own voice talking nonsense words. This was different. A mechanical sound. Or was that my mind breaking further open? When you first hear something like that it's so easy to doubt your senses, to believe that it's a fiction created by desperation, wishful thinking, and a failing psyche.

It was faint and far away, both muffled and distorted by the sound of the ocean. I made myself go still in order to hear it, to try and determine where it was. Not east, I thought. Probably not a Coast Guard rescue craft unless they'd gone out looking and were on the way back to the barn after giving me up as shark food. Wasn't west of me, either. I found Venus and used that to orient myself. The motor sound was off to the south. How far off, though?

In this gloom there was no way in hell anyone could see me. Could they hear me? The engine, though a ways off, had a throaty rumble. Something powerful but small. A boat engine, not a ship engine.

Going slow.

Slow.

In these waters at this time of night a slow engine could be a night fisherman out for yellowtail or bluefin tuna. Or maybe there were squidders. I rode a couple of swells upward and looked in that direction.

There.

A light.

Two lights. A bow light and the harsh white glow of a searchlight.

Someone was out looking for us. Had they found Top and Bunny? Please, please, let that be the case. Those men had followed me through hell and today they'd followed me into an ambush. If there was blame, then it was totally on me. They deserved better.

The boat was a couple of hundred yards off and it might as well have been on the far side of the moon. To them I'd be a dark dot on a dark ocean.

On the next swell I yelled as loud as I could.

"Ahoy the boat!"

Did it again on the next, and the next.

Kept doing it until my voice was sandpapered away.

Kept at it, though. Kept yelling. Hailing them. Begging for help.

When the engine noise changed from a rumble to a roar, I had that terrible feeling all survivors get when they see rescue within reach and then it begins to pass them by. I screamed and waved my arms, and the motion pushed me right down into the drink where I took a mouthful of water.

Then light filled the world. Bright as the sun, pure and perfect. And a voice bellowed louder than the motor.

"There!"

And another voice roared back, "Goddamn it, I can *see* him, Farm Boy. Why don't you drive the boat like you ain't drunk?"

I knew those voices.

Impossibly, I knew them.

When they got closer I knew the boat, too.

It was an XSR military interceptor. The boat Church had lent me, which had been stolen out from under me by Esteban Santoro. As the engine slowed to a muffled idle and the boat swung sideways toward me, I saw the faces of Top Sims and Bunny. Battered, worried, panicked, and relieved. I saw hands reaching toward me.

And they were real. No illusion, no wishful thinking. They were actually here. Somehow, impossibly, after all these hours and in all of this darkness, they'd found me.

I wanted to scream out their names.

A sudden swell picked me up and flung me toward Top and Bunny.

CHAPTER NINETY-TWO

Top and Bunny told me the story of how they found the XSR drifting in the water, the key still in it. They called in for help and there were at least a dozen other boats out looking for me. How the hell I managed to drift right through them is a logistical puzzle none of us will ever figure out. Top used the radio to call Church. He told him everything. And during that call he learned about what had happened to our air support.

Church directed them to a private marina in San Diego owned by one of his friends. DMS support team members helped us ashore and took each of us into a different cabana, where medical teams treated our wounds but asked no questions other than what they needed to know. My soaked and salt-caked clothes went into a trash can and an EMT brought me a Walmart bag with fresh clothes. New stuff with the tags still on them. Socks and shoes, too. I just finished dressing when there was a light tap on the door and Mr. Church came in. It was a small room with a shower stall, a dressing table, and two chairs.

He came and stood in front of me, studying my face, looking deeply into my eyes. I knew what he was doing.

"I'm me," I said.

Church made a small noncommittal sound and sat down on one of the chairs, waving me to the other.

"Tell me," he said.

"We don't have time."

"Brick is on his way here with a tactical support vehicle. Until he gets here we cannot and should not act. And I need to know what happened yesterday. Tell me what happened, and I do mean everything, Captain Ledger."

So I told him. Every single detail of what happened on the gas dock and on the salt. He listened without comment. When I was done he studied me for a long, uncomfortable time. Seconds cracked off and fell around us and the cabana was dead silent.

"And it is your assertion," Church said at last, "that you were not in full control of your actions?"

I shook my head very slowly and decisively. "I've been in enough fights to know the difference between losing my shit in the heat of the moment and not being in my own right mind. I know what happened."

Church nodded. "And what should we infer from that?"

"I had a lot of time to think out there," I told him. "There are a lot of pieces to this, so that so far it's felt like we were cruising the edges of things. Like we were catching glimpses of several different cases. ISIL and the Kill Switch. Gateway and all that interdimensional shit. The breakdown of the American intelligence community. The theft of SX-56. The Mullah of the Black Tent. The Unlearnable Truths. The Closers. The plague of . . . whatever you call it. Insanity, treason . . . the DMS falling apart."

"Yes," he said slowly.

"It's not a dozen cases," I said.

"No," he agreed.

"This is all the same goddamn thing."

"Yes."

"And I'm pretty sure I know who's behind it. I maybe even know why. It's just that it's crazy . . . and . . . I'm not sure I can trust my own judgment on this."

"Even after all of that time floating and thinking?"

"Don't joke," I said.

"Believe me, Captain, I am not joking. There are eleven dead in Oceanside, and another sixteen injured. Three of the injured are critical, including a six-year-old boy."

I closed my eyes because that hurt worse than any punch, knife cut, or bullet wound I've ever had. Much worse. I wanted to turn away from him, from those numbers, from the horror. But no matter where you turn, the truth is going to be right there in clear line of sight.

"There are videos of it on the Net," said Church. "You three were wearing balaclavas, which means your faces are not out there. Police are looking for three men matching your approximate physical descriptions. Luckily for us there are conflicting statements and the cell phone videos are shaky and unreliable. If need be, Bug can create a tapeworm to find all copies of these videos and erase or modify them. He's prepping that in case we need it."

"Jesus."

"I interviewed First Sergeant Sims and Master Sergeant Rabbit. They are both in shock and say that they don't remember much about what happened. Dr. Hu can test them for drugs and neurological damage, but I don't expect he'll find much. Will he, Captain?"

"No."

Church took his glasses off, removed a handkerchief from his pocket, and polished the lenses very slowly. He has very dark eyes. Brown with flecks of gold and green. They are not kind eyes. They are not forgiving eyes. And they are not young eyes. You can look at him and know—as I knew the first time I ever got a good look at him—that he is a man who has seen too much and who knows exactly how the world is constructed. He's studied the materials used in construction and he knows when and where it will break.

"The person you've encountered in your dreams," he said as he put his glasses back on. "You never saw his face."

"No."

"Do you think this is a real person?"

"Yes."

"Key question. Is this the person who you believe has been influencing your actions?"

"Yes."

"Is it your belief that he, and perhaps others like him, have used this technique to influence the actions of Sergeants Sims and Rabbit?"

I swallowed hard. "Yes."

"Is it your belief that this technique is responsible for the failure of other DMS field operatives?"

"Absolutely fucking yes."

"Speculate for me, Captain," said Church. "If such a thing as dreamwalking is possible, might it also be used to negatively influence field commanders and soldiers deployed in the Middle East?"

A day ago that question might have startled me. This wasn't yesterday. I said, "Yes. And I think this explains why our entire intelligence network is for shit. This dreamwalking thing may have been developed as a weapon to let us spy on our enemies, but I think it's pretty clear that it's being used against us. It's destroyed the operational effectiveness of the DMS and it's opened us up to ISIL and whoever else might be on the inside track of this. Can I prove it? No. Not yet. But do I believe it? Yes, I do."

"So," said Church, "do I."

"And I'll go you one better," I said. "That guy on the ISIL video, the Mullah of the Black Tent . . . ? Did you see his eyes?"

"I did."

"That was the same expression—the same *lack* of expression—I saw in the eyes of Top and Bunny. The same blankness I saw in Rudy and those surfer boys, and on some of the people on the gas dock in Oceanside. I caught a glimpse of it in Santoro's eyes, too."

"You think this is a signature?"

"Or a side effect of the dreamwalking," I said. "Yeah, I do. I think it shows that the conscious mind of the hijacked body has been—not sure what the word is . . . displaced, shoved back. Something like that. I think our Big Bad stepped into Santoro's body during the fight. I told you that his accent changed. That would make sense if the person doing the dreamwalking didn't have the same accent."

Church crossed his legs and then smoothed his tie. He nodded slowly. "Agreed. The Mullah was a cleric in a small village and his rise to become a leader and an effective military strategist happened too quickly to be reasonable. I would not be surprised to learn that the man himself is surprised by what he is doing. It's likely he thinks he is having religious visions. The clarity and veracity of these visions, coupled with the undeniable military gains, has cemented him as a prophet of jihad. This is a very dangerous thing, because most of Islam is not unified in their hatred of the United States. Until now it has only been a vocal and violent minority. The emergence of someone who demonstrates knowledge and abilities that are seemingly impossible outside of religious visions could—and very likely will—change that. Even our staunch Muslim allies might question their alliance with us, and more so with neutral Muslims. Our enemy has found a unique way to shove the world toward an actual war with Islam."

"And we can't prove that he's not a prophet," I said.

"No. Dreamwalking and the whole Stargate project isn't something the general public would either accept or believe."

"But they'll believe in a guy saying he's speaking for God." It wasn't a question. We have about eight thousand years of history to tell us how effective religion—or its manipulation—has been in starting wars.

I sat up. I was windburned, sunburned, and sore, but I managed. Anger is a useful fuel. "You need to get on the phone with the damn president and—"

"Oh, believe me, Captain, I've had several long conversations with the president," said Church. "As of two hours ago I am no longer the director or codirector of the Department of Military Sciences. I am no longer, in any capacity, an employee of the federal government. I am, in fact, likely to be under indictment by this time tomorrow."

I felt the blood drain from my face.

He said, "The DMS and all of its staff and resources are now under the management of the Central Intelligence Agency. Harcourt Bolton has been promoted to interim director pending reorganization. He will likely become full director of whatever the DMS will become, and it is likely to either be dissolved or folded into a minor department of the CIA. Our charter has been officially revoked. Federal marshals have been sent to each of our field offices to oversee the removal of personal items belonging to staff members. All employees and field agents are on unpaid suspension. Cleaning out desks and lockers was the only concession the president afforded me. Aunt Sallie has initiated a snowstorm protocol, which locks everyone out of MindReader except her, Bug, and me. Aunt Sallie and Bug are currently operating out of a safe house in Brooklyn."

He could have stood there and pummeled me with a baseball bat and done less damage to me.

"No . . . ," I breathed.

"Oh yes." Church gave me the strangest of smiles. "According to the president we are the bad guys, Captain Ledger. He has promised to file charges ranging from first-degree murder to conspiracy to commit treason. A warrant is already out for your arrest. Sergeants Sims and Rabbit will likely be charged, though right now POTUS does not know it was them on the gas dock. As team leader, you are in the crosshairs of a federal investigation."

"This is bullshit."

"It's a reality. The Department of Military Sciences, as we have known it, no longer exists."

CHAPTER NINETY-THREE

"What are we going to do?" I demanded. "Are we just going to bend over and take it? Jesus Christ, Church, we keep getting blindsided. First Hugo Vox turns out to be a traitor, then we find out that Vice President Collins is in bed—literally in bed—with Mother Night. It seems that no matter which way we turn, we get stabbed in the back. Now someone is messing with our minds. How are we supposed to fight this? I mean . . . is this it? Have they won?"

Church smiled. He seldom did that, and it was almost never a comforting thing to see.

"Tell me, Captain," he said calmly, "since coming to work for me, have you ever noticed in me a tendency for passive acceptance? Have you, in fact, ever known me to accept failure as an option?"

"No, but that's because you had the DMS and MindReader and . . ." I trailed off. It was the wrong answer and we both knew it.

"Presidents come and go," he said. "The war remains. I've been fighting this war for a very long time. Longer than you know. Over those years the war has taken a lot of different forms. Betrayal is not an uncommon occurrence. It is discouraging and it hurts, because the same optimism that gives us the will to fight also allows us to believe in the goodness of others. It is a tactical error to accept our own faith as a failing. That failure—the moral crime implicit in the betrayal—is owned entirely by those who betray our trust. By those who turn and stab the soldier fighting beside them. By those who take the sacred trust given them by the people they serve and use it as a sword against them. We can sit here and feel foolish and stupid for not having seen it, or we can waste time being awed by the sophistication and subtlety of our enemy. Neither choice, however, helps us get back up off the mat. And I, for one, have never been comfortable on my knees."

The room was very quiet.

He said, "We have been forced outside of our comfort zone before, and we've been forced to operate outside of the law. In those times I tend to look at the bigger picture, serving justice rather than a statute. It's been my experience that in moments of need you will bend a rule in order to accomplish what you know is right."

I nodded.

"When you told me about your dreams," he continued, "I found several items of particular interest. Having read the Stargate files, I know that it is possible, even probable, that the mental connection is not necessarily a one-way thing. You have certain aggressive tendencies, Captain, and you are a fiercely individual man."

"So what?"

"So maybe your dreams are more than that. More than fantasies. You described a place, a laboratory, with people sleeping in capsules. You described scale versions of the God Machines beside each one. What does that suggest?"

I licked my lips and fought to reclaim that dream image. It came to me with surprising clarity. More like a memory than some wild construct of nightmare. And suddenly I understood where Church was going with this.

"There has to be more than one person doing the dreamwalking," I said. "To control Top and Bunny, to slow me down, to manipulate the people on the dock. There has to be a . . . well, a team, I guess. A bunch of sleepwalkers."

"That would be my guess," Church said, nodding. "And they would have to be practiced at it. Focus your mind and tell me what else was in that lab."

I told him about the guard wearing an aluminum foil hat, and the other hats on the table. And the sign. Church nodded. "That makes a great deal of sense."

"It does?"

"During the Stargate project the researchers found that a helmet or skullcap lined with crystals, certain metals of low conductivity, and certain polymers blocked the psychic signals, even when a subject was in the presence of a person with pronounced abilities."

I had to smile. "So . . . all that stuff about wearing aluminum foil hats is true?"

"If I had to guess, it was a distortion based on leaked information from the Stargate program. Remember, to most of the people in the DIA and CIA the program was a joke and a failure. Very few people know that it was actually successful."

"Do I need to go out and buy a roll of Reynolds Wrap?"

"Something can be arranged," said Church. He made a very fast call to Dr. Hu.

"Is Hu still working at the DMS?" I asked when he was done.

"Bolton offered to keep him on and to promote him to deputy director of the DMS."

"I'll bet he lunged at that like a bass."

Church gave me a disapproving look. "Dr. Hu's response was to file his resignation. As soon as he was out of the parking garage he sent a coded signal to activate a computer virus that has since frozen all of his records. All of his research, past and present, is now locked. Any attempt to unlock those records receives the response *manducare stercore*. I believe you can translate the Latin."

I could. Eat shit.

"Hu did all that?"

"You have always underestimated him. Chemistry is against you both, but Dr. Hu is one of the family, Captain. Never doubt it."

I thought about my dream, of Hu fighting to save me, and of what Junie said about him. "If we get out of this," I said, "I'll buy him a beer."

"It's likely he would turn you down. He is part of the family but he still considers you to be a mouth-breathing Neanderthal. His words, repeated often," said Church. He looked at his watch. "My car will be here soon."

"Look, if this is all true, then that sleep lab is somewhere underground. A basement or subbasement. I think there's a full God Machine in there."

"Do you have any insight into where?"

"No. Maybe. I . . . I don't know. But there's something else," I said. "And I think it's really important. Maybe the most important thing. It was something Santoro said when his eyes glazed over. When he was taken over, I guess. He said, 'You're nothing but a thug, Ledger.' Sound like anyone you know?"

"Now isn't that interesting," said Mr. Church.

There was a knock on the door. Brick had arrived. Church got to his feet and glanced at me.

"We have been victims too long, Captain. It's time to go to war."

CHAPTER NINETY-FOUR

PACIFIC HOLIDAY MARINA AND YACHT CLUB
SAN DIEGO, CALIFORNIA
SEPTEMBER 10, 12:06 P.M.

Brick led us to the marina parking lot where a gorgeous Mercedes Sprinter luxury RV was parked.

"Welcome to the Junkyard," said Brick, patting the sleek silver-gray skin with real affection. When he opened the door and I climbed in I could see why Brick was so proud of it. The first time I'd met him he was driving a Mister Softee ice-cream truck that was actually a rolling arsenal. He had designed and kitted it out to provide massive tactical support for any kind of field mission up to and probably including a full-scale invasion of Russia. The RV was no different. Inside I saw a bank of advanced computer and communications equipment, but the rest of the interior was basically a gun rack. Rows of handguns and long guns, ranging from combat shotguns to the latest automatic rifles. Boxes of grenades—fragmentation, flash-bangs, smoke—and a bin filled with uniforms and Kevlar.

Brick chuckled. "Mike Harnick helped me trick her out. If it's not here, Joe, you don't need it. We got every single one of Dr. Hu's little electronic gizmos. I got a minigun mounted in the overhead dome, front and back chain guns, and if I press the right buttons I can lay down a nice barrage of mortars that would entertain even the most blasé of houseguests."

"Jesus H. Henry Christ on a hoverboard," I said.

"Until further notice," said Church, "the Junkyard is our mobile command center."

"To do what?" I asked as I dug black battle-dress trousers out of the bin. "What's our first move?"

There was a *click* behind me and the door to the tiny head opened and Harry Bolt stepped out. His face was flushed. "Maybe you should put some biohazard tape over that," he said as he quickly shut the door. "Oh, hi, Joe."

"Hey, kid. Where's Violin?"

"No idea," said Harry. "Once my dad started evicting everyone I lost track. Dad told me to get the heck out, too. He's really in a mood."

I started to say something foul and threatening, but Church cut me off.

"Captain," he said, "would you please describe to Mr. Bolt everything you can remember about the chamber with the sleep capsules."

"Everything?"

"Yes," said Church. "Mr. Bolt has joined the family."

So, as Brick drove and I went over the whole thing again, Harry listened with mingled surprise, reluctant acceptance, and horror. When I got to the part about the sign on the wall that read: PLAYROOM SECURITY NOTICE, Harry Bolt suddenly burst into tears. He caved forward and put his face in his hands and wept, and through his sobs I heard him say, "No, no, no, no, no, no, no, no, no . . ."

It didn't sound like denial, though. Not really. It sounded like the thing you say when your worst fears are realized. I sat down next to him and wrapped my arm around his quivering shoulders, and like a little kid he turned and buried his face against my chest. He kept saying no.

We both knew he meant yes.

I'd known it since that moment of dreadful clarity I had while floating out in the night-black ocean. Maybe I'd even come to suspect it before then, but it seemed so absurd, so impossible.

Except that it was neither. It fit all the facts, confirmed all the suppositions.

When he could speak, Harry told me the origin of that name. The Playroom.

It used to have pinball machines and a handball court and a six-lane bowling alley. Skee-Ball and video games, too. It's where he played, almost always alone, when he was a kid.

In his house.

In the basement of his home.

In the basement of the Bolton family home.

CHAPTER NINETY-FIVE

We sat in a vehicle filled with guns and pain and drew our plans for war.

Even though I had a strong suspicion that Bolton was our Big Bad, having it confirmed really hurt. Even after everything he'd done to Church, to the DMS, to me, it hurt. It was a betrayal by one of my longtime heroes. I worshiped that guy. I wanted it to not be true. I wanted to wake up, maybe still out in the ocean, and discover that this was all just a dream.

Only a bad dream.

Even if it meant I drowned.

The world needs its heroes. We already have enough villains.

But . . . Harcourt Bolton, Senior?

Goddamn, that hurt.

"Dad has a big house in Rancho Santa Fe," said Harry, his eyes red-rimmed, nose running, voice thick. "Huge, really. Too many rooms. It's built on the grounds of an old Spanish monastery and it has two levels of basements where the monks stored the wine they made."

He told us that the subbasement was expanded during Prohibition and became a speakeasy for rich locals. That's when it earned the nickname "the Playroom." When the Bolton family bought it, Harry's grandfather had turned the subbasement into a real playroom, installing the bowling alley and handball court. It was Harcourt who purchased the video game machines, because, as Harry put it, those games kept Harry out of sight when his father had business friends, work colleagues, or women over. After Harry went to college, his father closed the subbasement, claiming that it had needed to be overhauled because of asbestos in the ceilings. Once the repairs were done it was scheduled to be converted into a wine cellar, circling around to its original use.

"And you never looked to see if that was true?" I asked.

He gave me a funny look. "Why would I? The video games were long gone by then. Besides . . . I haven't been there at all except for Thanksgiving and Christmas, and those were always pretty dreary. Nothing lifts the soul more than having your superstar father go point-by-point through your personal and career failures."

"Turns out you're a better man than him, kid," I said.

It only made Harry cry again.

I turned to Church. "I'm thinking an airstrike would be pretty useful right about now. Worked on Gateway."

"And if the God Machine isn't actually there?" asked Church. "What then? Besides, right now the president still believes that Harcourt is his white knight. We have suspicions, not proof, and let's face it, we're being guided by something you saw in a dream. We have no political cards to play."

I got up and crossed to the weapons rack. "I'd love to go in guns blazing," I said. "But after what happened to Top and Bunny . . . and me . . ."

As if in answer to that statement, Church's phone rang. He answered it and I saw relief on his face. "How long, Doctor?"

He listened. I could feel my gut clench like a fist.

"Go to FreeTech. Tell Junie you need access to the model-making room. They have a full shop for making prototypes. Go." He made two more calls, one to Junie to tell her that Hu was on his way, and another to Toys to tell him to offer any support that Violin might need. Then he disconnected and turned to me. "Dr. Hu believes he can make a protective skullcap. FreeTech has the fabrication equipment. We don't have much time, so it might be crude and uncomfortable."

"I don't care if you have to nail it to my head. I can't go after the God Machine without it. What about my team?"

Church shook his head. "We can't risk involving anyone else. It will be hard enough for Dr. Hu to make one helmet in time."

"Shit."

"On the upside," said Church, "Ghost is at FreeTech with Junie. From what I read in the Stargate file, the process does not work on animals."

"He's been acting really weird around me," I said.

"More probably he's reacting to you being weird around him."

I grunted. "Ah. Okay. Then let's haul ass."

Brick hauled ass.

CHAPTER NINETY-SIX

I came over the hill, moving quickly but quietly. Ghost ranged ahead to find any traps or sentries. I hadn't given him a kill order so nobody died. Yet. The night was still young.

I was dressed all in black, armed to the teeth, face painted in camouflage colors. And I was wearing an aluminum foil hat.

Yeah, yeah, I know, it's not aluminum foil. It's a crystal-infused, polymer-lined, low-conductivity, aluminum-magnesium-alloy skullcap. You can tell me that all day and night, but at the end of the day, I was going hunting wearing a metal hat so people won't climb into my head. Joe Ledger, American Dweeb. I wanted to kill someone just because of the fucking hat. Let alone the other two or three hundred points on my Justifiable Homicide Greatest Hits list.

Harcourt fucking Bolton. Damn it all to hell. Why did it have to be him?

How could this country's greatest hero be willing to unleash something like SX-56 and slaughter all those children? How?

Resentment at growing older and feeling marginalized? It couldn't be that. There had to be a deeper meaning. Insanity, a brain tumor. Something.

His house was a sprawling mansion that looked like it belonged in medieval England. Or maybe Westeros. Gray stone walls that rose above acres of manicured lawn that was dark green despite the drought and the governor's water restrictions. The richer you are, the more you take laws as suggestions that you can choose to ignore. The house had eaves and turrets and even a suggestion of battlements. You could defend that place against the Normans. Or Saxons. Or whoever the hell the medieval English fought. It's been a long time since high school history and, as it turns out, I don't give a shit.

I crouched down and pulled out my Scout glasses. They're high-tech premarket devices developed for Church by a friend of his who worked at Google. Or possibly owns Google. They have excellent night vision, but the lenses can be cycled so that I can switch to ultraviolet, thermal scan, and even an overlay from a satellite. Nifty. Useful, too. It was still too light for night vision, so I used the heat-seeker function and *bam*, there they were. Sentries in nicely concealed posts dotted throughout the landscape. Ghost sniffed the air and probably knew their placement, height, weight, and what they had for dinner. He whuffed at me. Asking for the go order.

"Hold," I said quietly. He gave me a withering look. Telling me I was too timid.

Could he really tell that the Killer in me was still gone, or possibly dead? Maybe. There have been plenty of times when that killer's eyes looked out of my head and into the wolf's eyes in Ghost. We'd met on that primal level so many times that in the heat of the fight we didn't need words or commands. He knew because in those moments we were the same. Predators from an earlier age of the world.

I held my position as pack leader as much for that primitive aspect of my personality as for any of the training we did. Maybe another handler would have forged a different kind of relationship with Ghost. I'm not like other people.

Or . . . maybe that was changing. Maybe the fact was these dream-walking bastards had cut the Killer's throat while they were ransacking the house of my private thoughts. That might be a mixed metaphor, I don't know. You get the point. There was something wrong upstairs and I was afraid that without that aspect of my personality, I was going to die. I probably should have died already. I've been lucky.

Luck has a shelf life; ask any gambler. Ask any soldier.

We were moving through the trees, staying in the deepest shadows. I tapped my earbud. "Cowboy to Bug," I said quietly.

"I'm here, Cowboy," he said at once. He was at Auntie's Brooklyn safe house but it sounded like he was standing right beside me. "We just picked up your transponder on the satellite."

"Where's Big Daddy?" I asked. We'd given that nickname to Harcourt Bolton. I'd suggested Big Fucking Asshole, but Church overruled me.

"At the beach," said Bug. Meaning, still at the Pier.

"Okay."

"I have fresh intel, Cowboy," he said, and from the tone of his voice I knew it was bad.

"Hit me."

"I've hacked into Big Daddy's accounts and his personal computer," he said. It was something he wouldn't have done half a day ago. Now, all bets were off. "Bolton has been building a shell around himself for years. Layers of it. Shell corporations, offshore holdings, numbered accounts. You name it. Any way you can hide money, he's using it. No idea how much. We're hacking our way through it but it's complicated. Short version is that ten years ago he was borderline broke. He was one of the people really crushed when the economy crashed. His mansion was mortgaged to the hilt, he was behind on payments to a dozen banks. He kept it hidden pretty well, but he was about to lose it all. Then it turned around. He started suddenly making payments on time and paying back the principle."

"Where'd the money come from?"

"That's the thing, he reported it to the IRS as consulting and speaking fees and returns on investments in technology corporations. It'll take a team of forensic accountants to make sense of it all, though. He was very smart and very clever about it. Paid very heavy taxes so that he didn't raise flags. But MindReader was able to go deeper. A lot of his investments were in dummy corporations. He was using them to launder his own money. And, Cowboy, get this, some of those fake companies are tied to Middle East oil money."

"We can prove that?"

Bug laughed. "How? With information obtained illegally? Fruits of a poisoned tree."

"Okay, but—"

Before I could finish, Mr. Church's voice cut in as sharp and hard as a knife blade. "Deacon to Cowboy," he barked, "we have fresh intel. We believe we know how Big Daddy intends to use the SX-56."

"How?" I demanded.

"Freefall." He said that among the papers Aunt Sallie had obtained from Washington was a proposal for a device designed to work in concert with Kill Switch. The idea was to launch batches of small drones, each of which was rigged with a chemical self-destruct device that was kept in safe mode by electrical current. Stop the current for any reason and the chemicals mix and destroy the drone, but the blast isn't an incendiary. More like a big pop, seeding the air with the contents of the thin-walled plastic containers fixed to the underside of each drone. Shoot them down and they blow. Try to disarm them and they blow. Cut all power and they blow. Airbursts and prevailing winds are dangerous bedfellows for a bioweapon. Fly the drones over congested areas and let biology do the rest. Let the movements of people do it. Let the natural contact of humans to humans, parents to kids, person to person be the weapon that drives the plague.

And why not just fly the drones over the crowds and blow them up? Sure, that would work, that would spread the disease. But police and EMTs, the fire department, FEMA, the National Guard, and hundreds of other first and second responders would be able to step up and handle it. People would die, sure. Kids would die. But only a few. Not the thousands or tens of thousands that would contract the weaponized smallpox in the hours after the power went out. Kill Switch would do far more than kill the power. It was designed for use against technological cultures where the population relies on speedy and efficient response. The more civilized a person is, the more they panic when the lights go out.

Kill Switch turned off the power and Freefall filled the darkness with monsters.

I crouched in the shadows under the trees and felt my mind clenching into a fist.

Church said, "MindReader is tearing apart Bolton's accounting. We have been able to track deliveries of drone components to ten cities across the United States. I've called the president but he refuses to listen. Bolton apparently already told him that we were going to approach him with some kind of wild cover story. He's been ahead of us at every step. Erskine designed his drone weapon to operate via the Kill Switch. We're working on the code sequence but you need to locate the main God Machine or we'll have no chance at all of stopping this. Go!"

But I was already running.

CHAPTER NINETY-SEVEN

As I ran I called my "backup."

"Cowboy to Spykid."

And Harry Bolt said, "I wish you wouldn't fucking call me that. I need a better call sign. And I don't want Junior G-Man, Wonder Boy, Bambi, Scrappy-Do, Happy Meal, Fresh Meat, Zombie Bait, Boy Wonder, Shirley Temple, Red Shirt, Bear Cub, Son of a Gun, or any of the other stupid names you suggested."

"Really?" I said. "Now's the time for this?"

"I want to be called Jester."

"Jester? You think this shit's funny?"

"No," he said. "Because I *don't* think it's funny. The name's ironic."

"You're an idiot."

"I still want to be called Jester. It sounds cool."

There are times when banging your head against a tree really feels like the right choice. I said, "Sure. Jester. Whatever. Can we save the world now? Just asking, because we're not pressed for time at all."

A pause. "Okay, Cowboy. Jester is on station."

"Thank Jesus," I said. "Keep sharp and follow me in."

If Harry wasn't my best chance of finding my way into the house and down to the Playroom I'd have given him a lollipop and left him behind. He's a nice kid and all that, but he has no business being out in the field.

Lilith still hadn't gotten back to Church with fresh intel, but every instinct I possessed told me that we were fighting the clock. Fighting and maybe losing. Santoro had gotten the drives with the code sequence. He—or one of the other people working for Bolton—could be down in the Playroom punching those numbers into the God

Machine. Kids in ten cities across the country could be in the cross-hairs right goddamn now.

Add to that the damage from the blackouts. How many people would that affect? Depends on the cities. If it was New York, Chicago, Philadelphia, Los Angeles, places like that? Call it millions. Crashes, fires going unchecked, medical emergencies, and no one able to respond. People trapped in elevators and subway cars. People with pacemakers, people on life support, babies in neonatal units, patients in surgery. All of them plunged into darkness.

Or it could be even worse.

This could break us. It would simply be a matter of ISIL winning. This was a situation of terror proving that it was more powerful than sanity. This was a sword against which no shield would ever work. Fear and destruction wouldn't be something in the headlines. They would be the defining qualities of our lives.

Those of us who survived.

If I didn't find that code and the God Machine, I wasn't going to live long enough to see the fall. That's not a blessing. I'd burn for failing. I'm not particularly religious, but I know that much.

"I'm going in," I told Bug. "Jester . . . be ready, you hear me?"

"Ten-four," he said, using the wrong response. Idiot.

Ghost and I drifted along the line of hedges until we were at the wall. Then I drew my gun. For this part of the job I was using a Snellig A-220, a high-intensity gelatin dart filled with an amped-up version of the veterinary drug ketamine along with a powerful hallucinatory compound. We all call it "horsey." Dart someone with it and they go down right now and dream of psychedelic lobsters. Or so I've been told. Some of the guys have volunteered to try it and they tell wild stories. It's like a bad acid trip that puts you into a fucked-up version of *Alice in Wonderland*. You wake up hungover and disoriented. Horsey is designed to attack the nervous system like a neurotoxin, so it works faster than a bullet. You get hit and you go down.

Now, don't get me wrong . . . under any other circumstances I'd have been happy as hell to punch the tickets of anyone working for Bolton. But you can't ask questions of the dead, and if the code wasn't on the premises, then I wanted to be able to hold meaningful group therapy sessions with the guards. Somebody would know something and with the lives of all those kids in the balance, I wouldn't be in the mood to ask nicely.

JONATHAN MABERRY

I edged around the curve of one of the turrets. Two guards stood together, eyes roving back and forth across the grounds. Looking in the wrong direction. Watching the driveway, which was the only route in that wasn't covered by the motion sensors. I raised the Snellig.

Pop. Pop. They fell as surely as if I'd reached into their brain stems and flicked a switch on the nerve conduction.

Ghost bared his teeth at them, and I knew that if I hadn't given him a stand-down sign he'd have made sure they never woke up. He was in a mood.

Wish to hell I was. My nerves were shot and when I'd raised the gun I was half-sure the shakes would have spoiled my aim. Yeah, it was that bad. I needed my edge. I needed the Killer back.

Even so, even without him, I bent low and ran, dropped one more guard at the front door, and then I was inside. In the belly of the beast. Ghost was with me, but he was drifting farther and farther from my side. I didn't like the looks he was giving me, either.

Jesus Christ.

CHAPTER NINETY-EIGHT

THE BEACHVIEW APARTMENTS
ENCINITAS, CALIFORNIA
SEPTEMBER 10, 2:16 P.M.

Chief Petty Officer Lydia Ruiz pulled into the ten-car parking lot, eased into a slot between a squatty little Fiat and a PT Cruiser with wood side panels and a roof rack for surfboards. She killed the engine and got out of the car. The motor tinkled slightly as it began to cool.

A warm breeze blew off the water and the sun was high in a clear blue sky. Out on the water a boat full of whale watchers was cruising north from San Diego, its hull painted a white so bright and pure that it hurt her eyes to look at it. Lydia took a few steps toward the entrance, then paused and turned back to her car. The passenger door was still closed. Bunny hadn't moved at all.

Lydia went back to the car and came around to his side. Through the tinted glass she could see his face. Rigid, emotionless, blank. His sunglasses were tucked into the collar of his T-shirt, his blue eyes fixed on something that was not part of anything there in that moment. Seeing him like this twisted a knife in Lydia's heart.

"¿Conejito—?" she called. *Little bunny.* A joke because he was so tall and muscular. Except now he seemed small, diminished by the comprehensive loss of confidence in who he was, and total lack of understanding of what he'd done. The intel about Project Stargate and all that mind control stuff did not seem to help Bunny. It had still been his finger on the trigger.

She opened the door and touched his cheek with the backs of her fingers. When she did that he always closed his eyes and leaned his face into her touch. It was a thing he'd always done and it never failed to ignite the love flame deep in her heart.

Except he didn't do it now.

Instead he sat staring through the windshield glass as if it projected a movie he was commanded to watch. And Lydia was wise enough about combat trauma to recognize what was happening. The events on that gas dock had broken something inside Bunny. In his heart and maybe in his head.

Lydia knew that it could happen to any soldier no matter how they were hurt. The ones who were going to stay in the game knew how to manage their own scars, even use them. Doubt made you seek for truth. Fear made you cautious. They were pillars of wisdom and of survival. Except when they became the defining qualities of a person. That's when a soldier became a kind of landmine that could kill himself or anyone around him. On the battlefield it created fatal hesitation. It soured judgment and clouded focus. It planted poisoned seeds in the heart from which ugly flowers grew.

"Come on, baby," she said, pulling lightly on his arm.

He got out of the car and let her steer him to their house, but he did it like a robot. It chilled Lydia because it was like the man she loved had stepped out of his own body. She guided him to his favorite chair on their patio, opened a beer and set it on the table next to him, but Bunny didn't look at it, didn't take a sip. There were four old men playing bocce on the sand, and half a dozen surfers in black wetsuits sitting on their boards waiting for a wave. A line of pelicans rode on the wind out toward a fishing boat.

If Bunny saw any of it, he gave no sign.

Lydia sat next to him, her chair pulled close, her head resting against his shoulder. She didn't even know he was crying until she felt a tear fall onto her head.

CHAPTER NINETY-NINE

THE BLACK TENT
HOME OF THE MULLAH
ISLAMIC STATE OF IRAQ AND ASH-SHAM
MOBILE CAMP #7
SEPTEMBER 11, 12:16 A.M. LOCAL TIME

The Mullah rose from his narrow bed and walked out of his house. His staff and the gathered senior officers all turned as he approached. Their conversation died off but their faces were alight with expectation.

"Is it time?" asked the warlord who had been a skeptic less than a month ago. There was no doubt left in his eyes.

The Mullah looked at each of them in turn.

"It is time," he said.

CHAPTER ONE HUNDRED

Bolton did not live small, I'll give him that. This place must have cost twenty million. I couldn't afford to mow the lawn. Made me wonder how much of it was bought with innocent blood.

The Scout glasses told me that there were no motion sensors on the ground floor or the big double staircase.

"Cowboy to Jester," I said. "Ghost is coming for you. Follow him in."

I used hand signs to order Ghost to run back exactly the way we'd come in. He vanished like a puff of white smoke. While I waited for him to return with Harry, I removed a few sensors from my kit and placed them on the downstairs windows and doors. They uplinked to a small drone and both boosted its signal and focused it on the house. Looking for a large electronic signature. So far, nothing, and that was not encouraging. What if I was wrong? What if that whole dream was nothing more than that?

Bad questions. Letting my mind ask them was like throwing gasoline on a fire. I heard a sound and turned to see Ghost moving along the line of hedges with Harry running bent over behind him. The kid was not a good runner. His stride was too short and he did not appear to pay any attention to the irregularities in the lawn. And it was his lawn. When he reached me he was out of breath, his face damp with perspiration.

"Rule one," I told him. "Cardio."

"Yeah, yeah, blow me," he said, mopping sweat from his eyes. He looked around. "Dad really made a lot of changes to the place. Motion sensors, guards." He crouched in front of the door. "You were right, these are new locks. He didn't want me coming home and just waltzing in."

I almost said, *He didn't want you coming home at all.* Sooner or later it was going to catch up to Harry that the Closers were working for his dad. All of them. Including the ones who tried to kill Harry in Budapest. Maybe the kid already knew that and wasn't letting himself think about it. Or maybe he had that truth locked in a closet in his mind.

I removed another of Hu's doohickeys, peeled off the plastic tape to expose the adhesive, and gingerly attached it to the door. The little green light stayed green. But when I placed a second one on the frame the light turned red. An alarm, and a good one. No problem. I attached wires to the sensor and connected them to another of the signal rerouters, waited until the light turned green, and then let Harry pick the lock. The door clicked open. Easy as pie.

The inside of the house was all dark wood and expensive art, hardwood floors and rugs with complex patterns. Vases sat on little tables and a huge Bolton coat of arms hung over a stone fireplace that was bigger than my first apartment. There was a motto inscribed on the heraldry. *Vi et Virtute.*

Harry saw me looking and translated it. "By strength and valor."

He looked like he wanted to throw up. I placed my hand on his shoulder and whispered in his ear. "You're here, kid. It took courage to come in here. A lot of it. You could have stayed back at the Pier. You didn't. Hold on to that, it could be useful."

He nodded and wiped wetness from the corners of his eyes.

Ghost went ahead to sniff for guards and immediately returned to me, looking over his shoulder three times. Three guards down a hall that led to the kitchen. I could smell a faint whiff of grilled cheese and coffee. The entrance to the basement was in the kitchen. No way to avoid it. In other circumstances I'd have tossed in a flash-bang and then let Ghost go to town. But that would be noisy and we weren't ready for noise.

Not yet.

CHAPTER ONE HUNDRED ONE

Toys stood in the doorway and watched Dr. Hu work. The scientist was bent over a modeling press, making another of the protective skullcaps. Toys wore one already and he hated it. Apart from the fact that it was too small and hurt his head, it looked bloody ridiculous. Junie wore one, as well, as did Christel Sparks, the head of security. The two women stood on either side of Hu. Junie was working the forming press, and Sparks was standing guard, her hand resting on the holstered Glock she wore on her belt.

"How many more?" asked Toys.

The doctor looked up from his work. "I don't know. I might even be wasting my time. They haven't been tested yet. I've refined the design from the ones I gave Ledger and Bolton's son. Not sure if I made them better or worse."

"Wait . . . we don't even know if these sodding things will *work*?"

"No," said Hu.

"Bloody hell."

"Actually," said Sparks, "they don't work."

Hu didn't even glance at her. "And I suppose you're an expert on such things?"

"As a matter of fact," she said as she drew her sidearm, "I am."

She shot Dr. Hu in the back.

CHAPTER ONE HUNDRED TWO

First Sergeant Bradley Sims sat alone at a table in the mess, a coffee cup standing filled and cold nearby, a plate of eggs and bacon untouched. The TV was on and CNN was using its endless news cycle to dredge up every gory detail about the slaughter at the gas dock.

Top had come into the Pier to clear out his locker. The two U.S. marshals were with him throughout, each of them stone-faced. However, Top had talked them into letting him come in here for a last lunch before he left. Montana Parker, Brian Botley, and Sam Imura were also in the building because Director Bolton had wanted to interview them to see where they stood in terms of loyalty to their country and involvement with the recent catastrophes. Federal marshals dogged each of them, too. The rest of the staff had been sent home. It was all over. All crashing down. Top sipped his coffee and felt his heart breaking into pieces.

He closed his eyes and rubbed his face with his palms. He was so damn tired but he did not dare go to sleep. *They* would be waiting for him. The ones he'd murdered. They would be standing around his bed and Top knew that they always would be. For the rest of his life. Faces empty of life and painted with blood. Dead eyes watching him, dead hands lifted to point fingers at him.

"Top—?" said a voice. Sam Imura.

"Go away," he said without opening his eyes.

"Top, look at me," said Sam. He sounded confused.

"Go the fuck away."

"Top, what the hell are you doing?"

Anger overtook his remorse for a moment and Top dropped his hands and glared at Sam.

At Sam.

At . . .

Sam Imura lay on the floor, his face white with agony, his clothes torn. He sat there, legs spread wide, hands clamped over his stomach as red blood poured from between his fingers.

Top stared at him. "Wh-what—?"

This wasn't the mess hall. He wasn't even in that end of the facility. This was the hallway outside of the armory and the door was ajar. Sam lay on the floor beside it as if trying to block the exit with his body. Top felt something in his hand and he looked down to see a big serving fork clutched in his fist.

The fork, his hand, and his wrist were soaked with Sam's blood.

"What?" he repeated.

"T-Top . . . ," wheezed Sam, then his eyes rolled up and he slid sideways onto the floor and lay in a boneless sprawl.

"First Sergeant Sims," bellowed a voice, and Top turned to see Montana Parker behind him. A federal marshal lay unconscious at her feet. Another sat on the floor, his back against the wall, eyes closed as if sleeping.

But Montana . . .

She had her gun held in a two-hand grip, the barrel pointed at Top's chest.

"Drop your weapon and put your hands on your head," roared Montana. "Do it now."

"What?" he asked her.

He heard a sound behind him, half turned, saw Botley behind him, saw the gun in his hand. Pointed at Top.

CHAPTER ONE HUNDRED THREE

He sat on a low cushion, surrounded by the leaders of the groups who had come together because they now believed that he was a holy man. Or, if they did not believe that, they accepted him as a man of power.

Houston was still burying its dead.

The soldiers at Fort Rucker were preparing to bury theirs.

The staff at the Naval Auxiliary Landing Field on San Clemente Island were picking their dead out of the wreckage of the crashed helicopters.

Each time the Mullah said that he could reach out and switch off the power, he had done exactly that.

Now they gathered to watch the greatest stroke. The crippling blow. The streets of ten cities would be choked with the dead.

Burning with fires so hot that it would melt the hope and the hubris of the Americans.

The Mullah sat before them but he did not look at anyone. His eyes had gone totally dead and they each believed that he was in a spiritual trance. When he was like this, they knew, great things were about to happen.

CHAPTER ONE HUNDRED FOUR

I swapped out the magazine of the Snellig and, with Ghost behind me and Harry behind the dog, we drifted down the hallway to the kitchen. The hall connected to the kitchen at the corner, which meant that they couldn't see me until I reached the doorway. I held up a fist to signal Ghost and Harry to stop. I took a breath, let it out halfway, then wheeled around the corner. I saw three men in white shirts and loosened ties, jackets hung over the backs of chairs, microwave pulse pistols tucked into shoulder holsters, coffee cups and plates and an open bag of Cheetos. They were all looking at the TV hung on the wall. They were watching the news. A panel of experts was arguing about the Mullah's message, the threats, the predicted U.S. response, and the probable location of the ten target cities. One of the men was chewing a big mouthful of the grilled cheese sandwich he held. Another was standing by the stove making another sandwich. The third man was sitting there sipping his coffee.

I did not shout or yell or announce myself. That's stupid.

Instead I fired.

Gas darts caught both seated men on the back of their necks. They sprawled forward. Before the third guy even knew what was going on I was in motion. I put one hand on the table and launched myself, pivoting and bringing my feet up to kick him in the thigh and the side of the head. He caromed into the stove, rebounded and fell sideways, pulling the frying pan with him. As he fell he tried to bring the pan up to ward off my next kick. I stamped down on it and drove the scalding metal against his face. He started to shriek but then I kicked the pan away and pistol-whipped the scream right out of his mouth. His head hit a table leg and bounced back, and I hit him again. He flopped back, dazed and bleeding, burned and in pain, but not out.

I hadn't wanted him out.

"Ghost, watch!" I called, and the big dog swung around, crouched and—I think—prayed for someone to come along that he could bite. Harry stood there looking numb, his gun hanging limp in his hand.

I dropped onto the Closer, pinning his arms, caught his throat with one hand, and stuffed the barrel of the Snellig into his mouth. I wasn't nice about it. Teeth broke.

"How many?" I snarled.

He didn't want to tell me. Not how many, and not where. Too bad, because I really wanted to know.

CHAPTER ONE HUNDRED FIVE

Dr. William Hu staggered sideways, grabbed the side of the molding press, missed, and fell hard. Junie stood there, eyes wide, mouth open, her face and throat and chest splashed with bright, hot blood. Christel fired again and Hu twisted around, crying out in agony as blood exploded from his shoulder.

Junie screamed.

And then Toys flung himself across the room in a rugby tackle that drove Christel into a workbench. Tools and materials flew everywhere. Toys chopped down on Christel's wrist, smashing her bones against the edge of the table, sending the gun flying. Despite the agony she had to be feeling, Christel drove her other elbow into Toys's face. He twisted to take the blow on his cheek rather than his nose, but it still rocked him. Christel was a tall and powerful woman and she knew how to hit. She hammered backward again and again, driving him away from the table, forcing him to use his forearms to shield his face. As soon as he covered up, she kicked Toys in the groin with such savage force that it tore a whistling scream from him. He staggered backward and she followed with a series of vicious, powerful kicks. Toys threw his body away, dropping and rolling partway under the table to avoid her feet.

Christel used her good hand to snatch the fallen pistol from the floor, but as she raised it, Toys lashed out at her shins with both feet. The shot was powerful and very fast, and it completely knocked her legs backward, tilting Christel forward into a belly flop. She landed hard, striking knees and chin on the floor. Toys wheeled around, got to one knee, and kicked the gun out of her hand. Then he dove for it, came up with the pistol, and pointed it at the security woman's head.

"No!" cried Junie, rushing forward and slapping his hand away. "Don't. Toys—look at her eyes."

Christel was struggling to get up and come after him, and though her mouth wore a grimace of bloodlust, her eyes were totally dead.

"She's been taken over," said Junie.

Toys lowered the gun, then thought better of it, and reversed it in his grip. "Sorry, love, but needs must."

He whipped the butt of the pistol across the base of her skull. Christel's blank eyes rolled white and she collapsed. Toys, panting, stared past her to where William Hu lay in a rapidly spreading pool of blood.

"Christ!" bellowed Toys as he rushed forward. "Junie, call nine-one-one. Get me the medical kit, and—"

Before he could finish, Junie Flynn stabbed him in the back with a screwdriver.

He coughed, staggered, dropped the gun as he fell to his knees. He tried to reach behind him, tried to understand. Tried to beg for help. As he turned to reach for the handle of the screwdriver, Junie tore it free. He looked past the bloody tool and all the way up to her eyes. Her dead, dead eyes.

"No . . . ," he whispered.

She raised the screwdriver like a dagger and rushed at him.

CHAPTER ONE HUNDRED SIX

The Closer told me that there were fourteen other operatives in the house. That did not count the men outside. Most of them were down in the basement.

"Doing what?" I demanded.

"M-managing assets."

I cut a look at Harry Bolt, who was standing in the kitchen doorway with Ghost. Harry's face had gone a pale gray-green at the sight of the blood.

"Where's Santoro?" I asked the Closer, but he didn't know anyone by that name. I tried it a different way, reinforcing my request with a jab of my gun against his mashed lips. "Where's Priest?"

"Down . . . there," he said, and then he choked on the blood in his mouth and began coughing. Terrible coughs, that made his whole body twitch. I stood up, looked around the kitchen, sighed, and shot the man with a gas dart.

Harry came over and knelt to reposition the man and clear his airway. "He could choke to death," he said.

"He's lucky I didn't put a bullet through his brain pan," I said, then in a flash of anger I grabbed Harry's shoulder and hauled him to his feet, shook him like a rag doll, and thrust him backward against the table. "This is war, kid, grow the fuck up. Now get your shit together and find me a way down to the subbasement."

Harry pushed away from me, smoothing his clothes and looking scared and hurt. As he crossed the kitchen he shook his head as if unsure how someone like me could be one of the good guys. He had a lot to learn about how good guys win wars. It was always a mistake to confuse good with nice.

The cellar door turned out to be a fake. Beyond the wooden one was a steel security door. Top of the line and with a high-tech keycard scanner of a kind that is very tough to bypass.

A lot less tough, though, when you can pick the pocket of the assholes who were supposed to be guarding it. I used a bloodstained keycard to open the hundred-thousand-dollar lock. The door opened. No alarms rang.

"Ghost," I said, "ready."

The dog shifted to an angle where he could spring at anything or anyone who came out of the door I was about to open. He crouched, muscles etched like stone beneath his fur.

"Jester, watch my back."

"Ready," said Harry. He had his gun pointing down at the floor and he was sweating badly.

Chilled air wafted out at me from the stairwell and it carried a strange blend of machine oil, old meat, ozone, and mold. Ghost bared his teeth in a silent snarl. Fear or anger, it was impossible to say. Probably both.

Beyond the door was a lighted hallway that ran six feet to a set of stairs. I went in first, taking the steps quickly and silently, watching the corners as the stairs reached a landing and turned. Ghost swarmed down after me. I quick-looked around the bend and saw that the second flight took us down to a stone floor. The lights were on down there but I heard no conversation. Ghost came abreast of me and sniffed, then wagged his tail twice. No one in the immediate vicinity.

We went down into a room that was set up as a computer center, with twenty workstations and high-end electronics. Comfortable wheeled office chairs, a full coffee bar, area rugs over the stone, and even discreetly positioned speakers from which Mahler's Symphony No. 6 in A Minor played softly. Nothing but the best for the employees of a supervillain.

We moved over to the computers. The screens all had the same display. It chilled me to the bone.

KILL SWITCH PROTOCOL

And beneath that was a digital clock.
Yeah. Actual ticking clock? Check.
Shit.

As I watched, the clock went from 14:29 to 14:28.

Harry grabbed my arm. "Wait, does that mean they input the code?"

"Yes," I said. "It damn well does."

CHAPTER ONE HUNDRED SEVEN

Akbar had arranged ten laptops in a row, positioned so they could all watch as history unfolded before them. Each screen showed an image sent by a small fixed camera. Each of the video feeds showed cities viewed from a distance. Akbar had written the names of each in ink on the frame of the laptops.

> *New York*
> *Los Angeles*
> *Chicago*
> *Houston*
> *Philadelphia*
> *Phoenix*
> *San Antonio*
> *San Diego*
> *Dallas*
> *San Jose*

Ten American cities. Ten fields to be sown with the seeds of retribution, each by one touch of the fingers of God. On the bottom of each screen was a small digital counter. They were all in sync. 19:01:08. In less than twenty minutes the world was going to change. It was like raising a veil. A different world existed on the other side and nothing would ever—*could* ever—be the same again.

It made Akbar want to weep.

CHAPTER ONE HUNDRED EIGHT

THE COMCAST BUILDING
1701 JOHN F. KENNEDY BOULEVARD
PHILADELPHIA, PENNSYLVANIA
SEPTEMBER 10, 11:38 A.M. LOCAL TIME

His name was Trey Willis and he had worked as building supervisor since the tower opened in 2008. He had a staff of thirty and they kept the building clean, fully functional, and efficient. Trey had worked in maintenance and building supervisions for nearly twenty-two years and taught management courses three nights a week at Philadelphia Community College. He had a wife and three daughters, the eldest of whom was pre-med at Jefferson. His wife was a nurse practitioner in the neonatal unit at Children's Hospital. Trey had no criminal record and an honorable discharge after serving four years in the air national guard. He paid his taxes, went to church, had middling interest in politics, and planned on retiring to Ocean City, New Jersey, in five years. He already owned a little place there not two blocks from the beach.

Trey was absolutely the wrong person for the job he was undertaking. Which made him the right man.

All day he had felt a little uneasy and wondered if he was coming down with another migraine. He hadn't had one in years but something was definitely wrong with his head. Concentrating on anything, even little tasks, became increasingly difficult as the day wore on. Eventually it got so bad that he told his assistant to take over and Trey went to his office to close his eyes for a moment. Leaving early was never his plan. He hadn't taken a sick day in eleven years and wasn't going to let a headache break that record. So he locked his office door and stretched out on his couch.

It was the wind that woke him up.

Not the breeze from the air-conditioner. It was wind.

He opened his eyes and very nearly screamed.

He was no longer in his office. He wasn't even inside the building. Nor was he lying down.

Instead he found himself standing on the observation deck many stories above the busy traffic. He was alone.

Except . . .

Except that all around him were drones. The small kind that they sold at Target and Walmart. What were they called? Quadcopters? Like the kind that caused all that trouble last year.

Just . . .

. . . like . . .

. . . those.

And all of the little motors were humming.

Trey blinked, more than half sure that this was a dream, that once he woke up he'd still be down in his office. He blinked and blinked.

He was still on the deck but the drones were gone.

Of course they were. Why would he have drones? Where would he have gotten them? It was ridiculous.

Which is when he heard the buzz. When the sounds that were there registered in his stunned and startled mind. Trey turned and looked over the edge of the deck wall. The drones were there. All of them. Hovering like a swarm of hornets.

And then one by one they drifted away, going in different directions, flying to different parts of the crowded city. Trey felt something and looked down. Saw his hands. Saw his hands as they worked the controls of a device he held. He watched his hands move, saw his fingers manipulate the controls.

But try as he could Trey Willis could not stop his traitor hands from sending the drones out into the skies above Philadelphia.

CHAPTER ONE HUNDRED NINE

"Stand down!"

Three U.S. marshals came pelting down the hall, guns up and out. Top spun toward them, the bloody fork still clutched in his fist. Montana Parker and Brian Botley stood on the other side of him, each pointing their guns. Sam Imura lay on the floor, bleeding to death. The world had torn loose from its hinges and was tilting, falling, going sideways and down.

Then Montana shifted her gun away from Top and pointed it at the first marshal.

And fired. The bullet caught the man in the chest and knocked him backward. There was no blood even though the marshal wore no visible Kevlar.

"Top!" screamed Montana. *"Run—they're Closers!"*

The other marshals raised their weapons and Top saw that these were not ordinary guns. They were MPPs. Microwave pulse pistols.

Tok!

Tok!

The world seemed to explode into flames.

CHAPTER ONE HUNDRED TEN

I tapped my earbud for Church's. "Cowboy to Deacon," I barked.

"Go for Deacon."

"I am on site and have located a timer for the God Machine. We are on active countdown. Current reading is twelve minutes and fifty seconds."

"Understood," said Church crisply. "That confirms fresh intel from overseas." That was the code for Arklight, for Lilith. "We have a list of targets."

He read them off. He might as well have shot me. Those were the ten cities with the largest populations. The cities with the largest number of children. Total estimated population? Call it twenty-five million. How many kids? Half that, give or take. How many would be infected? How many would get sick? How many would die if the power was out? My mind did some ugly math. Conservative guess . . . a million kids. If we were lucky.

Lucky.

Good God in heaven. Ghost caught the fear that had to be surrounding us like a cloud. He whined. I plugged a MindReader patch into an open USB port on the console. The device flashed green.

"Deacon, is Bug online? Can he hack this system and shut it down remotely?"

Bug was right there. "Accessing it now, Cowboy."

"Tell me something good."

"Jesus, Cowboy," said Bug, "they've got a lot of anti-intrusion software in here. I mean . . . this is cutting-edge stuff. Wow. Nice code. This is sweet."

"Bug, do you see the timer?"

"Oh . . . crap. Yeah."

"Tell me you can stop this countdown."

He didn't tell me anything for ten seconds. Felt like ten years. My heart was rattling like machine-gun fire.

"No," Bug said. "There's a firewall that's going to take time to break through."

"How much time?"

His voice was weak. "Too much. Three, four hours. Joe, you're going to need to find Santoro or someone who knows how to turn the God Machine off."

"What would happen if I blew the goddamn thing up?"

"How would I know? But if it comes down to the wire, Cowboy, go for it. By then we'd have nothing to lose."

"Deacon," I said, "if I can't switch it off, I need you to back my play."

There was the slightest pause. "I have two of our Apaches on station, but understand this—you're too far underground. I can't guarantee anything."

"Shit," I said. I holstered my gas gun and drew my Sig Sauer. There are times for subtlety and there are times to put hair on the walls. "Harry, how do we get to the damn Playroom?"

He spun and ran. I followed, setting my Scout glasses to show me the countdown. We ran as fast as we could.

And hell seemed to follow us all.

CHAPTER ONE HUNDRED ELEVEN

Toys tried to crawl away, but Junie ran after him, chopping at him with the screwdriver. He stabbed back with kicks, knocking her off balance, knocking her down, but each time she got back up and charged again.

Her eyes were dead and empty, but her lips were pulled back from her white teeth. Drool swung in pendulous lines from her lips, and she was muttering a guttural, wordless noise.

"Gah . . . gah . . . gah . . . gah . . ."

The screwdriver rose and fell, rose and fell.

CHAPTER ONE HUNDRED TWELVE

We ran down a series of halls, through multiple rooms. Wine cellar, bulk storage, a woodworking shop, another for metalwork, two laboratories.

We found two Closers in the fifth room. Neither was Santoro. I pushed Harry behind.

"Ghost," I yelled. *"Hit! Hit! Hit!"*

He was a white missile. Fangs and claws and rage. It had been a long time since Ghost had been in a real fight. He was filled with nervous energy and the power that came with it. Speed born of fury and bloodlust. If you are on the receiving end of it, that is a nightmare beyond imagining. Ghost hit the nearest Closer and there was blood in the air before they struck the ground. Reinforced protective undergarments be damned. Ghost went for the throat. I shot the other Closer through the bridge of the nose. Protective undergarment, my hairy white ass.

I jumped over his body as he crashed down. Ghost straddled the flopping body of the first man. The Closer hadn't been able to so much as scream.

I didn't even look back to see if Harry was following. In the lens of my Scout glasses the digital numbers went from 10:45 to 10:44.

Ticking down to darkness.

CHAPTER ONE HUNDRED THIRTEEN

The wall beside Top burst outward in a fireball of burning plaster and brick, showering him, driving him back, burning his hands and face and arms. Montana lay on the floor where she'd fallen, but she rolled onto her belly and aimed her pistol, firing, firing, firing. The ankle of one of the Closers exploded into a red mess as the heavy slugs destroyed bone and ligaments. He screamed as he toppled sideways, and his timing was tragic. He fell directly into the path of his partner's next shot.

Tok!

The entire upper torso of the wounded Closer burst apart, hurling flaming meat everywhere. The flames slapped against the second Closer's thighs and his pants caught fire. Montana changed her angle and shot him in the mouth, blowing out the back of his head.

Top slapped at the flames on his own clothes, stepped on a piece of debris, lost his balance, and fell heavily against the opposite wall. A bullet burned past him, missing his neck by an inch. Top whirled to see Brian Botley, his eyes glazed as he raised his pistol and pointed it and fired. Top was moving, ducking, rushing. And then Brian was falling, and Top saw that the fork he'd dropped was now buried into the instep of Brian's foot. Brian kept firing as he fell . . .

. . . and he fell on the bucking gun. His body twitched once and then there was silence as a pool of dark red spread out beneath him.

Sam Imura, dazed and bleeding, lay there, his arm stretched for the long reach and stab. He reached over, rolled Brian onto his side, and took the gun. The weapon was smeared with blood, but Sam raised it anyway. His eyes were beginning to glaze over. Sam pointed the gun and had time to force out two strangled words.

"Top . . . *Run* . . ."

CHAPTER ONE HUNDRED FOURTEEN

07:19

We reached the stairway down to the subbasement. There was another steel door, another keypad. And four more guards.

They were ready for us. No way they hadn't heard the shots and yells. Four Closers, four pulse pistols. Me and a dog.

Short version.

They died.

I took a keycard from a dead hand and swiped it. The door opened. Ghost and I, both of us covered in blood, rushed inside. It burned me to know that the clock was ticking. It burned that I had no idea if there was even a way to stop this.

CHAPTER ONE HUNDRED FIFTEEN

Sam's shots were wild, hitting walls and floor and missing Top by inches.

Top dove, rolled, and came up with a pulse pistol, pivoted on his knees, fired. The wall beside Sam exploded, barraging the wounded sniper with burning chunks of sheetrock and shattered pieces of wooden studs. The force picked Sam up and flung him against the wall so hard that the sound of breaking bones was horribly sharp.

Then the air above Top sizzled as another Closer fired on him. He flattened out and rolled like a log, trying not to die, trying to bring the pulse pistol to bear. Nearby, Montana Parker crouched, the slide locked back on her weapon. She wasted precious seconds to swap out a dead magazine for one that might keep her alive.

Top saw the blast hit her.

One moment his friend and fellow warrior was there, raising her gun, ready to fight and kill, and the next she was gone.

Just gone.

The blast caught her dead center and exploded her. She never had time to even scream. Superheated blood and pieces of meat slapped against Top, getting in his mouth, burning his skin.

He screamed and screamed, even as he turned and brought up his own gun.

"Die, motherfucker!" he roared as he emptied the entire magazine into the Closers. Two of them went down, but more were coming.

More.

So many more.

And then the door at the far end of the hall burst open as a Closer came flying through, his limbs twisted, head twisted more than halfway around. The man struck the backs of the other Closers and dragged three of them to the floor. Everyone turned—the Closers and Top—to see two new figures enter the hallway.

A man and a woman. She was tall, with dark eyes that glittered like polished coal. He was a big and blocky man with tinted glasses and black gloves. She had two knives, one in each of her slim fists. He carried no weapons.

They each wore ungainly metal helmets.

The Closers raised their weapons.

And Violin and Mr. Church were upon them.

CHAPTER ONE HUNDRED SIXTEEN

BOLTON HOUSE
RANCHO SANTA FE, CALIFORNIA
SEPTEMBER 10, 2:45 P.M.

06:47

The corridor was exactly the same as the one in my dream.

That was freaky on a level that shook me to my marrow.

But at the same time it gave me a splinter of hope.

"This way!" yelled Harry, running ahead, but I was already going that way, running beneath rows of fluorescent lights. There were doors on both sides of the corridor, but unlike in my dream I did not stop to look in each one. I knew now where I was going. Maybe better than Harry did. He hadn't been here since this was actually his playroom.

The door to the laboratory was on my left. Another wasted second swiping a keycard. As the lock clicked I heard Ghost growl. I turned, bringing the Sig Sauer up.

The door directly opposite the lab opened and *he* was there.

Mr. Priest.

Esteban Santoro.

Closers crowded the doorway behind him. A lot of them.

And it was in that moment, when the odds were absolutely impossible, when it was three of us against eight of them, when the clock was running down and there was pretty much no chance I could win, that something happened. I could feel it. Way deep down inside.

It was not a battle heat. It was not fear. It was not any emotion that modern science or advanced psychology has a name for. It was something too old for that. Too primitive. Too elemental. As Santoro came at me, I felt the Killer awaken in my head. He had slept too long and we both knew it. Maybe he'd been driven into some kind of coma by the things we'd seen at Gateway, by illness, or by the rape of our shared mind by Bolton and his psychic vampires.

Who knows?

Who cares?

He came awake all at once. A killer, a monster, a beast. Beside me I heard the sound of Ghost's snarl change, too, as the dog—in the presence of his true pack leader—yielded control to the wolf within.

The hallway was narrow. Close quarters favors the few over the many.

It favors the savage over the civilized.

With a howl of inhuman fury and red delight, the Killer attacked, and the wolf charged with him.

CHAPTER ONE HUNDRED SEVENTEEN

Top Sims heard the screams and forced himself up. He was covered with hot debris from where the microwave blast had destroyed Montana Parker. His skin was flash-burned and most of the hair on his head was singed down to the scalp. He had to wipe blood and soot from his eyes in order to see what was happening, but when he did see it Top could only gape.

Violin and Church had entered the fight.

Violin moved like a dancer in a ballet whose story was about the end of the world. She lunged and pivoted, swept and leapt, ducked and pirouetted with a grace that made what she did both beautiful and appalling. Men screamed as she opened them and let their futures spill out. The walls seemed to almost glow with the bright red that flew like paint from the edges of her knife.

Beside her was Mr. Church, and never once had Top seen the big man fight. Church looked too old and too bulky to move with any kind of speed. A man Top always thought was well past the prime of life, past the point where he could wade into a battle and do anything but become collateral damage. As he watched Church fight, Top knew how very wrong he was. Top had never seen anyone fight like that. It was not karate or kung fu. If the fighting style had a name, Top was sure that it would be clinical. Mathematical. It was the opposite of Violin's elegant destruction because Church fought with no visible sense of style. His movements were machinelike, cold, and ruthlessly efficient. They were equations of deconstruction that took the problem of an armed attacker and subtracted all of the things about the opponent that allowed him to be a threat. What was left was no man at all. It was a broken thing that was permitted to fall because even his usefulness as a shield was gone.

Violin's face bore a smile of savage delight, and it was clear that she enjoyed the art of combat. For her this was gorgeous and she wrote a symphony in the screams she coaxed from horrified throats. Church wore no expression at all, except a cold disapproval etched into the lines around his mouth. These men stood between Church and what he wanted. That was it, that was the extent of the emotional connection.

And they died.

Closers. Fierce and deeply trained. Armed and armored.

They outnumbered Violin and Church five to one.

And it did not matter at all.

CHAPTER ONE HUNDRED EIGHTEEN

The Mullah and his people bent forward to watch the flocks of drones fly from rooftops in New York and Philadelphia, in San Diego and Boston, in each of the ten cities. There were four operatives per city and each operative released ten drones. A total of four hundred tiny machines fitted with tubes of SX-56—with the wrath of God.

The operatives were being released now, one by one, and the looks of confusion and horror on their faces were beautiful. The gathered warlords and generals saw them as the expressions of men and women who had been forced to do holy work and were now realizing it.

The Mullah knew different.

Or, at least, the Dreamer who squatted like an imp inside his mind knew different. The looks on those faces were fear and uncertainty, self-doubt and dread. They knew they had done something wrong, something bad, but they did not understand how or why. Most of them probably wouldn't even connect the launch of these drones to the power failure that was coming soon. So soon.

The Dreamer wished he could be there with each of them in the coming days to see how they reacted as the first news stories broke about the spread of a new and nearly untreatable form of a disease everyone in America thought was extinct. Seeing that would be nice, it would be fun.

But the Dreamer knew he would be too busy by then.

When the plague began sweeping the country, this fine and sterling nation would need the services of its greatest spy, its greatest warrior, its one unfailable hero.

While he slept in the back of his car in the parking lot of the Pier— slept and walked far in his dreams—Harcourt Bolton, Senior, smiled the contented smile of a happy man.

CHAPTER ONE HUNDRED NINETEEN

Microwave bursts turned the doorway into fire clouds of burning debris, but I ducked down and fired through the smoke. More by luck than skill I hit two of the Closers in the face; Ghost hit another with such force it drove the others back into the room. Harry Bolt fired his gun but God only knows what he was aiming at. Bullets binged and whanged down the hall, killing two of the overhead lights.

Santoro tried to shoot me but I was too close. I knew I couldn't kill him, because I needed something from him. That didn't mean I couldn't hurt him. I buried the barrel of the pistol against his belly and fired four shots. I figured he'd be wearing the same body armor, but at that range no protective padding in the world is going to keep you from feeling the foot-pounds of impact. It folded him in half. As he bent forward I kneed him in the crotch and then punched him four times in the face, breaking his nose, cracking an eyebrow. He'd beaten me once because someone had been in my head holding me back, keeping the Killer on a leash.

That wasn't going to happen now. Oh, hell no.

I swept his leg and hammered him to the concrete floor with an overhand knuckle punch to the floating ribs.

"Stay down," I roared, then I grabbed Harry by the collar and flung him away from me. Inside the room Ghost was rolling around on the floor tearing red chunks out of a guy. A second man sat nearby trying to hold his throat in place, and failing. The other Closers were climbing to their feet, raising their guns, caught in a moment of indecision between killing Ghost and killing me.

One of them swung his gun toward Ghost's head, but I put two rounds through the man's face. Then I emptied the magazine into the others. When the slide locked back I used the gun to crush the throat of one of the others. That left two. There was no time to reload, no time to even draw my knife. Fuck it. I'd been training for moments like this since I was fifteen. If the Joe Ledger I'd been as a kid died the day those older teens attacked Helen and me, then the one who was born on that day has no mercy in his soul. Not in moments like these.

I leapt over a dying man and hit one of the two remaining Closers with a leaping palm shot on the point of the jaw that spun him halfway around, but it spun his head farther. Too far. He corkscrewed into the ground, dead or dying. The last man tried to make a fight of it. He lashed out with a short chopping roundhouse. One of those devastating Thai boxing kicks that would have shattered my leg had it landed right. But he put too much hip into it, trying for torque power instead of whipping snap. It should have been a follow-up move, or maybe it's that he's used to fighting slower opponents. I shifted right into the path and took his shin on my bent thigh. It hurt, sure. But in the middle of a fight it's not pain that matters—it's damage, and he didn't do any. I did. I punched his forearm muscles hard enough to lame them, chambered, and short-punched him in the chest. That turned him and lifted his chin and I used the open Y of my other hand to smash him in the Adam's apple. He staggered backward, making dying fish sounds.

"Joe!" cried Harry, and I turned to see Santoro pulling him backward, one arm wrapped around the kid's throat, the other trying to reverse the grip on the gun he'd just ripped out of Harry's hand. I grabbed the guy whose throat I'd just crushed, spun him, and used him as a shield as I drove toward Santoro. The assassin fired five shots and each one of them pounded into the dying guy's back, but the undergarment kept them from passing through to me. The slide locked back just as Harry stamped down on Santoro's foot. The kid pivoted and drove an elbow into the man's face. Santoro stumbled back, stared at me as I threw my now-dead shield away, and then he turned and bolted down the hall.

I pelted after him, yelling back at Harry, "Get into the lab! Call Bug. Find the God Machine. Ghost, go with!"

Santoro ran from me and I ran after.

I caught up to him as he fumbled a swipe card through the slot on a reader to open the last door in the hallway. I hit him hard with a flying tackle and we both went crashing into the room.

CHAPTER ONE HUNDRED TWENTY

Top staggered out of the armory as Church came hurrying over. The big man's clothes were spattered with blood, his mouth hard, eyes filled with fire. Church knelt by Sam Imura and placed two fingers against his throat and raised an eyelid.

"He's alive."

Top was closer to Brian Botley, but when he felt for a pulse he found nothing at all.

"Where's Bolton?" demanded Church.

Top licked his lips. "I . . . haven't seen him."

Church half turned to Violin. "Find him. *Go.*"

She leapt over the dead like a gazelle and vanished down the hall.

Church tapped the helmet he wore. "If you can walk, there's a duffel bag with more of these. It's in the hall outside of the conference room. Don't pick up a weapon until you put one on, understood? Bring me one for Sam, too."

"Yes, sir." Top was in no shape to run, but he ran anyway.

Church settled Sam against the wall and applied pressure to his wounds. Top came shambling back with the duffel bag, a helmet pushed down on his own burned scalp. He handed a cap to Church, who fitted it carefully over Sam's head. Then Church bent and picked up a fallen microwave pistol.

"Stay with him," he said as he rose.

Top caught a brief glimpse of Church's face as he turned to continue his hunt. The man's expression was not the detached and mechanical face he'd worn when fighting the Closers. There was emotion now. There was desperation and there was hate. Few things frightened Top Sims. The look in Church's eyes did.

CHAPTER ONE HUNDRED TWENTY-ONE

The room we entered was one I had been in before. I knew it even as Santoro and I went crashing and thrashing along the floor, rolling among lengths of pipe, knocking over worktables and scattering tools. The chamber was massive, and from the leftover fixtures on the walls I could tell that this used to be the Bolton family bowling alley. A place of fun, a place to relax.

Except now the room was dominated by something huge that gleamed with silver and copper and gold and steel.

The God Machine. Huge, *real*. Glowing with power. I kicked Santoro away and back-rolled to my feet. It reeked of wrongness. It was as alien a thing as any monstrosity I'd seen in my dreams.

Santoro rose, his face dripping with blood. He stood near the circular mouth of the machine, and behind him were dozens of gemstones. A fortune in cut diamonds, topazes, rubies, emeralds, and sapphires. They were socketed into the copper sheeting, and behind each a bright light flashed in sequence. Santoro saw me gaping at it and he grinned at me with red-streaked teeth. "You're too late, Ledger. The code has been input and our weapons are already in the sky. Even if you killed me now there's nothing that can stop this."

I whipped the rapid-release folding knife from its pocket clip and with a flick of the wrist the blade glittered in my hand. "I'm going to keep cutting parts off of you until you tell me how to shut it down. How's that sound, motherfucker?"

Santoro beckoned me with little flips of his fingers. "You have to beat me first. We're one and one, my friend. Let's see who wins the final round."

Off to my left I heard a sound and risked a slanting look. It was a twisted shape that almost, but not quite, looked human. He wore white pajamas that were smeared with food and snot and piss and blood. His skin was wrinkled and puckered and blistered. He was exactly as I'd seen him in my dream.

I said, "Hello, Prospero."

What was left of Prospero Bell smiled at me with white teeth in a burned red face. His eyes glittered with emerald fire every bit as bright as the gems on his machine. There was pain in those eyes, and wildness, and absolutely no trace of sanity. As he stepped forward I heard a tinkling sound and realized that the boy had a metal cuff locked around his ankle, and a chain that trailed back to a squalid corner of the room where there was a soiled cot, a filthy toilet, a card table, and a chair. Beyond that was an elaborate computer workstation that was as clean as the rest of Prospero's cell was dirty. And I understood how it worked. The young man was a prisoner here, a captive of Harcourt Bolton for God knew how many years. Since the Ballard academy had burned down, maybe. He was allowed to continue his work but the chain did not allow him to reach the mouth of the God Machine. A slave forced to toil in the shadow of what he believed was his salvation. I felt so bad for the kid, but the clock was ticking.

04:18

"You're wearing your hat this time," said Prospero Bell, pointing at my skullcap. "You're safe from the monsters."

Prospero took a step toward me, but the chain brought him up short.

"Get back, boy," snarled Santoro. "This man is dangerous."

"Prospero," I said quickly, "I know you want to go home."

"They won't let me," said the prisoner.

I took a chance. "*I* will. Do you know what they're going to do with your God Machine? They're using it to control Kill Switch devices in ten cities. They have hundreds of drones in the air, each one rigged to blow when the power goes out. Each of those drones is carrying weaponized smallpox. Do you know that? Did they tell you that's what they were doing with your machine?"

"Don't listen to him," snapped Santoro. "He's just trying to confuse you."

"No," I said, "Harcourt Bolton has replicated dozens of the Kill

Switch devices. They're in the ten biggest cities in America. He's going to kill millions of people, Prospero. Most of them are children, like you were when your father stole the God Machine from you. . . ."

But the prisoner shook his head. "Children like me? No . . . there are no children like me. And what do I care? They said that once the sequence is finalized they'll let me go home. I want to go home. That's all I ever wanted to do."

"Prospero, listen to me," I said, feeling each tick of the clock like a crack of thunder, "they're never going to let you go home."

"He's lying," warned Santoro.

"The machines will kill millions of people, Prospero. Millions."

Prospero shrugged. "They're not my people."

"Yes, they are," I said. "Some of them are."

The boy stared at me. "What?"

"He's lying," said Santoro. "You know you're unique. That's why we love you. That's why we keep you safe, yes?"

04:16

"Prospero . . . I *know* someone who's like you," I said. "Her name is Junie Flynn. She was born in the same place as you. They called it a hive. She looks just like you. She could be your sister. Or maybe she *is* your sister."

Prospero's eyes went wide. "Sister . . . ? Yes . . . I dreamed I had a sister. . . ."

"He's trying to confuse you," said Santoro. He began shifting toward my blind side. I saw it and compensated, but I kept between Santoro and Prospero.

"I'm telling you the truth, kid," I said. "She *does* look like you. And she knows about you. She wants to meet you. She wants to share her secrets with you."

"What do you mean?"

"Junie knows she's not from here, either," I said. "She knows she doesn't belong here. She knows she's from another place."

"He's making it up," snapped Santoro, but Prospero was listening to me. Very closely.

I fished inside my head for something, some way to prove it. And those strange words floated to the surface of my need. In as clear a voice as I could, I looked at Prospero and said, *"Ph'nglui mglw'nafh Cthulhu R'lyeh wgah'nagl fhtagn."*

I have no idea what it means, or if it really means anything. Lovecraft wrote it into one of his stories, and I heard it in my head. I had to take a chance.

Prospero Bell closed his eyes. "Please," he whispered. "I just want to go home."

"Then *help* me," I begged, "and I'll help you. How do I stop it? Help me save your sister and I will help you go home. I swear it by everything I love. Give me the reset code."

Tears glittered in the corner of those burned eyes, and Prospero said, "The reset sequence is—"

"No!" cried Santoro, and he attacked. He hooked a toe under one of the lengths of pipe, flipped it up, caught it, and swung it at my head with shocking speed and power. I ducked fast, but the pipe still caught me a glancing blow. I staggered, bells exploding in my head. I ran sideways, fighting for balance, trying to clear my eyes, and saw him come at me again. I jumped forward this time, crashing into him and slamming his shoulders hard against the side of the machine.

It was the wrong thing to do. The impact hit something and suddenly all of the lights flashed at once and there was a heavy, bass *whoooom*. The lights ringing the gateway flared so bright it stabbed my eyes. I shoved Santoro away and tried to run, but it wasn't something that could *be* outrun. It was like trying to outrun the sound of a scream. It was like trying to outrun a tsunami. It rose above me and wrapped around me and smashed down on me and it took me. It was at once totally alien and yet disturbingly familiar.

I'd felt this before. Down, down, down in the cold bottom of the world. When the machine Erskine had built in the ancient city had pulsed and then exhaled its foul breath all over Top, Bunny, and me. The breath of something evil and hungry and strange. Then it had only been a puff of that air. Now it was a roar.

Now it was a scream that burst from the mouth of the gate and slammed into me, lifting me physically off the ground, hurling me across the room like I was nothing. Spitting me out like a piece of gristle. The wall was there. It seemed to reach for me. To want to hurt me.

And it did.

I spun, curled, tried to position myself to take the impact in a way that wouldn't ruin me. I hit. God, I hit. Shoulder. Head. Hip. The pain was like falling into boiling water. It was everywhere. Inside and out. I collapsed onto the metal floor as the God Wave washed over me and filled the room.

And filled me.

The lights in the room stayed on. The lights inside my head went out. The last thing I saw was the digital display on the inside of my goggles.

03:59

CHAPTER ONE HUNDRED TWENTY-TWO

Lydia left Bunny on the patio while she went in to take a shower. She was quick about it, though, and pulled her robe on over wet, bare skin. Her attempts to entice him into the shower with her had been answered by a single, slow shake of the head. No words.

As soon as she stepped into the living room, though, she knew something was wrong. Badly wrong. The couch cushions were missing and the gun safe hidden beneath them had been opened. Boxes of ammunition, spare magazines, cleaning kits, rags, and three handguns lay scattered across the floor. A six-shot nickel-plated Smith & Wesson Special lay in a growing pool of gun oil that ran from a plastic bottle that had been stepped on. Oily footprints led in a wandering trail out to the patio, but when she ran to the French doors, the patio was empty. One of the guns was missing. A Glock 26. The trigger lock had been removed and lay where it had fallen. There was no time to count the magazines to see if one was missing, but a box of .9mm shells had been torn open and bullets littered the floor.

"*¡Ay, Dios!*"

Lydia ran to the slat-wood rail and looked wildly up and down the beach. The bocce players were still involved in their game and the sound of their laughter floated to her on the breeze. Somehow the normalcy of that sound and the accompanying ordinary happiness twisted the day into an even worse shape. The oily footprints ended at the patio rail and she leaned out to see deep prints punched into the sand. They started toward the water, then turned sharply and vanished around the far side of the apartment complex. Lydia vaulted the rail, not caring that she was unarmed and wore only a damp bathrobe.

What did that matter? She landed running, pivoted in the sand, and tore along the side of the building. Even then, even as panic turned her heart to ice and exploded red poppies before her eyes, she did not lose herself. She didn't scream Bunny's name. She knew that it could have the exact opposite effect. Her screams would be filled with fear and all that they would become was a starter pistol for whatever Bunny was going to do.

At the corner of the building she skidded into a turn and then froze.

Bunny was there, kneeling on the sand between two decorative bottle palms. The barrel of the Glock pushed up hard into the soft underside of his chin. He did not look at her. His eyes were glazed, empty, like glass. There wasn't even an expression of pain on his face. There was absolutely nothing.

Lydia was very still. "Bunny," she said in as calm a voice as she could force past the stricture in her throat. "Listen to me. I need you to put the gun down."

She repeated it several times, making it a statement of calm command. Not asking questions, not asking if he could hear her. Bunny was too close to the edge to allow him a choice. She needed him to obey. That was all. It was the only thing tethering either of them to the world.

"Put the gun down, Bunny," she said as she very carefully edged closer. Her heart wanted to add a plea, to beg, to call on his love for her, but she knew better. This was a tightrope stretched across the abyss and it needed only a single breath to make him fall. His face was as red as flame, his hand glistened with sweat, and his huge muscles were rigid with some kind of awful internal conflict. Each separate muscle stood out in sharp relief as if he had committed himself to a total struggle against some opponent of monstrous strength. His blond hair hung in sodden spikes over his brow; beads of moisture covered his face like rainwater. Bunny's body shuddered with the strain. And yet there was still no trace of expression on his face.

"Master Sergeant Rabbit," she said, putting steel in her voice, "you will lower your weapon right now."

That did it. Somehow, that reached him. The pressure of the barrel eased, the hand holding it seemed to fall as if the weight of intent was too much for even those muscles to bear. The Glock came down, down, down . . .

And then Lydia moved.

She stepped in, clamped one hand over the gun, wrapping her fingers tight to provide resistance to the slide in case he fired, aware that it probably wouldn't work. But at the same moment she used her other hand to strike the nerves on the top of his wrist. Lydia was very strong and she knew how and where to hit. She was certain that never in her life, not in all her years of combat, had she moved faster or hit with greater force and precision. She leg-checked his arm, using body weight to jerk his arm straight, to weaken the elbow in a moment of hyperextension; then she pivoted and took the gun from him. She put everything she had into the movement because she knew how strong this man was, and how quick.

With the gun in her hand she pirouetted and danced backward, releasing the magazine, racking the slide to eject the round in the chamber, doing everything right because there was so much to lose if she did anything wrong.

Except that Bunny never moved.

Never resisted.

Did not try to hold on to the weapon.

He knelt there, staring at nothing. Saying nothing.

Being nothing.

And then he fell face-forward onto the sand without even trying to break his fall.

CHAPTER ONE HUNDRED TWENTY-THREE

I woke to the sound of weeping.

At first I was afraid it was my own sobs I heard, that I was broken. But as I struggled to come fully awake it was clear that the sobs were not inside my head or in my chest. They were close, though. And male.

I forced my eyes open. The lab was gone. The walls were gone. Maybe I was gone. My brain was too battered to tell. The guy kept weeping. After a minute or maybe an hour, I rolled over onto my hands and knees, coughed, spat, blinked my eyes clear. Looked around.

He was there. A dozen feet away, huddled into a quivering ball against a stone wall. Long, jagged cracks ran from ceiling to floor and a few zigzagged out across the ground. The place was ruined, dying. Big chunks of masonry were heaped around, dust drifting like pale ghosts from the impact points. The computers at the far end of the lab were smoking and as I watched, a few small tongues of fire began to lick at the metal housing. The stink of burning plastic and rubber filled the air. Other smells, too. Cloth. And . . . flesh. That was one of the odors I wish was not stored in my personal inventory, but it was. And I knew it well enough to recognize it now. Someone was burning. People smell different than animals when they burn.

This was a person. Or maybe more than one. I sat back on my heels and tried to make sense of what happened. The lab was wrecked as if it had been struck by something worse than the God Wave. Maybe an earthquake? The lights around the inner rings of the gate were still glowing with hellish light. Steam curled out of the mouth of the tunnel and roiled against the rough stone of the ceiling. Several of the fluorescent lights had torn loose from their bolts and hung precariously by wires.

I turned to the man who lay against the wall. He wasn't wearing a lab coat and he wasn't dressed like a Closer. For a crazy moment I thought it was Toys. It looked like him, though that was impossible. Toys was in San Diego. A thousand miles from here.

But . . . he wore the same clothes Toys had worn when he stayed at my house. Same shirt and pants. Same sandals. Same wristwatch. My brain seemed to slip out of gear. How could Toys be here? How?

I crawled to him. He was facing away from me, arms wrapped around his head. I could see pale scars crisscrossed on his hands and wrists. Toys had those same scars. He'd gotten them when he'd thrown himself across Circe O'Tree at the hospital when Nicodemus and his Kingsmen stormed the hospital to try and kill Church's pregnant daughter. Toys and Junie had shielded her with their bodies and both would carry those scars forever.

I said, "Toys—?"

The sobs instantly stopped at the sound of my voice. Or, maybe, at the sound of his name.

Then the weeping man rolled over, his body whipcord taut, and past the shelter of his protective wrists he stared at me with familiar eyes.

"L-Ledger . . . ?" he whispered in a voice thick with fear and surprise. "How . . . ?"

"Toys? How the hell are you even here?" I demanded. "How did you get here? What are you *doing* here?"

Tears streamed from his fever-bright eyes. "I tried to save her, Ledger. God help me, I tried. Please . . . *please* . . . I tried."

I hauled myself to my feet. The room swung around me, refusing to settle. There was thunder in my head and blood in my mouth. "What the hell are you talking about?"

He tried to answer, but he simply could not. Instead he stretched out his arm and with a hand that shook with the palsy of absolute terror, he pointed to something behind me. I did not want to turn. No fucking way. Whatever was happening here was all wrong. I'd hit my head, I knew that. Nothing was probably what it seemed. Everything was suspect. Nothing that I'd done since Gateway was to be trusted. I knew that. The mycotoxins. The viruses. They were messing with me. Rudy said so. Hu said so. I was delusional. Everything was a bad dream.

That's what I told myself as I turned to follow the direction of his pointing finger. No matter what was there, no matter what it was that had torn Toys down like this, no matter what horror my concussed brain wanted to show me was going to be a lie.

I turned.

I saw.

I screamed.

She was there. Across the room. Against the wall. High on the wall. Heavy iron spikes driven all the way through the precious, familiar flesh. Bloody spike-heads sticking out from wrists and ankles and stomach and breastbone. Long, tangled blond hair hung in sweat-soaked twists down her naked body. Her breasts, empty of blood, sagged. Her head hung down so that I could not see her face. I didn't need to. I knew those lines, those curves. I was more intimately familiar with the landscape of that woman than with anyone I'd ever known. The pale flesh, the paler scars. Each freckle and mole.

"I'm sorry," said Toys, his voice filling with fresh tears. "They needed a sacrifice and I had no choice. No choice."

My scream drowned out his words. I did not scream at him. I did not scream his name, nor did I howl out a denial. No, the shriek torn from my chest was a single word. A name. *Her* name.

Junie.

On the other side of the room the God Machine pulsed.

And the God Machine pulsed again. A fresh wave hit me.

Someone shook me awake and as I came up out of blackness a hand clamped itself over my mouth and a voice whispered directly into my ear.

"Quiet. They'll hear you. They're right outside."

A female voice. Not familiar, no one I knew, and yet . . .

Somehow I *did* know her.

I opened my eyes. We were inside a school bus. A big damn yellow school bus. Small, pale faces peered in silent horror over the backs of seats. Dozens of them. Scuffed and dirty, some of them streaked with blood. So many young eyes, each filled with bottomless horror. In some I saw the dangerous vacuity that spoke of shock and trauma that may already have run too deep.

The woman who spoke removed her hand from my mouth and shifted to help me sit up. She was a cop, but no one I knew. A big blonde with lots of curves and a beautiful face that was set into hardness. Blue eyes and a tight-lipped mouth. Blood and dirt smeared on her clothes.

"You good?" she asked, her voice low but not a whisper. Whispers carry. Cops and soldiers know that. She was a cop, but she had the soldier look. Battle horrors leave a certain stamp on a person, a particular light in the eyes, and she had that. There was a small black ID badge pinned to her breast. It said FOX.

"What's going on?" I asked, pitching my voice low, too. "Where am I? Who are these children? And who are you?"

I saw doubt flicker over her face. "Oh, for fuck's sake, don't tell me you got some kind of amnesia bullshit. You didn't get hit *that* hard, you pussy."

There was a dull ache on my forehead and I touched it. My fingers came away red with blood. "What happened?"

Officer Fox took a single short breath before answering, as if she needed the moment to control her anger. "How much don't you remember? Do you know who the fuck you are, at least?"

"Captain Ledger," I said.

"Captain? You demoting yourself?"

"What?"

"Last I heard you were a full bird colonel," she said. "But we can run with captain. Whatever. I don't fucking care as long as you know who you are."

"It's captain," I said. "You're Officer Fox?"

"Then you *do* remember?"

"I read your name tag."

"Balls. We're trying not to die and you're checking out my tits."

"Your name tag," I repeated. "Who are you and what's happening?"

"What's the last thing you remember?"

There were sounds outside. The distant chatter of automatic gunfire, a few hollow pops of small arms. Growls.

Growls?

"I was in the Playroom," I said. "Got hit with a God Wave and—"

She punched me. In the chest. Hard.

"No," she snapped. "Don't go getting stupid on me. I don't know what the shit a God Wave is, but that's not part of what's happening. This is here and now. This is Stebbins County and we are in deep shit. Can you remember anything about that? About Lucifer 113?"

Yeah, I knew about that microscopic monster. It was the bastard child of a Cold War bioweapons program. But all that knowledge was from a report. One of thousands I had to read over the years to keep track and get perspective. Nothing from an active case.

"It's the God Wave," I insisted. "It's screwing everything up."

"Come the Christ on, Ledger," growled Fox. "Sam talked about you like you had the biggest dick in Special Forces and you're babbling about some religious surfer bullshit? I need you to get your head out of your ass and get back in the game, because we are in deep shit."

"Sam? Sam Imura? Is Sam here?"

A shadow crossed her face. "He . . . was. I told you what happened at the food depository. He fell . . . they . . ." She shook her head. "It doesn't matter. We're here and we need to do something."

The gunfire was trailing off. There were fewer shots but the growls were getting louder. Closer.

"They're coming back!" cried one of the children, and they all started crying. Too much, too loud. I could hear the way those sounds changed the noises from outside. The growls got louder, more insistent.

No. They weren't growls. They were moans. And that fast I knew what they were. Even though it was impossible, I *knew*.

I caught Fox's wrist in a tight grip. "Listen to me," I said urgently. "I have a head injury and I can't remember much. But if those are *walkers* out there, then you need to bring me up to speed real damn quick. I need a sitrep and don't paint it with pretty colors."

She gave me a strange look. Almost a smile. A little relief, maybe. A small warrior's smile. She nodded.

"Short version of a bad story," she said. "I'm Officer Desdemona Fox. Dez. We're south of Roanoke and we're trying to get to Ashville. We have three school buses. Used to have more but . . ." Tears glistened in her eyes, hard as diamonds. She pawed at them and plunged ahead. "Sam and his team helped us get out, but we lost most of them. We had to go off the main roads because of the traffic jams. A whole wave of those dead bastards hit us two hours ago. You and your boys came out of no-fucking-where and we made it ten more miles down the road. Then we got hit by another surge of them and you got nailed by debris when you didn't duck fast enough when the grenade went off. What'd I leave out that you need to know?"

"How bad is it?" I demanded. "How far has it spread?"

The look she gave me was one of hard, unflinching fatalism. It was the reason there was no trace of hope or optimism in her eyes. "It's everywhere, man. How can you not know that? This is the actual end."

Suddenly hands began pounding on the outside of the bus. Heavy, soft, artless thumps. Nothing fast, nothing precise. Just the battering of mindless need. I knew that sound. The hungry dead. The relentless dead.

I'd fought this before. It was how I got into the DMS. Sebastian Gault had developed a prion-based pathogen that turned people into something straight out of *The Walking Dead*. Except this wasn't TV. This was the world and we'd had to do terrible things to save it. So many people died to put the monster back into its cage. Then it surfaced again after Artemisia Bliss stole the *seif al din* pathogen from the secure facility where it had been locked away. She'd unleashed it on a subway train in New York, at a Best Buy in Pennsylvania, and at a science fiction convention in Atlanta. Worst day for civilian deaths in American history. Again, my team and I had been forced to pull triggers and cut throats in order to save the nation—hell, the entire world—from consuming itself. No joke, no exaggeration.

So what happened? How was I on a school bus with all these kids and a cop telling me that some *other* bioweapon, Lucifer 113, had slipped its chain? How could I not have prevented this? Where was the DMS when the Devil got out of its cage? How was it possible that the apparatus of defense that Church had built could have failed on so spectacular a level?

How? The dead hammered on the bus. The children screamed.

"This isn't real," I told her.

"Fuck you," she said, and punched me again. Harder. "Look around you. These kids are all that's left of my town. Every bus is filled with kids. *Kids.* Look at them. Listen to them, for Christ's sake. Not real? God, I want to kick your teeth down your throat. This is happening and it's happening right now. You're supposed to be a genuine goddamn American hero, Ledger. Why don't you Velcro your nutsack back on and act like it."

The dead began hammering on the side of the bus with renewed intensity.

I struggled to get to my feet.

And the God Wave hit me again.

* * *

I stood on the side of an overturned school bus.

Dez Fox was gone. The bus was years old, wrapped in creeper vines, rusted and dead. There was a sound behind me and a young man climbed up to stand next to me. At first I thought it was Sam, but I was wrong. He was younger, taller, slimmer. His eyes were sadder. He had a katana slung over his shoulder, angled for an overhand draw. His name was Tom, but I don't know how I knew that.

"There's a trail through the trees," Tom said, nodding off to my left. "Heads up into the hills. Zoms won't go uphill unless they're chasing something."

"I taught you that, kiddo," I said. My voice sounded different. Older, filled with hard use and gravel. The kind of voice you could get if you screamed enough.

Far ahead we could see movement on the road as first one and then several emaciated figures staggered out of the tall weeds.

"Time to go, Tom," I said.

We turned and walked the length of the school bus. He dropped lightly to the ground and then offered a hand to help me down. It was disconcerting to realize I needed it. In the distance on the other side of the bus the dead had caught our scent and they began to moan. We faded into the trees, heading uphill.

The God Wave took me away before I saw where we were going.

And then I stood on the shores of a black ocean.

Creatures roiled and twisted in the surf. Dark shapes that made no sense to a sane mind. Out on the horizon there was a mist, white as milk, rolling in. It churned, too, as if there were things moving inside it, approaching where I stood. If it reached me while I stood there they would consume me. No question about it.

"It's beautiful here," said a voice, and I turned to see a handsome young man standing beside me. He was whole and straight. No burns, no madness flickering like candle flame in his eyes. And he could have been Junie's twin brother.

"I guess you'd have to know how to look at it," I said.

Prospero nodded. "It's not your home."

"No."

There were storm clouds above us and something moved inside of them, too. Not animals, not beasts. Machines. As I watched, a half dozen of them broke from the clouds and soared above us. Two groups of three. Each of the machines was triangular in shape. They were elegant and they soared above us toward a row of mountains that towered miles and miles into this impossible sky.

"Not outer space," said Prospero. "You know that, right?"

"I guess I do."

"That's too far to travel."

"Yes."

"But here," he gestured to the nightmare world around us, "my home is right next door to yours."

"Prospero," I said, "my world is dying. My people are going to burn when all the lights go out. Children are going to get sick and die. I can't do this without you."

He said nothing as he turned to watch the triangular craft dwindle into tiny dots.

"Your father and Harcourt Bolton have stolen your machine and they are using it to destroy everyone I love."

He smiled. "My father is dead. He shot himself, did you know that? They broke him up and threw him away. Poor Daddy."

"Okay . . . but Bolton is still trying to steal what you made. He's turning you into a monster by exploiting what you built."

"I *am* a monster. I come from a world of monsters."

I turned to him. "Maybe that's true, Prospero, but you're not evil. You never were. In my world *Bolton* is the monster. And he is definitely evil. He keeps you in chains. You're the monster in his basement. And he will never let you go home." I gestured to the world. "You're dreaming this, but you're still a prisoner in that basement."

Tears broke and ran down his face. "All I ever wanted was to go home."

"Help me stop Bolton and I promise you that you can go home."

He looked at me shrewdly. "You're really in love with someone who comes from here? A woman like me?"

"Her name is Junie Flynn. She's your sister, Prospero, and I love her with my whole heart and soul. That has to be worth something, Prospero. It has to mean something."

He opened his mouth to speak but then the God Wave hit me again. And I was gone.

CHAPTER ONE HUNDRED TWENTY-FOUR

Harcourt Bolton slept and dreamed and smiled as the seconds ran down.

He did not see the elevator doors open there on the parking garage. He did not see the woman and the man step off. Did not see her point with a knife toward the parked SUV. The windows were smoked and he was content that he could not be seen.

He had forty Closers in the building. The last of the DMS was being exterminated here, and soon, with federal marshals, FBI agents, NSA, Secret Service, and Homeland to work with, he would shut down every last field office. It was already in motion. Nothing could stop it now.

He lay on the seat he'd put back, and he floated inside the mind of the Mullah, and he was content.

Until the window beside him exploded inward.

The sound, the flying safety glass, the sheer shock of it tore him out of the Mullah's mind and out of the dream state. Then hands reached through and tore him out of the car, dragging him through the window as teeth of glass ripped at him. Violin and Mr. Church dumped him on the hard concrete and squatted down in front of him.

"Harcourt," said Church, "you disappoint me."

Bolton went for his gun. Church took it away from him and handed it to Violin. She removed the magazine, ejected the round, and then threw the weapon away.

"Harcourt, you have one chance here," said Church. "Tell me how to stop the countdown. We have the code, but we need to know what to do with it."

Bolton pulled himself up so that his back was against the car. His clothes were torn and he was bleeding from a dozen cuts.

"Oh really, Deacon?" he said, laughing in Church's face. "And what will you offer me? A plea bargain? My life? What?"

"What do you want?" asked Church, his voice soft, almost gentle. "What can I offer you that would mean anything to you? Just ask. Tell me what will get this done."

Bolton spat in Church's face. "You're a monster, Deacon. You know that? I even tried to crawl inside your head. Jesus Christ, that was scary as hell. But I *know* who you are. I know what you are."

"Then we both know," said Church as he wiped the spittle from his face. "How does that help us help each other?"

Bolton sneered. "Even if I told you what to do, you couldn't do it." He looked at his watch. "You have less than two minutes."

"Tell me and we'll try."

"No, you ass, you have to be there, at the God Machine. You have to input the first ten values of pi. That code cancels out the first one and—"

"No," said Church.

A slow smile formed on Bolton's face.

"You're lying to me," said Church as he straightened. He tapped his earbud. "You heard?"

CHAPTER ONE HUNDRED TWENTY-FIVE

01:04

"I heard," I said.

I stood in front of the God Machine. My clothes were torn and streaked with black muck from that alien ocean. Blood leaked hot and wet from my ears and nostrils and from the corners of my eyes. My hands were shaking with palsy. It felt like I'd been away for hours or days, but it had been seconds. Even time seemed fractured.

I turned to Prospero Bell.

"There is no way to stop it. Not even Bolton can do it now."

Prospero, burned and crooked with damage and disease, smiled at me. His clothes were filthy but his teeth were so white.

"If I do this," he said, "you have to promise me."

"Anything," I said, "I swear."

"Swear on her. On my sister. On Junie," he said. He looked down at the broken length of chain that was still locked to his ankle, and at the pipe I'd used to smash two of the links. Then he looked up at me again. "Swear on her."

I was about to fall down. "I swear on my love for her. I swear, Prospero. I swear on Junie Flynn."

"Okay," he said.

He hobbled over to the machine. We were alone there. When the God Machine swallowed us, I went one way and Esteban Santoro went somewhere else. I came back and, so far, he hadn't.

"Hurry," I begged.

Prospero bent and kissed the metal skin of the God Machine. The jewels were flashing faster and faster now as the thing cycled up to send the signal to all of those other machines.

00:31

His fingers were crooked from damage, the tendons shortened by the fires that had burned him. But they danced over the surface of the jewels. He touched the emerald first, and then the topaz twice, then the diamond, then the ruby five times. Moving faster. "There is an operational code," he said, "and that's the one I gave to Bolton. It's the calculation of three stars that can be seen from Antarctica. To use the God Machine as a global device, you input those coordinates."

I nodded. I knew this. My legs buckled and I dropped to my knees.

00:25

"But there is a master code. That resets the entire system. It's the coordinates of those stars on the day my ancestors first came here," he said. "A billion years ago." He turned to me. "That's how you'll send me home, too. You understand?"

00:14

"For the love of God, Prospero . . ."

"And then you put in the coordinates for the stars today. That's the secret. That completes the energetic circle."

He smiled and tapped the last numbers in. The same numbers Dr. Kang had found, and then the other set.

00:00:07

The lights all went off and we were plunged into darkness.

Total darkness.

I seemed to swim in it.

The only thing I could see was the digital display on the inside of my goggles.

00:00:02

Steady, unblinking. Burned into the moment.

I bent my head and wept.

CHAPTER ONE HUNDRED TWENTY-SIX

THE COMCAST BUILDING
1701 JOHN F. KENNEDY BOULEVARD
PHILADELPHIA, PENNSYLVANIA
SEPTEMBER 10, 11:54 A.M. LOCAL TIME

Trey Willis stood on the deck, staring in blank wonder as the small quadcopters drifted back toward him. He almost ran, but he didn't. Not because something held him in place—he was free now. But because he had to know what was going to happen.

The little machines flew back toward him, toward the control device he held.

One by one they settled back onto the deck in exactly the same place where they'd been before they'd swarmed off. It took a lot of courage for Trey to set down the device and pick up one of the drones. When he saw the plastic tanks on the bottom he recoiled, set it down, and went running for help.

The only thing he did first was to place the control device on the ground and smash it with his heel.

CHAPTER ONE HUNDRED TWENTY-SEVEN

I sat on the edge of a filthy bed, my head in my hands. Alone. All alone.

It was Ghost who found me. He led Harry Bolt down the hall and into the chamber. Harry was covered in blood and soot, and his eyes were crazed. Harry stopped in the doorway and looked around, confused. I sat against the wall of a vast and empty chamber. Prospero's bed, chains, and a few pieces of debris were the only things in there with me.

"But . . . but . . . ," stammered Harry, confused and frightened, "I thought the machine would be in here. There's nowhere else it could be."

I raised my head to look at him. "It was here. So was Prospero."

"But, where'd it *go*? I mean . . . how'd they get it out of here? And where's Prospero?"

Ghost went over and sniffed a spot on the floor where some of Santoro's blood was spattered. He cocked a leg and pissed all over it. Then Ghost came over and began licking my face. I wrapped my arms around my furry friend and buried my face in his ruff and left Harry to answer his own questions.

I don't remember passing out at all.

EPILOGUE

1.
Head injury.

Yeah.

Another damn coma. Only two days this time. Lucky me? Not really. Actually, looking back on my life since joining the DMS I'm not really sure where my life falls in relation to the whole "luck" thing.

I woke up. I'm alive and my brain still works.

Hey, if you have your health you have everything, right?

Right?

2.
I woke to news and heartbreak.

Montana Parker and Brian Botley had died in the battle at the Pier. They were gone. And it was touch and go for Sam Imura and Toys. The surgeons earned their pay keeping them both on this side of the dirt. Sam lost ten inches of intestine. Toys had some kidney and lung damage. Bunny was going to be in therapy for a long time. Maybe Top, too, but he's tougher than the rest of us.

Violin came to visit me. She brought flowers and food. Harry Bolt came to visit; he brought flowers and food. Every-damn-body else at the DMS came to visit. They brought flowers and they ate most of the food. The president did not come to visit. He sent the vice president. He brought flowers but no food.

Junie spent half of each day in my room and half in with Toys. She was going to need a lot of help getting over it. Sure, it wasn't her doing those things, but tell that to her, or Top or Bunny. Tell any of the dozens of people around the country who woke up to find themselves standing on rooftops surrounded by drones filled with small-pox. Cops, lawyers, doctors, and shrinks may never sort it out. Maybe historians will.

I tried watching it all on the news. There was one international story about a vicious fight that erupted among disparate factions who had recently set aside their political and religious differences to follow what they thought was a new prophet. When a holy plague failed to sweep across America there was a bit of a backlash. Right now we're all watching as the Taliban, al-Qaeda, and a dozen other groups gouge chunks out of the ISIL leadership. I'd like to think that they'll gang up so hard that they'll crush ISIL flat. I'd like to believe in Santa Claus, too.

But it's fun to watch.

The retaliation by our own government was severe. Some say it's too harsh, but I'll see their outrage and raise a weaponized plagued aimed at our kids.

Church came to visit me. He brought cookies.

I said, "Please tell me that the Gateway technology's not going to wind up going to another black budget group."

"Aunt Sallie has assembled a team," Church told me. "It's being taken care of."

"I don't even want to hear about any of this going to FreeTech. None of it."

Church nodded. "We're on the same page."

"Good."

"Good," he agreed. We sat for a long time in silence. He'd brought a box of Nilla wafers and a package of Oreos. We each had some.

"So," I said, "are there still warrants out for us?"

"I'm happy to report that they've been withdrawn," he said. He removed a letter from his jacket pocket. "And you might find this interesting."

The stationery was remarkably crisp and was embossed with the presidential seal. The letter was a newly drafted and signed executive order for a revised charter for the DMS. I read it and whistled.

"What in the wide blue hell did you have to do to get POTUS to give you *this*?" I demanded. "It makes our old charter look like obfuscatory gibberish."

"I didn't even have to ask," he said. "This was hand-delivered within twenty-four hours of the raid in Rancho Santa Fe. I had Bug share your radio and body-camera feed with the White House. They saw and heard everything."

I almost smiled, but the stitches in my mouth turned it into a wince. "You took Bolton alive, right? What have you done with him?"

Church tucked the charter away, patted my leg, and left without answering.

Junie came in and crawled onto my bed and we held each other.

3.

Dr. William Hu was in intensive care for two weeks. We all came to visit him. Once I got out of the hospital, Junie and I were there every day. Aunt Sallie flew out from Brooklyn. So did Bug. So did a lot of people. The bullet had done a lot of damage. They operated on him three times and he survived each procedure. He woke up on the fifteenth day and saw that I was sitting beside his bed. He looked at me. I looked at him. He licked his lips and I gave him some water out of a bendy straw.

"The . . . children . . . ?" he asked, his voice as thin as a whisper. "The lights?"

"The lights stayed on," I said. "We kept the monster in the box."

Hu smiled and closed his eyes.

The machines around him started screaming.

The doctors and nurses came running; they pushed me out of the way. There was a lot of yelling. I stood in the hallway watching them fight to keep him alive. They fought every bit as hard as I'd fought Santoro. As Toys and Junie had fought. As Church and Violin had fought. As Harry had fought.

They fought and fought.

But you can't win every battle.

No, you can't.

Goddamn it, you can't. I stood there, numb and empty, and for a moment I thought I heard Hu's voice. I turned and caught a fleeting glimpse of him going through the fire door. He cut a look over his shoulder and gave me a sarcastic smirk. When I blinked the fire door was shut.

I leaned slowly against the wall.

Slid down.

Sat there while they switched off the machines one by one.

4.

Everyone came to the funeral.

Even the president.

Church met him at the entrance to the chapel and would not move. I joined him. So did Top and Bunny, Toys, Junie, Aunt Sallie. All of us. Even Harry Bolt and Violin joined the blockade.

The president stood on the steps, surrounded by his Secret Service entourage and all of his people. Mr. Church did not say a single word. He didn't have to.

After five long minutes the president shook his head and turned away. His motorcade drove away with all of the usual lights and sirens.

5.

Deconstructing it all will take time.

If I thought it would be the trial of the century, I was wrong. None of the true facts ever got out. Harcourt Bolton, Senior, went away somewhere. Not sure where. The public thinks he's dead. The Closers *are* all dead. The dream team from the Playroom are in a secure psychiatric facility. Harry Bolt had gone around the room smashing the sleeping capsules, and apparently that caused a short resulting in traumatic brain damage to each of the dreamwalkers. They're still alive but they're vegetables. God only knows what we can or should do to them. The guards at that facility and everyone on the staff have to wear those damn aluminum foil hats just in case. Maybe it will ultimately prove too costly to keep them. Too costly in too many ways. Personally? I'm sorry I wasn't awake enough down in Bolton's basement to put a bullet in each one of them. Would have simplified things. Might even have made me feel better, or achieve a sense of justice. Or something.

Those are not thoughts I share with Junie. Or even Rudy, who's recovering from knee replacement and nose reconstruction. He says that he forgives me, but I haven't managed yet to forgive myself. Nor has Circe forgiven me yet. Fair enough.

And as far as Prospero Bell? The official story is still that he died after he and his friend, Leviticus King, set fire to their school. No need to amend that story with troublesome facts. We know what happened. That's enough.

For me, I can't ever look at the world the same way. Sure, I know that the monsters I saw weren't part of my world. But on the way to that world I saw things about this world that hurt me. Things that eat at me. I saw the end of the world. I saw what I would become as things fell apart. Or maybe *might* become. Which means what, exactly? Am

I doomed to live out that future? Will some old Cold War bioweapon turn everything into a wasteland picked over by the hungry dead? Is that my reward for all these years of fighting? Is the future a fixed point that we travel to with the certainty of a bullet drilling a hot hole through the air toward a stationary target?

God, I hope not.

Mr. Church says he doesn't believe in prophecy. He says it's been wrong too many times. He says that nearly all of the prophets have been wrong. What do they call it in fiction? Unreliable narrators.

But I saw it. This isn't a Ouija board. This was me standing ankle deep in blood. If that is what's coming, can I stop it? Change it? Save it? If so, how? Do I stay on the clock and stay in the fight so that I'm poised and ready? How soon before that would drive me absolutely out of what's left of my mind? Or do I throw the universe a curve and lay down my arms, turn my back, walk off? In that dark future I was still a soldier. What happens to the future if I stop being that? Will it change destiny or insure it?

Those are impossible questions to answer.

Time, as they say, will tell. But forewarned is forearmed. We know about the Lucifer 113 pathogen. Church is looking into it. He's going to see what he can do to stop it from ever being released. Maybe I can help. Maybe I can go find the people involved and put bullets in their heads. As a public service, you understand.

Which opens another door of speculation. What if that was a fantasy of a damaged mind under great stress? I had a head injury, after all. It's entirely possible, even likely, that this was nothing more than a trauma-born hallucination. How does that give me license to go kill people?

You see the problem?

The Kill Switch may be gone, but I believe there is still a darkness coming. The question is how to hold a light to keep it from becoming absolute.

So where does that leave the world? This world, I mean. The world of now.

That's a damn good question. In my darkest hours I wondered how many times we could be knocked down and still manage to get back onto our feet. There's that old saying from the Japanese martial arts that's a favorite of Mr. Church. *Nanakorobi yaoki.* Fall seven times, get up eight. It's a great philosophy, but after a while it's harder to

JONATHAN MABERRY

make it work. The knees don't want to flex, the back is too sore, the heart is heavy. What if you manage it one more time and they hit you again and drive you back down? And again? And again?

The Modern Man in my soul wants to stay down, to hide, to burrow into the sand so that no one else takes another swing. The Cop wants to figure it out, to lie low until he's sure there are no more punches coming. Both effects are the same; whether fear or caution, the sad fact is that the bad guys have put you down on the deck and maybe this is the last time.

But the Killer in my soul—the Warrior, whatever it is I call him or he wants to be called—he sees it differently. He's too primitive to give up. He operates on the level of immediate need. It's live or die. It's fight or die. It's kill or be killed.

6.

On a sunny Southern California day twenty-eight days after the God Machine fired, I came into the office to find Sam Imura there, walking carefully, looking pale and thin. The others drifted in and we went up to the deck to watch the ocean. I'd brought with me a whole sack full of sandwiches. There's a guy named Jake Witkowski who has a food truck near the Pier and he invented a sandwich for me. Rudy says that these things are more dangerous than anything we face when we roll out as a team. The "Joe Ledger Special" is a homemade bacon cheddar brat, sliced open and topped with a steak patty with grilled pepper and onions, piled high with a homemade cheese sauce, homemade whiskey BBQ sauce, and crushed Fritos. Anytime I feel one of my arteries opening, I have Jake make me one of these. Food for the soul.

We all sat on the deck and ate them. Me and what was left of my team, my family. Ghost, too. It was a farewell dinner in a lot of ways. Brian and Montana were gone. Dr. Hu was gone. At least half of the DMS field agents had been adversely impacted by the Dreamwalking intrusions. A lot of them were dead. A lot of them had quit or asked for transfers to desk jobs. The whole DMS had collapsed down almost to the size it was when I first joined. We were a broken machine, and even with our new charter, none of us felt up to the task of fixing it. Maybe it would never be fixed. Maybe this was the end of us.

Echo Team was falling apart around me. Lydia had submitted her letter of resignation from the DMS and had accepted the job of head of security for FreeTech. And Sam . . . ? He said that he wanted to go back to California for a while and spend time with his family while he healed. When I asked if he was going to come back to Echo Team, he said, "We'll see." Which I took to mean, "No."

Things were coming to an end.

Or . . . maybe it was like chess. The pieces are removed from the board one by one but you still have to play the game with what you have left. I had Top and Bunny.

I hoped.

As I munched my sandwich I looked at some photos Harry Bolt had sent me from his cell phone. The kind of pictures tourists ask passersby to take. Harry seated at a table at a sidewalk café in Paris. Short, dumpy, silly, and ineffectual Harry Bolt. World's worst spy. Son of a madman who nearly ruined the whole country. Seated at a table with a gorgeous brunette with dark eyes, a mysterious smile, and an outrageous hat. I showed the photo to the guys.

"Well, kiss my ass," said Top.

Bunny looked at it, and shook his head. "No. That doesn't fit inside my head."

"Why not?" asked Sam. "Kid's richer than God. He's going to be a chick magnet."

"But him and *Violin*?" asked Bunny, shaking his head. "Seriously?"

No one could believe it. We all had a beer to shake it off. One beer didn't do the whole job, so we had another. And another.

Which is where Church found us.

He came and stood there, looking down at us, at what we were eating, at the rows of empty beer bottles, and then out to sea. Finally he took a thick stack of folded papers from the inner pocket of his suit coat and handed them to me. First-class plane tickets. Hotel and car rentals. My name was on the top one, then Junie, and then everyone. A hotel in Hawaii, right on the beach. The flight was for ten thirty tomorrow morning. We all looked at the tickets and then up at him, attentive as schoolchildren.

"The world will have to turn without you for a couple of weeks," he said, then he turned and walked away. I caught up with him at the door.

"Whoa, wait a minute," I said. "Look, Boss, I appreciate the gestures, but we can't go off the clock now, we're just getting back on our feet and—"

Church said, "When was the last time you took a vacation, Captain? You live at the beach but you don't act like it. When is the last time you went swimming when it didn't involve having a boat shot out from under you? When is the last time you took a day off when it didn't involve a hospital stay? When is the last time you went fishing, played tennis, rode a bicycle, slept in a hammock, hiked in the mountains, played catch with your dog, spent unstructured time with the woman you love?"

I opened my mouth to reply but I had nothing to say.

"The war will still be here," Church said quietly.

"But—"

"If I need you," he said with a faint smile, "I'll call."

7.

We were on the beach in Hanalei Bay on Kauai's north shore.

Junie was wearing a string bikini that tested the limits of public decency. I was very okay with that. Twenty feet away Bunny was sprawled on a chaise lounge in a Speedo that I was less okay with. They don't call them banana hammocks for nothing. Lydia was seated nearby, smearing her legs with oil. Top was in a chaise lounge, snoring quietly, a peach-colored fedora covering his face.

That was how it was and how it had been for day after gorgeous uncomplicated day. Dangerous drinks with little paper umbrellas. Lotion glistening on sun-dark skin. Tourist hats pulled low over dark sunglasses. To passersby we must have looked strange. Not one of us, not even Junie, was unmarked by the weapons of war. Knives and bullets, teeth and claws. People gave us strange looks and moved on. At least for the first few days. As our tans deepened and we became familiar faces there were more smiles directed our way. Fewer frowns. Parents didn't pull their kids to another part of the beach.

We baked. We ate. We drank.

We relaxed, I think.

In the depths of the dark tropical nights, as the fragrant flowers perfumed the air, Junie and I made love. Sweet and slow and gentle. Afterward, sweaty and spent, I lay in her arms and listened to the world be the world. No gunfire, no screams.

On days like this one, though, as we all lay sprawled on chairs and towels, it seemed to me that we had crossed a line, reached a place, achieved a state. Relaxation isn't really the right word. Peace, maybe. Or a calm before the next storm.

Church said that the war would still be there. He said that if he needed us he'd call.

My cell phone sat on the table beside my chair, day after day, and didn't ring.

It did not ring.

Until it did.